"YOU SAVED MY LIFE. SURELY THAT MUST COUNT FOR SOMETHING."

Gillian leaned forward and very softly touched her lips to his. Dante didn't think. He reacted. The need to have her, made overpowering and fierce these past days, raced through his every vein, pounding in his head like a hammer. He pulled her against him and kissed her deeply, reveling in the taste of her and the quickness of her breathing.

"Oh, God. You make me feel as if I could conquer anything."

She looked at him, eyes glazed. "You can."

Dante swept his hand beneath her back and lowered her to the carpet in front of the fire, waiting for her response.

She kissed his cheek, his ear, his forehead, and finally his mouth. Dante could feel Gillian's pulse beat strong against his lips.

Lifting his head, he looked down at her in the glowing light. "I don't even know your true name."

Stealing Heaven

by

Jaclyn Reding

A TOPAZ BOOK

TOPAZ

Published by the Penguin Group
Penguin Books USA Inc., 375 Hudson Street,
New York, New York 10014, U.S.A.
Penguin Books Ltd, 27 Wrights Lane,
London W8 5TZ, England
Penguin Books Australia Ltd, Ringwood,
Victoria, Australia
Penguin Books Canada Ltd, 10 Alcorn Avenue,
Toronto, Ontario, Canada M4V 3B2
Penguin Books (N.Z.) Ltd, 182–190 Wairau Road,
Auckland 10, New Zealand

Penguin Books Ltd, Registered Offices:
Harmondsworth, Middlesex, England

First published by Topaz, an imprint of Dutton Signet,
a division of Penguin Books USA Inc.

First Printing, September, 1996
10 9 8 7 6 5 4 3 2 1

There are four men in my life,
excepting my son and my husband.

The first of them is silent and strong,
and the best father a girl could ever ask for.

The second of them is sometimes temperamental,
but when you need him, he will always be there.

The third is the charmer, with curly golden locks
and dimples that can melt any heart.

And the fourth, well, he is simply one of a kind;
he can bring a smile to your darkest day
and leave your eyes watering with laughter.

To my father, Fred Adamowicz,
and my brothers,
Michael, John, and Mark.

If ever a girl had her choice,
I couldn't have found any better.

The things we remember best
are those better forgotten.
                    —Baltasar Gracian

Chapter One

Breathing, hot and heavy and blowing just beside the lobe of her left ear. It was that sound which first woke Gillian from sleep.

At first she thought she must be dreaming. She lay still a moment, hovering between sleep and waking. Until the breathing came again. It only took her another moment. She jerked away, pulling up her knees, wanting nothing but to put a safe distance between herself and whoever, or whatever, was there beside her on her bed, in her bedchamber, alone with her. The moment she stirred, two hands grabbed her ankles, pulling her down. She struggled to break free, and the breathing someone came heavily over her upper body.

She realized then there were two of them.

Gillian opened her mouth to scream, and a gloved hand clamped down hard over her mouth. An odd smell, pungent and peppery, nearly overcame her.

"Hello, Gillian."

A man's voice spoke to her, deep and chilling, characteristic of a nightmare. Gillian drew a frightened breath, unable to move, barely able to breathe. His face was so near to her, she could smell the ale he'd recently drunk on his breath. The other intruder, the one at her feet, tightened his gloved fingers around her bare ankles.

Gillian tightened her fingers into the sheets. What could she possibly do? The men had her completely caught. She wondered what they wanted, why they were here. She wondered who they were. The one at her feet sneezed.

"Shut up, you idiot," his partner hissed. He moved his hand away from Gillian's mouth, only for a moment before shoving a thick cloth in its place, cutting off any sound she might have made.

He took her chin then with unkind fingers, gloved fingers that stroked over her skin with the smallest amount of pressure meant to gain her full attention. It succeeded.

"This will go a lot easier for you, Gillian, if you do not fight us. You cannot get away. I would suggest you accept that now."

Why were they doing this? Gillian tried to twist her head, searching the darkness for their faces. The fire in the stone hearth at the foot of her bed had died, not even a vague flicker of it remaining to light her chamber. Adding to the dreadful atmosphere were the oddlooking shadows moving here and there in the muted moonlight that came through the open balcony door.

Gillian struggled as they began to bind her ankles, then her wrists with her hands crossed awkwardly before her. The knotty cord chafed at her skin; the gag and her fear were nearly suffocating her. They yanked a coarse cloth hood that smelled of dampness and mildew over her head, blocking her sight, before proceeding to haul her none too gently from the bed.

"To the door."

Gillian could see nothing, and she could barely breathe through the vile-smelling hood. Still, she felt she should try to fight them. She had never been one to accept the inevitable without first trying to change it. At least once. She waited, and when the moment came, she kicked forward with both legs, hoping at least to catch the one at her feet with a hard blow to his gut. She failed and his partner simply slung her over his shoulder with her head and upper body hanging down his back. Gillian still didn't give up. She bucked and rolled, trying to twist away from him, until he grabbed her leg hard and dug his fingers painfully into the vulnerable soft flesh at the back of her knee, effectively crippling her.

"I will tell you this only once more, Gillian, so listen to me well. Cease your struggling. It is senseless, useless. We are two and you are one, a smaller one, a helpless one. Now we mean to take you out the same way we came, which is over your bedchamber balcony from the garden. If you fight us, and we drop you, you'll only succeed in breaking your neck in the fall. That is how your family will find you on the morrow, and that wouldn't be at all pleasant. Do you understand?"

Gillian weighed the intruder's words. She couldn't see. She couldn't move with any degree of freedom. She certainly didn't want her family to find her dead. She nodded silently.

"Good girl," he said, and Gillian realized a nagging familiarity to his voice. Where had she heard him before?

As he started to carry her from her bedchamber, Gillian tried to imagine who he could be, why she knew his voice. Obviously, he knew her, he had termed her familiar. Why was he doing this to her?

Gillian realized that the two men weren't planning to kill her. They could have accomplished that in the first seconds after she had realized they were there. No, these two men had gone through too much in their efforts to take her. They wanted something from her, something she could give them. But what was it? Money? Ransom? Yes, that had to be it. Everyone knew her father was rich as Plutus. He was a marquess with holdings throughout England and Scotland, and held part in a number of lucrative dealings, or so Gillian had overheard oft enough about the periphery of many a ballroom.

These men knew this, had kidnapped her for it, and were planning to demand a ransom from her father for her safe return, a ransom he would immediately pay without the slightest hesitation, of course. Her father loved her. He would never allow her to come to harm. He would do whatever these men asked of him, and then, when she was safely returned, he would send her brothers, all three of them, to punish these brutes for their actions.

It would be an adventure, like the romantic tales she liked to read in which the damsel is saved from the vile villain by the hero, a hero was is always handsome and always strong. Only, in this particular adventure, there would be two villains, and there would be no hero, handsome or strong, coming for her. These men would take her someplace secret, most probably an old, abandoned castle in the remote countryside where no one lived within miles. And after her father paid them whatever amount they would demand of him, she would be returned to her family safe and un-harmed.

Yes, that was it.

That had to be it.

Now if they would just get on with it, for the blood was rushing downward as she hung over the intruder's shoulders, causing her head to pound like a drum beating over and over and over.

"You go over first, and when you reach the ground,

I'll lower her down to you," said the first voice, the familiar voice, to his accomplice.

"Why do I have to go down first? I went up first. You go down."

"Listen to me, you idiot," answered the familiar voice, his impatience crisp in his voice now. "Gillian may be a mere slip of a girl, but I don't think you've the strength to hold her. The heaviest thing you've ever toted without some degree of assistance is a tankard of ale, and that was only from table to mouth."

"And you're Hercules?"

"I've lifted two tankards, and I have managed to keep upright this long holding her as I am with her hanging over my shoulder. Don't let's bungle this now when we've just cleared the first hurdle. The rest will be easy, mere stumbling stones. Stop squabbling like a bloody shrew and climb over the railing."

The next thing Gillian heard was a scraping sound followed after by a soft, solid thump. The second voice came a moment later, farther away than before.

"All right, I'm ready for her. You can lower the lass down to me now."

Gillian slid down and off her abductor's shoulder. She stood before him, wavering on unsteady feet. This one, the one with the familiar voice, seemed to be the one most in command, more inclined to issuing orders than taking them. Who was he? And who was the other one? Why couldn't she place his voice?

He grabbed Gillian's arm then. The cool night air blew about her bare ankles. Her toes curled against the stone balcony floor.

"I would advise you to listen to me, Gillian, and listen to me well," he said, his voice coming softly beside her ear. "I know this is something to which you're not accustomed since you never believed I had anything of merit to say, but in this case, since I have you, and with you, your life in my hands, I would think it more than prudent. I'm going to hold you by your arms and lower you feet first to the ground. I will have to lean over the balcony railing in order to do so. I will be supported by a rope which I have secured to the railing. You will be supported only by me. If you struggle, Gillian, even a little, you will cause me to lose my hold on you. Although the distance to the ground isn't all that great, with your feet and hands bound as they are, you would have little chance for a safe landing. At the least, you would fracture your ankle. Perhaps both of them. Snapping your neck is another possibility. Keep still, and this will go a lot easier for us all."

Gillian did as he said, tensing every muscle when she felt herself being lifted and propped upon the railing. Her feet dangled dangerously over the edge, nothing beneath them. She waited for him to proceed, wondering what would happen to her if this person, who hadn't lifted anything heavier than two tankards of ale during the course of his life, couldn't support her weight after all? What if he dropped her regardless of how still she kept?

He reached around under her arms from behind. His hands strayed to her breasts. She felt him cover her, his fingers curving around her, touching her, invading her through the thin fabric of her nightrail. Gillian shrank from his touch.

"That's not keeping still, Gillian."

Gillian closed her eyes. She would have liked to have cursed him to Barathrum, and if not for the wadded-up cloth shoved nearly down her throat, she would have. Instead, she made a mental note to cuff him one good with her hand balled tightly into a fist and aimed upward straight for his jaw the first chance she found, just as Archie had taught her.

Thank heavens for older brothers.

It seemed like an eternity as he lowered her to the ground before she felt the second one below her grasping her ankles. He wrapped his arms around her upper legs and when she was released from above, she tumbled backward, landing hard on her bottom on the damp garden floor. The one on the balcony had been right. His partner hadn't been able to hold her weight, even for a second. Gillian tried to push herself aright before he grabbed her by her bound hands and hauled her up to stand.

"I got her!"

"Shut your trap," hissed the other one from above. "Do you want to wake the entire house with your crowing? Gillian has brothers, three of them, who are each of them much larger and stronger than either of us. If they hear you, they will come down and beat us to a bloody pulp."

The thought occurred to Gillian to somehow make a noise to do just that, but with the gag and this moldy makeshift hood on her head, she decided her chances of success remote. The city had fallen silent, and with the fire in her hearth having gone down, she guessed the hour quite late. Everyone inside the house would be well in the arms of Morpheus, never suspecting that she was at that very moment being dragged, bound and gagged, from her bed, from under their very noses, by two unknown intruders.

There came another thump as the other intruder, the one with the groping hands and the peppery smell about him, dropped to the ground nearby. "All right, you take her feet, I'll take her arms, and we'll get her to the coach."

They carried Gillian off and into the night, dropping her twice before they jerked to an abrupt halt.

"Wait here," said the familiar one, leaning Gillian back against him. "I hear something." He paused. "Someone's coming."

Gillian listened. She heard the sound of a horse and coach traveling slowly along a cobbled street. She tried to scream, despite the gag, when she thought the coach close by, but the intruder holding her arms quickly clamped his hand down over the hood to stifle any sound she might make.

After the coach had gone, he grabbed her roughly by her arms. "Another stunt like that, Gillian, and you'll force me to employ stricter measures to ensure your cooperation.

"All right," he then said to the other one, who was still holding her feet. "I think they're safely gone now. We've not much farther to go. The coach is waiting just around that corner. We're almost there."

"Help me get her inside," came the first voice when they reached the coach, and the two of them, one pulling her and the other pushing her upward from behind, maneuvered her inside. Gillian fell face forward onto the seat. The two men climbed in behind her. They lifted her, sitting her on the seat seconds before the coach door slammed shut.

"Drive!" one of them yelled, rapping on the roof. The coach lurched forward. Gillian tried desperately to keep herself from falling, inching her way back onto the coach seat.

"Are you sure the driver knows the way to go?"

"Aye. I told him to take the back alleys and byways to the east into the city, in case we're seen leaving by anyone, then split off at the cross to the North Road and onward to Scotland."

Gillian listened closely. *Scotland?* Why on earth would they be going all the way to Scotland if they intended to demand a ransom from her father? Surely they could have found a closer place to hide her.

"Good work, my friend." There was a pause. "Well, then, I would guess the time is now appropriate to remove Gillian's mask."

He removed the mildew-smelling hood from her head. Gillian took in a long, slow breath of the clean night air through her nose. She blinked in the darkness. She could make out the twin silhouettes of her abductors sitting across from her on the opposite coach bench. She could not see their faces, even by squinting.

One of them reached forward and withdrew the cloth gag from her mouth.

"Well, my dear, what do you have to say for yourself?"

Gillian couldn't say anything, not at first, for the cloth had taken up any moisture from her mouth. Finally, she lifted her chin, trying to sound as fearless and intimidating as she could.

"I have nothing to say to you, sir, at least not until I know the identity of the person I am addressing."

He chuckled, a rusty sound that gave Gillian an involuntary shudder. "It appears Lady Gillian still hasn't figured out who we are, although I should have expected no less. She has never paid either of us more than a passing interest during our entire acquaintanceship."

He reached and yanked open the small linen curtain that covered the coach window. Moonlight filtered in just enough for her to make out their faces.

"This is not well done of you," Gillian said, recognizing them both. "Either of you."

"It seems I was mistaken," the first one said. "She does know who we are." The Honorable Garrick Fitzwilliam then turned to his accomplice, smiling. "You owe me five quid, Ozzie."

"Aye," answered the other fishing in his coat pocket. " 'Tis the last of my quarterly after paying the coachman, you know." Sir Ozwell Gilhooly reached up, scratching his bewigged head.

"Not to worry, my friend," said Garrick, smiling. "Once Lady Gillian and I are safely wed, and I have her well with the threat of child after plowing her straight for a fortnight or so, our pockets will be filled to overflowing with her father's precious guineas."

"Marry you!" Gillian nearly laughed at the absurdity of his suggestion, and indeed would have if not for the fact that her hands and feet were still tightly bound, which did illustrate his determination in the venture. "I wouldn't marry you if you were the last bloody idiot in England."

"Tut, my dear. I'll not have my bride using such language. I do not find it a comely quality in a wife."

Gillian stared at him. His dark eyes danced in the moonlight. He leaned forward, and his face, a face that Gillian had always thought looked as sneaky as a pointed-nosed wharf rat, was fully illuminated in the light. A stray lock of his sandy brown hair fell down over his high forehead just above his right eye. He stared at her, and a cold shudder passed through her.

"And I assure you, Gillian, you will be my wife. With or without your consent."

It was the utter confidence with which he spoke that gave Gillian pause. Garrick was serious. Deadly serious. He had abducted her from her bedchamber in the middle of the night, from the very bosom of her family, to carry her off to wed her. There would be no ransom, no abandoned castle. And this surely was not going to be an adventure.

"Perhaps you could tell me how you propose to wed me without—"

Scotland. Gillian lost her words as she remembered what Sir Ozwell had said about their intended escape route. Indeed, Garrick had never planned to ransom her. He intended to spirit her off, out of the country, to Gretna Green, where marriages could be had as easily and as cheaply as a new pair of kidskin gloves. No posting of the banns. No waiting to secure a proper license. Just a simple ceremony and they would be man and wife. The thought of it sickened Gillian to the depths of her stomach.

"I see, dear Gillian, from the expression on that lovely, albeit unexceptional, face of yours, that you've already answered your own question. And," Garrick went on, extracting a small dark bottle from inside his coat pocket, "I have paid a visit to an apothecary who proved most easy to bribe. If need be, I will drug you to prevent you from creating a scene straight out of some romantic drama."

Sir Ozwell broke in. "You never said anything about drugging the lass, Garrick."

"Did you honestly think she would willingly consent to the vows out of simple fear after we kidnapped her? Any other mutton-piece at court, perhaps, but not Gillian. She is far too obstinate for that. And given that, what else might you expect me to do? Cinch you into your sister's stays and paste your face with Spanish red so you could stand in for her?"

Gillian frowned. "I never would have thought you so vile. Your mother would be ashamed were she to see what you have become."

Garrick sat back in his seat and gave Gillian a sinister grin. "Yes, well, Mother died birthing the tenth of her ungrateful sons. Killed the babe with her, a thing my father has never forgiven her for. One cannot have too many sons, a thing you will do well to remember, for I expect you will birth me at least five or six of them in the first decade of our marriage. Perhaps, Gillian, you should blame my mother for the predicament you now find yourself in. Had she done the birthing of her sons right, I would have been the first and not the fifth. I would have had the title of my father, the title my brother, the undeserving Allistair, will have. Along with that title went any advantage I might have had in securing myself a wealthy wife. With that title I wouldn't have had to tolerate disrespect from overprivileged young women like yourself. I would have had a proper upbringing, an upbringing that wouldn't allow me to so much as consider committing such a vile act as I am now. Without Mother here to pass on her more saintly virtues, my father was free to instill his 'Do whatever you must to get ahead' code of living in each of his sons. Which is what I am doing now. I have been planning our little meeting for some time, Gillian, some time indeed. I've watched you as you flitted about the best ballrooms, turning your nose up at me at every chance you found. I daresay, I know you so well, I could predict every move you make even before you make it."

Gillian narrowed her eyes on him. "What could you possibly know of me?"

"You're a creature of habit, dear Gillian, and your routine became quickly predictable. Chocolate and rolls for breakfast at eight, usually in the solarium, always alone, with your nose stuck inside one of those inane French romances you favor so well. For a woman of your uncommon intelligence, Gillian, I would have thought your reading more suited to treatise and discourse."

Gillian frowned at him. "Sorry to disappoint."

Garrick grinned, pleased. "You pass the remainder of the morning either out visiting acquaintances with your mother or one of your brothers' wives, or in your chamber, reading and answering correspondence—you are a devoted letter writer—followed by a light dinner with tea, usually around one. Occasionally, you try your hand at limning, though I must say your talents as an artist are at best primitive. I have never once witnessed your practicing at stitchery."

"I do not find it a pastime that holds my interest."

"Fortunately, for you, I am willing to overlook that small imperfection."

"How very good of you."

Garrick chuckled, going on. "Your afternoons, Gillian, are devoted to music. Monday and Tuesday you practice the harpsichord, Wednesday and Thursday the treble recorder, and Friday and Saturday, oddly enough, the bass viola da gamba. I hadn't thought that an instrument often undertaken by ladies, what with the obstruction of the skirts hindering its proper placement. Tell me, dear Gillian," Garrick said, running a finger along her knee, "how is it you manage to position such a large object so easily between your legs?"

Gillian moved her legs away from him. "I am fond of its sound."

He laughed, and went on. "You sup with your family, all of them, including the children, promptly at seven, after which you attend whatever social event you deem worthy of your presence. Again, this is always under the proper chaperonage of your mother or one of your brothers' wives. I must say you are very conscientious on that end. It did make my plans for you rather difficult, though not, as you can see, impossible. You retire to your chamber anywhere between midnight and two, whereupon waking, the whole cycle begins anew. Have I chanced to leave anything out?"

Gillian stared at him, speechless, appalled, and, perhaps a little frightened.

How had Garrick managed to learn so much about her, things she hadn't even noticed about herself until he'd just now recited them? He must have hidden himself in the rue bushes outside the house, or worse, somewhere inside—in the buttery closet?—mentally recording her every movement. How hadn't she noticed him? Was what he'd said true? Was she so caught up in her own interests that she had failed to see the very danger going on around her?

"So, as you can see, I have thought of everything,

Gillian. Rest assured, there is no possible way for you to escape."

Gillian stared at Garrick, silent as a stone set in high ground. What could she do?

The coach seat creaked as Garrick sat back, puffed up with confidence in himself. "Now I would suggest you accustom yourself to that space there, for you will be occupying it from now until we reach Scotland. We will wed there, and then we will honeymoon as private guests of my good friend here, Sir Ozwell, after which we will return to London in grand ceremony as husband and wife."

Gillian sat back, not because Garrick had told her to; she hadn't even heard the last of his provocative litany. She was beginning to formulate a plan of her own, a plan for her to escape.

Marry Garrick Fitzwilliam?

It was absurd.

It was, quite simply, ridiculous.

And, beyond that, it would never come to pass as long as Gillian had a breath left in her body.

Garrick may believe he had thought of everything, but there were always possibilities even the most twisted mind overlooked. Hadn't the villain in her stories always been confident of success? And hadn't he always been brought down? Gillian knew she would find a way to save herself. It would take nearly a fortnight to reach Scotland, perhaps even longer once they reached the rougher, less easily traveled roads in the North Country. They would have to make time for nourishment and to rest the horses. They would have to stop to relieve themselves. Surely, he didn't intend to stand beside her while she performed that most personal of functions?

Or did he?

No, something would present itself. A possibility for escape would come about even before this man, the

*Dis*honorable Garrick Fitzwilliam, had a chance to recognize it.

And when that opportunity arose, Gillian would be waiting for it, and she would seize it before either of the men could do anything more than blink.

Chapter Two

Derbyshire, England

Dante Tremaine, third Earl of Morgan and fifth Viscount Wyldewoode, stared silently out the narrow opening afforded by the small curtain on the coach window. It was raining, not just raining, but pouring in thick and heavy sheets that pelted the coach's windows like a spray of tiny pebbles thrown up by the gusting wind. The night was grim, and the moon had concealed itself behind a cover of fat clouds as if to say that even it wasn't particularly pleased to see him. It would, however, make occasional appearances, allowing the least affirmation that the coach was still riding on the road and hadn't wandered off it to vanish into the boggy moorland.

Progress had slowed markedly during the past hour or more. The rain had turned the road to mud, mud that was now sucking the coach wheels deeper into the worn wheel tracks. Since the coach was now winding its way through the Lower Pennines instead of driving along the swifter flatlands, it was all the more likely they wouldn't arrive at Wyldewoode until well after midnight.

Damned bloody rain.

Dante slouched on the cracked leather seat, one booted foot propped on the edge of the opposite bench, listening to the cadence of the rain on the rooftop. His chin, darkened with three days' growth of a beard, rested irritably on his knuckles as he contemplated the foul weather and his equally foul mood.

He hated the rain. Every time some misfortune had come upon him during the course of his life, it had come about in the midst of a downpour. In a life which consisted thus far of two and thirty years, it had become downright predictable. Fifty-nine had been one of the more probative years. First his brother, then his father had died, and England had been nearly crippled by a downpour that rivaled the Great Deluge. What more should he have expected now on this, his return journey to England, a journey that was to take him to face his mother's grave?

Of course, Dante didn't know if it had been raining the day his mother had died. He hadn't been there. He had been across the Channel in France, where he'd spent the past three years, idling away his time at the court of the Sun King, Louis XIV. For all he knew, the weather could have been clear and sunny that late August day when his mother, Helena, had expired from the plague, alone with only her most faithful servants to attend her. It had, however, been pouring the day Dante had received the post, informing him of her passing.

The weather during the twelve months since, the three hundred and fifty-two days actually, was another matter of mystery to him. Instead of being here, at his home in England, where he wanted to be, where he knew he belonged, he had lingered in France, awaiting word from King Charles II permitting him to return home to pay his final respects to his mother. The day the king's messenger had come, finally granting him leave to return, had been a pleasant one, he remembered, not a dark cloud in the clear blue summer sky.

Dante had headed out the following morning on the first ship bound for Dover, and he hadn't looked back,

not once, as the boat carrying him across the water
back to his homeland had sailed from Calais.

That was nearly a week ago now, for Dante had left
Dover just five days before, in the gleaming black
Morgan coach that had been waiting for him on the
docks when he'd arrived. The coachman, a squat sort
of man named, aptly enough, Stubbs, whom Dante had
never before seen or heard of, and who spoke with a
terrible stutter, said he'd been given instruction by
Renny, the Morgan steward, to be there to meet him.
Dante hadn't bothered to ask Stubbs how Renny would
have known he'd be returning at all, let alone how he
knew he'd be arriving on that particular day. Truth-
fully, he didn't care.

The coach jerked suddenly, taking Dante from his
thoughts as it veered sharply to the right. Dante's slum-
bering valet, Penhurst, pitched forward from the opposite coach seat, nearly onto Dante's lap. The coach
lurched forward and sideways to a hard and abrupt halt.

"I beg your pardon, my lord," Penhurst said, his expression confused and hazy from a sleep which had
likely been filled with visions of sunnier days and far
more agreeable climes.

"No need," Dante said, peering out the window, trying to see what could have caused the disturbance.

"Have we run off the road, my lord?"

"I'm not certain, Penhurst. With the clouds obstruct-
ing the moon, I can't see more than six inches through
the window." Dante threw open the door. A blast of
chilled night air struck him full face. "What the devil is
going on out there, Stubbs?"

There passed a silent moment. The coach lurched
again and Dante had to grab hold of the door frame to
keep from falling out. Then he heard the sound of
someone running.

"Stubbs!" Dante shouted, louder this time, "are you
all right, man?"

When there was still no response, Dante reached for his flintlock inside the compartment hidden beneath the coach seat.

"Highwaymen?" Penhurst whispered, the whites of his eyes showing in the moonlight that had suddenly come out from behind the clouds, lighting the coach's interior.

"Perhaps." Dante slid forward and peered around the door. The rain had stopped. Surely, that was a good sign.

"Stay here, Penhurst. There's a second pistol hidden in the seat there. It is fully loaded. Take it and cock it and be ready should I need you."

"But, my lord Morgan, I've never discharged a firearm in my life. I've never even held one. I wouldn't know the first thing of how to—"

Dante quickly strapped on his rapier. "Just be sure to cock it all the way back, not halfway, and act as if you know what you're about should we find ourselves faced with more than one highwayman. They are known to sometimes travel in pairs."

"Aye, my lord, but what if . . ."

Dante vanished into the night. He slipped around to the back of the coach, coming up along the opposite side. He could hear Penhurst inside fumbling for the pistol in the darkness. He said a silent prayer the valet didn't end up shooting himself in the process. Dante couldn't see a thing, nor could he hear a sound, except the jingling of the reins with the occasional movement of the team to his right. The smell of rain and horse sweat filled the cold night air. A light drizzle began to fall.

Dante could see in the faint moonlight, that the coach was set at an odd angle just off the roadway. Tall, wet grass blew around the tops of his jackboots in the gusting wind. The icy air cut through the cambric of his shirt. He peered at the coach seat and found it empty.

Had Stubbs perhaps fallen asleep at the reins and tumbled over the side? Had he been waylaid? Dante searched for his stout body lying in the grass. He pivoted about at the sound of running footsteps coming toward him from behind, lowered the flintlock, cocked it, and trained his sights toward the noise.

"Halt, or be shot where you are!"

"L-Lord M-M-Morgan," came a winded voice, " 'tis m-me, S-Stubbs."

"Deuce take it." Dante lowered his pistol. "What in perdition were you doing, man? I nearly shot you through."

"I s-saw something in th-the road just as we c-c-came around th-that bend. I had t-to run us off the r-road s-so I wo-wouldn't hit it."

Stubbs's stutter had worsened, punctuated by his attempts at catching his breath from running.

"Relax, Stubbs. Take long, deep breaths and calm yourself."

The coachman did as he was bid, bending at the waist, puffing up his jowly cheeks, and blowing out his mouth as if he were trying to bring up a fire from an ember. Finally, he stood, peering up at Dante from shoulder height.

"I th-thought it was a deer ly-lying there in the m-middle of the road l-like that. I ran b-back to s-see if it w-were still alive. B-but it w-, it w-, it w- . . ." His stuttering suddenly overcame him so that he couldn't finish his sentence at all.

Dante clapped him once, hard between the shoulder blades, knocking him forward. "It's all right, Stubbs. Calm yourself. Take two more deep breaths. That's good. Now talk slowly. What did you find lying in the road?"

"I th-think it w-were a b-body, m-my lord."

A body?

Dante pulled on the coachman's arm. "Show me where it is."

They started back the way Stubbs had come. Dante couldn't see clearly with the thick cover of trees that surrounded them. He wondered how Stubbs had concluded that what he'd seen had been a body at all. Surely, it was his imagination running wild. Surely, it had been an animal standing in the road that most probably had run off by now, frightened by the coach and Stubbs's confounded stuttering. But as they rounded the bend in the road, coming into a clearing, Dante saw it, just as Stubbs had said. There in the mottled moonlight, a figure lay on its side in the middle of the road several yards away. A light-colored garment covered it, but two bare legs curled distinctly under it.

Dante came to a standstill. It was a body—bloody hell—where a body shouldn't be. He remembered how the coach had lurched. He grabbed Stubbs by the sleeve.

"Are you certain you didn't hit it?" he asked, his tone deadly serious.

"I m-missed it, I'm s-sure of it, m-milord. I sw-swear I d-didn't, I d-didn't . . ."

Stubbs began to puff and wheeze once again.

"All right, Stubbs. Stay here and try to calm yourself." Dante pushed his pistol into the man's trembling hands. "Listen to me. This could possibly be a trap set by a highwayman, an attempt to distract us so we can be successfully waylaid. I will go forward to see what is going on here. I want you to shoot if you hear or see anything that is at all suspicious."

"B-but, my lord, I d-don't know h-how to sh-sh-shoot a g-gun!"

A coachman who didn't know how to fire a weapon? What idiot had employed the man? "Just hold the pistol up as though you know what you're doing. I will return in a few minutes."

Dante left Stubbs and started toward the body. He pulled his rapier free from its scabbard. He glanced back at the coachman, who was standing at the same spot he'd left him, holding the pistol up with two hands that Dante could see trembling even in the faint moonlight. He was taking in long deep breaths, whistling them out in the silence as he exhaled. The barrel of the pistol was aimed straight for Dante's back.

"Stubbs, point that thing away from me, please. Should your finger accidentally hit the trigger, I'll end up shot, and that's not the way I wish my life to end, here on this road, in the remote parts of Derbyshire."

"Aye, m-milord."

Dante stopped when he reached the motionless body. Its back was to him, one thin arm flung forward to shield the face. It had every appearance of being dead. He glanced around and seeing nothing suspicious, he hunkered down beside it.

"Can you hear me?" Dante said softly, watching for a movement.

There was none.

Dante set one hand on the body's shoulder, immediately noticing how cold the skin was, how thinly it was stretched over the fragile bones beneath it. His initial suspicions that whoever this was would not be found alive mounted. He pulled gently, turning the body to face him. He sucked in a sharp breath when he saw that the body lying there in the road was actually a young woman.

He couldn't see her face clearly in the night, but he recognized her fine bone structure and the distinct outline of her breasts beneath the thin white covering over her. She didn't move. She didn't speak. He couldn't detect if she was still breathing. The realization that she might be dead filled him with a strange sense of sadness and loss.

Dante nudged her. "Can you hear me, miss?"

No response.

"Stubbs!" he shouted, dropping his rapier, "go back to the coach and fetch a lamp. And get my cloak from Penhurst inside. Hurry, man!"

It seemed to take Stubbs a long time, too long, to return. Dante didn't move from where he knelt. He felt along the woman's wrist for a pulse. He released a breath when he found one. It was a weak one, but at least she was still alive. He didn't take his fingers from it.

Dante moved so that he could see the girl's face more clearly in the faint moonlight. Full lashes, spiked from the rain, rested lightly on her cheeks. Her skin was pale, and her lips were slightly parted. Without knowing why or even realizing it, Dante lowered his head and lightly touched his mouth to hers. Her lips were soft, supple. He thought he detected a slight movement in response, but he pulled away when he heard a noise coming from behind. He turned to see a light swinging erratically back and forth moving toward him.

"H-here it is, m-milord. I h-have the l-lamp. And I h-have your cl-cloak, too."

"Good work, Stubbs. Hold the lamp up and shine the light over her."

The face revealed was delicate, marred only by splotches of mud from the road and a raised bruise at the hairline. Dante gently pushed two fingers through the wet strands, probing the swollen skin. When he brought his hand back, his fingers were stained red with fresh blood in the lamplight.

" 'Tis a g-girl, m-milord!"

"That she is, Stubbs, and she's had an injury to her head. I won't be able to tell how severe it is until we have benefit of better lighting. How far are we from the nearest village?"

"Eyam w-would be th-the c-closest by. We'll h-have to t-turn off the m-main road to g-get there. It's a sm-small village, and T-Tideswell is only another qu-quarter hour or s-so, m-milord."

"Give me the cloak, Stubbs."

Dante lifted the girl and wrapped her in it until her small body was completely covered by the voluminous fabric.

"Let us get her into the coach and to Eyam as fast as you can take us, Stubbs."

"Is sh-she d-dead, m-milord?"

"No, but as far as I can tell it is only by the slightest of margins. We must hurry if we hope to have any chance at saving her."

Dante took the girl gently into his arms and followed behind Stubbs and the lamplight as they retraced their steps back to the coach. He lifted one booted foot on the closed coach door and kicked hard. It immediately sprang open.

"Halt or I'll shoot!"

"Calm yourself, Penhurst. I'm no highway man."

Dante set the girl carefully on the seat before taking the lamp from Stubbs. He hung it from a small hook in the ceiling.

Penhurst was pressed as far back on the coach seat as he possibly could be. His eyes were wide and terrified, his mouth fixed in a grimace. In his shaking hands he held the pistol Dante had given him. The butt of the thing was aimed for Dante's chest, Penhurst's two hands clutching the thick metal barrel close against himself. The muzzle was pointed dangerously downward.

"If you don't take immediate precautions, Penhurst, you'll greatly hinder any hopes you might have at procreating. You've got that thing aimed straight at your nether parts."

Penhurst's face lit with alarm, and he nearly dropped the pistol in his haste to set it aside.

Dante took the flintlock and released the cock. "Remind me, Penhurst, at the first opportunity, to teach you and Stubbs here the proper handling of a weapon. It's one of the two basic things every man should know."

"What be th-the second, m-my lord?" Stubbs asked from behind.

"The proper handling of a female, of course, although I don't rightfully know which I would consider more treacherous. Which would you say, Penhurst?"

Dante was trying to ease Penhurst's obvious distress, without much success, for the valet didn't respond. Instead he peered curiously at the cloaked bundle Dante had set on the seat across from him.

"What is it, my lord?"

"*It*, my good man, is a girl, soaked to the skin, wearing naught but her smallclothes, and she's injured. A nasty gash to the head that I fear is far worse than it first appeared. We're going to move on to the nearest village and see if we can locate a physician to help her."

Dante gently pulled the girl against him, seeking to warm her with the heat of his own body, as Stubbs snapped the reins and the team started forward. He slid his fingers along the slender column of her neck for her pulse once again. He was glad to note that she was already growing warmer. He found a pulsebeat just above her collarbone and let his fingers linger there. With his other hand he tried to brush some of the road dirt from her cheek.

She was young, eighteen perhaps, and so thin she looked as if she would blow away in a strong wind. He couldn't tell the color of her hair, for it was wet and sticking close to her skull. Her lashes were thick and dark, her bottom lip slightly fuller than the top. Dante wondered what she was doing in the middle of the road and in the middle of the night. He wondered how she'd been injured. He thought to himself that she was quite lovely—not an elegant beauty, one that takes away your breath with wonder, but a charming picture that leaves one feeling intrigued.

"Do you have a handkerchief, Penhurst?"

The valet produced one immediately, as if he'd simply been awaiting the request.

Dante took the cloth and pressed it gently to the wound on the girl's forehead. There was still blood, but it seemed to be slowing. Dante took hope. He looked up and he could see Penhurst sitting across from him, watching closely as Dante had studied the girl's face. He didn't say a word. They passed the next quarter hour in silence until the coach finally began to slow.

"We must be at Eyam," Dante said, parting the curtain to peer outside.

In the moonlight, now fully out with the passing of the rain clouds, he could see two figures standing in the middle of the roadway, hindering their passage.

As they came to a halt, Dante recognized they were men, one of them hold a burning torch, its smoke twisting upward in a dark, ominous spiral.

The other held a musket aimed straight for the coach.

Chapter Three

One of the men came toward the coach, swinging the flaming torch outward as if to hold them at bay. "Halt! Turn your coach and go back. Ye'll go no farther."

"B-but m-milord M-Morgan must needs s-see a physician r-right away."

The musket man trained his sights on poor Stubbs. "Ye'll not find one in Eyam."

"B-but . . ."

Dante laid the girl back gently against the coach seat. He didn't want to leave her, but he also didn't much like the looks of things outside, especially the reckless manner in which the gunman was wielding his musket. Judging from his brief experience with Stubbs thus far, Dante would have guessed the man near to an apoplectic fit by now. It was time he took hold of the matter before someone ended up getting his head shot off, that someone more than likely being Stubbs.

Dante grabbed his flintlock and pushed the coach door open. "What is the trouble here, gentlemen?"

He started walking toward the pair, coming up beside Stubbs and holding his pistol close against his side. The gunman shifted, aiming the musket barrel on him now.

"I said ye'll go no farther!"

Dante halted. "A moment, my good man. There was once an old Romany who told me it is extremely unwise to kill a man before you know his name. It doesn't

bode well with the powers above us"—he glanced star-
ward—"if you take my meaning." He extended his
hand. "I'm Dante Tremaine, the Earl of Morgan.
We've encountered a bit of a complication, and I'm
only looking for some place to stop to—"

The gunman eyed Dante's outstretched hand, but
didn't move to take it. Nor did he lower his musket.
"No one comes into Eyam, not even yer lordship. 'Tis
the only way we can control the spread of the plague."

"Plague," Dante said, taking a cautious step forward.
"Have you not heard? The plague is gone now, and
even if it wasn't we've not come from London, my
good man. I only just returned from the Continent. We
landed at Dover, and we traveled straight from there to
here and—"

"I said halt!" the gunman said, cocking the musket
fully now. His finger was ready on the trigger. "It's the
last warning I'll be giving ye. I've orders to shoot anyone what tries to get past the boundaries, and I means
to see to them."

Dante eyed the two small poles topped by red-
colored cloths fashioned into makeshift flags on either
side of the men along the roadway. "I can assure you,
gentlemen, we do not bring the plague with us."

"It's not that we fear ye might be bringin' the plague
into Eyam. We've already got the deadly sickness.
We're overrun with it. It's nearly a year ago now since
our village tailor, old Edward Cooper, opened a box of
clothes and patterns delivered him from London. He
didn't know the box was carrying the plague with it.
Struck down his whole family in that first month, it
did. Then came the others. We must have lost nearly
half the village by now. No one's really counted.
We're afraid to. Most of us wanted to leave for safer
places but Rector Mompesson, he told us it was our
duty as Christians to stop the plague from killing any
others by staying put here in Eyam. We've secluded

the entire village to keep the disease from spreading outside the village. No one is allowed in or out past these boundary lines."

Dante stared at the man. He could not believe what he was hearing. He wondered why he hadn't noticed before then the gaunt hopelessness that hung about the man like a shroud. They, both of them, had eyes that were hooded with their fear. "Do you mean to say your entire village has been cut off from civilization for a year now? How can you possibly continue to survive? Where do you get your essentials?"

"His Lordship, the Earl of Devonshire, sends supplies to us by carrier from Chatsworth. They leave them at the southern boundary before dawn. We come to pick them up at midday and leave money in a hole we dug in a stream there. The water washes the coin so the infection will not spread to any others."

"But how can you continue on like this with no monies coming into the village?"

The torchman spat in the dirt. "We can't. Everyone knows the plague is here, so no one with any sense would buy goods coming from Eyam. Those what aren't dying from the plague will soon be dying from starvation. We try to ration what supplies we can, but even that won't last for long. That thief, Marshall Howe, he's the only one getting rich off the bloody plague."

"Marshall Howe?"

"Aye. He's a big, foul-mouthed bastard who took to acting as parish burier for the dead, but not for any Christian reasons, mind ye. He took the job only by claiming as his right all money and possessions left by the dead with no heirs. Lost his wife and young son, he did, but he doesn't trouble over it. All he cares is how fat his pockets are growing off the dead. He's profiting off the plague whilst the rest of us are starving and praying for its end."

Dante had heard enough. "Penhurst get me my traveling satchel from under the coach seat." He looked back to the two men. "Gentlemen, I've a young girl we found lying unconscious in the road not far from here. She's a bad blow to her head. I do not think she'll survive much longer without medical attention. Would either of you know where I might find a physician close by to tend her?"

The musketman only then lowered his gun. "Found her nearby, you say? A blow to her head? Were I you, milord, I'd be to setting her back down quick as ye can. Could be she's from the village and found a way to escape. Could be she's infected with the plague. Probably tried to beg a ride on a passing coach, and they whacked her in the head to keep her away. In either case, ye'll be hard-pressed to find a quack what will look at her."

Dante took the satchel from Penhurst, removed a small leather pouch from inside, and tossed it in the direction of the two men. It chinged in the still night air, skittering in the roadway.

"Take the coin inside, gentlemen, and make certain it is used to buy the needed supplies for your villagers."

The torchman had already scooped the pouch up and was counting out the coin from inside into his palm. "Look, Mackie. There's enough here to keep everyone fed for a month! 'Tis a bloomin' fortune. God bless ye and keep ye, Lord Morgan."

"Wyldewoode, my family seat, is located not far from here, near Castleton. As soon as I arrive there and have settled, I'll send additional supplies to your village through Lord Devonshire. If you have need of anything in particular, let me know of it, and I will see you receive it. Tell Rector Mompesson what your village has done to prevent the disease from spreading is the most courageous and selfless act I've ever seen. I pray you do not lose another soul to plague. You are all of you to be commended for your bravery."

Dante turned to leave, releasing the catch on his flintlock a second time now.

"Godspeed, Lord Morgan," said the torchman.

"Aye," added the musketman called Mackie, " 'tis a gentleman, ye are, and a good Christian, milord."

As Dante started back toward the coach, his heart felt cold and heavy in his chest, knowing the hopeless plight of those poor people. He could take no real satisfaction from his deed. His paltry donation could do nothing to bring back those who had already gone on to the hereafter.

Would this disease never end? For nearly two years the plague had held England in its thrall. It was said there wasn't a family who hadn't been touched by it in some way. It took the good, the bad, the innocent, the condemned. Yes, there had been outbreaks before during his lifetime, but never of this magnitude. This time it had taken his mother. The more Puritan-minded called the plague God's punishment for the loose and libertine response that had come about in the wake of the reign of the Protectorate. Others said it was the beginning to the end of the world, the Lord's long-promised Judgment Day.

No one knew what the next day would hold. Everyone was desperate for atonement. Everyone had begun to question their past way of living. Even Dante.

When Dante reached the coach door, Penhurst stepped from the shadows, drawing up close beside him.

"My lord Morgan, do you think what they said could be true?"

"What is that, Penhurst?" Dante said, redepositing the flintlock in its place.

Penhurst eyed the cloaked bundle inside the coach through the open door. "I heard what those two men said about the girl. Do you think she could possibly be carrying the plague?"

Dante looked at his valet. He thought of his mother dying from the disease, of the reports of how it could spread on the wind, infecting all it came into contact with. So many had died already, countless many. He remembered the girl's slight body lying in the middle of that roadway. Her face had been so deathly pale. He remembered the blood from the wound on her head, blood that hadn't been brought on by any plague. He knew what he must do.

"No, Penhurst. While I understand and appreciate your concerns, this girl is injured and is in need of help. I could not leave her to die alone on the road, which is surely what would happen, when odds are she doesn't even carry the disease. She would expire from exposure alone. What kind of man would I be were I to so much as consider such a thing?"

"Yes, my lord, but, perhaps you could just take her to the next village and leave her there—"

"Penhurst, if I didn't know you better, I might believe you were suddenly showing misogynist tendencies. We are nothing if not gentlemen, my good man, out to set the world to rights, to secure safety for any damsel in distress."

"Pardon my forwardness, my lord, but was it not the last time in coming to the aid of another damsel in distress that sent us to France for the space of the past three years?"

Forward or not, Dante could not deny the truth of Penhurst's statement. He had paid dearly for that little escapade. It had been his first real experience in self-study. He hadn't much liked what he saw and he swore it would never happen again. Still, it didn't change the situation now.

"I'm sorry, Penhurst," Dante said, "but I must do what any gentleman would do in a like situation. No true gentleman would desert this young woman. Nor can I drive about the countryside, looking for a village that will take her. Faith, none will take her if there is such a strong plague fear among the nearby areas as it would seem from the two men there. No, I will take the young woman with us to Wyldewoode, and I will minister to her there myself. Once she has mended, I will then happily return her to her people."

Penhurst stared at him. "As you wish, my lord."

Dante smiled, clapping the valet on the back. "Now come, my good man, let us stop worrying and be off before the rain begins again and fills our boot tops to overflowing."

The darkness was comforting, and it was only with some effort that she managed to open her eyes. She blinked slowly, hesitantly, trying to focus against the bright and blinding sunlight that awaited her on the other side.

She lay still for some time, her eyes moving about, noticing everything, recognizing nothing around her. She was lying on an unfamiliar bed, pale peach damask draped about the posts above her. The eggshell walls were adorned here and there with feminine knickknackery, tiny statuettes set on a wall shelf, a small painting of lovely spring flowers framed in gold leaf beside it. It was the sort of room that greeted people when they woke, filling them with the joy of a renewal, instead of making them want to bury their heads beneath the pillows again to sleep away the remainder of the day.

She started to sit up, but the moment she tried to lift her head, a sharp pain shot straight through her skull. She lifted a hand to her temple where it seemed to hurt the worst, startled when her hand touched cloth and not hair and skin as she'd expected.

She probed at the cloth lightly with her fingers. It

Jaclyn Reding

was a bandage that wound around to the back of her head. What had happened? Had she been injured? Obviously, she had, but how badly? Gingerly she sat upright and looked over her person for any other bandages. She was wearing a nightrail made of soft cambric that was decorated along the front with ivory lace and tiny seed pearls. It was lovely and she realized that it wasn't her own for she knew she'd never seen such a delicate feminine creation in her life.

She slid her legs over the side of the bed and stood, wavering slightly. Volumes of the soft fabric swirled down around her legs, caressing her skin as it pooled around her feet at the carpeted floor. Now she was certain of it. This exquisite garment had definitely been fashioned for another, someone who was much taller than she.

She walked slowly across the room, her bare feet sinking into the thick Aubusson carpet. Rich furnishings of fruitwood inlayed with mother-of-pearl decorated the tasteful and airy chamber. Twin armchairs upholstered in peach damask flanked the tall casement windows. She looked outside. The view beyond was breathtaking. A rich green lawn stretching as far as the eye could reach, meticulously cared for with trimmed topiary, beds bursting with colorful flowers, and a small serene pond off to one side greeted her. Below, on a flagstone-paved courtyard framed with huge pots of bright flowers, she watched a maid as she shook the dust out from a small rug. She didn't recognize her. She didn't recognize anything. The house, the trees, the room she stood in, everything around her was foreign to her. Even the clothes she wore were unfamiliar, almost as if she'd woken to find herself in a dream.

Yes, that was it, she thought. She must be dreaming. And what a lovely and curious dream it was.

She decided to start back for the bed, thinking to lie down, close her eyes, and wait for this chimeric scene to conclude. Her head had begun to throb a little, persistent though not painful, where the bandage was. She hoped that when she woke, she would remember the rest of the dream, remember why she was here in this strange and beautiful house, wearing someone else's clothes with a bandage wound around her head.

She froze when she turned and noticed a man standing in the doorway across the room. He watched her with a smile in his warm dark eyes.

"Good morning," he said to her. His voice was deep, rich, the sort of voice that drew attention with just the sound of it.

"Good morning," she replied, wondering who this man was who had suddenly appeared in her dream.

He advanced into the room. "How do you feel?"

"Fine, well, a little light-headed, but I guess that's only to be expected."

Dreams did seem to have a sort of whimsical effect on a person's sensibilities, as if every movement was executed a little slower than when awake.

"I should think so."

So he knew this was a dream as well. How interesting, she thought, finding she quite liked his smile.

"Are you in any pain?" he asked.

Pain? Why would a dream cause her any pain, unless, of course, it was a nightmare, but thus far, this dream didn't appear to have the trappings of being nasty.

She shrugged. "No, I don't believe so. Should I be?"

"Not necessarily. I am glad to hear you are feeling well, but I think it might be better if you returned to bed now. We wouldn't want to aggravate your condition with too much activity too soon."

She nodded, thinking she could probably agree with most anything this man said to her. He had a most persuasive air about him. She started toward the bed, wondering where this odd dream might lead. Her head was growing lighter.

Her conjured-up dream man, who was really quite handsome now that she saw him closer, came to stand at the side of the bed. He was dressed casually, wearing a cambric shirt that was unfastened at his neck. His breeches were tan and snug. He wore brown, well-worn jackboots reaching to just below his knees. His hair was cut short to the nape of his neck, and it was the darkest black she'd ever seen—another result of the dream, no doubt. A small bit of it fell appealingly over his eyes, eyes that were an odd shade of golden brown, like shimmering amber, perhaps. She wanted to touch his hair. He was very tall, not like any man she'd ever encountered. Ruggedly crafted, he towered over her as only a man in a dream would.

"Is there anything I can get for you?" he asked.

"No," she answered, smiling slightly to herself. "You're very handsome," she added, knowing she would never dare say anything so forward were she awake. She only had spoken now because this was a dream, this man was indeed very handsome, and she was feeling rather reckless.

The man smiled, and two dimples appeared on either side of his generous mouth. She felt the urge to reach out and touch them, but decided that might be taking things a bit too far, even in a dream.

"Thank you," he said. "Why don't you just lie back and close your eyes to rest."

"But then you'll go away, and I don't want you to leave just yet."

His smile deepened. So did the dimples. The urge to touch them grew.

"All right, I suppose I can stay for a little while." He lowered himself into a chair beside the bed. "What would you like to talk about?"

"Where am I?"

"You are at my house, at my family estate, Wyldewoode, in Derbyshire."

"It is a very pretty house, I mean what I could see of it from the window. The flowers in the garden are lovely, and this room is very lovely, too."

"This is my mother's room."

"Oh. Won't she be displeased to find me in her bed? Where will she sleep?"

Her dream man's face darkened at the question. "My mother died last year."

"I'm so very sorry. What happened to her?"

"The plague."

"How truly terrible for you, but at least you weren't taken by the sickness as well."

The man looked down at the floor. Any trace of the dimples was definitely gone now. She frowned.

"I wasn't here when my mother died," he said softly. "I couldn't be here."

This dream was in dire need of some uplifting. "How did I get here, to your house, I mean?"

"You don't remember?"

She thought for a moment, but nothing came to mind. This didn't alarm her, though, for this was a dream, and everyone knew things weren't always what they were supposed to be in dreams. She shrugged, saying matter-of-factly, "No, I'm afraid I don't remember."

"I found you lying in the road not far from here. You had been injured."

She raised a hand to the bandage on her head. She had completely forgotten about that.

"Do you know how you came to be there?" he asked. "No."

"Can you tell me where you are from, so I can send a message to your family to let them know you are safe?"

She thought, but, again, nothing came to mind. How funny dreams could be. "No."

The man looked at her, an odd expression on his face. "No, you cannot tell me where you are from, or no, you will not tell me?"

She shrugged. "No, I cannot tell you. I don't know where I am from."

"Can you tell me who your family are?"

She shook her head. She was not at all worried. Any moment now she would be waking from this dream. "No."

"Can you tell me your name?"

"No."

"Do you know your age?"

"No."

"Do you know what color your eyes are?"

She thought, and then giggled. "No, I do not."

Her responses seemed to be causing him a great deal of distress. She reached out and patted his hand reassuringly. She liked the warm, rough feel of his skin. "It is all right, sir. You see, when I wake up, everything will be back to the way it was, before I started dreaming this dream, I mean. There really is no need to worry yourself."

He looked at her, his face grave. "I'm afraid this is no dream, miss."

She smiled. "Of course, it is."

"I assure you it is not."

His dead-on serious tone began to alarm her. "Don't tease me so, sir. Of course this is a dream. Why else would I wake to find myself here, in your house, wearing someone else's clothing, where I recognize nothing, where I know no one, and where I am unable to remember my name or where I come from?"

Chapter Four

"You did what!"

Clare Forrester's elegant features fixed into a mask of anger as she all but leapt from her chair. "How could you be so stupid? You lost Gillian? What in bloody perdition happened to her?"

Garrick had expected Clare to be upset, even angry by his words, so her reaction did not really come as any surprise. What he did find difficult to believe was that she would voice her feelings so loudly, especially since only a single door separated them from the assembly room they'd just slipped from, an assembly room that was presently filled with nearly half of London's more cultured society, including every member of Clare's family. Should the two of them be discovered together, alone as they were in this dark and quite secluded antechamber, their affair would surely be exposed. While that didn't really give Garrick cause for concern—in truth it would only do his repute a good turn—it might bring Clare a bit of unwanted trouble, and that most assuredly from her husband.

"Tell me exactly what happened," Clare said, her words clipped. "And I want every last detail."

"As best as I can figure, I seem to have lost Gillian somewhere in the wilds of Derbyshire," said Garrick, calmly inspecting a fingernail. "It was late at night, and it was indeed raining rather hard. The coach had slowed as we moved over a stretch of rough road. It was fast growing cold inside the coach. Ozzie was sleeping, snoring like a drunk really, oblivious of both the cold and the coach bounding over the rugged road. I had poured myself a bit of brandy to warm me. Being a gentleman, I offered some to Gillian. I was concerned for her health because she had begun to sneeze earlier that day and had she had grown a bit pale. Gillian took the brandy and made to drink, but instead of swallowing it she tossed it into my eyes. I was blinded. I never saw her leave, but when my vision finally cleared, she was indeed gone, leaving the coach door flapping in the wind."

"Idiot!" Clare spat, an unappealing response for her. She began pacing the floor, her silk skirts sweeping any tracings of dust from the floorboards of the seemingly neglected chamber. "How could you have been so enormously stupid?"

Garrick stared at her, allowing time for her tirade to expend itself. Clare might be angry with him. She might even call him unpleasant names and question his intelligence, but Garrick had learned since they'd first become lovers to take Clare's bouts of temper in stride. He could accomplish this only because he knew that later that evening, when they were naked and he was thrusting inside of her, Clare would look at him entirely differently. No longer elegant or even angry, she would look at him with that particular gleam in her lovely green eyes, a gleam that told him he was ultimately her master. The satisfaction he found in the promise of this gleam allowed him to tolerate her viper's tongue now instead of slapping her into the submissive silence she deserved.

"What does it matter, really?" Garrick said then, attempting to calm her. "You wanted Gillian gone, and she is gone. As I see it, everything went according to plan. And if anyone should be irritated, it is me. I lost out on any reward for my part in this scheme when the insolent little chit nearly blinded me with that brandy before she jumped like a fool from the coach."

"Tell me something." Clare came to stand before him, hands placed at her narrow corseted waist. Her breasts were pushed up to the point of near-bursting from her strict bodice, rising and falling rapidly with her irritation. Garrick felt an urge to touch them, but wisely tempered that urge.

"Did you not hear me when I told you why I wanted you to take Gillian from here and wed her?"

Actually, Garrick tried his best not to listen to Clare whenever she hatched one of her reckless schemes. They were usually vicious, and oftentimes senselessly cruel, such as the time she'd arranged to have certain mandatory stitches loosened on the gown of a young woman she had taken a dislike to. The result had been an unexpected halt to a rather invigorating performance of the galliard in a crowded court ballroom. Reflecting on it now, Garrick could still hear Clare's wicked laughter as the poor thing had stood there frozen before all of London society, her skirts pooled at her ankles, her privy parts exposed to all and sundry. However, Garrick now recalled that at the particular moment when Clare had been detailing her plans for Gillian, he had indeed heard her. "As I remember it, you were concerned because Gillian had nearly uncovered your little secret. You wanted her gone so no one would suspect what you were really involved in."

Clare sat down, her pale green silk skirts swirling about the carved scrolled feet of the elegant high back chair. She shook her head, saying, "Gillian would have figured it out. She would have figured out all of it, given the time."

"Yes, Gillian was a rather bright girl, wasn't she? I do believe she would have gotten to the heart of matters sometime. It is a good thing you convinced me I should wed her."

"If that is an attempt at flattery, you can abandon it. It was the fifty thousand pounds she was to bring in dowry that convinced you, not me."

"But it was still a risky wager Clare, even for me. After all, who was to say I'd ever realize Gillian's dowry? I am wont to believe that her father, your father-in-law, the good marquess, would have been less than pleased with a son-in-law who had resorted to abduction in order to secure himself a wife, especially when his daughter was the unwilling bride. He might have even had the union annulled."

"Given that you were not to return to London until you had Gillian well with child, I should think an annulment less than a threat to your reward, as you call it. Lord Adamley would never risk the disgrace of having Gillian unwed with a bastard in her belly. He would not have liked it, having his daughter wed by such circumstances, but then he would have had no choice, really. He would have had to accept you. He would never allow Gillian to endure the scandal. That is precisely why heiresses are abducted into marriage so successfully."

"Yes, well, more importantly you are still free from the burden of Gillian's curiosity. She can no longer question your activities." Garrick was pleased with himself that he'd managed to sound as if he actually cared.

Clare narrowed her eyes. "But I am certainly not free from the possibility that Gillian might turn up at any given moment. I will have to delay my plans now, at least until I am certain of what became of her."

"I really don't think you've anything to worry about."

"It is there you are wrong. I do have to worry." Clare frowned, making the lines around her mouth deepen unattractively. "Because of you I will now be forced to continue to live in the same house with my husband's family, all of them. You cannot possibly imagine what it is like, having to see them each day and act as if I do not hate them. Have you any idea how truly confining it is to live here?"

Garrick shrugged. "Not really."

"I must see them every day, and I must be pleasant if I wish even a modicum of peace. I am allowed no freedoms; my every moment is either spent with them or questioned by them. I have no privacy, and worse than that, because there are so many of them, I must sleep in the same bedchamber as my husband. Reginald refuses to leave Adamley House, and he refuses to allow me a house of my own, even though he has every pound of my dowry totally at his disposal. This house is already filled to bursting, what with Marcellus and that mousy wife of his producing children like rabbits, I swear I cannot even relieve myself in peace."

Suddenly, Garrick was very glad things had turned out as they had for, fifty thousand in dowry or not, it sounded as if he would have come out at the disadvantage in these doings. "Gillian's disappearance will undoubtedly still create a scandal that will prove to be a minor thorn at least in the good marquess's side. That should give you some taste of satisfaction."

Clare smiled. "It is true, but he deserves far worse. It is because of him I am still wed to his worthless son. You should count yourself fortunate I hadn't yet arranged for the marquess to find Gillian's diary with my recently added entry indicating she had eloped with you. It might have been a bit difficult for you, explaining a dead bride. It actually worked out better since the marquess has already considered the possibility of Gillian having eloped, with my subtle suggestion, of course. But to him it is only a possibility right now. Another is that she may have been kidnapped. Either way the marquess is caught. He is not in a position politically to endure a scandal. Faith, thus far he hasn't even alerted the authorities to Gillian's disappearance. He cannot for if she was kidnapped, he knows what it would do to her, and to this family, once she returns. She would be ruined, as would any possibility of an advantageous marriage. But if Gillian eloped, that is an entirely different sort of scandal. So instead he has hired some sort of investigator to see if he can discover what happened to her."

"An investigator?" Garrick felt a slight tightening in his stomach. "What if the man finds something out? What if he discovers my involvement somehow?"

"I wouldn't worry. This investigator has an even smaller brain than that idiot Ozwell you persist in associating with. I believe his initial theory was pirates who came into her bedchamber and spirited her away into white slavery. I daresay he'll be occupied on that end for quite some time. They have no way of knowing where Gillian is or who took her, but the marquess will not alert the authorities of her disappearance, yet. It's amusing really. Lord Adamley spends his nights sitting all alone in his study until well into the wee hours, worrying himself senseless. I cannot say which is more worrisome to him though, the fact that his daughter has vanished to parts unknown, or the potential for scandal and what it might to do his political career."

"A result, no doubt, of that nasty little episode you presented him with not so many years ago."

Clare frowned at the mention of her one well-known failure. It had been a brilliant plan, really, to rid herself of her marriage to Reginald Forrester, eldest son of the Marquess of Adamley, but due to unforeseen complications, it hadn't come off. Instead, it had left her utterly and publicly humiliated. It was not a feeling she wished to experience again. Nor did she plan to.

"Which is precisely why the marquess will not yet allow anyone outside the family to know Gillian is missing," Clare said. "He has hired his investigator and has paid him handsomely to keep quiet about whatever he might finally discover. Further, he has instructed everyone in the household to explain away Gillian's sudden absence as a visit to an ailing aunt in the country. He has threatened to dismiss any servant who speaks otherwise. He will not even consider that Gillian might not return. And I am telling you now, Garrick, Gillian must return. That is one point on which the marquess and I agree. I cannot proceed further with my plans until I am certain what has become of her. You must find her and wed her before she has the chance to find her way back on her own and tell everything. If she does that, it will not be just me who will suffer. You will be implicated as well."

Listening to her now, Garrick wondered why he'd ever agreed to take part in this plan in the first place. And then he remembered. It had been the same night Clare had slipped that interesting little gold ring over his rod, which had kept him hard for hours.

"And my reward is marriage to the freethinking Gillian and virtual imprisonment at Adamley House," he said. "That fifty thousand in dowry is beginning to sound less appealing by the minute."

"There are other advantages you haven't yet considered," Clare added, sensing his fading enthusiasm. "As Gillian's husband, living in this house, you would have complete access to me as well. There would be no more thirty-second trysts against uncomfortable casks in buttery closets. We would be living under the same roof. The possibilities would be virtually endless."

Garrick looked at her. "Sounds tempting."

"It can be more than temptation. All you need do is find her, and it can be reality." Clare stood and sidled over to Garrick. She licked her fingertip with the tip of her tongue and touched it to his lips. "You grant me this one small favor, and I promise your rewards will be beyond anything you could have imagined."

Garrick schooled his instinctive male response as Clare curled her body against his and offered him her mouth. Even as he kissed her, it perturbed him to no end that Clare believed him so raw as to think a dip between her thighs that much more satisfying than anyone else's. One woman was as good as another, after all. Still, thinking again of the little gold ring, Garrick had to admit Clare was quite inventive. Despite that he was fast growing weary of her relentless self-infatuation, he decided it would be best to maintain her belief that she was in control, and that he was content merely to do her bidding. The less intelligent she thought him, the easier it would be for him to escape the aftermath should her plan be uncovered.

"So what is it you wish me to do from here?" he asked, pulling away. "I certainly cannot leave London to go traipsing about the English countryside looking for Gillian now. It might seem a little suspicious were I to disappear at the same time as Gillian. I'd be the first one they'd look to. While I am willing to take an outside part in your little schemes, I am not willing to face the possibility of hanging for murder."

Clare fell silent. It was not a thing she did often, but Garrick knew she could not deny the truth of his words.

"Then, send someone after her," she said after a few minutes of careful contemplation. "You can have that bumbling idiot, Gilhooly, see to the task since you've already involved him in this. No one would question his leaving town. They probably wouldn't even notice, and certainly no one would believe him clever enough to have pulled off Gillian's abduction. He is a consummate fool. I cannot for the life of me figure out why you countenance him."

For much the same reason I do you, Garrick thought. *For the moment anyway, you both serve me a purpose.*

"Ozzie is quite capable of seeing to it," Garrick

said, ready to say anything now just to be quit of her. While she might know wonderful things to do to his body, she also had a talent for wearing his patience thin.

"Just make certain he leaves no stone unturned," Clare said. "Gillian can't have gone far from where you lost her. Derbyshire is quite remote. She has no money, no food, she doesn't even have any clothes beyond her nightrail. Just find her and we will proceed as originally planned."

Garrick stood, peering at Clare with unconcealed lust. Hopes of the little gold ring had risen, among other things. "Will I be seeing you later?"

"No." Clare checked her appearance in the looking glass near the door. She turned and wiped the remnants of her lip rouge from his mouth. "It is far too dangerous with Gillian's recent disappearance. I cannot risk any connection to her abduction. Just send me a message when you have found her, and we will proceed from there. Until then, I would suggest you keep yourself as visible as you possibly can."

That would not a problem, Garrick thought as he emerged undetected from the antechamber to meld into the crowded assembly room once again. A few people standing nearby glanced in his general direction, but quickly returned to their prior interests.

Garrick had no intention of searching for Gillian. Why should he when he knew what he hadn't already told Clare? After Gillian had escaped, he had stopped the coach and had gone back to look for her. Actually, he had been ready to choke the breath from her for having tossed the brandy in his face. His eyes stung now just thinking of it. Garrick had found Gillian that night. She had been lying in the road, still and silent. He had seen the blood trickling down the side of her face, mixing with the rain and puddling beneath her head. He hadn't remained long enough to check for a pulse.

He'd left her there, knowing that if the fall from the coach hadn't killed her, lying there injured in the icy rain in the middle of that deserted road certainly would.

"I'm afraid your suspicions were correct, Lord Morgan," the physician from the nearby village of Castleton said, peering closely into her eyes. His face was so near to hers she could smell the distinctive odor on his breath of the onions he'd eaten with his dinner.

"She has lost her memory," answered the man she'd thought she'd created in her dream, the man she now knew as "Morgan."

The physician nodded, removing his small, round gold-rimmed spectacles. He rubbed them clean with the wadded-into-a-ball handkerchief he'd extracted from his coat pocket. "The blow to the head appears to have been caused more from a fall than from a direct strike, as evidenced by the abrasive rather than blunt nature of the wound. As well, it has most assuredly caused the lapse in the girl's memory. I've treated and dressed the wound, but you'll need to watch the bandages for sign of any additional bleeding. You'll also need to change the dressings daily to prevent infection. As for the plague, I have found nothing to indicate that she carries the infection."

Morgan nodded, seemingly relieved at the prognosis. "Will her memory eventually return?"

The physician looked over at her, exhaling a heavy, onion-tinged breath. "Quite often it does, but it really depends on the magnitude of the injury, and even if it does, the timing is never certain. Memory loss is a selective affliction; it never quite affects two victims in the same manner. Some will lose the memory of their names, their family and friends, others will lose even the ability to speak. They have to be instructed in everything again, as if they were a newborn babe. Fortunately, this young woman's condition is not that far gone. I read a pamphlet on it recently. Fascinating condition. Odd things might trigger a memory, and fragments of her past may start to come to her first, like pieces of a vague and often confusing puzzle, before she will ever remember everything. It could be days, weeks, even months before she can remember who she is and where she comes from. Or," he added finally, "she may never remember at all."

Dante looked over to the girl and realized that she was listening intently to their conversation. He didn't wish to frighten her any further than she was already. "I'm sure everything will return to her very soon," he said, directing the physician to the door. "Thank you for your assistance, Dr. Greentree."

"Of course. The wound is fast on its way to mending, and she is in otherwise good health. A mite thin, but nothing some of Mrs. Leeds's cooking won't cure. It was a good thing you came upon her when you did. Another hour in that rain and she'd have never woken to see daylight again. Do send for me if you need anything else."

Dante closed the door behind the physician. He stood there a moment, repeating everything the physician had said in his head, then turned back to face the still-silent girl. She was sitting stiffly on the bed as she had been since the moment she had realized she wasn't, in fact, dreaming, but was in a strange house filled with strange people with absolutely no recollection of how she'd gotten there or even who she was.

Dante walked slowly toward the bed and smiled. "Is there anything I can get for you?"

"You mean other than my memory?"

She was staring down at the floor, troubled. Her eyes, a smoky, seductive gray were narrowed and focused as if she were concentrating very hard on the pattern woven through the carpet, trying to find some hint of her past within its intricate designs. Her hair, freshly brushed and which had revealed itself upon drying to be an uncommonly lovely shade of reddish blond, like golden copper, fell about her shoulders and down her back in soft, full curls. She was an entrancing sight.

"I'm sorry," she said, peering at the carpet again. "I don't wish to sound churlish or at all ungrateful for all you have done. You have been very kind to me. It is just so very disconcerting to wake and find myself not even knowing my own name."

"Beatrice!"

The girl snapped her head up. "Is that it? Is that my name?"

Dante didn't answer. He was staring at something as he crossed the room, stooping just before he reached the door. When he stood again, he held in his arms a large, furry gray cat whose long tail was curling playfully underneath his chin. He pulled the tail down. It snaked its way back, tickling under his nose. He pulled it down again, this time tucking it under his arm.

"No, though I wish I had, I'm sorry to say I was not suddenly blessed with the knowledge of your name. I mean, your name could be Beatrice for all I know of it, but the Beatrice I was calling to"—he scratched the cat's head—"this mischievous Beatrice, was just preparing to stretch her claws into the peach silk coverlet, a thing she knows quite well she is not supposed to do. But, you know, you will need a name, even if it is a temporary one until you recover the memory of your true one. And I would think Beatrice as good a name as any other."

He was trying to distract her, to take her thoughts away from her troubles. He realized success in that when she smiled, lighting up those slate eyes to a delightful sparkling silver.

"Beatrice will do fine," she said.

"Well, then, Beatrice it is."

Dante set the cat atop the bed. She promptly padded over to the other Beatrice, curling up in the small nest created by her sitting cross-legged as she was beneath the bedcovers. Beatrice stroked her fingers through the cat's thick fur.

"It would seem even Beatrice the Cat agrees," he said.

She smiled up at him, and then her smile slowly faded into that same lost expression of unknowing which had been there before.

"Is there anything that Beatrice the Lady would like? Are you hungry? Thirsty, perhaps?"

"A bath," she said, looking up at him. "I would very much like to have a bath."

"Then a bath you will have. I will request a tub and water and send up one of the maids to attend to you. I might even manage to locate you a cake of Mrs. Leeds's rose and lime blossom soap. My mother used nothing else."

He started from the room, stopping just before he reached the door. "Since you've no clothing of your own besides that which we found you in, please avail yourself of anything in the wardrobe there. The clothes were my mother's. You are of similar size, though she was a bit taller, but they should fit reasonably well. If any alterations are necessary, I'll have one of the maids see to them, at least until we can summon a seamstress to make you some clothing of your own. And you needn't worry about there being any chance of infection from the plague. My mother died while she was in London. Since she divided her time equally either here or there, she kept ample clothing in both places so as to avoid the task of packing numerous trunks and lugging them across the countryside. These clothes have remained here at Wyldewoode the entire time."

Beatrice nodded. "Thank you. I'm certain they will do just fine. You needn't go to any trouble."

"It is nothing more than I would do for anyone else in your situation. When you are finished with your bath, I will be in the dining room. Your maid can direct you. I would be honored if you would join me for an early supper."

She nodded again, smiling. "Thank you again."

Dante started to leave.

"Excuse me?"

He turned. "Yes?"

"You have given me a name, but I don't yet know yours. I mean I have heard you called 'Morgan,' but I'm not sure if that is your Christian name or your title. Thus, I am not certain as to how I should address you."

Dante smiled, bowing gallantly. "Well, then, allow me to introduce myself to you, Beatrice. I am Dante Tremaine, Earl of Morgan and Viscount Wyldewoode, of Wyldewoode Estate in Derbyshire. Those who know me well call me either 'Dante' or 'Morgan.' You have my permission to employ whichever you prefer."

And with that, Dante turned, thinking as he went, *others know me simply as the Rakehell Earl.*

Chapter Five

Dante sat alone at the far end of the long polished walnut table in the dining room with its high ceiling and tall windows that faced onto Wyldewoode's southern lawn. It was a lawn that was pleasing to the eye, rich and emerald green. It stretched farther than the swift could fly, dotted here and there with large-limbed oak and beech trees that would offer ample shade on a warm summer's day. Far off in the distance, beyond the lush Derwent valley and the dark gritstone Stannage cliffs, rose majestic Higgar Tor, its misshapen peak vanishing into the low-hanging clouds.

Dante sat in solitude, oblivious of this incredible panorama. The only sound was the distant echoing tick of the case clock against the opposite wall. A glass of the rich Burgundy wine he'd brought with him from France sat untouched on the table before him. He twisted the stem of the glass negligently between his thumb and finger as he stared out the windows, contemplating the odd arrival of the mysterious Beatrice in his life.

Beatrice, he'd come to decide over the past three quarters of an hour, was obviously a lady of refinement. Her speech, her mannerisms, everything about her bespoke a life of gentle advantage and carefully arranged breeding. Even with the loss of her memory, she had retained the knowledge of proper address and deportment. And having seen the smooth white skin on her delicate hands, Dante also knew this girl had never seen a day of menial labor.

Dante knew every family of noble blood in Derbyshire and the surrounding areas. He could think of none who would have a daughter of her age, which he judged perhaps eighteen or nineteen. He'd also been away from English society for nearly three years. A great many things could have taken place during that time. She could be a young newly wedded wife to a neighboring land holder, though Dante rather doubted that, noting as he had the absence of a ring on the appropriate finger.

The one thing, the *only* thing concerning this mysterious girl of which he was absolutely certain was that he wanted her.

He'd been trying to deny it since the moment he'd kissed her after finding her lying in the road, but the more he learned about her, the more that wanting grew. Beatrice was unlike any woman he'd ever encountered. She was as unconcealed as an open book. She never thought to hide anything; she had no need to. She was innocent of the ways of men and women; she had to be, for she seemed completely oblivious of the very air between them and the way it became charged when they were in the same room. That alone made Dante only want her more.

Perhaps it was that he hadn't been with a woman in nearly six months. He thought of Claudette, his last mistress, a lovely young brunette with lush breasts, whose husband preferred the company of young men to his pretty wife. She hadn't been overly pleased with Dante when he'd severed their relationship. No doubt she soon found another to console herself with. Claudette had been the last of many adieus he'd said to his previous existence, for he was determined to live a new life, a respectable life, a life in which the games of such seductions were forbidden.

Forbidden. He had to wonder if that might be the most likely reason for his attraction to Beatrice. She was in his care, after all, and thus she was vulnerable. She was a temptation he could not allow himself to give in to, not if he wished to embark on his new life with any success. And he was determined to succeed, to avoid any of his past trademark involvements, such as had given him the name of the Rakehell Earl.

Dante wondered then if Beatrice had come to him from the heavens perhaps, as some sort of test on his determination to adhere to the path of respectability. For she surely was an angel, all pale white skin and soft hair, those full lips begging to be kissed, her breasts . . .

He shook his head. No, he would simply have to ignore the way his body responded to her. He would find out who she was and return her where she belonged as soon as he possibly could, or before he expired from unsated lust, whichever came first.

He would need to make inquiries. His first inclination had been to write to Cassia, his friend, Rolfe's, wife, for if anyone would know everyone who moved about in the ever-changing circle of English society, it would be she. In fact, while Beatrice had bathed, he'd drafted a letter to Cassia, sending it off by messenger to Sussex at their country seat, Ravenwood. Dante doubted Rolfe and Cassia would be in London since the city had been deserted at the coming of the plague. The members of court were only now just returning at the rearrival of King Charles earlier in the year.

But it could take weeks for him to hear back from Cassia, if she was at Ravenwood at all, and he didn't want to delay that long in looking for Beatrice's family. He couldn't delay. Her family would certainly be worried about her. And while he was determined to abide by a life of respectability, he really had no wish to test himself so soon. It would be better to simply avoid temptation. He would need to begin searching for Beatrice's family now, immediately, before he heard from Cassia. And there was one person here at Wyldewoode who, if any noble alliance had taken place within the whole of England, would most assuredly know of it.

"You wished to see me, my lord?"

Dante sat up in his chair. "Renny, my good man, come in. Have a seat, if you will?"

Renny had been the Wyldewoode steward since Dante's father had become the earl in 1638 upon the demise of his father, Ruthbert, the first Earl of Morgan. The steward's full name was Reynard de Haviland Frobisher, a mouthful for even the most able of speakers. Though proud of his heritage, Renny didn't much relish the thought of being known throughout life as something like Frobisher, thinking it sounded like some odd sort of fish. He'd settled on Renny when he'd been a boy. It was simple and straight, and had been immediately adopted by everyone, excepting his mother who even now, at the age of two and seventy, still insisted on calling him by his full name— and all three of them—whenever she referred to him.

During Dante's absence, a three-year period of neglect actually, Renny had been single-handedly seeing to the affairs at Wyldewoode. Five and fifty and of medium build, Renny sported a trim mustache and small pointed beard, his peppered gray hair worn chin length in the style popular during the reign of the previous King Charles nearly three decades before. He also favored the tight-fitting, small-waisted doublet and wide white falling band collar of that era as well, but despite his outdated taste in hairstyle and clothing, he was as sharp as a rapier blade and cunning as the legendary fox for which he was named.

"Renny, I wish to thank you for running the estate so

well in my absence and for taking care with my mother's passing as you did. Your success in having her removed from London to be interred here at Wyldewoode was remarkable, given the fact that I have learned so many of the plague's victims are buried in the mass plague pits long before any family member has had the chance to claim them."

"Lady Helena held a special place in her heart for Wyldewoode, my lord. She came here as a young newly wedded lady and, if you'll pardon my forwardness, turned a rather old, unfeeling relic of a building into a home."

Dante smiled. Everyone had been fond of Helena. "She was a remarkable woman."

"That she was, my lord. And I could not have lived with myself if I hadn't done everything I could to see her laid to rest here where she belonged."

"I still don't know how you managed to accomplish it."

Renny frowned dolefully, twisting the pointed end of his beard between his thumb and forefinger. "While the plague is swift in its coming, my lord, it is often reluctant to take its leave. When I finally heard of the arrival of the disease in London, in a letter sent to me by my sister, who was attending to your mother while in London, it was already several months into what had started as a small outbreak and had by then grown to epidemic proportion. I fully expected Lady Helena to return to Wyldewoode after the arrival of my sister's letter, but when several weeks passed with no word, I began to grow concerned. When I learned that the king and court had vacated Whitehall for Hampton Court, I knew something was amiss. I was in the process of packing to leave for London when I received a second letter from my sister."

Renny's frown deepened. "She told me that your mother had remained in the city because Miss Nesta, your mother's abigail, had contracted the sickness, and Lady Helena refused to leave her. Did you know that many servants who had shown any symptom of sickness, plague or not, had been thrown to the streets without a shilling to keep them?"

Dante frowned. "I had not heard."

"Other noblemen simply closed up their dwellings in the city, abandoning their servants without funds enough to depart the city for safety themselves. The city gates were being guarded, and no one without a certificate of health signed by Lord Mayor Sir John Lawrence himself could pass through. My sister also indicated she feared greatly for your mother's health because she had herself begun exhibiting early signs of the disease."

Dante closed his eyes, faced as he had been the past twelve months with the overwhelming guilt that while he'd been away, safely ensconced in France, his mother had been left virtually alone to face the epidemic. She, as well as all the others, had been his responsibility. As the Earl of Morgan, he should have been there to see to their survival, and would have if not . . .

"I am sorry, my lord," Renny broke in. "Perhaps I should not go any further."

Dante opened his eyes, knowing he had to hear it, all of it. It would be the only way in which he could put his mother's death, and his conscience, to rest. "It is all right, Renny. Please go on."

"If it is any ease to you, my lord, Lady Helena did not suffer as badly as many, for she had applied to an apothecary, a brave man named Boghurst who stayed on in the city to treat the ill. Mr. Boghurst's curatives are said to have saved many. When I arrived in London, I had a difficult time of it getting through the city gates. The guards thought I was crazed for wanting to enter the city when everyone else was so desperate to leave. I was warned that I would not be allowed out again."

Dante looked at him. "Why did you go on, Renny?"

"I could not in all conscience abandon Lady Helena. I knew had you been able to be here, you would have done the same."

"That is true, but she was my mother, Renny. She was not tied to you by blood."

"Some ties, my lord, are even stronger than blood. I, and members of my family, had served your father and with him your mother for nearly three decades. Lady Helena was a most gracious lady."

Renny's words dropped off as he went back in his mind, reminiscing on earlier, happier times, times before the wars, before Cromwell, and now plague had come to England. They were carefree times marked by laughter and joy, of hopes and dreams for the future.

"So many doors on the houses in the city were marked with a God's mark, the red painted cross. Once it was known a plague victim resided within a house, the doors were marked and everyone inside was confined for forty days. With each new victim, another forty days. It was said some families hadn't seen the light of day for several months. But there was no cross on the door at Morgan House. All was quiet, and I thought Lady Helena had finally left the city."

"But she hadn't," said Dante.

Renny shook his head. "My sister quickly drew me inside and shut up the door. She told me that some of the infected, mad with the disease, had taken to pounding on doors, demanding money, else they would break inside and infect the entire household. There were no watchmen to call."

"I have seen such as that during the wars. Desperation tends to bring men to foul acts."

Renny nodded. "I found Lady Helena lying on her bed, feverish and unconscious. Her breathing was labored, and though her eyes were slightly opened, I don't think she ever knew I was there. When I saw the small plague token swelling on the side of her neck, I knew I was too late. I knew it wouldn't be much longer."

Dante drew a slow breath before asking what he knew he had to ask. "She passed quickly?"

"Aye, my lord. She did not last the night. The death carts came by several times, collecting the dead to be buried in the pits, but I could not bring myself to summon them. I could not allow Lady Helena to be taken. Instead, my sister and I wrapped her in a white sheet we had fashioned into a shroud and tried to think of a way past the guarded gates. It was a few days later, in the first week of September, that we finally found a way past. I am sorry, my lord, but we had to sell what we could for money to bribe the gate guards with."

Dante shook his head. "There is nothing to be sorry for."

"We returned to Wyldewoode, and after laying Lady Helena to rest beside your father, my sister and I segregated ourselves in the old gatekeeper's cottage. We waited forty days, and when neither of us showed signs of sickness, we returned to the house. It was then I wrote to you, my lord."

"After which I wrote to the king several times, requesting allowance to return to the country. He finally responded to me then. My earlier letters, written when I first learned of the plague outbreak, were never answered."

"Most probably your letters never reached His Majesty until he returned to Whitehall in early February of this year. Affairs of state were in chaos, I would imagine."

Dante nodded. "Which would explain why it took an additional six months for him to respond." He let out a heavy breath, wishing he could somehow change the past. He supposed a great many wished the same. "Had I known the magnitude of the situation here, Renny, the true epidemic proportions of the disease, I would have come back to England sooner, with or without His Majesty's blessing."

Chapter Six

"I've not heard of any marriages taking place with anyone who would fit the young lady's description, my lord," Renny said, having finished apprising Dante of past events at Wyldewoode during his three year absence. They had scheduled a full reviewing of the account books for the following day. "The number of matrimonial alliances has dropped considerably," he added, "with the coming of the plague."

"Thank you, Renny," Dante said. "Please make whatever inquiries possible. Otherwise, it seems we shall just have to wait until Cassia receives my letter."

"Aye, my lord." Renny hesitated. "I would guess then Miss Beatrice will be staying with us for a while?"

Dante looked at him, wondering at the underlying question he detected. "She has nowhere else to go at the moment, Renny, thus she will have to remain here."

"Yes, of course, my lord," Renny said excusing himself with an odd smile, leaving Dante to return to his Burgundy, and his thoughts, in the dining room.

Dante glanced up when Beatrice entered the room a moment later. Her coppery blond hair shone in the sunlight beaming in through the tall windows. A fresh bandage covered the wound on her head. The gown she'd chosen from his mother's wardrobe was a pale seashell pink that complimented the natural coloring of her cheeks. The wide, rounded neckline, decorated with gold-threaded Brussels lace, showed her shoulders and the rise of her breasts to innocent advantage. It fit well, and as she took the seat to the left of him, she gave the appearance of sweet, untouched beauty.

And she would remain untouched, he told himself, even if it killed him.

"I trust you are feeling better," Dante said, trying not to notice the way her tongue had just come out to moisten her lower lip. He took a measured breath at the tightening he felt in his groin. She was only a child, a child who was in his care. Why did he suddenly want nothing more than to kiss her?

"I am feeling much better, thank you, my lord. Thank you for the use of your mother's clothing as well. She had such beautiful things, and you were correct in saying we were of similar size. Except for the height, I mean, but I have found a way to hold the skirts while I walk to prevent myself from tripping and falling on my face."

He smiled. "We will have a seamstress employed to remedy that problem. I wouldn't want you to sustain another injury to your head."

"Perhaps it would serve to knock my memory back in place."

"Perhaps, but that is not an experiment I particularly wish to undertake. Are you hungry?"

Beatrice nodded with enthusiasm. "Starving."

"Good. Mrs. Leeds has most likely prepared something delicious. She is a wonderful cook."

The double doors behind him opened, and two footmen wearing blue and yellow livery entered carrying trays. They set out on the table several covered dishes that contained what appeared to Beatrice to be a veritable feast. Surely, there would be more than just the two of them dining? With all this food, there was enough to feed at least a half dozen people.

Beatrice smiled, waiting while one of the footmen emptied a ladle of steaming cockle and oyster soup into the porcelain bowl before her. Her stomach instantly and quite audibly voiced its approval of the first course in the otherwise silent room.

"Excuse me, my lord," she said, her cheeks reddening.

"Mrs. Leeds would be pleased to know that the very aroma of her soup caused such a reaction. Now," he went on, taking one of the still steaming, oven-fresh rolls from a linen-covered basket, "if you want a real treat, dip the end of this into your soup and let it soak into the bread."

"My lord, I couldn't. It wouldn't be at all proper." She paused for a moment. "It's odd, you know, because I don't really know why it wouldn't be proper. I just do."

"Some lessons in life take more than a knocking on the head to erase. Some lessons stay with us no matter the circumstances."

Beatrice stared at him, at a loss. Dante smiled and handed her a roll. "Take a chance, Beatrice. Life isn't fun without a little bit of risk."

Beatrice took the roll and tentatively lowered the end of it into the soup. She glanced at him one more time, uncertain, then took a small bite, careful not to dribble any of the soup on her chin.

"You were right, my lord. It is delicious, unlike anything I've ever tasted before. I never would have thought to do such a thing. Wherever did you learn it?"

"When I was a boy, my brother, William, and I would visit Mrs. Leeds in the kitchen when we knew she was making our favorite lemon pudding. But she wouldn't give us a bite until we had both first eaten a full bowl of the soup she always seemed to have simmering over the fire and at least two of her rolls. Being boys possessed of a minimal amount of patience, William and I would race to see who would finish the soup first and thereby attain the pudding before the other. Sopping up the soup with the roll proved to be a great time-saving device."

Beatrice giggled. "How inventive. Where is your brother now?"

Dante frowned. "William was killed during the Cromwellian wars. He is buried here at Wyldewoode with my father and mother and my infant sister, Elizabeth."

"I am so very sorry, my lord. Have you any other family?"

"No. I am the last Tremaine."

Beatrice looked down at her soup. She suddenly didn't feel so hungry. "I guess we are both of us orphans then."

Dante didn't respond. The room was silent for several minutes.

"I was thinking," Dante said, motioning for the footman to remove the soup, "it is still early, and if you are feeling up to it, I would be honored if you would accompany me on a walk about the grounds. Perhaps I could show you the inside on the morrow, so that you won't be walking into closets thinking they are chambers."

"That would be very nice, my lord. Thank you. I am sorry to have to impose on you like this."

"There is no imposition; I am quite happy to help you. I have already sent off for some assistance in trying to find out your true identity. There really is nothing more that can be done right now, so let us just concentrate on getting you healed, both physically and mentally, agreed?"

Beatrice looked at him and smiled. "Agreed."

Dante hadn't lived at his family's ancestral home since he'd left to attend Oxford. In fact, the last time he'd been to the estate at all had been at the death of his father nearly ten years before, and then only long

enough to see to his affairs and officially assume the
Morgan title. Being away had served to put to rest certain memories, memories he would have preferred forgotten. Now that he had returned, those same memories
were raising their ugly heads once again.

"Your home is lovely, my lord. Is it very old?"

"The house you see now isn't really all that old by
Derbyshire standards. It was built by my grandfather,
the first Earl of Morgan, during the reign of Elizabeth.
There was another structure, older and smaller, that
still stands along the northern fringes of the estate, and
yet another that lies mostly in ruins nearby to it. That
was the home of the first Tremaine who lived here, the
one who gave the land its name."

"Goodness, you must trace your family all the way
back to Domesday."

Dante looked down at Beatrice. He suddenly wondered what it would be like to have no memory of who
he was, where he had come from, to not even know his
name. In that thought, he could not help but envy Beatrice her affliction.

"The first Tremaine of which there is any record was
a man named Godric de Tremayne who came to live
here in the fourteenth century in the reign of Edward II.
He was the last from what was by all accounts a family
of fighters, a proud family, and a family that had nearly
been destroyed by another plague."

"That would have been the plague of 1348. It removed nearly half the population of England," Beatrice
said.

Dante looked at her, intrigued that she should know
something even most well-educated young women did
not. He went on. "Yes. Godric de Tremayne somehow
survived the threat of that plague and wed a Cornish
lass named Roseia. They settled here on this land,
named it Wyldewoode for the dense forest that sur-
rounds it on three sides, and built the first structure, the

one that now lies in ruins. They had seventeen children, thirteen of whom remarkably reached adulthood and carried the family through another three centuries until this plague came to England. It is ironic, for this plague has left only one Tremaine survivor as well."

They had come around by way of the northern facade to the western side of the house. Dante stopped. Ahead, in the distance beneath a canopy of huge oak with thick leaves and widespread boughs, enclosed by a crude gray stone wall, lay the final resting place of nearly every Tremaine for the past three centuries. The sun had hidden itself behind the clouds. Dante could not deny the sudden chill. He went no farther.

"Your family is buried there," Beatrice said softly.

"Yes."

"I understand from the maid you sent to assist me that you came home to Wyldewoode to pay your final respects to your mother. It must be very painful for you, losing her. I will leave you now to your privacy."

Dante took her arm, stopping her. "If you wouldn't mind, I would rather that you stay."

Beatrice nodded and touched his hand gently. Together they walked toward the small cemetery.

They stopped beside the graves of his father and mother, where they had been laid to rest beside one another. Their two other children lay on either side of them.

"William was named after our father," Dante said suddenly. It was something he needed to say, and he was glad to have Beatrice there to listen. "He was the firstborn, the one who should have been the heir. He died fighting for the royalist cause during the civil wars. My sister, Elizabeth, was stillborn the same year my father died. I never knew her."

In saying that, Dante suddenly realized he was indeed the last of a family who had survived plague and war and adversity. It would be his responsibility, whether they carried on or faded into obscurity. Had his mother lived, he would still have been the one, the only one who could continue. Why did the responsibility he'd carried all along suddenly now become so real to him? Had his ancestor, Godric, felt the same three hundred years earlier?

Through his entire adult life, from the age of sixteen when he'd first become a man with the willing eighteen-year-old bride of the doddering Earl of Easthorpe, Dante hadn't given more than passing thought to the future. It had gone from a method of managing to remain detached to a code of conduct to which he religiously adhered.

He had never bedded a virgin, for he refused to be responsible for ruining the future of any young girl whom he had no intention of wedding. Widows, though in great supply since the wars, were much the same, not that they would be ruined, but in that he had no intention of wedding any of them either. The women Dante did take company with were always wedded, and always unhappily, for he also refused to be responsible for ruining a happy union. In an age when marriages were arranged as easily as appointments at one's tailor, unhappy unions were, like widows, in great supply.

However, now, after fifteen years of that life, the repercussions had begun to take their toll. In the months since his mother's death, Dante had come to disdain his indulgent lifestyle. His carefree, careless outlook on life had begun to pall, causing him to question his morality, and with it his own mortality. There were no guarantees he would live so long as next year. War, and now the plague, had taken many before their time—too many—leaving families without heirs, wives without husbands and sons, bringing many a noble line to extinction.

Who was to say he was not exempt from the same?

How did he know he wouldn't retire to his bed that very evening, never to rise again? And what would he have left behind him? What would Dante Charles William Ruthbert Tremaine, the third and perhaps last Earl of Morgan, leave behind him as a legacy?

His only legacy, Dante realized sourly, was that he would be known forever through history as the Rake-hell Earl of Morgan, a man who had bedded more women than he cared to count, the last and certainly the most ruinous of the Tremaines.

Chapter Seven

Dante lowered himself onto the small crude stone bench next to his mother's grave. Beatrice sat quietly beside him, allowing him his thoughts. For a long while he just sat there, staring out in the distance, watching but not really seeing the sun as it set on the far Pennine peaks, listening to but not hearing the sounds of the ending day. Dusk fell quickly, and the wind began to awaken with the brewing threat of yet another storm, stirring the thick leaves on the gnarled oak branches overhead.

A familiar mewing broke through blowing wind. Dante looked down to see Beatrice, the cat, rubbing against his legs.

"Glad to see you managed to survive without me here to save your hide all these years, Fur Ball." He scratched her head. He glanced at Beatrice. "Believe it or not, your feline namesake is nearing a quarter century in age."

Beatrice looked at him. "Surely, you're teasing me, my lord."

"Not at all. I was eight years old when she first came into my life. She very nearly ended it all then, and would have had I not been running across the south lawn on my way to the frog pond, angling line in hand. I remember well her mewling cry for help. She sounded like a gate that had been left too long without oiling. She had climbed to the uppermost branches of a huge oak tree and obviously hadn't given a thought as to how she would find her way down. And upon discovering her, I scrambled up to save her, neglecting the same thought."

"So there were two of you stuck up in the tree then?"

Dante smirked. "I sat there, clutching this terrified kitten, her claws digging into my neck, hollering as loud as my eight-year-old lungs would allow. I had never climbed that high before, and the ground looked so far away. I would that it had been anyone but my father who came in answer to my cries. But it was him. I remember seeing him, his face set in its perpetual frown, at the base of that tree. Suddenly, the tree didn't seem so frightening. I don't recall what angered him more, that I'd climbed so high after a mere cat, or that there were tears running down my cheeks. My father was not a man given to emotion. I remember him ordering me to climb down and forget the 'flea-ridden creature.' I refused and begged him to help us down, the two of us together. I remember seeing him turn, leaving with his departing bit of wisdom. It stuck with me throughout my life."

"What did he say?"

"He told me to be a man and find my own way."

Beatrice frowned. "What did you do?"

"Just what he told me. I had little choice really. I eventually worked my way down, with Beatrice clutched under my arm. After that day I was convinced my father hated me. It took me years to finally understand that he didn't hate me; he just couldn't be bothered with me. You see, as the younger son, in his eyes, I held no importance in his life. William had been raised strictly by our father, groomed as the heir, his duty to the Morgan title drilled into his head since the moment he came squalling into the world. I had been brought up solely by my mother's indulgent hand. My mother had had little say in William's life. He had been virtually whisked away from her at birth, his nourishment provided by a hired wet nurse, his every other physical need seen to by my father."

"It sounds terribly cruel, both to you and your mother."

Dante shook his head. "It wasn't that my father was a cruel man; indeed he accorded my mother every respect he felt due her. He was simply the product of generations of men who believed that strength and honor and emotional detachment were the only qualities needed in a man. The softer needs, like sensitivity and understanding, were something not required. My mother's needs were therefore considered frivolous female whimsy. She'd done her duty; she'd delivered the heir, and nothing more was expected of her in his upbringing."

Dante smiled then. "Until I came along. Things were vastly different the next time. My mother's first step into staking her claim on me, her second son, had been in her choice of names. Against my father's wishes, while he was away to London, she'd birthed and christened me, naming me for her favorite poet. Poetry was another thing my father felt was foolish whimsy. How to discharge a weapon, how to issue orders effectively, these were the things William's childhood had been filled with in preparation for his future role. An advantageous marriage had already been arranged by the time he turned fourteen. I had the privileges of noble birth without having to bear the responsibilities my brother did."

"But, then, you are the earl now."

"Yes. Fate does have a way of stepping in, working her unexpected play. I don't think my father ever could come to terms with it. I remember the day he summoned me to his study shortly after William's burial in the Wyldewoode cemetery. He told me I was to wed my brother's betrothed. It was as if I had no say in the matter."

"What did you do?"

"I refused, of course. He wanted me to wed the girl, who was two years my senior, had overlarge dark eyes and a face that resembled a stoat. I think that was when he finally realized it wasn't William standing before him."

"He gave up on the match then?" Beatrice asked, her eyes hopeful.

"Not exactly. He threatened to disown me. I saved him the trouble by leaving Wyldewoode, vowing never to return again." Dante hesitated. "My father died three weeks later when he collapsed while atop one of the tall ladders in the library reaching for a book. He broke his neck in the fall. And I returned to Wyldewoode, not as the irresponsible second son, but as the new earl, the third Earl of Morgan. I imagine he cannot rest in peace over that one fact alone."

Dante stood then. He held out his hand to Beatrice. "Enough of this depressing history. I think perhaps we should go inside. It is getting cold, and I don't want you to catch a chill."

Beatrice stood and started with him toward the house. As they walked, Dante's head was filled with questions. Should he have bowed to his father's wishes that long-ago day, wedding his brother's intended for the sake of the Morgan title? Would things be any different now if he had? Somehow he didn't believe so, for he knew, if he had, he would only be trapped in a marriage with a woman who inspired nothing in him but distaste. The woman Dante would wed would be as beautiful as his mother, with Helena's spirit and strength and intelligence.

Even as he thought this, Dante found himself looking down at the woman who walked beside him.

* * *

She didn't even know her name.

Beatrice set the hairbrush down and stared at her reflection in the glass. Nothing, not a hint of recognition struck her in the face that stared back at her.

Where had she gotten gray eyes? Had her mother, or her father, had them? And her hair, such an odd shade. Not really blond, yet not red either, as nameless a color as she was a person. She noticed a small white scar on her forehead at the hairline that wouldn't have been visible if not for the bandage on her head. The scar had long since healed, too faded to have been from her current injury. How had she gotten it? Another bump on the head, perhaps? Did this mean she was habitually clumsy?

Beatrice stood and walked over to the fruitwood writing table set near the hearth. She dipped the goose quill in the crystal inkwell and wrote out a single word on the blank sheet of parchment atop the table.

Beatrice.

It didn't feel at all natural to write. In fact, it was really rather awkward. It took effort just to remember to respond to it. It wasn't her real name, she knew that. So, if it wasn't, then what was? She tried several more names; Mary, Anne, even Elizabeth. They, all of them, left only an empty feeling within.

Beatrice walked about the room. As she did, she wondered how old she was and realized she might never know when her birthday passed. It could be tomorrow. It could have been yesterday. But then, she thought, she could just claim her birthday as the day Dante Tremaine, the Earl of Morgan, had found her and had saved her life.

She remembered sitting with him in the small cemetery earlier. She could feel his sadness, a sadness that ran so very deep. He was such an interesting and complex man. At times, as when she'd first awoke to find herself there, he was laughing and carefree. At others it seemed he bore the weight of the world on his shoulders. He had done so much for her. He'd saved her life. She wished she could do something for him in return, but what could she possibly do?

She didn't even know her name.

"As you can see, the Tremaines are a family of collectors. My ancestors refused to discard anything. I remember once, when I was a young boy, I opened a small wooden box I found tucked away in a root cellar, and you wouldn't believe what was inside."

"What?" Beatrice asked, pushing back the same coppery curl from her eyes, something she had done a number of times now during the past two hours.

"It was filled with gloves."

"What?"

"Left-handed gloves, to be precise. Countless many, all of different styles and sizes. There were kid gloves, gloves made of fine silk and decorated with fine beading. There were gloves that reached beyond your elbows. But none of them, not a single one, was made for the right hand. I haven't been able to decide if somewhere, back in my family history, there lived someone who had only one hand, or if instead I come from a line of glove bandits."

Beatrice giggled. "Left-handed glove bandits, it would seem." She stopped laughing suddenly, and her smile faded to a distant, unhappy frown.

"What is it?" Dante asked.

"I was just wondering whether I could possibly have any glove bandits in my family as well, but I . . ."

Dante took her hand, angry with himself for bringing such sadness to her silver eyes. "I'm sorry. I should have realized that hearing about my family would only make you long for your own."

"No, it is all right. How can one long for something they don't even know they have? And I do enjoy hearing about your family." She took a deep breath, smiling. "What room are we at now?" She motioned toward the door before them.

All morning, Dante had taken her, room by room, floor by floor, acquainting her with each section of the massive Elizabethan house. It was shaped like an *E,* in honor of the queen, and was constructed with a combination of both the local gritstone and limestone. The colorful flowers from the surrounding park and gardens only set off the natural rock more. The effect was lovely.

Beatrice found it funny, appealingly so, that each chamber within the house had its own history, and with it, its own distinction.

There was the Acorn Room, on the second floor at the northwest corner, so named because it had remained empty for an extended period once many years earlier, during which a family of red squirrels had taken up residence within it, piling their winter stores in every corner.

There was the Eloping Room from whence at various times during the past century at least three young ladies had escaped to run off and wed their true loves. There were rooms named for the colors that decorated them, and still others named for months of the year. There was even a room called the *Peu de Chose,* so known simply because nothing of any import had ever occurred within it.

At first Beatrice had found it strange, this concept of naming a room, but now, having seen the number contained within Wyldewoode's weathered stone walls, she realized it actually made good sense. What other way could one possibly keep account of them?

"This room," Dante said, grasping the door handle, "is known quite simply as the Music Room."

He pushed the door, stepping back to allow Beatrice

to precede him. She took three steps inside before she stopped.

It was a lovely room, filled with sunlight from the tall windows that lined the far wall. A huge colorful arras, depicting a cheerful scene of cherubic children dancing beneath a beribboned maypole, hung over the face of one wall. A burr-walnut harpsichord stood across the room, nearer to the windows, its gleaming case decorated with mother-of-pearl marquetry. Beside this, a harp, a lovely *arpa doppia*, stood with the sunlight glistening on its double set of strings. Various other instruments were set on stands or in cases about the perimeter of the room.

Twin walnut settees, covered in pale yellow silk brocade, were arranged in the center of the room, where the acoustics would be best. A carved embroidery stand stood nearby, a half-finished sampler stretched across it, a threaded needle tucked within the cloth at its edge.

Beatrice moved forward. She felt oddly drawn to this place. She sat down on the small bench before the harpsichord and without thinking or saying a word began to play. Dante remained to the side. Beatrice played and played, her fingers striking the keys, skimming over both keyboards with ease, and as she concluded the piece, she began to laugh aloud.

"What is it you find so funny, Beatrice?"

"Do you hear it?" she answered cheerfully.

"Do I hear what?"

"The song I am playing, do you hear it?"

"Yes."

"Do you recognize it?"

"Yes. It is one of the more popular compositions I've heard."

Beatrice laughed aloud. "I'm laughing because I have never heard it before. At least I don't remember ever hearing it, but for some strange reason I know how to play it, as if I've been playing it all my life."

She stood then, her eyes alight with glee. "Isn't that funny? I know how to play the harpsichord, Dante, although I haven't the faintest idea what it is I'm playing."

She spun about, picking up a carved treble recorder. "May I?"

Dante nodded. "By all means."

She began playing again, this time a lively tune.

"What is that called?" Beatrice asked when she'd finished.

"I don't know if it really has a name. It's just a children's song that tells about when Old London Bridge was burned to the ground by two warring Norse kings."

Beatrice thought for a moment. She began to hum the tune softly, then, after a few moments, she began to sing.

> *London bridge is broken down,*
> *Gold is won and bright renown.*
> *Shields resounding,*
> *War horns sounding,*
> *Hildur shouting in the din,*
> *Arrows singing, mailcoats ringing,*
> *Odin makes our Olaf win.*

She was laughing aloud by the time she finished. Dante couldn't help but smile, too. Her happiness was infectious, lighting up the room. She came forward and threw her arms around him. "I remember it, my lord, every word of it. I do still have a memory."

And then she kissed him quickly, on the mouth, before stepping away, spinning about like a carefree child.

Dante didn't say a word. He couldn't. He was fighting the rush of his reaction to the feel of her breasts pressed against him, the sweet taste of her mouth. His heart was pounding. He had trouble catching his breath.

"I wonder what else I can play," Beatrice said, oblivious of the chord of chaos she'd just struck in him. She started to position herself behind a large standing bass viola da gamba.

"Beatrice, I wouldn't think that an instrument in your repertory. Perhaps the violin instead . . ."

Dante rooted himself to the floor, falling dumb. Beatrice had managed rather deftly to seat herself behind the tall instrument, and without hesitation had pulled her skirts back between her legs to allow her to properly position the large instrument. She lifted the bow and began moving it over the strings, unaware that in doing so, she had exposed a goodly portion of her stockinged calves to him.

Blood began to rush through Dante's entire body as he watched Beatrice hugging her knees around the viola's wooden case, silk garters tied above them, begging to be loosened. Her fingers directed the bow, caressing the taut strings while she played a slow seductive strain. She closed her eyes, overcome with the music, her head dropping languidly to the side. All Dante could do was watch, imagining himself in place of the viola, his mouth running over her smooth, white neck while his body moved with hers in rhythm with the song.

He hadn't even noticed she'd stopped playing the thing until she called out to him. "Dante? My lord?"

"Yes?" His throat was so tight, he barely choked the word out. Good God, what was wrong with him? He was sweating as if he'd just run a race. He tugged on his neckcloth to loosen it.

"Is everything all right, my lord?"

Dante's rattled senses returned. "Yes, of course. That is quite an accomplishment, Beatrice. Most ladies do not undertake to play the viola da gamba, especially the bass. In fact, I don't believe I know of a single one."

"Whyever not? Its sound is rather inspiring."

Inspiring? Well, he could think of a few other words that would much better describe what he was presently feeling.

"Ladies usually find their skirts hinder the instrument's positioning, though you seem to have found a way around that." Dante remembered the way she'd pushed back her skirts, her legs brushing the sides of the viola. The tightening within him returned. He flushed, a thing he'd never done in his life. He had to get out of this room—immediately.

"Shall we go on?" he asked turning away. "We're nearly finished touring. We've only the library left to see, and I've a few matters dealing with the estate to contend with this afternoon. Perhaps you'd enjoy looking through Wyldewoode's collection of books while I am occupied with my steward?"

Beatrice smiled. "That would be splendid. I thank you, my lord, for taking time from your responsibilities to show me about. I hope I wasn't too much of a distraction for you."

Distraction.

Good God. Her choice of words was extraordinary.

If ever there was the perfect word to describe Dante's state of mind from the moment he had found this girl lying rain-soaked in the road, it was most definitely distraction.

Chapter Eight

The view was breathtaking. Beyond breathtaking, it simply was not to be believed.

They had crested a high hill, the horses puffing and pawing at the ground from their swift run, when Dante drew his stallion, a magnificent chestnut he called Fury, to a halt.

"There," he said, pointing outward with his gloved hand, "it is visible just beyond that stand of trees. That is Castle Peveril."

Beatrice raised a hand to her eyes to better see. It was a crude-looking structure, and looked to have been fashioned of the very stone from which it jutted. The top of its one large turret disappeared into the afternoon mist that clung to the rocky mountainside, giving it an ethereal appearance, as if it had surfaced from a dream. "It is just what one would imagine in a fairy tale."

Dante loosened the reins, allowing Fury to munch on the sweet grass at his feet. Beatrice did the same for her mount, a quiet little dappled gray mare called Sugarloaf, a name which probably had something to do with her fondness for the same. She removed her wide-brimmed, plumed hat and smoothed back her hair from her face. It had come loose from their ride, an invigorating one that took them over grassy fields and rocky fence lines. Beatrice took in a deep, restorative breath, allowing the cool mountain air to fill her lungs.

"The castle was never meant to serve as a permanent dwelling," Dante said, sitting lax in the saddle. Beatrice thought looked handsome in his contrasting black coat and breeches and crisp white shirt. Very handsome, indeed. "The castle was actually constructed nearly five hundred years ago, soon after the Conquest, more as a watchtower for the village and surrounding lands."

Beatrice nodded and looked again at the castle, noticing its crumbling foundation. "It is in ruins?"

"Yes, it has fallen into disuse since the Peverils were dispossessed by Edward III. It has been used in the past as a prison for debtors and robbers, but mostly it stands vacant. If you look between the trees there, you might be able to see the mouth of the Devil's Cave lying just beneath the castle's curtain wall on the escarpment."

Beatrice cocked her head. "Oh, yes, I do see it now. It looks rather sinister, does it not? A good name for it, the Devil's Cave. Can we go inside of it to explore?"

Dante chuckled at her question. "I'm afraid it would take us too long to reach the cave from the village. The pathway up the mountainside is difficult to navigate, even in daylight. Night will have fallen long before we'd ever reach it."

Beatrice frowned, disappointed.

Dante looked at her a moment. He gathered the reins. "Follow me."

"Where are we going? I thought you said we were headed for the village."

"We are. But we've a bit of spare time to deviate from our course."

Beatrice lightly touched her heels to Sugarloaf and followed Dante along the narrow wooded path that ran beside a small rolling brook. Except for the sounds of the water and the horses moving along the path, the wood was quiet and still. The area looked as if it had never seen humankind. It was untouched, natural, and beautiful.

A short time later, Dante pulled Fury to a halt at the foot of a rocky outcropping.

He swung down from the saddle. "We'll have to walk from here. It isn't much farther."

He helped Beatrice from her horse, then began leading the way.

"Where are we going?" she asked again, picking her way alongside him on the obscure path, which he seemed to find rather easily.

"You will see."

He was being purposely obtuse, and Beatrice hated it. There was nothing she could do about it. She hated that even more. They rounded a bend in the trail, and Dante climbed over a small natural barrier of rocks. He turned to help Beatrice over after him.

"There it is."

He pointed to a small opening set nichelike in a catstep on the hillside. It was nearly hidden by the dense growth around it, and had he not pointed to it, she would probably have never seen it. Beatrice looked at Dante.

"What is it?"

"That, Beatrice, is a cave. You said you wanted to see one. Here is one my brother and I used to play in when we were boys."

Beatrice cocked her head doubtfully. "But it looks rather small, not at all like the other one."

"Not all cave openings are as large as the Devil's Cave below the castle. This particular one, though, is deceptive in appearance. You have to duck down in order to enter, but once inside, there is room enough for a man to stand fully upright."

Beatrice eyed the cave opening. "I am not so certain that it is a good idea, Dante."

"You said you wanted to see the inside of a cave."

Dante took a step toward the cave, extending his hand. "Unless, of course, you are more squeak than wool . . ."

Dante's teasing words triggered something in Beatrice's head, a voice that seemed to come from far away.

Come on, bratchet, you're not afraid are you?

She must have looked as if she might fall to her feet because Dante was suddenly there beside her, taking her elbow, holding her steady. His eyes were dark with concern.

"What is it? Did you feel as if you might faint? Your face lost all expression. The air at this elevation does tend to be a bit thinner than the lowlands, but I didn't think it would . . ."

Beatrice gripped his coat sleeve. What she'd heard had been a memory. The first memory she'd had since waking. "No, it is all right, really. I just heard something, like someone's voice in my head, teasing me as you just were." She looked at him. "Whoever it was called me 'bratchet.' "

"My brother used to call me that. It is a common enough nickname where children are concerned. Dr. Greentree said you would probably begin to remember odd things that might not mean very much at first. Could you discern if it was a male or female voice?"

Beatrice tried to recall. "I'm not certain. It's as if it was just there, so clear, and now it is gone." She closed her eyes, frustrated at the unknown. "Why can't I remember?"

Dante squeezed her hand. "It will take a little time, Beatrice, but at least you are beginning to remember something. That is progress, isn't it? Don't fret over it, and it will come. In the meantime, let's go into the cave, and perhaps something else will cause you to recall another memory."

Beatrice nodded and followed him to the cave.

Dante had been correct in saying the entrance was deceptive, for as soon as Beatrice ducked through, there was room enough for both of them to stand upright. It was also very, very dark.

"Come along," Dante said, taking her hand.

Beatrice didn't budge. "But there isn't enough light. We won't be able to see where we are going."

"It is only dark until we get around this rather uglylooking formation here. My brother and I were convinced this was a calcified troll who used to guard the cave entrance hundreds of years ago. There are a few turns, which I think I can still navigate, and then there will be light in the next chamber from another opening above us."

Beatrice reluctantly allowed Dante to lead her through. Actually, she clung to his arm, afraid if she lost him, she'd never find her way out. True to his word, they emerged moments later into a large chamber lit where the rock wall had separated high above, creating a narrow opening. Several smaller trails led off from the main chamber deeper into the mountain belly, but they appeared too small and certainly too dark for them to enter without a lamp.

Beatrice's eyes followed the cavern wall higher and higher still. It seemed to go on forever. The chamber was indeed stunning. She could hear water dripping down one wall, echoing rhythmically within the many openings around them. Oddly shaped formations of dripstone decorated the inner cavern, glistening with hidden fires in the sunlight. It had an almost magical quality to it. Beatrice removed her glove and ran her hand over the smooth, rippling surface of the stone, noticing the way it would sparkle with blue and violet radiance when the light hit it just right.

"What sort of stone is this?" she asked.

"Mostly limestone, although it carries the properties of another, rare sort of stone that is found only in the

Treak Cliff hills. Derbyshire tradition has it that it possesses unusual powers."

"Indeed? What is it called?"

"It is amythesine spar, although locally it is known simply as Blue John."

"Blue John," she repeated, turning. "It is a lovely stone, oh—"

She had moved and the toe of her boot caught on the hem of her overlong riding skirt. She pitched forward, landing straight in Dante's arms.

Beatrice looked up at him to beg his pardon. The words never came. She was so close to him that she could see the tiny flecks of gold in his dark eyes. He was bent back slightly, leaning against the rock wall, holding her. He didn't release her. She didn't attempt to pull away. She was caught, unable to tear her eyes away from his. She took in a breath and held it when he lowered his head to her.

His kiss came a second later. Beatrice was afraid to move, fearful of losing the riot of sensations that were surging through her. A giddy, excited warmth made her instinctively press against Dante. Her hands were splayed against his chest, and she could feel his deep breathing as he moved his mouth seductively over hers.

She felt his mouth leave hers, kissing along her jawline to her ear. She dropped her head back, clinging now to the opening of his coat as he continued kissing her, moving downward along her neck, his hand brushing the side of her breast. His touch was thrilling, exciting. She hoped he would never stop.

He did.

"Good God, what in bloody hell am I doing?"

Beatrice opened her eyes just as Dante set her away from him. He moved from the wall then a good three feet. She didn't know what to do, what to say. She felt terribly awkward, uncertain, confused. Why had he stopped kissing her. Had she done it wrong?

"My lord?"

It was the expression of bewilderment on Beatrice's face that sent Dante to feeling lower than a snake. He felt her respond to his kiss and he knew she was wondering why he'd pushed her away as he had. He also knew if he hadn't pushed her away, he'd have done the one thing he'd always vowed never to do. He would have seduced an innocent, and it would have been the easiest thing he'd ever done in his life.

"I am truly sorry, Beatrice," he finally blurted out. "I should not have kissed you like that. It was not well done of me."

Beatrice blinked. She didn't say a word. It only made his compunction double.

"We'd best be getting on to the village now," he said finally and started back the way they'd come, leaving Beatrice little choice but to follow.

Outside, he helped her onto her mount, placing his hands quickly at her waist and lifting her into the saddle. He swung up onto Fury's back and wordlessly headed back down the mountain pass.

They rode in comparative silence until they reached the outskirts of the village a half hour later. Castleton lay nestled in a valley below Castle Peveril, surrounded on three sides by rocky hill land. Quaint stone cottages that looked as if they were stacked upon one another lined the dusty cart path that served as the main roadway leading into the small village square. The window openings were decorated with brilliant flower boxes, while freshly-washed laundry hung out to dry in the summer sun. Wherever they passed, heads would poke out windows to see who the newcomers were. Murmurs of excitement would follow.

They stopped at the square, and Dante dismounted, tying Fury to a tether post. He helped Beatrice down. An open-air market had been set up on the other side of the square. Villagers teemed about while children played cheerfully in the shade.

"I'll be going to the posting house. Perhaps you'd like to look about the shop stalls while I'm gone?"

Beatrice smiled and nodded. She watched him go.

When he reached the edge of the square, Dante turned to look back at her. Beatrice was browsing through some trinkets and chatting with the woman who was selling them. He had forced himself not to look at her during their ride from the cave. He knew if he chanced to glance into those silver eyes, he would return to that mindless, careless state that had caused him to throw all his newfound morals to the wind. He knew he would kiss her again.

She must think him an utter cad. He'd taken advantage of a situation that even now he wondered if he'd somehow set up unconsciously. His errand to post the letter to Lord Devonshire at Chatsworth could have easily been seen to by Renny or a footman, but he had decided to see to it himself. It gave him an excuse to be with Beatrice. He knew they would be alone. Going into that cave had only ensured it. He could have warned her to watch her step inside the cave, but he hadn't, and worse, he had taken full advantage of the situation that had virtually fallen into his lap.

Still, he could not deny her response to his kiss. It had been genuine, eager, and had fueled his blood to the boiling point. Dante had been with women who rivaled Venus in beauty who had never inspired that sort of response in him. What was it about this petite, ungraceful creature that just the thought of having her, made him hard to the point of very real pain?

It boggled the mind.

Beatrice browsed through the shop stalls, glancing through the delicate laces and pretty fabrics. She barely noticed them. All that was on her mind was Dante, and the kiss they had shared.

She just didn't know what to make of it. When she had stumbled into Dante's arms and had glanced into his eyes, she had seen the intensity, and had felt it in kind with his kiss. Returning his kiss had seemed the only natural reaction.

It was his response, or lack thereof, that left her confused.

Perhaps Dante feared she had taken offense at his kissing her. She certainly hadn't told him to stop. Perhaps, instead, he thought her the forward one for having kissed him back. Oh dear, that could cause problems. If only she hadn't tripped. But then, if she hadn't tripped, she wouldn't have fallen against him, and he wouldn't have kissed her at all.

What mattered now was what could she do about it? They certainly couldn't go on, pretending nothing had happened. That was only making the air between them more awkward. She thought on it a bit longer, trying to come up with a plan. The only solution was for her to express to Dante that the kiss had had no outward effect on her at all.

It had been a kiss. Nothing more. In other words, a lie.

"Are you ready to leave, Beatrice? I've finished at the posting house, and it will be getting dark soon. We need to start back for Wyldewoode."

The sound of his voice startled her. She turned to him and smiled. "Yes, of course, Dante, but before we go, I should like to say something to you."

He waited politely for her to go on.

"It occurred to me while you were off to the posting house that you might be thinking I was upset when you kissed me in the cave earlier."

Dante glanced over at the peddler, an elderly man

who seemed to have very keen hearing, for he'd taken a step closer at Beatrice's impulsive statement. "I see."

"Well, I simply wished to assure you that I was not upset by it at all. I mean, it was nice, but it wasn't anything that should be given further thought."

Where had this come from? Dante had to force himself not to smile. "Oh?"

"Yes. Please don't be offended by it, my lord. I'm sure you are a very good kisser, as kissers go. Have you much experience at it?"

"You could say my experience is a bit more extensive than yours."

"I, of course, have nothing to compare. And thus, I hope you can understand why I say it is best forgotten. Let us simply pretend it never took place and go back to where we were before. I mean, it really wasn't anything to arouse the passions. I guess I am just not by nature a passionate person."

Dante just looked at her. The peddler stifled a grin. "I see."

"I thought you should know that," she added, smiling, seemingly pleased with herself. "I wouldn't want what occurred between us to cause any difficulty."

She certainly was making this rather insignificant event significant, Dante thought. He wasn't fool enough not to realize what she was really doing. "Well, I thank you for your honesty, Beatrice. I am happy to see you weren't in any way injured by the experience, but I guess someone of a dispassionate nature would certainly know if they had been."

"Exactly," she said, "that is what I am. A person of a dispassionate nature."

With that she turned her attentions to the merchandise for sale. "Please, my lord, think nothing further of it."

Dante stood beside her, studying her. He had kissed many women in his life, and his experience told him

Beatrice had certainly not been as unaffected by it as she put on. He had felt her response; it had spurred his own onward. It wasn't arrogance or self-complacency that caused him to reject her little ruse, and that's precisely what it was—a ruse. He knew she had been as affected by the kiss as he, and just to be certain of it, he would prove it.

Beatrice started to walk away, heading back toward where the horses waited. Before she got far, Dante reached out and grabbed her hand, pulling her around to face him. Before she could say anything, he had taken her into his embrace and was kissing her again. He kissed her until he felt her hands clutching at his coat. He kissed her until he felt her knees buckling beneath her. He continued kissing her, and only when he knew he had proven his point, did he finally lift his head from hers.

Beatrice's eyes were glazed, her lips were parted, and her breathing was coming swiftly. The marketplace had come to a virtual standstill.

"It is getting late, and we really should be starting back for Wyldewoode," he said softly.

He set her on unsteady feet and turned. As he made for the horses, Dante thought he had never before met, or kissed, a more passionate person of a dispassionate nature.

Chapter Nine

"My lord, I am so glad you are home."

Renny was waiting for them on the front steps when they returned to Wyldewoode. It was nearing nightfall, but even in the fading light, Dante could see that the steward looked as though he'd just seen the devil as he came rushing down the steps to meet them.

Dante swung down from Fury. "What is it, man?"

"There are visitors, my lord. I told them you were away, and that we didn't know when to expect you back, but they insisted on remaining. They have been here since just after midday, my lord."

"I trust you offered them refreshment?" Dante said, immediately assuming that the visitors must be Cassia and Rolfe having come in response to his letter.

It never occurred to him that his letter had only been posted a few days before, and that they would never have had the time to travel to Wyldewoode so quickly.

"Yes, my lord, although they would take only tea, nothing more. They are waiting for you in the parlor." And then Renny added, his voice dropping oddly low, "Perhaps Miss Beatrice would be better served to allow you time to handle the situation on your own."

"Nonsense, Renny. I've been expecting them. It is because of Beatrice that they have come. It is best to get to the heart of matters straightaway."

Actually, Dante was thinking that the sooner he introduced Beatrice to Cassia, the sooner they might find out Beatrice's true identity, and the sooner he could send her off to where she belonged before he ended up tossing his newfound respectability to the wind. Kissing her in the marketplace had been a mistake. He knew that now. He had wanted to prove to Beatrice that he knew she was lying, that he knew their first kiss had meant more than she let on, which he had. But he had also proven to himself that his attraction to her was fast moving beyond mere attraction to absolute infatuation. That meant only one thing.

Danger.

Dante motioned for Beatrice to follow and threw open the door to the parlor. "I hope you weren't kept waiting too long."

Dante halted in the doorway when he saw who awaited him inside. Beatrice, following close behind him, collided with his back, but he hardly noticed, for his every attention was fixed on the two figures sitting in the parlor. They were not Cassia and Rolfe, nor were they anyone he'd ever seen before. There was a woman, who sat with a backbone as inflexible as iron, looking at him with her black gown fastened tightly to her raised chin, her hair pulled back so severely it made her eyes appear slanted. Her thin-lipped mouth was pinched in a frown.

With her was a small girl with fat dark curls framing a tiny face that held an expression of pure fear. The expression, he noticed, was directed at him.

"Excuse me," he said, "I had thought you would be someone else."

"Evidently," the woman said. That one word alone carried an unmistakable tone of contempt.

"May I inquire as to your name and purpose for being here?" he asked after a moment of tense silence.

"I am the child's governess, Abigail Stoutwell. *Miss* Abigail Stoutwell," she added, apparently feeling the distinction necessary. "And this is Lady Phoebe

Havelock, at least she was Lady Phoebe Havelock until it was discovered she is in truth your bastard daughter."

There was no sound, not even the audible gasp that usually followed a pronouncement of this gravity. For Dante it wasn't shock or disbelief that first came upon him at the woman's recitation. Instead, it was anger, pure, and fierce.

"A moment if you would, Miss Stoutwell," he managed. He turned to Beatrice, who looked oddly calm standing beside him. "Beatrice, I would appreciate it if you would take the child from the room while I discuss the situation with Miss Stoutwell."

Beatrice said nothing, just calmly walked over to the girl and held out her hand. The child placed hers in it and walked with Beatrice silently from the room. Dante watched them go. He turned back to the woman.

"I find it difficult to understand how a person who speaks with such open venom could ever be considered suitable to rear a child."

Miss Stoutwell was quite obviously undaunted by his opinion of her. Her mouth rose in a sneer. "My references are beyond reproach."

"Then you would be wise not to add my name to the list. Now perhaps you could explain yourself in more socially acceptable terms?"

The woman extended her arm. Fisted in her bony hand was a letter. Dante took it and turned, crossing the room to the window to read it in private.

May this letter serve as notice to all and sundry who may read it that His Lordship, Roger Havelock, the Marquess of Overton, does hereby release all relation and responsibility, financial and otherwise, to the child known as Lady Phoebe Havelock to her true and rightful father in blood, Dante Tremaine, the Earl of Morgan.

Dante read the letter a second time, then a third. When he was certain he'd read it right, he then turned on the objectionable Miss Stoutwell.

"What in bloody hell is the meaning of this?" he asked, shoving the paper under the woman's lofty nose.

"Precisely what is reads, Lord Morgan. His Lordship, the Marquess of Overton, has recently been made aware that his wife, the marchioness, had at one time been involved in an assignation with you, the result of which was the child he believed these past five years to be his daughter. He has been advised to terminate his relationship with the child and has delivered her to you."

"What does Eliza have to say about this? Surely, she would never have agreed to—"

"Lady Overton is dead. She was taken by the plague earlier this year."

Dante felt a terrible chill run through him. Eliza was dead? Dear God, no.

"While going through Lady Overton's personal effects," Miss Stoutwell went on, "Lord Overton came upon a letter his wife had written"—she paused—"to you. In it she told you of your child, Lady Phoebe. It was dated not long after the child had been born. Apparently, Lady Overton never saw fit to post it."

"Yet she never destroyed it."

"Perhaps she was simply waiting for a more fitting time, after the child had been given the benefit of upbringing as the Marquess of Overton's child."

Dante was in grave danger of doing Miss Stoutwell bodily harm, and he knew it. He took a deep breath, tempering his anger. "I'll thank you to keep your opinions to yourself, Miss Stoutwell. They have no bearing on the situation."

She sniffed, but wisely did not speak.

Dante walked over to the windows, leaning his

forearm against the wall. He thought of Eliza, poor, sweet Eliza. She had been an innocent, but had quickly learned of the darker side of life in her marriage to the well-respected marquess. She would be far better off now that she was dead. Overton had been a monstrous man long before he had found that letter. There would be no telling what he would have done had he learned of it while she'd still been alive.

"How old is she?" he asked, still staring out the window.

"She reached her fifth year this February past."

Dante counted back the months during which he had been involved with Eliza. He closed his eyes when he confirmed Phoebe was indeed his daughter.

"Has she been told?"

"Lady Phoebe is aware that the man she believed to be her father is not really her father. She knows that her mother is dead and that we traveled here to meet her true father."

Hence the expression of terror on her face at his entrance.

Dante turned. "And that is all?"

Miss Stoutwell's cold eyes glared at him. "Yes."

Somehow he didn't quite believe her.

Dante moved from the window. "Thank you, Miss Stoutwell. You may go now."

The governess stood. "Go? What do you mean? I am the child's governess. I am the only person she knows."

Dante halted right in front of her. He stared at her, and the look on his face caused her to fall back on the chair. "Correction, Miss Stoutwell, you *were* Phoebe's governess. As the letter states, the child is now my responsibility, and in my first duty as such I am dismissing you. Without references. Being uprooted from her home and sent here to meet a stranger must be terrifying enough. I will not compound that terror by forcing the child to suffer your presence, and your influence in her life, another second. You may leave by the same route you came in. Take your baggage with you, but leave Phoebe's belongings here. You may return to His Lordship, the marquess, although I'd wager you'll find this need for the services of a governess greatly diminished upon your arrival. Good day, Miss Stoutwell, and Godspeed."

She stared at him disbelieving, then stood and slowly walked from the room. Dante remained in the center of the room, watching her departure, secure in the knowledge that it was the last time he would ever have to face that virago again. Still, even after she'd gone, he stood there longer, wondering if he'd imagined the whole thing.

Never in his maddest dreams could he have conjured up something this unbelievable. He had a child. A daughter. He'd been a father for the past five years. And he hadn't known it.

Dante walked over to the chair that faced out onto the lawn and sat down, resting his face in his hands, his elbows on his knees, eyes fixed on nothing in particular.

He could still remember the first time he'd seen Eliza Havelock. She'd been newly wed, having just returned to court after a honeymoon at her new husband's country seat. She and her husband, the marquess, had been presented at court, and Dante remembered thinking that the bride had looked a bit pale, gaunt almost, but he'd put it off as too many sleepless nights spent with her new husband. He had forgotten about it as quickly as he'd considered it.

He was soon to discover the truth.

His relationship with Eliza had been a special one, the closest thing to marriage Dante had ever come by. They had been friends as well as lovers. He had talked freely with her as he did with no other, for he had known he could trust her above anyone else.

Oddly, it had been Eliza who had ended their involvement. She had come to him late one night, telling him she needed to get away from court, from London. Dante knew what she had really been saying, that in truth she needed to get away from him, because she was intelligent enough to realize he would never have an affection for her as deep as she did for him. As he thought back on it now, he realized she must have known then that she carried his child.

And she hadn't told him because she hadn't wanted him to feel that obligation to her had he known the truth.

Eliza had left after making love to him one last time, and Dante had let her go. She had returned to her husband's country house, and to her husband's bed, so that he would never know, so he would have no reason to believe the child wasn't really his. She had been so very careful, little Eliza, keeping her secret hidden so well that no one had suspected a thing. . . .

Until the plague.

Bloody damnable plague.

Outside a heavy rain began to fall.

Dante closed his eyes and said a silent prayer for the hope that Eliza would find peace in the hereafter, the peace she had never known while living among mortals.

Chapter Ten

Dante found Beatrice with Phoebe in the Music Room, the two of them sitting together on the carved bench set before the harpsichord. Beatrice was showing Phoebe how best to position her fingers on the keys to play. They looked natural and right sitting there together.

Dante didn't intrude, not at first. He watched as Beatrice played a simple tune and took an uninterrupted study of Phoebe, this child who was now his.

Even if he had initially questioned Miss Stoutwell's claim of his paternity, once faced with Phoebe there would have been no doubt. She had his hair, "black as Derbyshire gritstone," Mrs. Leeds used to say, and she had his mother's sky blue eyes. He hadn't seen Phoebe smile, but somehow he knew when she did, like his mother, those eyes would light up with the brilliance of the star-filled night sky.

She was a Tremaine through and through, but then, when he looked at her closely, he could see the delicate features, the inherent grace of her mother, Eliza, shining through.

Dante smiled as Phoebe repeated the short measure Beatrice had just played, misplaying only one key.

"That was very good, Phoebe," he said, coming into the room.

Phoebe jerked about on the bench. Her face lost its expression of delight and fell to fearful trepidation. Dante noticed this. He would have to be an idiot not to realize it was a result of a long-formed habit. He wondered if Overton had ever beaten her. He would kill the coward if he had.

Dante smiled at Phoebe. "It is all right, Phoebe. No one is going to hurt you here."

Phoebe just looked at him as if conversing with a man was completely beyond her. Actually, she looked as if she expected him to swallow her whole.

He hunkered down in front of her, trying to be anything less than intimidating. "I'd wager you had a long journey to come here today. My steward, Renny, told me you haven't eaten anything all day. Are you very hungry?"

She stared at him, then, slowly, she nodded.

"Mrs. Leeds, our cook, makes the best treacle gingerbread in the world. Do you like gingerbread?"

Phoebe gave another small nod.

"I happen to know that she always has some cooling in the kitchen. Would you like to go there and have some? And, perhaps, a nice cup of milk with it?"

"Yes, thank you, sir."

Her voice was small, innocent, and it did something to Dante he couldn't quite describe. Suddenly, he knew he would do anything he could to see this child never lived in fear again. Suddenly he knew he would die for her. "I'll see if I can find Renny to take you to the kitchen."

Dante didn't have to go far, for Renny had appeared on cue at the door.

"Renny, my good man, would you take Lady Phoebe to the kitchen and see if Mrs. Leeds would be kind enough to give her some of her gingerbread and a cup of milk?"

Renny nodded. "Very good, my lord."

Dante looked back at Phoebe. "Phoebe, this is Renny. He is very kind, and he loves children especially pretty little girls like you. If you go with him, he will take you to meet Mrs. Leeds and he will get you a bit of that gingerbread I promised you. He may even find you some lemon curd to spread upon it."

The child looked at Beatrice, as if to ask if she should leave. Beatrice smiled. Phoebe looked over at Renny, weighing her decision a moment longer, then slipped down off the bench and walked slowly to him. Halfway there, she stopped and turned.

"Where is Miss Stoutwell?" she asked.

Dante wasn't certain as to how he should respond. Despite his immediate aversion to the governess, he could not deny that she was the only person with whom this child was familiar. Having her gone too might upset Phoebe, but he couldn't very well lie to her either. Finally, he decided to be truthful, but vague.

"Miss Stoutwell has gone, Phoebe. She will not be coming back. You will stay with me and live here now."

Phoebe considered this. "Oh," she said simply, then turned and took Renny's waiting hand before leaving the room.

"She is a lovely child," Beatrice said once they were alone. "And very bright."

"Yes, she is." Dante was silent, then said, "You are probably wondering what all this is about."

"It really isn't any of my business, Lord Morgan."

If he really wanted to, Dante could agree with that statement, but something inside of him pushed at him to explain, to make her understand. He needed her to know. "I would prefer it if you heard the truth, Beatrice. I find at times like these it is not nearly as damning as rumor."

Beatrice shrugged. "If that's what you would like."

Dante leaned against the harpsichord, thinking. After a few moments he looked at her. "Beatrice, I have done some things in my life of which I am not very proud."

"I think you would be sorely pressed to find anyone who did not share your feelings, Dante. I cannot recall having ever crossed paths with a true paragon."

Dante smiled. For someone with no memory of the past, she was rather wise. "Ah, yes, well, those are knowing words coming from someone who has nothing of which to be ashamed."

"How do you know? I could very well have something terrible in my past, so terrible that it caused me to lose my memory just so I could forget it. I guess that is the one good thing about not knowing who I am. I cannot remember things I might regret."

"If having something terrible in one's past could cause one to lose memory, I should have succumbed to it a long time ago."

Beatrice touched his hand. "I'm certain whatever you have done isn't anything so awful. Things often tend to seem larger than life when kept in our own minds. Once said, you might find it really isn't all that bad."

Dante took a deep breath. They would soon find out. "Phoebe is my daughter, but her mother was never my wife."

There was only a momentary pause. "Not at all uncommon I would think."

"Actually, she was someone else's wife."

"Oh."

Dante continued. "It was a balmy night in early summer when I first met Eliza. There had been a masque performance at Whitehall held on the green along the riverside. I had stepped away; I don't readily recall why. I only remember hearing Eliza's soft sobs in the silence of the night.

"I remember coming around a bend near an ornamental hedge. I found Eliza siting alone on a stone bench beneath the heavy branches of a tree. Her face was buried in her hands, and her slender back shook as she cried. I startled her at my approach. She immediately attempted to hide her tearstained face. I handed her my handkerchief and asked if there was anything I could do to help. She responded by beginning to sob once again."

Dante fell silent a moment. He had not been looking for a liaison that night; he was already involved with another, but something about Eliza, the helpless, defenseless gleam in her eyes in the moonlight had caused him to sit beside her on that bench and hold her in his arms as she cried. What followed had been inevitable.

"Why was Eliza crying?" Beatrice asked.

"Eliza, I then learned, was newly wed and had spent the better part of her wedding journey alone, for after a disastrous wedding night with her new husband, an experience she'd been ill-prepared for, her husband, the Marquess of Overton, chose to spend his time elsewhere. He did, however, communicate to her his utter disgust with her on every occasion he could, reviling her until, after a fortnight's time, he'd taken away any ounce of self-worth she had ever had. No one should be made to feel so absolutely worthless. I offered her comfort, and we became"—he paused—"*involved* for a number of months."

"You fell in love with her."

Dante shook his head. "I'm afraid it was never that simple. I believe Eliza did feel a strong affection for me, she probably loved me, but unfortunately, I never came to feel the same for her. I cared for her very much, but I couldn't honestly say I loved her."

"At least you were honest enough not to mislead her into thinking you did."

"I might be many things, Beatrice, but dishonest isn't one of them. That is one thing I can state unequivocally. I just never was very good at lying. So, no, I never misled Eliza into believing I loved her. Since learning about Phoebe, though, I have come to the conclusion that when Eliza discovered she was with child, she decided to end our involvement. She never told me about the child. I did not know about Phoebe's existence until today."

"That was evident from the look on your face," Beatrice said. "But why would Phoebe's mother suddenly decide you must know the truth now? Why would she send her daughter away?"

"Eliza is dead, Beatrice. She was taken by the plague early this year. Her husband learned the truth about Phoebe when he found a letter among Eliza's effects. It was a letter she had written to me years ago but had never sent, a letter in which she stated I was Phoebe's natural father. As a result, the marquess no longer wants the child, so he has sent her here to me."

Beatrice frowned. "That is truly despicable. How can a person love a child for all those years and suddenly discard her so lightly?"

"As I said, the marquess was not the kindest of men. From the fear on her face when she looks at me, it would seem it is something Phoebe knows well. This man, probably the only man she has ever known in her short life, has made her fearful of all others."

Beatrice actually looked angry. "Well, then Phoebe is better off without him."

Dante watched her. She wasn't saying anything about his relationship with Eliza. "So you do not think me a reprobate now, my having told you the truth of my involvement with Phoebe's mother?"

"Don't be absurd, Dante. You offered solace to someone who had unjustly been brought low. How could I condemn you for that? Had you known of Phoebe before today, I have little doubt you would have taken responsibility for her, as any gentleman would."

"Many would say a gentleman wouldn't have involved himself with a married woman in the first place."

"So Phoebe's mother, Eliza, was supposed to spend the rest of her life with a man who mistreated her? She was never to know happiness? No doubt it was an arranged marriage."

"Yes."

"A marriage should never be a financial transaction. It only results in anguish." She looked at him, then added, "I don't even know why I feel so strongly about that, but I do."

Dante could but smile. "It would seem you're a bit of a freethinker."

Beatrice stood. "Perhaps. I wouldn't rightly know. What I do know is that all this freethinking has given me an appetite. Would you care to join me in a slice of gingerbread, my lord?"

And that was the end of that.

Dante peered inside the room that was lit by a single candle, no more. Phoebe was sitting up on the bed, knees bent beneath her white linen nightgown, her hair tumbling about her shoulders in dark curls, as she stared fixedly at something she held in her hand.

"Hello," he said, coming inside.

Phoebe closed her hand around the object, concealing it from him. She turned her head and stared.

Dante came forward and sat on the edge of the bed. "Do you like your new room, Phoebe?"

"Yes, sir."

"This was my room when I was a boy. I used to have an army of wooden soldiers standing by the window over there. I used to talk to them at night when everyone else was asleep. They are very good listeners, you know. I think they are packed away in storage up in the garret. If you'd like, I could get them down for you and . . ."

She continued to stare at him.

Dante smiled. "I guess toy soldiers wouldn't much interest a little girl."

Still, she didn't respond, so Dante decided to forgo the preamble and cut straight to his reasons for coming there. "Phoebe, I thought you might be confused about why you were brought here."

"You are my father," she said matter-of-factly.

"Yes, I am. Do you understand what that means?"

"Yes. The man Momma was married to was not my father really. Nobody knew until she died. She used to tell me about you when she would read to me. She said you were a gentleman. But I wasn't supposed to tell anyone else about you. It was a secret, but Momma forgot to hide it."

Dante stared at her. "You are very bright, Phoebe."

"Momma said she didn't want me to grow up like she did. I can read and write my name. She taught me. I can cipher a little. She said girls weren't ever taught things because people didn't want them to be smart. She said that was wrong, and she didn't want me to be like that."

"Your mother was a very bright woman, too. But since she is gone and I am your father, you will be living here with me now. Does that displease you?"

"Miss Stoutwell said it wouldn't really matter that you were my real father. She said you would probably send me away to a boarding school. She said you probably were a Papist, so you might even send me to a con-, con . . ." She searched for the word.

"A convent?"

"Yes. She said that gentlemen like you didn't want young children. They sent them away to live in convents until they were old enough to marry whoever they had chosen for them. Will I be going away to the convent soon, sir?"

Dante frowned. "No, Phoebe, you will not be going away soon. You will not be going away at all. In the first place, I am not Catholic, although I have friends who are, and they are very nice people. A person's choice of religion does not make them terrible."

"Miss Stoutwell said Papists are evil."

"Miss Stoutwell is wrong about that and a great many other things as well. What else did she tell you?"

"She said Mama was a whore and that you were a rakehell who seduced Momma and fornicated with her when she was already married."

Good God, but that women was a termagant. Dante was glad he'd already sent the pious Miss Stoutwell packing, for if she'd still been at Wyldewoode, he felt certain he'd be throttling her right now.

"She said that I was a bas-, bas . . ."

"Bastard," Dante finished.

"Yes, and that was shameful, and no one would ever want me. She said that you would beat me if I was bad, and that I should be quiet and speak only when told to until I grew up and then I could become a governess like her."

Not bloody likely, Dante thought, releasing a slow, measured breath. It was the only way he could keep himself from slamming his fist into the wall. Throttling was too good for that vicious harpy. She should be damned to perdition for filling this child's head with such verbal absurdity.

"Now, Phoebe, I want you to listen to me very closely. You should never be ashamed of who you are, or who your mother was, because she was a very special person, as you are."

"Momma used to read me stories when I would go to sleep."

Dante suddenly imagined Eliza, sweet Eliza, sitting

beside Phoebe just as he was now, reading her fairy tales as she drifted off to sleep. Eliza always had been given to whimsy, filled with belief in knights and dragon slayers. It pulled at something inside him, knowing she had still retained that wondrous quality despite the ugliness of her marriage.

"Miss Stoutwell said stories were the work of the devil," Phoebe said then, breaking into his thoughts.

"Miss Stoutwell is the work of the—" He caught himself. "Phoebe, Miss Stoutwell was not a good person to tell you all those things. They are simply not true. Miss Stoutwell didn't like your mother, and that is why she told you those things. Was Miss Stoutwell ever mean to you?"

"She hit my hand with her stick once for taking a sweet cake from the kitchen. It made me cry. Then she wouldn't give me any supper."

"Did you like your mother, Phoebe?"

"Yes, sir, very much. She didn't like Miss Stoutwell. She said Miss Stoutwell was a pig." Phoebe shook her head. "No, not a pig. I think she said Miss Stoutwell was a prig. What is a prig, sir?"

"A prig is a person who doesn't care if what they say or believe hurts someone else's feelings."

"Like Miss Stoutwell."

"Precisely, and since you know this, you must also know that nothing she said to you means anything. She was not a nice person, and that is why I sent her away."

"I am glad you sent her away. Momma wanted to send her away, but he wouldn't let her."

"The marquess?"

Phoebe nodded.

"Phoebe, you must always remember your mother the way you just described her to me."

"She used to play with me and my dolls, and she would sing to me."

"Always remember those things about your mother

and forget what Miss Stoutwell or the marquess might have said because they didn't really know your mother as you or I did."

Phoebe frowned, then. "I miss Momma." She took her hand out from under her legs. She opened her fingers to reveal a small pendant with a portrait of Eliza attached to a thin gold chain.

Dante looked at the likeness and felt nothing but sadness. "I know you miss her, Phoebe. You keep this pendant with you, and your mother will never be far from you. Ever." He waited a moment. "Is there anything you want to ask me?"

He braced himself for questions about his relationship with Eliza—why he hadn't taken her away from her abusive husband, why he had allowed her to leave London, why he hadn't attempted to see her again—questions he was asking himself.

Phoebe looked at him. "What did you call your soldiers?"

Dante smiled. "They were called 'The Cavaliers,' Phoebe."

"Cav-a-leers?"

"Yes. They fought for King Charles I."

"He had his head chopped off."

"Yes, he did. His cavalier soldiers had long hair, and they dressed in fine clothes. They also were very skilled with swords. I wanted to be one of them."

Phoebe's eyes were lit with interest. "Did you fight with your sword just like them?"

"I was too young to fight with them, but I did learn how to use a sword."

"Will you show me?"

"Young ladies do not—" He stopped himself. Why couldn't he teach his daughter how to wield a sword? Eliza certainly would have. "Yes, Phoebe, I will show you how to use a sword. Not right now, though. It is far too late, and you are far too tired. It is time for you to go to sleep now."

Dante pulled back the covers, and Phoebe lay down on the bed. She clutched the chain with Eliza's picture in her tiny hand. She looked up at him, and Dante would have sworn he saw Eliza looking at him through her. He smiled. "Good night, Phoebe."

"Good night, sir."

Dante started for the door.

"Sir?"

"Yes, Phoebe?"

"Perhaps tomorrow you could see if the soldiers are still packed away in the garret?"

"Come on," Dante said, pulling Beatrice up from her chair. The book she'd been reading dropped to the floor.

"What's the matter?" she asked, thinking whatever it was, it must be urgent. Perhaps Phoebe had run away. Perhaps that abominable Miss Stoutwell had taken her. "Is Phoebe all right?"

"She is fine. We had a nice talk, and she is sleeping in her new bedchamber."

"Then what is so urgent?"

"Beatrice, we are on a mission."

Dante started for the stairs. He grabbed a burning branch of candles from the table by the door and started climbing the stairs. On the third floor he took Beatrice down a hallway where he came to a halt at the foot of a narrow flight of steps. At the top, set in the ceiling, was a small trapdoor.

"Where are you going?"

"*We* are going up to the garret. I realized when I took you on that tour of the house, I neglected to show you the garret."

Beatrice looked at him. She wondered if he'd lost his mind. "That really isn't necessary."

"Come on now. It is perfectly safe. The ghosts have been gone for quite some time, except, perhaps, for the 'Duchess.' "

"The 'Duchess?' "

"Yes, it is said she was a guest here at a ball given by my grandfather, the first Earl of Morgan. At least they think she was. She was found murdered in the garret, with a whack from an axe. Her head was never found. She used to haunt the garret, searching for her lost head, at least they think it was her. One can never tell, what with her head being gone and all."

Beatrice slanted him a look of amusement. "Why don't you simply ask her?"

"You do not belive me, do you, Beatrice? Well, don't say I didn't give you fair warning." He handed her the branch. "You hold the candles while I push open the trapdoor."

They climbed the stairs. Dante slid the iron bolt free and pushed the door upward. It thudded backward against the floor above them. He climbed up through the opening, then reached down for the light.

"All right, give me your hand." He chuckled. "I promise I will give it back."

He took Beatrice's hand and guided her up into the shadowy garret.

The ceiling was low, leaving Dante to duck his head in places. Beatrice had no trouble standing. The flickering branch of candles sent dancing shadows across the walls, illuminating the dusty trunks and various pieces of furniture that were stored all around them.

"What exactly are we looking for?" Beatrice asked, eyeing a dark corner where she'd just heard the distinct sound of scampering creatures.

"Toy soldiers. I promised Phoebe I would fetch them down for her. I've an appointment tomorrow morning to meet with a neighboring landholder in the village, so I won't have time to get them for her when it's light."

Beatrice smiled. Dante could very well have sent a servant to find the soldiers in the morning, but he hadn't. He had wanted to get them for Phoebe himself. She liked that. "So where shall we begin looking?"

Dante surveyed the area. "I'll look over here. You might wish to stay close by." He grinned. "In case our friend, the 'Duchess,' decides to pay us a visit."

"Perhaps we should send down for tea," Beatrice said, rolling her eyes at him. "Then, again, she wouldn't be able to drink it, would she, without her head?"

Dante chuckled as Beatrice lifted the lid on a trunk near her feet. She fingered through bundles of correspondence that had been neatly stacked and tied with string. She could see that the letters were addressed to Dante's mother, the countess. Setting the bundles back, she lowered the lid and moved on to another. Something fell with a loud thud to the right, making her jump.

"Ah," Dante said from across the room, "perhaps it is the 'Duchess' coming to look for her head."

Beatrice frowned. She wasn't about to tell him she'd just nearly jumped out of her skin. "Don't be absurd. There is no ghost here. It is just the darkness . . . and all the shadows . . ."

Dante popped his head around a large wardrobe, grinning. He obviously knew her words were directed more at herself than at him.

"Keep looking," she said and lifted the lid on another trunk.

This one was full of clothes, children's clothes. She took the topmost garment, holding it up by the arms. It was a small coat, the color indistinct in the darkness, one arm torn at the shoulder. Beneath it was a miniature pair of breeches with well-worn knees. "Were these yours?"

Dante looked over to her. "I would have to assume they are since they are damaged. My brother was fastidious about his clothes. He always walked on a pathway, never straying, while I preferred to frolic in mud puddles and streams."

"Seems a vastly more interesting route to take," Beatrice said, folding the coat and placing it back in the trunk. She closed it and then moved on. She removed a cloth that covered a tall flat object leaning against a chest of drawers. Beneath the cloth was revealed a portrait of two children sitting beside a huge wolfhound. She moved the candle branch near to it to better see.

One child stood beside the dog, his hand placed negligently at its head. He had sandy-colored hair and clear, soft blue eyes. The other child, sitting crosslegged before the dog, had hair black as sin and golden eyes lit with mischief.

"It isn't all too difficult to figure out which one is me, is it?" Dante asked, suddenly standing beside her.

"That is William, your brother?"

"Yes. Even then he had the look of a future earl—poised, confident. I simply had the look of more trouble to come, or so Mrs. Leeds was fond of saying."

"I happen to know that Mrs. Leeds is extremely fond of you. She even told me how you are having fresh food stores sent over to that village that has been struck by the plague."

The wind suddenly blew up outside, causing a mournful whistle to echo through the garret rafters. "It would seem the 'Duchess' doesn't agree with Mrs. Leeds and her opinion of me."

Beatrice replaced the cover on the portrait. "You really shouldn't tease me so, my lord," she said, moving away from him around a tall wardrobe. "It isn't very gentlemanly of y—"

Beatrice froze. She took in a frightened gasp.

There, poised near a small oxeye window, silhouetted in the moonlight behind it, was a body, a body whose head was clearly missing.

Chapter Eleven

Dante came immediately forward, drawn by Beatrice's gasp. "What is it, Beatrice? Did you injure yourself? What is wrong?"

Beatrice didn't respond. She couldn't. She couldn't even move. She just stared at the headless figure, while the wind wailed about outside like a lost soul.

Or was it a lost head?

Beside her, Dante began to chuckle. He didn't just chuckle, he laughed, loud and deep. His revelry brought Beatrice out of her terrified trance. She narrowed her eyes at him, unable to believe he was making fun of her.

"It's just a seamstress's figure," he said, bringing the candle branch closer to the shadowy figure.

The figure took on a much different perspective in the light, not nearly so frightening. Beatrice felt utterly ridiculous.

"It was my mother's." Dante was still smiling like a goon. "Did you think, dear Beatrice, that perhaps the 'Duchess' had come for her head?"

Beatrice wanted to slap him; in fact, she took a swipe at him as he turned. She missed him. "Don't be absurd. The figure merely startled me. What sort of a reaction did you expect with all your ghoulish talk of ghosts and the like?" She stepped around him, her heart still pounding in her throat. "Have you given up yet on finding those soldiers for Phoebe?"

He started off in a different direction. "No, not yet. I know they are up here somewhere. My mother never discarded anything. And since Phoebe asked for them, I would really like to find them for her. I think they might be over here—"

Dante was cut off by a loud, crashing sound of splintering wood. In the midst of all the noise, he vanished. A loud thud came from beneath the garret somewhere. And then, silence.

Beatrice grabbed the candle branch. "Dante? Are you there?"

There was no response.

"If this is another of your inane pranks, I swear I will . . ."

She looked to where she'd last seen him. Stepping closer, she could see that the floor had given way, leaving a gaping hole where Dante had last stood.

"Oh, dear Lord."

Beatrice raced to the trapdoor, hurrying down the stairs to the lower level. There, on the landing, amid a pile of broken floorboards and settling dust, lay Dante, flat on his back. He wasn't moving. She prayed he wasn't dead.

"Dante? Can you hear me?"

He groaned.

"Oh, thank God," she said and went to him.

"You are thanking the Lord for my having fallen through the floor?" he said, rubbing the back of his head. He tried to sit up among the rubble. "I guess that is what I get for laughing at you."

"Wait!" Beatrice set the branch down and pushed Dante back, throwing herself over him. He knocked his head on the floor again. He groaned louder. "Let me see if anything is broken," she said.

"If it wasn't before, it is now."

Beatrice ran her hands over Dante's arms and chest

and down to his hips. She began to move her hands downward, probing at his thighs. Dante moaned again.

"Does that hurt?" she asked, running her fingers along his inner thigh, trying to locate his injury. "Is it broken?"

Dante grabbed her wrist.

"It does hurt, doesn't it? Oh, dear, I better go and get some help. I . . . "

Her words trailed off at his intense stare. He wasn't moving. He wasn't groaning. His eyes were burning at her so fiercely she stilled.

"No, Beatrice, my leg certainly isn't broken, and if you keep touching me like that, we're going to need more than help."

She looked down at him, saw what he was talking about, then quickly glanced away. Her faced flushed. "Oh."

They stayed as they were for several minutes.

She hadn't moved her hand from his leg.

"It would probably be best if you got off me now, Beatrice."

"Yes, I think in this instance you are right, my lord."

Still, her hand rested on his thigh.

"And you can let go of my leg now, too. I assure you I am fine."

Beatrice hadn't even realized she still rested her hand so improperly. She immediately moved it and pushed herself back to stand. She waited while Dante did the same, looking down at the floor while he shook his head to clear it.

"Are you all right?" she finally asked.

"Just a knock on the head. Nothing serious." He took the candle branch and looked up at the gaping hole in the ceiling. "In light of things as they are, perhaps it would be best for both of us if I asked Renny to see to the soldiers in the morning."

Beatrice simply nodded. She couldn't have agreed more.

Dante sat in the library, the fire warm on his legs, the brandy in his stomach warmer still. It was late. The last time he remembered hearing the clock chime had been at half past midnight. He wasn't tired. His head was too full for sleep, and he often did his best thinking at times like these, when the house was at its quietest, no servants to interrupt, no business to see to, no children to tuck into bed . . .

Dante still floundered at his newfound paternity. Never in his wildest dreams could he have imagined he would be solely responsible for the continued existence of another human being, especially a small, doll-like creature who resembled him so much it was frightening. He'd always planned on having children, but whenever he had thought of it, it had always held the future tense. Words like "someday" and "when I'm older" came to mind, but someday had suddenly arrived, coming sooner then he could have ever thought it could.

And, perhaps, narrow-mindedly, on those odd occasions when he had thought of his future progeny, it had always been of sons.

Dante recalled how Phoebe had so naively named herself a bastard, repeating with a child's innocence what had been said to her, while not really knowing what it entailed.

But Dante realized all too easily what it would mean for her. Phoebe would undoubtedly become known as "the Rakehell Earl's Bastard Child." She would be ostracized, ridiculed, and even held to account for his transgressions, transgressions that had occurred far before she'd been conceived. Dante couldn't allow that. He wouldn't allow it.

King Charles himself refused to allow his own illegitimate children to bear the stigma of bastardy; he simply ennobled them. And though Dante didn't have that authority, he would do whatever he had to assure Phoebe didn't suffer for her birth. Whatever he had to.

"Oh, excuse me. I hadn't expected to find anyone here at this hour."

Dante looked up. Beatrice stood framed in the doorway, lovely in her nightclothes. His insides instantly tightened.

What was it about this woman? She wasn't anything like the women he usually preferred, women who were dark-haired like himself, tall, statuesque, who were elegant and confident. Beatrice was an utter contrast to that image. She was short, the top of her head barely reaching his chin, and her hair was an indescribable shade of reddish blond that seemed to change in a second's time.

Yet here she stood, that same indescribable hair hanging about her shoulders, shining coppery in the muted firelight, and wearing a modest nightrail, a virgin's nightrail made up of white linen and girlish buttons that fastened to her neck. Her bare toes were curled against the polished wooden floor, for God's sake, and she looked more inviting than if she wore a sheer confection cut to her navel.

It was perplexing. Indeed, most perplexing.

"Hello, Beatrice," Dante said, trying to quash the image of her dropping that damned virgin's nightrail to her ankles and walking to him naked.

"I wasn't altogether truthful when I said I hadn't expected anyone to be about at this hour. I mean, I saw the light when I was on the stairs, so I knew it must be you here. Actually, I was hoping it was you."

Dante might have thought to ask what exactly she meant by that statement, that is if his mind hadn't been occupied elsewhere, on her legs and hips as he watched her walk into the room.

"Couldn't you sleep either?" she asked.

He shook his head.

"Just now, when I came in, you were thinking about Phoebe, weren't you?" She didn't wait for him to answer. "Somehow, from the look on your face, I knew you were."

Beatrice circled around to sit in the chair beside him. She folded her legs beneath her, leaned her elbow on the arm of the chair, and rested her chin on her hand. "Would you like to talk about it?"

"There really isn't anything to say. I was merely realizing the many obstacles Phoebe is going to face for having the misfortune of being my child."

"How could having you for her father be a misfortune? You obviously care for her more than the man she has known as a father up until now. You would never send her away as he did. Never."

Dante shook his head. "There are things you don't know about me, Beatrice. Things I have done. Things I'm not very proud of."

Beatrice peered at him. "There may be things I don't know about you from your past, but I do know about who you are now. You are a kind, honorable, and giving man. You are honest enough to admit you didn't love Phoebe's mother, but you did care for her very much, and you are genuinely grieved over her death. You care enough about Phoebe to want to protect her, from that horrible Miss Stoutwell, and now from whatever you think the circumstances of her birth might bring to her."

"But it's because of me that she must face these things. Don't you see, if I hadn't been who I am, what I am, she wouldn't be forced to face life labeled as a bast—"

"If it hadn't been for who you are," Beatrice broke

in, "she wouldn't be Phoebe, and her mother wouldn't have known the small amount of happiness she had in her short life."

"But what kind of life can I offer her? I cannot give Phoebe what she deserves. I wouldn't presume to replace the mother who birthed her and who loved her more than anything else in life. And, logically, I cannot even hope that she will not someday face ridicule and disdain for having been born the wrong side of the blanket. She is a beautiful child, Beatrice. She should be showered with love, pampered and spoiled. She should be able to come out in society like any other young girl, have young men falling at their feet in adoration of her eyebrows, composing pages of poetry in tribute to her. All I can offer her is my home and my financial support. Had she known what awaited her when she left the life she knew before, I'd wager she would have preferred to remain where she'd been."

"There is one other thing you can offer her, Dante. One thing she would never have received from Miss Stoutwell or Eliza's husband. You can offer her love."

Dante shook his head. "I should have listened."

"Listened to whom?"

"To everyone who warned me something like this would someday happen. I always thought I was above their well-intentioned hints and not so subtle comments. Those simply didn't apply to me. I was infallible. But I was wrong, and now I've brought an innocent child into the midst of the quagmire, a quagmire of my own making."

Dante stared into the fire, hating himself more than he ever thought possible. He heard Beatrice stand and walk in front of him. He turned his head when she knelt before him. He didn't want to look into her eyes and see pity. He started when he felt her gentle hand lightly touch his cheek.

"I don't know anything about that part of your life,

but I do know something else. You saved my life, and you have saved Phoebe's as well, even if it is in a different way. Surely, that must count for something, for it means everything to me."

Beatrice leaned forward and very softly touched her lips to his. Dante didn't think; he didn't want to. He simply reacted. The need to have her, made overpowering and fierce these past days, raced through his every vein, pounding in his head like a hammer. He pulled her against him and kissed her fully, deeply, his tongue stroking hers, tasting her, reveling in the kiss, taking her until her fingers were clinging to his shoulders and her breath was coming quickly.

"Dante," she whispered.

"Oh, God, Beatrice," he groaned into her mouth. "You make me feel as if I could conquer anything."

She looked at him, her eyes shimmering in the firelight. "You can."

Dante swept his hand beneath her back and lowered her to the carpet in front of the fire. Beatrice moved her hands to his neck, her fingers easing back through his hair. She kissed his cheek, his ear, his forehead as he moved his mouth down to her throat. He could feel her pulse strong against his lips. Her skin tasted so sweet. He lifted his head and looked down at her in the glowing light.

Beatrice blinked. She smiled. She touched the tip of her tongue innocently to her lips. Her breasts were rising and falling, taut against the fabric of her nightrail. Several of the tiny buttons at her neck had loosened, the fabric parting, inviting him to part it further still. He wanted her so badly his ears rang, but even as he realized this, he knew he couldn't take her. It would be heaven, but he just couldn't take her.

"Dear God, what am I doing?" he whispered roughly, dropping his head against her shoulder.

Beatrice stilled. "What is wrong?"

Dante lifted his head. "I cannot do this, Beatrice. It isn't right or proper. I don't even know your true name."

"It doesn't matter."

"Yes, it does. Someday, when you do remember who you are, and when you know who I really am, it will matter, and then you would never be able to forgive me. Much as I want this now, God how I want this, I would never be able to forgive myself for it."

Dante released Beatrice and stood. He looked down at her and saw the disappointment on her face, the inability to comprehend his actions or his words. If he didn't go now, he knew he never would. Despite the fact that his body burned for her like no other, Dante turned quickly and left the room.

Beatrice awoke early that morning just as dawn was breaking over the mist-covered hills. Dante was gone. He'd left a message with Renny, reminding her of his meeting in Castleton, adding that he most probably wouldn't be back until late that afternoon. He did suggest that she might wish to take Phoebe about the house while he was away.

Which was precisely what she did, after they had finished a hearty breakfast of eggs with ham, and rolls with tea—sweetened milk for Phoebe.

Remarkably, Beatrice remembered most of the names for the many rooms they encountered, even the *Peu de Chose.*

"Pu-de-shoze?" Phoebe attempted as they closed the door on the small nondescript room. "What does it mean?"

"A *peu de chose,* Phoebe, is something which is of little significance, scarcely noticeable, something without distinction."

"Like I am?"

Beatrice halted and looked down at her. "Phoebe, why would you think something like that?"

"Because I don't belong anywhere. Miss Stoutwell said I was like too much extra baggage. Something that just couldn't be helped, but that wasn't really wanted either." She smiled a little then. "But, then, Lord Morgan, my father, he told me Miss Stoutwell was a fool and that she was wicked and that I shouldn't believe anything she ever said to me."

Beatrice knelt down before her. "And Lord Morgan is right, Phoebe. You should not believe anything that Miss Stoutwell person told you. She is a fool, and even more than that she is a terrible person to have told you those things. Let me ask you something. Do you think I am a wicked person?"

Phoebe shook her head. "No. You are nice. You don't make me feel like I am stupid."

"Because you are not stupid. You are very, very bright. Your mother was a very smart lady to have taught you so many things at your young age. I know if she could be here with you now, she would tell you these same things I am. Everyone has significance, Phoebe. Even I do, and I don't even know my real name. I told you I had lost my memory when I was hurt, but even with that I know I have a purpose. We all do."

"What is a purpose?"

"A purpose is a reason, a very good reason for something. Like the sun's purpose is to shine and light the day, or the rain's purpose is to cause things to grow. Do you understand?"

"Yes," Phoebe said. "But what would the purpose for me be?"

"It's quite simple really," Beatrice said, taking her hand as she led her down the hall. "I've thought over it a lot lately, Phoebe and I've come to a conclusion. You and I, we share a common purpose. We have both come here separately, but for much the same reason. The two of us, Phoebe, have come here to save your father."

Chapter Twelve

"Morgan, I must confess I was a bit surprised when I received your letter requesting this meeting."

The Earl of Devonshire, a man nearly ten years Dante's senior, who wore a wig of bushy dark curls and a suit of rich burgundy velvet, stood from his chair in the small taproom of the Goosehill Arms Tavern to shake Dante's outstretched hand.

"Thank you for agreeing to see me so quickly, Lord Devonshire."

The earl sat down, motioning to the serving girl for another round of ale. He waited until they'd been served, and watched sternly as the serving girl delivered Dante a flagrant wink and swish of her hips, before going on.

"You realize there is nothing I can do to repair your status at court, Morgan."

Dante couldn't fault the man his impression. In fact, he should have seen that coming. "I have no intention of asking that of you, my lord. That isn't at all my purpose for requesting this meeting."

"So what is your purpose?"

Straight as an arrow toward its target, never straying from its course, but then Devonshire always had been direct. Actually Dante preferred it to social artifice. "As you are aware, my lord, I have been absent from Derbyshire and from England for quite some time."

"Aye." Devonshire took a swallow of his ale. A bit

of it dribbled onto his chin. He wiped it away with a napkin. "How did you find things at Wyldewoode when you returned?"

"Very well, my lord. I am very fortunate, given that I haven't been there myself to see to things."

"How was Versailles?"

Dante smiled. "Much the same as they are at Whitehall, I would imagine, only spoken in a different tongue." He went on. "Reports of the plague reached us at Versailles, but they never really described the enormity of the epidemic. I only realized the true proportions of it when my own mother was struck down with the disease and died a number of months ago."

Devonshire nodded over another swallow of ale. "Helena was one of the last great ladies. Lady Devonshire, as you know, was very fond of her. Your mother will be missed by many."

"Myself most of all, my lord. It weighs heavily on my conscience that I could not be with her when she passed." Dante paused a moment, and when he saw Devonshire wasn't making any effort to respond, he went on. "But that isn't the purpose of my request to meet with you either, though the plague does play a part in it. You see, while traveling to Wyldewoode from Dover, I came to need the services of a physician."

Dante paused. He decided it would be better to avoid his reasons for needing the physician, thereby necessitating that he divulge the presence of a young unwed lady in his house. Any lady known to be alone in the company of the Rakehell Earl would certainly be ruined, regardless of who she might turn out to be or how honorable he'd been. Vagueness was definitely the better course. "My coachman stopped just outside a local village; I should say he was stopped at a barricade blocking passage into this village."

Devonshire nodded. "Eyam. I know their plight well."

"So I was told. It is a noble and selfless thing those good people are doing, maintaining the disease within their bounds, and they are dying in great numbers for it."

"Rector Mompesson is a man well ahead of his time. If only half of the afflicted throughout England had followed the same methods of quarantine, this disease would not have obliterated nearly a third of the population of England by now."

Dante was startled at the number. "Is that the true toll?"

"Aye, and those are only the known cases of plague. Many refused to admit to the disease for fear of retribution. Who can say how many others there truly are?"

"Which is my reason for asking you here, my lord. The men at the barricade at Eyam told me you were seeing to their food stores. I, as well, have had fresh supplies delivered from Wyldewoode, but I feel this isn't enough. The people need to purchase cloth for clothing, tallow for candles, coal for burning. Admittedly, this would be a costly venture."

Devonshire sat up a bit, his interest growing. "What is it you are proposing, Morgan?"

Like Devonshire, Dante came straight to the point. "My father shared an interest with you in the corn mill at Calver."

"Aye." Devonshire leaned forward, listening carefully now.

"I seem to recall your offering to purchase his share a number of years before his death, but he refused."

"Stubborn man, your father."

"That he was, my lord. I, however, am not. I recently did some research into the production at that mill during the past three years of my absence. It is doing quite well, it seems."

"There was the cost of repairs last year, but otherwise . . . "

"Are you still interested in purchasing the Morgan interest in that mill?"

Lord Devonshire looked at Dante. "I was after your father for nearly a decade to sell me his interest in that mill, but he refused every offer I made. It wasn't a matter of the monies, of course. It was more a game to him."

"You are correct in that, my lord." Dante smiled. "I remember once my father's solicitor told me his refusing to sell the mill interest to you was a bit like playing chess, on a board built to grander scale, of course."

Devonshire nodded. "Knowing this as you do, why then would you want to sell your interest in the mill now, Morgan? Are you in need of funds? Behind in debts?"

"On the contrary, my lord. In reviewing the Morgan ledgers, it would appear I am on solid financial footing, rather remarkable given my absence."

"You employ honest people."

" 'Pay them well and they will pay you back in kind,' my father used to say."

"Wise man, your father. A good head for business. Which makes me all the more curious as to why would you wish to remove yourself from a profitable venture such as that at the Calver mill?"

"Let me just say I wish to simplify my assets."

Dante removed a folded piece of foolscap from his coat pocket. He held it out to Lord Devonshire. "I think you will find this a reasonable sum in exchange for the Morgan interest of the mill."

Devonshire took the paper. He glanced at Dante over the top of the page. His eyes gave away nothing. Finally, he said, "I will write to my solicitor in London to see that the funds are transferred to your accounts immediately."

"Which brings me to the one condition on the sale, my lord," Dante broke in. "I should like you to hear it and consider it before any transaction is made final."

"Which is?"

"I do not wish the monies from the sale placed in my personal accounts. Instead, I wish for you to place them in a separate account solely for the use of the people of Eyam. I would that this were an anonymous transaction with no mention of my involvement in it. I will trust that you will oversee the funds and assure they are used accordingly. In all my father's business with you, chess game or not, he always said you were a fair and honest man, my lord, albeit a stubborn one."

Devonshire grinned, downing the remainder of his ale. He stood and shook Dante's hand. "I don't know quite how to say this without stepping outside the proper bounds, but I'm proud of you, Morgan, and your father would be too, after he throttled you for selling that interest to me, of course."

Dante smiled, nodding. "Thank you, my lord."

Devonshire flipped a crown to the serving girl for the ale. He started to leave, then turned back. "If you don't mind my asking, Morgan, why the request for anonymity?"

Dante looked at him. "I know you must be thinking it would be a prime opportunity to remove some of that dark blot I've left on the Morgan name, as indeed it would be, which is precisely why I wish the transaction to remain private. I wish no ulterior motive attached to this. It would only belie its true intent. This is simply something I feel compelled to do. Perhaps it is due to my mother's passing. I cannot say. And besides," he added, grinning, "it wouldn't do to have the Rakehell Earl of Morgan known as a philanthropic soul."

Taking this, Devonshire turned, shaking his head as he went.

Dante remained in the taproom through another slow tankard of ale. He was pleased with the outcome of his meeting. He knew he could trust Lord Devonshire to comply with his wishes, and he also wouldn't allow a single pence of the monies to go anywhere but where they were intended to go—to Eyam.

Dante stood to leave, declining another open invitation from the serving maid. As he stepped outside, he took in a deep breath, wanting nothing more than to get back to Wyldewoode, and Beatrice, as soon as Fury would take him. He didn't know why, perhaps it was the cleansing of his conscience that he felt at having helped the people of Eyam, or Devonshire's reluctant nod of approval. Whatever it was, it had made him feel as if he'd finally embarked upon a new road, a road to a new life. And whenever he pictured this new life, it included Beatrice.

The ride to Castleton early that morning had been quiet and filled with reflection. Dante had thought of Beatrice, of her total acceptance of him and her acceptance of Phoebe, despite the circumstances of her birth. He realized he could not allow Beatrice to leave his life. He didn't really care that he didn't know her name. Finding her had been the start of something wonderful for him, the beginning of his new life. A life he wanted to share with her.

Dante paused before untethering Fury when he spotted a small jeweler's stall in the market square.

"Good day, milord," the proprietress said as he approached. "What can I do for ye?"

Dante browsed through the trinkets she had on display. "I'm looking for something, a gift, but I want it to be something special."

"For a lady, milord?" she asked, grinning.

"You could say that." Finally, his eyes caught

something, a sparkle of yellow and blue and violet. He lifted up the gold chain attached to it, watching the sunlight play across the rounded stone.

"Aye," the woman said, "I see you've a liking for the Blue John stone."

"I know a lady who expressed a certain fondness for it."

"Well, that be a special stone, it is. Blessed by an ancient wise woman to guarantee happiness and true love to the one what wears it."

Dante removed a guinea from his pocket and handed it to the woman. "Will that do?"

"Amply so, my lord," the woman said, eyes wide. "Amply so, indeed."

Back at Wyldewoode Dante took the stairs two at a time to the front door. He didn't notice the coach that was pulled just to the side of the main house. The traveling valise set at the foot of the stairs failed to catch his attention as well.

"Renny, my good man," he said as he encountered the steward in the entrance hall, "where can I find Beatrice?"

"I believe she is in the east parlor, my lord. But—"

Dante strode past him. At the parlor he grabbed the door handles and pushed the double doors open.

"Beatrice, I—"

His words died on his lips. Beatrice wasn't alone in the parlor. A striking brunette sat across from her. She turned around to look at him from her place on the settee. She smiled brilliantly when she saw him there.

"We've been waiting ages for you, Dante, dear. What on earth took you so long to return?"

Cassia Brodrigan, the Marchioness Seagrave, stood from her chair, her dark eyes sparking with amusement. She wore a smart-looking dark blue traveling habit, layers of white lace at her throat. Rich chestnut hair tumbled in twisted ringlets about her face, a face that still managed, despite the three years that had passed, to cause Dante to stare in mute admiration. The reaction was much the same for any man who beheld her—to the continued annoyance of her husband, Rolfe.

Rolfe and Dante had been friends since Oxford, along with their third "partner," Hadrian Ross, a marquess who now resided in Ireland with his wife, Mara, and their children. The three of them had fought in the wars during which, at one time or another, each had saved one of the others' lives. Cassia had come into Rolfe's life not long before Dante's departure for France. She was everything his friend had needed. And for Cassia, Rolfe had been much the same.

Cassia chuckled. "Well, are you going to stand there gaping like some sort of dumbstruck ninny, or are you going to come over here and deliver me a proper welcome?"

Dante found his head, crossed the room and hugged Cassia to him. "Cassia, when did you arrive? And where is Rolfe?" He looked about the room. "I expected you'd send word first before traveling all the way here from Sussex."

"Well, I wasn't even certain you had gotten back yet," Cassia said, kissing him lightly on the cheek. "I was up in Lancashire, seeing to the sale of the estate there and decided to stop at Wyldewoode on my way back to the city to see if you'd come home yet." She glanced over her shoulder, nodding in Beatrice's direction. "And I see now that you have."

"You didn't receive my letter then?"

"Letter?"

"The one I wrote to you when I first returned to England. Actually, it's most likely just now arriving at Ravenwood. I suppose Rolfe will be there to receive it.

It's good you came here, Cassia. I am in need of your help on a matter . . . " He paused, looking over Cassia's shoulder to where Beatrice still sat, watching and listening to their every word. "You've met Beatrice?"

"Yes, I have indeed met her. This lovely girl was just beginning to tell me how you two came to meet. Something about how you found her lying abandoned on the road in the rain in the middle of the night?"

"It is a long story." Dante took Cassia's hand and led her back to the middle of the room. He sat across from her. "When I found her, Beatrice had suffered an injury to her head."

"The bandage on her head did give that bit of news away," Cassia said, smiling.

Dante looked at Beatrice, then back to Cassia. "As a result, she has no memory of who she is."

"Only that she is called Beatrice?" Cassia knit her brow. "How odd."

"No," Dante said, "she doesn't remember what her real name is. Beatrice is simply a name we decided to call her."

"Surely, you could have come up with something better than that, Dante," Cassia said, rolling her eyes. "She's far too lovely for such an ugly appellation. I would think Juliet or Victoria much more appropriate than Beatrice. I mean you may as well have named her Barbara after that Castlemaine creature at Whitehall who does nothing but spread ill will."

Cassia was just one of the many who held King Charles's longest-standing paramour, Barbara Palmer, Lady Castlemaine, in disaffection. And for good reason.

"Actually it is the cat's name," Beatrice interjected.

"Barbara is your cat's name?" Cassia asked. "Good God, Dante, have you forgotten it was that same woman who was responsible for sending you to France?"

"No, Cassia, I have not forgotten. And I wouldn't name my chamber pot for her. *Beatrice* is my cat's name. My mother named her that because of the way she always followed after me like a lovesick girl when I was a boy."

"Ah, yes, Beatrice, the true love of your poet name-sake. So, in turn, you decided you should give this poor girl your cat's name?" Cassia looked at Dante, clearly appalled. "Dante, what were you thinking?"

"It just came about that way. She goes by Beatrice, at least until we can find out what her true name is. If we find out what it is. We haven't had any luck thus far. This really is a puzzle that looks to have been crafted by Gordius."

Cassia's eyes lit with excitement. "Oh, I do love a mystery. Have you any clues yet?"

"Not really," said Beatrice.

"Other than that we have discovered she loves to read and she is proficient at several instruments, the most interesting of which is the viola da gamba."

Cassia turned to Beatrice. "How ever do you manage that, my dear? 'Tis a rather large instrument for a lady to play, especially for one of your delicate size."

"It's only a matter of positioning it correctly. If you're interested, I'd be happy to show you."

"It sounds intriguing."

Dante broke in. "Perhaps another time."

The two ladies looked at him.

"The only other thing we know," he went on, "is that Beatrice was left lying injured in the road in the middle of the night, wearing nothing but her nightrail."

"I see," Cassia said. "An admittedly peculiar clue." She thought for a moment, then turned again to Beatrice. "Do you still have the nightrail, dear?"

"I believe so. I think it is somewhere in my chamber."

Cassia smiled. "Good. Why don't you bring it to me so I can have a look at it? In fact," she added, "why don't you go and get it right now, Beatrice dear?"

Chapter Thirteen

Beatrice left Dante and Cassia to fetch the nightrail. When she had gone, Cassia leaned closer to Dante, watching him keenly.

"What the devil is going on here, Dante? I dare say never in my maddest dreams would I have expected to arrive here to find you living virtually alone with a lovely young girl who has no idea who she is. You've only been back in England a short while. Are you trying to make up for time past?"

"That is not the case at all, Cassia. I have left that part of my life in France. This situation with Beatrice is just as I told you. I found her lying in the road. Actually, my coachman found her first. He very nearly ran her over. When I went back with him to check, I found she was injured. She was nearly dead. In any case, she clearly didn't belong there. What was I to do? Leave her to die?"

"Certainly not. She is obviously not some wayward waif out to cheat a rich and gullible gent. She speaks too well and is far too charming for that. But, charming or not, surely you realize you must return her to wherever it is she belongs. Have you sent out dispatches to see if anyone fitting her description has come up missing?"

"I set Renny on it. There has been no report."

"And that is all?"

"And I wrote to you, knowing with your court

affiliations you would be the most likely person to help discover her true identity. However, you weren't at Ravenwood, because you were off riding about the north country. You are right in saying that Beatrice is not a waif. She is of the quality. One need only to look at her and listen to her speak to know that. She is in relatively good health, so she must have had some means to keep her, yet no one has come looking for her, in and of itself an odd thing, wouldn't you think? I am left, therefore, to assume no one knows or cares she is missing."

"Are you saying you think she might have run away?"

"It is a possibility I have considered. And, if that is the case, would I want to return her somewhere she isn't wanted or doesn't wish to be? That is why I have not pursued more public avenues in searching for her identity. By the by, Cassia, what made you think I had returned to Wyldewoode? In fact, how did you know I would be returning to England at all?"

Cassia grinned. She had, of course, known he would eventually figure that out. "I was aware His Majesty had granted you permission to return home. After learning of your mother's passing, and of Renny's success in removing her to Derbyshire, I also knew Wyldewoode would be the first place you would come upon returning. Allowing adequate time to travel, I figured if you weren't here already, you would be soon, so I decided to take a roundabout route and see for myself."

"But how did you know when His Majesty sent off his response to me in France?"

Her smile widened. "Because I stood right there beside him while he wrote it and sealed it. I even handed it to the courier who was to take it to you."

Dante looked at her, the picture coming clear. "It

was because of you the king allowed my return to England."

"Let us simply say I was able to persuade His Majesty to give the matter his full and immediate consideration."

"How, madam, did you manage that? No, don't tell me. I'm don't think I want to know, especially if it is something that might compromise your name as a happy and devotedly wed lady."

"Of course not, Dante. My days as gossip-fodder at Whitehall are long since passed. Rolfe, actually, was the one who suggested I speak with His Majesty on your behalf."

"Your powers of persuasion are to be commended then, Cassia."

She smiled. "It really was quite simple. It took very little effort, actually. I wagered His Majesty over a game of chess. You know we have long been at opposite ends of the board. He says I'm the only opponent who doesn't purposely allow him to win for fear of falling out of favor. The terms on this particular wager were that if I won, he was to allow you back to England immediately."

"And if he emerged the victor?"

"Let us just say it was never a question of whether you would be allowed back, but how soon." She frowned. "As well as seeing to His Majesty's own personal little amusement."

"Which was?"

"If I lost, I was to compliment Lady Castlemaine on her stylish gown, in front of the court." She smiled, shaking her head. "His Majesty really is quite incorrigible."

Dante grinned. "I am relieved you won. I know how difficult it would have been for you, having to publicly give your approval to anything concerning Lady

Castlemaine. And I would hate to think how many more months I would have passed at Versailles."

"So am I." Cassia squeezed his hand. "On both accounts." Her voice dropped to a whisper. "I have a confession to make to you. I have missed you terribly."

"The feeling is mutual, madam. How is Rolfe faring these days?"

Cassia laughed out loud. "Obstinate as the day he was born. Even worse since my condition was confirmed. I swear sometimes he's worse than a mother hen with one chick."

"Excuse me, madam? Your condition?"

"Oh, dear, yes, Dante, we are expecting the next generation Brodrigan early in the new year."

Dante laughed out loud. "That is good news, Cassia. Rolfe must be fair splitting with pride."

"Splitting with worry is more the fitting description. He was thoroughly put out with me when I told him I was going off to Lancashire. Refused to allow it at first, but I was persistent."

"You mean stubborn."

She punched him on his arm. "Enough from you. To be bluntly honest, Dante, I had to get away from him, just for a little while, else I'd have bolted myself into the pantry till Christmastide. He was hounding me day and night: 'Sit down, Cassia. Get your rest, Cassia.' He started quoting Mara Ross as if she spouted the gospel. Do you believe she sent him a letter with a list of instructions. Instructions! Remind me I must pull that red hair of hers for that when next I see her. You see, as I figure it, when Rolfe sees I've survived a fortnight of traveling through the countryside alone, he'll have to give up this nonsensical worriment. Women have been birthing babies for centuries, you know."

"I am vaguely aware of that fact. I am curious, though, as to how you managed to convince Rolfe to give in and consent for you to go Lancashire by yourself at all. I don't think I've ever met anyone who could change his mind when he's set on something. Especially when it comes to you."

Cassia's voice softened. "I didn't actually convince him."

"Cassia . . . "

"It was late the night I left Ravenwood. I didn't wish to wake him. He had been working so hard, and he was exhausted, snoring his head off in our bedchamber loud enough to wake a corpse. Believe me when I say a coach ride was much more appealing at that moment than the idea of bedding down with him. I left him a note detailing my planned route, and I took Quigman, my groom, with me for protection. I've sent Rolfe a post each day to inform him of our progress and to assure him I haven't been waylaid or anything like that."

Dante shook his head. "I'm surprised he didn't give chase the minute he found you gone. Rolfe must be growing soft in his old age. He'd never have allowed something like that to pass in our younger days. One time, during the wars, he followed an enemy courier for six straight days through freezing rain in the Scottish Highlands just so he could see who the letter the poor fool was carrying went to. It mattered naught to him that it ended up being for nothing. It was a letter some Roundhead captain had sent to his wife, but Rolfe wasn't willing to take any chances. He treated that mission as if the courier carried covert instructions written by Cromwell himself."

"Yes, but this is different. And I am safe."

"Still, I don't envy you your arrival home, Cassia. Rolfe will most probably be waiting for you at the door with leg shackles in hand."

"Rolfe wouldn't do that."

Dante raised a disagreeing brow.

Cassia shrugged. "Well, I'll just face that possibility when the time comes. Besides, I'm to meet him in

London after leaving here, at least that is where I told him I would be going next, to see our solicitor, Mr. Finchley, in order to make final the Lancashire property transfer. Now enough of me and the possible punishments that await me from my husband. Let us get back to the subject at hand. What precisely is going on with you and Beatrice, Dante? Somehow I am wont to believe there is more here than first meets the eye."

"I have been completely aboveboard, Cassia. My intentions are honorable."

"Of course they are, dear. Beatrice isn't married."

Dante frowned.

"What is it? She is married then, isn't she? Oh, dear, that could put a bit of a twist on things, couldn't it? She would be fair game then, and well, quite frankly, she wouldn't stand a chance."

"Beatrice is not married, Cassia, not that I am aware of." And then he added, "At least she isn't wed yet."

Cassia stared at him. "Don't tell me you are thinking of wedding the girl?"

Dante stood and made for the sideboard to pour himself a much needed glass of port. "Believe me when I say, Cassia, my intentions upon returning to England were to spend the rest of my days counting my blessings that I was home again and all in one piece. I've had my fill of assignations. More than my fill. I was going to grow old replete in my bachelorhood, but things have taken a turn and"—he paused to hand Cassia a glass of port—"the thought to take a wife had recently occurred to me."

Cassia took a small sip. "You do realize, Dante, you cannot possibly wed someone whose name you do not even know."

"Marriages are performed under assumed names quite frequently in this part of England."

Cassia stared at him. "Tell me something, is it that

you have honestly tried and cannot find out who Beatrice is, or is it that you do not truly wish to know?"

"A wife who has no memory could know nothing of the past. More specifically, my past."

"Do you hear yourself speaking? Do you think she will never find out the truth? What if her memory returns and you learn that she knows very well who the Rakehell Earl of Morgan is? If she has been in London for any extended amount of time, chances are she has at least heard of you. Absence, my dear, tends to make legends out of the most trifling of scandals, and even if Beatrice doesn't know who you are, do you really believe she will never discover you've been with other women? A number of them?"

"She already has."

Cassia looked at him.

"Eliza Havelock. There is a child involved." He paused. "I have a daughter, Cassia."

Cassia's mouth fell open.

"Good God, Dante."

"Eliza was taken by the plague," Dante explained. "Phoebe has been sent here to live with me now."

"Is this what has spurred on your recent thoughts of marriage? To obtain a convenient mother for this child?"

"I did not know of Phoebe's existence before yesterday when I arrived home to find her waiting for me in this very room. It seems Eliza left behind a letter in her effects, naming me as her daughter's true father. When Overton discovered this, he immediately sent the child here. He has effectively washed his hands of her. He wants nothing further to do with her. I had already considered the idea of wedding Beatrice, but I wouldn't be truthful if I told you Phoebe's arrival in my life hadn't all but decided me."

Cassia shook her head. "Poor thing—the child I mean. Phoebe you say? Lovely name. She must be frightened half to death. And Beatrice must be confused at the very least. What does she have to say?"

"Remarkably, she said Overton was despicable for abandoning her and that Phoebe was better off without him. She painted me as some sort of hero for caring about Eliza when Overton had treated her so poorly. It never occurred to her that in doing so, I was also committing adultery."

"Don't you see that is precisely why you must find out who Beatrice truly is? Even if she doesn't care about the past, what if you wed this girl, involve the child, and months from now another husband shows up at your doorstep? That might be a bit awkward to explain. And Phoebe would end up losing another mother. It isn't fair to the child, Dante. And it isn't fair to Beatrice."

"What if we never find out who Beatrice really is? What should I do then? Leave her at the nearest village and forget I ever found her? I can't do that, Cassia. I won't."

Cassia looked at Dante. They'd grown close, and despite that he'd been away for much of their acquaintanceship, they had corresponded frequently. Cassia and Rolfe had visited Dante a number of times in France during his exile. Cassia had come to know Dante well, and she loved him even with his shortcomings. Not in any of his previous affiliations with women had she ever heard him speak so passionately. In fact, if a relationship had ever threatened to turn to more than a passing fancy, he deserted it. Immediately. Entanglement was something Dante furiously avoided. And the knowledge that this girl had spun her own web about him delighted Cassia to no end. She smiled softly. "She must be rather extraordinary."

"Who is extraordinary?" Beatrice asked, coming into the room.

Dante and Cassia both turned to look at her, smiling and silent.

"I am sorry it took me so long. I had trouble finding the nightrail." She held it out. "You'll have to excuse its condition, Lady Seagrave. It has seen better days."

Cassia took the garment and looked at it closely. Though torn, the lace on the collar was fine Valenciennes, the fabric a light and soft lawn. One sleeve had been rent at the shoulder seam, and the fabric was stained with dirt from the road and spots of blood from Beatrice's injury. Cassia turned the garment inside out and peered closely at the stitching along the hem, then examined the full sleeve. Finally, she set the garment on the table in front of them all.

"Madame Olga."

Dante and Beatrice looked at her.

Cassia picked the nightrail up again. "This was made at Madame Olga's shop on St. James's."

"How do you know this?" Beatrice asked.

"Do you see this small fleur-de-lis stitched into the sleeve? This is her cachet. She marks all of her garments with it. See." Cassia pulled back the cuff on her gown to reveal a like design. "I frequent Madame Olga's as well when I am in town. It would seem you come from a background of some means, Beatrice, for Madame Olga's clients pay dearly for the distinction of her handiwork. This should be quite simple, really, solving the question of your identity. All we need do is take this nightrail to Madame Olga and ask her who purchased it. She should recognize it. I'll send Quigman, my groom, on ahead with a letter to Rolfe, informing him of our arrival in the city. First light tomorrow, we shall set off for London. By week's end, Beatrice, I have every confidence we will have found out who you are."

* * *

After an evening of furious packing and preparing, they left Wyldewoode early the following day, bound for London—and the truth.

Two coaches, one carrying their baggage, and the other carrying Cassia, Phoebe, Dante, and Beatrice, rolled down the gravel drive leading away from Wyldewoode toward the North and South Road to London.

Yet, instead of feeling excited at their journey, for deep down she knew she was returning from where she'd come, Beatrice found herself filled with fearful hesitation. This troubled her. Why wouldn't the prospect of finding out who she really was fill her with anticipation?

"I went to London once," Phoebe said, sliding closer beside her on the coach seat. "Momma took me with her to see the 'Nice Lady,' and we had cheesecake tarts with sugared berries on top." Phoebe's face darkened then. "Mama died after we went back home to Dorset. Miss Stoutwell said she tried to tell Momma she should never have gone to the city. Miss Stoutwell told me that the only reason she died was because she took me there and that I could have died, too. She said Momma was selfish for taking me there. I liked the 'Nice Lady.' "

"Perhaps we can see the 'Nice Lady' again," Beatrice said. "Do you know her name?"

Phoebe shook her head. "But she lived in a pretty house with lots of flowers all around."

"There are flowers at my house in London, too," Cassia broke in, "and our cook makes wonderful cheesecake tarts. There is a place called the Tower where there are wild animals like lions and bears. Perhaps we can go there."

As Cassia told Phoebe more about the things to see in London, Beatrice watched out the back coach window as Wyldewoode's weathered gray and white facade grew tinier and tinier still, windows winking in the sunlight like shimmering diamonds. She watched until they had rounded a bend in the drive and the house disappeared behind the thick trees, trying not to acknowledge the niggling and intruding doubt that she would most likely never return.

Wyldewoode was the most beautiful place she'd ever remembered seeing. She guessed that wasn't saying much, since she had no memory of anywhere else, but still, she loved everything about it—the colorful hedges that lined the semicircle drive, the numerous rooms each with their own name, the servants who had come to treat her as if she had belonged there, its intriguing history, and the untamed, untouched beauty of the countryside. What she loved most about Wyldewoode was how it made her feel. Safe, secure, at home.

Beatrice touched the Blue John pendant on the necklace Dante had given her that morning. He had told her to always wear it so that wherever this journey to London eventually took her, she would have a small piece of Wyldewoode with her. She needed that, for leaving now was like standing on the edge of a tall cliff, ready to leap, yet not certain how far the drop was below it. Wyldewoode was all she really knew in life, all, except for the man sitting across from her on the coach seat, the same man she saw standing beside her on that cliff, taking the leap with her.

Chapter Fourteen

London

The plague was gone.

The city was alive again, its long imposed moratorium at last at an end. The streets were filled with people, scores of them walking about in the early morning sun, exchanging friendly greetings, pausing to chat about the events of the past fifteen months. Beyond that, they were grateful just to be alive.

Costermongers pushed simple carts, crying out above the city noise. Children scampered about, giggling delightedly at a scurrying chicken. The aroma of bread baking in hot ovens along Baker's Alley filled the air. Freshly washed laundry hung from taut lines strung up between the houses, timber-framed houses whose projecting upper stories nearly touched each other across the streets. One could almost hope to believe that a deadly plague hadn't swept a dark unforgiving hand through the city streets, were it not for the reminders in the slowly fading red crosses painted on so many doors, and the vast numbers of new graves in every churchyard.

As the carriage rolled slowly down the narrow crowded street, Beatrice took in everything she saw, every shop sign, every dwelling, searching for something that might trigger her memory. Faces she'd never seen turned toward her in greeting as they slowed to wait for the road to clear ahead. Even London Bridge, with its houses upon houses strung across the Thames, was unknown to her. Dante pointed out a place called Whitehall to her, a palace that didn't really look like a palace, where King Charles and all his courtiers lived.

"Don't become discouraged if you don't recognize anything immediately," Dante said, reading her thoughts. "The city is new to me as well. I've been away the past three years. I'm not at all certain I can remember my way about."

Beatrice smiled at him, knowing he was trying to ease her anxiety, and turned to look out the window once again.

Soon after they stopped in front of a large timber-framed house with an impressive four-level facade that sat on a quiet, shaded street in a place called Piccadilly.

"Here we are," Cassia said, pushing the coach door open before the coachman could climb down off his seat. "Home at long last."

Collectively they had decided they should stay at Seagrave House, Cassia and Rolfe's city residence, since Dante's town house, Morgan House, had been shut up after Helena's death. Servants would have to be rehired, cleaning and provisions would have to be seen to, and Dante wasn't willing to leave Beatrice now to see to its reopening. That had pleased Beatrice.

"Well, I must be dreaming," came a deep male voice from outside the coach. "This surely cannot be my wayward wife returning from her cross-country crusade."

Beatrice peeked outside the coach window. A tall man with dark hair and a look in his eye that at once told he wasn't really angry, but sincerely relieved to see his wife, had appeared at the front doorway. Quite obviously this was Cassia's husband, Rolfe, Marquess of Seagrave.

Cassia raced forward to greet him. "Hello, my love.

I've missed you terribly." She snaked her hands around his neck, pulling his head down to hers for a kiss.

"I hope you're not thinking that kiss will save you from my anger, madam." His expression turned grave. "I was most displeased when I learned you'd gone, Cassia. I would that I had been given the choice of whether to accompany you on your Lancashire journey."

Cassia stepped back and spun around in a circle, her full skirts swirling about her feet. "As you can see, dear husband, I am none the worse for having made the journey without you, and it is all the better that I had, for I acquired a few companions in Derbyshire for the trip to the city. There really would have been no room for you in the coach."

Rolfe looked over to the coach. Beatrice stepped down, smiling slightly. He didn't recognize her, of course, but he returned the smile nonetheless. Dante emerged behind her, and Rolfe's friendly smile broke into a wide grin.

"Good God, the fires of perdition must finally be extinguished. The prodigal has come home at last."

Rolfe clasped Dante to him, then stepped back to shake his hand, thumping him hard on the back.

"I wouldn't slay the fatted calf just yet, my friend," Dante said, grinning. "It is good to see you, Rolfe. It has been a long time."

"Too long, at least a year or more since Cassia and I last traveled to France."

"More," Dante confirmed.

"I was sorry to hear of Helena's passing, Dante. The plague was unmerciful in its wrath. Had we known, we would have tried to get you home sooner."

Dante nodded. "Thank you, Rolfe. And thank you for your efforts in seeing me returned. I guess we should count ourselves fortunate we didn't lose any others to the epidemic."

"Aye." Rolfe then noticed Phoebe peeking around the coach door. "And who have we here?"

Phoebe vanished.

Dante reached a hand inside the coach. "It is all right, Phoebe. Lord Seagrave is my friend and a very nice man."

Phoebe emerged slowly from the coach, holding Dante's hand tightly. She came down and stood in front of Beatrice, pressing herself back against her skirts.

Cassia motioned for Beatrice to come forward. Phoebe stayed close to her skirts.

"Rolfe, I would like you to meet a friend of ours. You may call her Beatrice."

"It is a pleasure to make your acquaintance, Beatrice. The child, she is yours?"

"Heavens no. She is Dante's daughter."

Rolfe looked at Dante. "Is that so?"

"It's a long story."

"And one better told indoors, I would guess. Let us take this conversation inside where you can all rest your travel-weary bones."

Rolfe took Cassia's hand and started for the house.

"He seems very nice," Beatrice said when Dante offered her his arm. She took Phoebe's hand with the other.

"He is one of only two people whom I have always held closer to me brothers. The other one is my friend Hadrian Ross, the Marquess of Kulhaven."

"Ah, yes, Hadrian," Rolfe said, having heard Dante's last comment. "Our dear friend and his lovely redhaired wife should be arriving in the city within the next few days. Their post came to Ravenwood just after you'd gone, Cassia."

"Isn't that delightful?" Cassia said. "Now we'll all be together. I guess my going to Lancashire was a good thing after all."

"That, my dear, has yet to be decided," answered Rolfe.

Once inside, their cloaks seen to, tea simmering in the pot, Dante spent the next hour apprising Rolfe of the events of the past two weeks, with Cassia's assistance, of course.

"So you've come to London, hoping to discover your true identity?" Rolfe said to Beatrice.

"Yes. Cassia thought I might have originally come from the city. We're hoping if I have family, they are living here."

"And what brought you to that conclusion, madam?" Rolfe asked his wife.

"It's quite simple, really. The nightrail Beatrice was wearing when Dante discovered her in the roadway that night bears the mark of Madame Olga."

"Ah, yes, your wonderful dressmaker. And since you are one of her most prolific clients, you surely recognized this immediately."

Cassia grinned. "Of course."

"It is odd, though," Rolfe said, "I have been in the city for nearly a week now and have not heard any report of a missing person. I assume you come from a family of some means, Beatrice, judging from your mannerisms and the fact that you wore a garment styled by someone as exclusive as Madame Olga."

"And given the few odd recollections Beatrice has had," Dante added, "we cannot rule out the possibility that someone may have attempted to bring her to harm intentionally. Especially now that we learn there has been no hue and cry for her return."

The foursome fell silent as each contemplated this turn of events.

"I've got it!" Cassia suddenly said. "Cordelia!"

Rolfe groaned. "Oh, are we in for trouble."

"Excuse me?" Beatrice asked. "Who is Cordelia?"

"Cordelia is my friend. She lives here in the city at

Whitehall. She would know at once if there was a report made of your disappearance at court. I thought first to visit His Majesty and ask him directly, but then that might arouse curiosities we do not necessarily wish aroused. I had also intended to bring you with me to Madame Olga's, to ask her about your nightrail, but now, I think that wouldn't be a wise course either."

"Why not?"

"Because," Rolfe finished for his wife, "if someone wished to harm you, we certainly wouldn't want to alert them to your return to the city."

"I agree. We must proceed with caution," Dante added.

"Precisely." Cassia stood and walked to a small writing desk set in the corner of the room. "I will send a message to Cordelia at the palace immediately, asking her to come here this afternoon for an early dinner. If we're lucky, she might even recognize you, Beatrice, which would make the matter of discovering your identity vastly simpler."

Every head turned when Beatrice entered the dining parlor later that evening.

"So this is the girl," said a smartly dressed brunette, wearing a gown of ice blue satin. Every accessory, in fact, including the nosegay of flowers worn at her left shoulder, was made of the same color.

"Come closer," she said, smiling at Beatrice and holding out her hands to her. "You must be terribly confused, my dear."

"That is putting it mildly."

The woman smiled. "I am Cordelia Fanshaw. This is my husband, Percival, the Earl of Haslit. Please call me Cordelia." Cordelia peered closely at her. "You know you do look a bit familiar to me, but I cannot place from where." She narrowed her eyes a moment longer, then shook her head. "No, I am sorry, but I do not recognize you. Percy and I had left London for a spell before the plague outbreak when we were called away to the country."

She glanced at her husband who had removed himself to the other side of the room with Rolfe. Cordelia lowered her voice to a whisper. "Percy's mother was having another of her many 'dying spells.' Every three or four months, if she doesn't see my husband, she invents new and improved illnesses to bring him to visit her. It's really most annoying. When Percy learned from a post that the plague was in the city, we decided to extend our visit in the country. We missed a full season before the plague, and have been gone another fifteen months since, so there is a good chance I have never met you, dear. I'm sorry."

Percival, a huge man with an inappropriate name, Beatrice thought, had come back. "We were with my mother in Dorset for nearly nineteen months."

"Nineteen months and eleven days, Percy dear," Cordelia corrected, smiling. She winked at Beatrice, conveying her relief at having her lengthy visit with her mother-in-law at an end. "But, I have been back at court for nearly two months now, and I haven't heard anything about anyone having come up missing. You say she's been with you nearly a fortnight, Dante? Do you know your age, my dear?"

"No."

"Well, you appear to be young. Perhaps you'd not come out at court as yet."

"That is possible," Cassia said, "but she had come to the city on at least one occasion, for she did acquire a nightrail made by Madame Olga."

"Have you asked Madame Olga?" Cordelia inquired.

"No," Dante broke in. "There exists the possibility that someone intended to bring Beatrice to harm. We must be careful not to let out that she is safe."

"I see." Cordelia thought a moment. "I just had a thought."

"Oh, no," Rolfe said. "Here comes trouble."

Cordelia slanted him a glance. "Rolfe, you are going to give this darling girl the impression that you don't like me."

"My lady, I worship you, all the way to your fashionably matching shoes."

"Cassia, how do you countenance this man?"

Cassia grinned. "It is exceedingly difficult."

Cordelia shook her head. "This is what I propose. Cassia, you and I will go to see Madame Olga. We will show her the nightrail and ask if she knows for whom she made it. We can tell her it belonged to a young girl who came to the fête you had when you reopened Ravenwood."

"We had over two hundred guests there."

"Precisely. We will tell Madame Olga we do not know the name of this young girl, but we will describe Beatrice to her."

Cassia's eyes lit up. "Yes, that way we will not reveal anything we do not want Madame Olga to know, and we will avoid any speculation. You are a genius, Cordelia."

Cordelia grinned and squeezed Beatrice's hand. "Leave it to us, my dear."

The tiny silver bell that hung above the door in the quaint but stylish shop tinkled softly as Cassia and Cordelia walked through.

A small woman, her burnished red hair pulled into a fashionable topknot fringed with curled ribbons, poked her head around the doorway of the back room.

"La! My ladies, it is so good to see you!"

Madame Olga had come to London from France shortly after the Restoration of Charles II to the throne. She had opened a small shop in a less fashionable section of town and had made a modest living. Her notoriety had come with the assistance of Cassia, who, after hiring Madame Olga on a whim and having been delighted with her work, convinced the queen, Catherine of Braganza to employ the dressmaker's services as well. It wasn't long before every fashionable lady at court was vying for one of Madame Olga's original designs, nor was it long before Madame Olga had moved her shop to the more prestigious St. James's Street.

Ever mindful of the circumstances of her success, Madame Olga never required an appointment from Cassia or any of her close friends.

"Good day to you, Madame Olga," Cassia said. "How are you?"

She raised her eyes heavenward. "We are so busy, what with everyone returning to the city all at once. Fifteen months of gowns, and they all want them yesterday. I have my girls working day and night to complete the work, but for you, I will see that your order is first in line."

Cassia smiled. "That will not be necessary today, Madame, although I will be requiring some gowns with a little more allowance in the front very soon."

"La! You are with child!" Madame embraced Cassia, kissing her cheek.

"Yes, but that is not the purpose for our visit." She held the nightrail out to Madame Olga. "I am trying to locate the owner of this garment, Madame. The lady in question was at the opening of Ravenwood a while ago, and she left it behind. It bears your mark, so I was hoping you might recognize it."

Madame Olga took the nightrail and held it up so it hung full-length. "Good heavens, what happened to this? It is ruined."

Cassia hesitated. She should have known Madame would question the garment's condition. She struggled for a reasonable explanation.

Cordelia stepped forward, sparing her.

"Confidentially, Madame, Lady Seagrave is of the belief that the nightrail was actually stolen from its proper owner. She found a maid with it, you see. Actually, she found it on the maid, who was just returning from a midnight tryst with one of the grooms. You know how these things are. Lady Seagrave feels terribly that someone in her employ has behaved thusly, and she wishes to recompense the true owner of the garment."

Cassia stared at Cordelia, amazed. Had she not known the truth, she would have believed the concocted tale without question.

"I hope you dismissed that ill-behaved maid," Madame said, reexamining the nightrail. "Whoever the lady was who owned this, she would have been slight, like me, but much thinner." She scrutinized the stitching. "These stitches were made by Natalia. I know the work of all my girls. Let me go and get her for you. Perhaps she will remember."

Madame left them, only to reappear moments later. A petite young blond girl stood beside her. "Natalia, this is one of yours?" Madame asked.

Natalia looked at the nightrail and nodded. "Yes."

"Can you tell us who it was made for?"

The girl examined the garment carefully, then rattled back her response to Madame in quick Russian. Cassia and Cordelia waited while Madame listened to the girl, thanked Natalia, and sent her off. She turned to them then, smiling broadly.

"Yes, yes, now I remember her. She is a charming girl, very smart that one. Lovely hair and eyes. Oddly enough, she plays the viola da gamba. I know this because I must make her gowns more full in the skirts to allow her better access to the instrument. I should have known it was hers at once." She shook her head. "I must be getting old. It is just so difficult to remember everyone I see."

"Madame," Cassia said, pulling her back to their purpose for coming there, "are you able to tell us the lady's name?"

"What? Oh, yes. Of course, my lady. She is Lady Gillian Forrester, the Marquess of Adamley's youngest child and only daughter."

Chapter Fifteen

"She is Gillian Forrester," Cassia said, closing her eyes against the reaction she knew would follow.

"Oh, good God!" exclaimed Rolfe.

Dante didn't say a word, not at first. He felt a fierce chill wash over him when Cassia had spoken the familiar name. He looked at Cassia, fearing her answer to the question he was about to pose. He had good reason to. "Is she any relation?"

"Oh, yes," Cordelia said, plopping into the seat beside her husband. Percy leaned his bulk over and kissed her affectionately on the cheek.

"It wouldn't, by any chance, be a distant relation?" Dante asked. "A cousin? Thrice removed?"

Cassia smiled ruefully at the bleak hope in his voice. "It was a good try, Dante, but I am afraid not. It seems our Beatrice is in fact the youngest child, and only daughter, of the Marquess of Adamley. She is also the sister of Reginald, Archebald, and Marcellus Forrester, all with whom, we know, you are well acquainted, Dante."

Dante dropped his head into his hands and groaned aloud at his unbelievable misfortune. Was this a joke? It had to be. Reality was never this punitive. "I never knew they had a sister."

"Given the circumstances of your association with the Forresters, they most probably preferred you didn't know of the existence of this particular twig of the family tree. Actually, Gillian is their only sister. She was raised in the country by her mother, while her father and the boys spent their time in London. She was too young, fifteen, I believe, to have been involved in what took place five years ago. Her parents, who I am told are intensely protective of her, no doubt shielded her from the scandal involving you and her brother Reginald."

"Thank God she is resting upstairs and isn't present to hear this," Rolfe said, quickly filling a glass with brandy. He pressed it into Dante's hand. "Here, you need this more than I."

Dante took a swallow of it. "You know as well as I there should never have been a scandal in the first place, Rolfe."

"A difficult thing it would have been to avoid," Cassia said, "when all of court was already abuzz with rumors of your assignation with Reginald's wife."

"Falsehood, all of it. I never did anything more than kiss Clare's hand in greeting. There are a great many other men who cannot hope to claim that distant of an association with her."

"Not according to Clare."

"Cassia, you know Clare's claim of an assignation between us is unfounded. Moreover, it's an out-and-out lie. She made it known to me, and everyone else for that matter, that she wanted a more intimate association. Pressing her breasts into my face every chance she got was one of her more subtle overtures, but still I refused her. I had known both Reginald and Archie from Oxford. Rolfe can vouch that we burned down many a candle playing at cards till the small hours with both of them when we should have been studying."

Rolfe sat back in his chair. "It was you and Hadrian who played at cards with Reggie and Archie till the small hours. I passed my nights studying and then would spend the next day allowing both you and

Hadrian access to my labors. Without me, neither of you would have made it through the university."

Dante frowned at him. "I admit I may be guilty of many things, and the occasional collusion at school is no exception, but one thing I would never do is cuckold a friend. I considered Reggie one. Reggie was mad for Clare, even though everyone knew she wed him only because he'd one day take his father's place as marquess. She started the rumors of our illusional affair in effort to get back at me for refusing her repeated requests to share my bed. I knew nothing about it until that day Reggie, with Archie and Marcellus acting as his seconds, came upon me all horn mad at my tailor's, demanding I meet him at dawn in St. James's Park to settle the *affaire d'honneur*."

"At least you had sense enough to avoid dueling with him," Rolfe said.

"You think Reggie could have bested me?"

"With your talent at the sword? You would have destroyed him, which would have only fueled the rumors into a raging scandal the likes of which Whitehall has never seen. You were right to refuse his challenge, Dante, even if you did end up humiliating Reggie more than Clare and her tales of false assignations ever could."

Dante returned to his chair, his face grave. "I never meant to humiliate Reginald. I only wanted him to let it go, leave off as it was. But he wouldn't. He just kept pushing me. It started with letters threatening me, then it turned public. Everywhere I went, Reggie would surface, brothers in tow, and he would goad me until I had no choice but to thrust back at him, figuratively, with the truth."

"That his son wasn't truly his own," Cassia finished.

Dante looked about the room. Cordelia and Percy, who knew nothing of what was being discussed, were sitting on the settee, wisely silent.

"I never actually told Reginald that Alec was Limley's get," Dante said in defense of himself. "I merely suggested that he might benefit from discreetly following Clare on one occasion when she went on her Wednesday afternoon 'shopping' expedition. I guessed right when I figured Reginald intelligent enough to put it all together when he saw Clare with Alec meeting Limley at the Garden. She never took that boy with her anywhere, and Alec's resemblance to Limley when they are together is beyond remarkable."

Cassia sighed in resignation. "It was foolish of Clare to meet with Lord Limley in so public a place as Mulberry Garden, and on so regular a schedule. I believe, on that occasion, poor Reginald was indeed the proverbial last to know. It was quite a blow to him, discovering that Alec wasn't of his blood. He doted on that boy. I saw him once when he took Alec with him hunting in the park, parading the boy out in front of all of Whitehall as his heir. Unfortunately, now, it is Alec who suffers the brand of his illegitimacy, for neither his father nor his mother will have anything to do with him."

Dante shook his head. "I never should have told Reggie to follow Clare that day. It was wrong. I should have just left matters as they were."

"Admittedly, you were younger then, and more easily provoked," Rolfe said. "And Reggie would have found out about Clare's involvement with Limley eventually, Dante. It was only a matter of time. Everyone at court knew of Clare's numerous assignations. They also knew Alec's true parentage. As you said, the resemblance to Limley was remarkable, and Clare wasn't one given to discretion. I would venture to guess Reginald already suspected the truth. You merely confirmed it for him before someone else could."

"Yes, but at the expense of the child, and at the expense of a man's pride, a man I held as friend. It is not something of which I am proud."

Rolfe refused to allow Dante to shoulder all the blame. "It was a comedown, yes, but what else could you have done? Should you have faced Reginald in a duel at St. James's? Had you done that, one of you, most probably Reginald, would be dead now. In doing so, you would have been all but admitting your guilt to something you did not do. Reginald refused to accept your denial of Clare's accusations and your attempts to walk away from the whole mess. You forget, Dante, I was present at that last confrontation, when Reginald walked up bold as Beauchamp and all but called you a coward for refusing to face him. He didn't leave it off at that, either. He went on, accusing you of bedding most every woman at court, ruining innocent daughters and wives alike. I'm surprised he didn't try to say you'd bedded Queen Catherine, although we all know how ludicrous that would have been—all while Clare stood there grinning like Medea at the outcome of her handiwork. It went beyond simple speculation at that point, Dante, and became character assassination."

"I saw this same thing happen with my mother and father," Cassia broke in, "neither of whom lived exemplary lives. They only succeeded in destroying each other in the end, and left me to bear the brunt of it."

"I haven't lived the most exemplary of lives either, Cassia," Dante said, "in case you've forgotten."

"Perhaps, but you never ruined anyone. I know you, Dante, and you would never intentionally hurt a soul. In fact, it was your trying to avoid doing just that with Reginald and Clare that got you into the mess you were in. Reginald knew Clare's accusations were false. He doesn't strike me as stupid, but he was too hot-tempered and prideful to admit it."

Dante was silent, thoughtful. After a few moments he looked back at his friends. "So what am I to do now? March up to Adamley House and announce to all and sundry that I found their long lost daughter and sister lying in the road somewhere in the wilds of Derbyshire and, oh, yes, by the by, she has absolutely no recollection of who she is or who they are whatsoever?"

Newport, the Adamley butler, was to be commended on his composure. He barely showed a reaction upon his discovering Dante standing at the door, announcing himself and his request to speak with the marquess directly. In fact, if Dante hadn't been watching specifically for it, he never would have noticed the slight twitching that showed itself above the man's rheumy right eye, a sure sign that the past five years had done little to erase history.

"You may wait there," Newport said grimly, motioning toward the small space beside the door reserved for messengers and the like, "while I see if his lordship is available to see you."

Dante watched the aging Newport turn, wondering if the man's noticeable slowness was a result of his advanced age, or if it was indicative of his reluctance to see to his task.

When the butler had gone, disappearing somewhere within the bowels of Adamley House, Dante took the opportunity to look around at the entrance hall of this place Beatrice—or rather Gillian—called home.

Rich furnishings, ancient and priceless tapestries over polished paneled walls—all of it was meant to impress upon the visitor the mighty marquess's wealth and stature. There was even a full suit of armor in the foyer facing the door, complete with a mace clutched in its gauntleted hand. Dante barely gave it notice. Instead, he found himself picturing Gillian sitting inside the side parlor, whose interior he could barely glimpse through its slightly open door, knees curled beneath her as she read a favorite book. He found himself smiling as he thought back to the quiet nights they had passed at Wyldewoode, sitting by the fire, how he had been able to detect what was happening in the story just by watching the expression on her face.

Gillian. It was a name that suited her far better than Beatrice. Gillian was different. Gillian was an original. He'd never met anyone like her. And somehow he knew he never would again.

Once he'd first learned her true identity, and once the resulting shock of it had waned, Dante decided it would be best to delay telling Gillian the truth until after he had met with her family. Rolfe and Cassia had agreed. While Dante wanted to be the one to explain everything to her, he also wanted to see what the Forresters' response would be. He wanted to find out why he had found her lying in the road that night. He wanted to know why no one had come looking for her.

From his personal experience with her family, the possibility of her having run away became far more likely in his opinion. If so, it would appear she had stolen away in a hurry, without even pausing to change into proper clothing.

And if that was the case, he had no intention of returning her.

So caught was he by these thoughts, Dante barely noticed the movement on the stairwell above him. Barely. Lemon yellow sateen swirled about two slippered feet as they made their descent. A slim waist caught up in pale blue silk, and full breasts edged with a hint of blond Brussels lace, with soft chestnut colored ringlets framing a deceptively innocent-looking face. The picture was complete.

Clare Forrester, the Countess of Trisbane, and the future Marchioness of Adamley, stopped the instant she noticed Dante standing at the bottom of the stairs. She didn't say anything to him, just swept her gaze over the length of him before staring directly at his eyes. A long moment passed before Dante nodded his head, then watched as Clare turned and vanished down the far hall.

Thinking back on it, he should have recognized the chill that had come upon him like a spectre seconds before she appeared.

Moments later Newport returned, his expression enhanced by an advanced degree of hauteur.

"I am to inform you that his lordship is occupied at the moment and will be unable to see you, Lord Morgan. You may leave a message, if you wish."

"Did you tell Lord Adamley I am here on an urgent matter, that I must see him immediately?"

"Yes, of course, but his lordship cannot—"

"Never mind. I'll tell him myself."

Dante shoved past Newport, heading back the way the butler had just come. He ignored the sounds of protest he heard coming from behind him, knowing his younger, longer-legged stride would easily outdistance Newport's aged one. He had no idea really where he was going, but left to their own, his legs took him straight to a closed door at the end of the hall. He barely stopped. He didn't bother to knock, but grasped the door handle firmly in his hand and pushed the door open, entering without preamble.

Alexander Forrester, Marquess of Adamley, was seated behind his gleaming walnut and mother-of-pearl desk, his face hidden behind the letter he was reading.

"I trust he left quietly, Newport."

"No, my lord, he did not."

The marquess stood with a speed and dexterity that belied his advanced age. "Morgan, what the devil do you think you are doing?"

"Perhaps you've forgotten already, my lord, I had requested an audience with you."

"Which I declined, or was I not clear? You are not

wanted here, Morgan, so leave now before I have you thrown out bodily."

"As I told Newport, I have an important matter to discuss with you. Perhaps he wasn't the clear one."

"He relayed your message quite succinctly, as I'm certain he did as well with my response. Newport is most adept at handling rabble like you. There is nothing that you and I need to discuss."

"I assure you this is a matter of great import—"

"Begone, Morgan. I will not say it again."

"—about your daughter."

The marquess was silenced. He looked at Dante, and his eyes took on a cloud, not of anger, but of great and obvious fear. Dante watched him closely. "What do you know about Gillian, Morgan?"

"I know that your daughter is alive and well."

Relief finally allowed the marquess to release his pent-up breath. "Bless the saints. Where is she?"

"She is safe."

"I asked you where she is, Morgan."

"And I will tell you, my lord, in good time, after we have had a few minutes to talk. That is if you can now spare the time."

"Of course I can spare the time. I've been worried half to death about her. Where has she . . . ?" The marquess remained standing, his eyes suddenly growing dark with suspicion. "What is this, Morgan? Is it ransom? Is that what you're about now? You no longer are satisfied with ruining marriages, so you've now resorted to extortion? Get to it then. How much will it take for you to return Gillian to us?"

Dante wasn't sure he heard the man right. "What?"

"Out with it, man, you kidnapped Gillian from us for a reason, did you not? I should have known it was you all along, but I had believed you were still in France. And I thought Gillian had eloped, but there is no way I will ever believe my daughter would have run off to wed the likes of you. King Charles had sense enough to send you away. I thought certain you'd never be permitted back. Had I known you had returned, I would have come after you, and Gillian, long before now. What is this, Morgan, your twisted way of wreaking more havoc on my house? If you've so much as harmed a hair on her head, I swear I will see you dead before you have the chance to blink—"

"I don't know what you are rambling about, Lord Adamley. I have simply come here to assure you that your daughter is safe and alive."

"Then where is she? You certainly haven't brought her with you, so you must want something from me before you will return her to us. If you even have her, that is if this isn't your demented idea of a joke." He shook his head. "This is something I would have thought beneath even you."

Dante remained silent. The marquess looked at him. "You do have her, don't you? I can see it in your eyes. You have her, and you want something for her. Why else would you have kidnapped her in the first place?"

"You have taken leave of your senses, my lord. I did not kidnap Gillian."

"Lady Gillian to you, Morgan."

"Perhaps you should sit down and calm yourself, allowing me a moment to explain how I came to find her."

The marquess stared at Dante. He didn't want to listen to him. He didn't want to spend another second in his company, but he also was intelligent enough to know he had no choice in the matter. Without Dante, he might never see his daughter again. It wasn't a chance he wished to risk. Slowly he lowered himself into his chair and sat, watching Dante with ill-concealed hatred in his eyes, waiting.

"You have said Gilli—Lady Gillian was kidnapped, my lord? From where?"

"From right here at Adamley House. She was whisked out of her bed in the middle of the night."

"Are you certain she was kidnapped? Have you considered that she may have left willingly, or for that matter purposely?"

"That is nonsense now that I know she is with you. My Gillian would never have run off with you."

Dante went on. "When did this happen?"

"What do you mean? You ought to know since you're the one who took her—"

"Lord Adamley, I will only say this once more, so listen to me well. I did *not* kidnap your daughter. I did not even know you had a daughter until this morning when I finally discovered who in blue blazes she was. Now, when did she disappear?"

"Over a fortnight ago. Why?"

"Interestingly enough, I found her a fortnight ago, in Derbyshire."

"Derbyshire? How would she have gotten there? It's too far for her to have walked."

"I cannot say, but I found her lying in the rain, in the middle of the road, soaked to the skin, wearing her nightrail. You are correct in saying she didn't walk."

"Her nightrail!" The marquess stood again. "What the devil is going on here, Morgan? Why haven't you brought her home before now?"

Dante let out a slow breath. "As I have already told you, I did not know who she was until just a couple of hours ago."

"She must have told you her name. Surely, that would have been enough to lead you back here."

"No, my lord, Gillian did not tell me her name." He paused. "She couldn't."

"What do you mean, she couldn't tell you her name? Has she been struck dumb? Is she unable to hear? What are you talking about, Morgan?"

Dante stood, staring straight into the marquess's

angry eyes. "Gillian could not tell me her name. Nor could she tell me her family name, or even where she came from. I'm afraid, my lord, your daughter has lost her memory."

Chapter Sixteen

"You have precisely five minutes to tell me what in bloody hell you are up to, Morgan, before I have you brought up on charges and thrown into the Tower for kidnapping and—and moral turpitude! This is outrageous! This is unbelievable, even for you! What could you possibly hope to gain by this ridiculous story?"

Before Dante could respond to the marquess's angry outburst, he felt himself yanked backward. Seconds later, a fist, closed and tight, slammed into his jaw.

He had no chance to defend himself. His arms were pulled behind his back, and a forearm was clamped hard against his chest.

Across from him, struggling to break free from Archebald's hold, was Reginald Forrester, Gillian's oldest brother, ready to deliver Dante another blow.

"I thought Newport was off his head when he told me Morgan was here in this house," Reginald said. "At least I planted him a good one before you throw him out, Father."

"Calm yourself, Reginald," the marquess said. "You've only just recovered from your illness. Taxing your strength might cause you to suffer another setback."

Dante worked his jaw to see if it was broken. It wasn't, but then looking at Reginald, he didn't think he would have had the strength to. In the five years since Dante had last seen him, Reginald had aged well beyond his years. His once dark hair was now peppered with gray and he looked as if he'd lost a good deal of weight. He'd always been a man of moderate build. Now his clothes hung on him and his eyes were sunken and shadowed. He also seemed to have trouble catching his breath.

"I would guess that is you with a hold me, Marcellus," Dante said then, "since the other two are here in front of me and Newport doesn't have the strength to so much as carry a tune with any success. You can release me now. It should stand to reason since I'm surrounded by furious Forresters, I'm not going to cuff your brother one in return."

Marcellus, a tall, thin man who was much stronger than he looked, slowly loosened his hold on Dante. He stayed closed by Dante's side, silent yet alert, lest his assistance be needed again.

Dante rubbed his jaw as he looked at Reginald. "I suppose I deserved that, Trisbane, though you did take me at a disadvantage. Nonetheless, you can call us even."

"You can go to blazes, Morgan!" Reginald spat at him. "We are far from even. You deserve far worse. You're just lucky Archie's got a hold on me, else I'd have beat the bloody—"

"That will do, Reginald," the marquess broke in, silencing anything further from his eldest son. "You cannot kill Morgan here in my study, at least, not yet. Not until he tells us where he has Gillian."

Marcellus came closer to Dante. "You know where Gillian is? She is safe? She is alive?"

Dante nodded. He'd always liked Marcellus, whom he had found the calmest and most reasonable of the Forrester boys. The third son, he had entered into the law profession and had acquired a propitious position at court. Marcellus had always kept a sound head. Dante even recalled his having tried to sway Reginald from throwing down the glove that long-ago day. "Your sister is well and fine, Marcellus." And then he added, "Physically anyway."

"What do you mean by that nonsense, Morgan?" Reginald broke in. "If you so much as laid a finger on Gillian, I swear I will—"

"Shut up, Reggie," Marcellus said. "Your mouth runs faster and with less tact than a cheap harlot." He turned back to Dante. "Where is Gillian, Dante?"

"She is well and safe—"

"Probably warming his bed at Morgan House," Reggie interrupted.

"That is your sister you're speaking of, Reginald," the marquess said, "not your wife. If you cannot keep a civil tongue, I will have Archie remove you from the room at once."

Reginald glared at his father with a bitterness that had been three decades in the making. Their mutual resentment extended far beyond Reginald's poor choice in a wife and the dark cloud from the events five years before. It was a resentment that had been rooted in Reginald's birth.

"Give off, Archie," Reginald finally grumbled. "I won't touch him."

"Father?" Archie asked. The second son, the soldier, Archie had always been an accomplished strategist. Unfortunately, his talents had become obsolete when he had had to resign his military commission after being wounded early on in the Cromwellian wars. Experience had obviously taught him not to trust his brother's word.

"Let him go, but stay close, should I have need of you again."

Reginald and Archie sat on the bench near the window. Dante took one of the chairs before the marquess's desk, Marcellus the other. The marquess returned to his chair last, leaning forward on his forearms atop the desk. Oddly, it was Marcellus who spoke first.

"Dante, tell us what has happened to Gillian."

"It was late when I first found her, nearly midnight, about a fortnight ago. I was traveling by coach to Wyldewoode. No one had been there to tend to matters since my mother died."

"I was sorry to learn of Helena's death," Marcellus said. "She was a true lady in every sense of the word."

"Thank you," Dante said. He went on then, "We were almost to Wyldewoode when my driver had to pull the coach off the road in order to avoid hitting something he saw lying in the road. He said it was a body. We went back and discovered that the body was that of a young woman, who I have only recently learned is your sister, Gillian."

"What do you mean you only recently learned who she is? Gillian didn't tell you her name?"

"Gillian sustained an injury to her head that has caused her to lose her memory. The nearest physician to Wyldewoode, Dr. Greentree of Castleton, examined her and treated the wound, but he said it could take time for her to regain her memory. As of now, she has yet to do so."

Marcellus took this in. "So you're saying Gillian does not know her name?"

"No, she does not."

"Did she know you?"

"No, but oddly enough she has retained her memory of other things."

"Other things?" Archie asked from behind.

Dante turned back to look. It was then he noticed the smooth wooden cane Archie employed years earlier. His war injury, it seemed, remained with him. "She knows a proper curtsy, social address, she can cipher better than Renny, my steward, and she plays the viola da gamba as if she's wielded a bow since birth."

"It is Gilly." Marcellus's eyes shone with the unshed tears of relief at hearing this final confirmation that his sister was indeed alive. "But you say she doesn't know who we are."

"Which is why I did not bring her with me today. I am especially glad, now that I hear from your father the circumstances of her disappearance. He said she was kidnapped."

"I have never believed Clare's drivel that she eloped," Marcellus said. "Gillian just wouldn't do that. I have been of the belief that she was forcibly abducted from her bedchamber late after we had all retired. No one heard a thing."

"How do we know it wasn't you who took her?" Reginald said, breaking in.

"Because Dante most probably wasn't even on English soil when she disappeared," Marcellus answered. He looked at Dante. "I had heard His Majesty had given his consent for you to return."

"Yes."

"When did you return, Morgan?" Archie asked.

"We landed at Dover on the thirteenth."

"Gillian was taken on the fifteenth," Reggie said. "Ample time for you to have come to London to take her, especially considering we wouldn't have known you were back in England yet."

Marcellus sighed impatiently. "Reggie, Dante's mother just died of the plague. He was coming back to pay his final respects to her. I don't think he would have had the abduction of our sister foremost in his mind."

"Don't be so quick to discount the idea, Marcellus," Reggie said. "I know Morgan a lot better than you. I wouldn't put anything past him."

Marcellus shook his head hopelessly at his brother. He turned to Dante. "When can we see her?"

"There are a few things I wish to get clear before I proceed any further."

"You haven't the right to ask anything of us," Reginald said.

"I think he does," Marcellus broke in. "He has Gillian, so I think it would be wise if we just answered Morgan's questions. We have expressed our distrust of him. He has every right not to trust us either."

Dante nodded to Marcellus. "Firstly, I would like to know why no efforts have been made by your family to find her."

Marcellus looked at his father. "You said you had hired investigators."

The marquess's face colored a bit. "I sent a man on it. He utilized a number of men. They found nothing."

"You sent a man?" Marcellus was genuinely surprised. "I only agreed not to report Gillian's disappearance to the authorities because you assured me you would hire a team of investigators to find her. Why the devil wouldn't you have done it, Father?"

"Because I had no way of knowing whether Gillian had gone willingly or unwillingly. Think of your sister's good name. If she had been kidnapped, when she did return to court, she would be ruined. But if no one knew about the abduction, she would be safe. I also had good reason, before I knew of Morgan's involvement of course, to suspect she might have eloped. And if she had eloped, then circumstances would have been completely different. I was simply waiting to see if I could find out what had really happened."

Marcellus shook his head in disgust. He turned to Dante. "Had I known there wasn't a team of men looking for her, scandal or not, I would have reported Gillian's disappearance. I would have had every man in His Majesty's service combing through England in search of her."

Dante looked at him. He believed him. "You are certain Gillian did not leave here because she wanted to?"

"I would be hard pressed to believe that, Dante. Gillian seemed happy enough here. She had her own interests and was enjoying her coming out into society. We won't know, of course, until she can tell us. Seeing us all might help to bring Gillian's memory back. Would you consider bringing her here to Adamley House?"

"What do you mean asking him when you can see your own sister?" the marquess broke in. "We will have Gillian back here at Adamley House directly."

"Lord Adamley, I would advise you to proceed slowly and with great caution where Gillian's welfare is concerned," Dante said. "Any upset and she could lose whatever weak grasp she may have on her memory at all."

"Damnation, Morgan! Where my daughter belongs is with her family, not out amid strangers, and certainly not with you. I am not entirely convinced you didn't kidnap her, then have an attack of conscience that spurred you to bring her back. And as for this nonsense about her losing her memory, I can assure you as soon as she sees us again, she will remember everything. I know my Gilly. She is arrow sharp. She will have her wits about her again. Then, perhaps she can tell us who it was who spirited her out of her bed in the middle of the night."

"That would be beneficial information," Dante said, "were she to regain her memory, of course."

"The only way we will ever know that is if you bring her to us. In any case, you certainly have no right to her. I give you twenty-four hours to go back to wherever you have her and bring her to us, or you can be sure I will send the Lord Mayor himself to fetch Gillian home."

* * *

Lethe, the river of oblivion, rolls her watery labyrinth whereof who drinks forthwith his former state and being forgets, forgets both joy and grief, pleasure and pain . . .

"Hello, Beatrice."

Gillian looked up from the book she was reading and smiled when she spotted Dante standing on the garden path before her.

"I didn't hear you coming."

Dante walked forward, taking a seat on the stone bench beside her. They were in a small private alcove formed by a canopy of various flowering vines. The sun was shining, and the air was filled with the mingling scents of the garden flowers. A small fountain bubbled nearby.

Dante lifted Gillian's book from her lap and glanced at its title.

"Milton?"

Gillian nodded. "It seems I am fond of the myths and legends. I was just reading this poem describing a river called Lethe."

Dante set the book aside, tucking its ribbon inside to mark her place. "Ah, yes, the river of forgetfulness, if memory serves."

Gillian giggled at his unintended pun. "It seems Lethe has effected you as well, my lord."

"Were you perhaps wondering if your current condition was brought on by a stolen sip from its waters?"

Gillian smiled. "I missed you at supper."

"Accept my apologies. I had an errand to see to."

"So Cassia said."

"Where is Phoebe?"

"She is with Cassia. I believe she was going to give Phoebe an art lesson. Cassia is a talented artist, you know."

"I know." Dante stared down at the crushed shell pathway. He looked as if he were searching for something to say, something that was causing him great distress.

"Is something bothering you?" Gillian took his hand, pressing it softly between her two. "Your errand, was it an unpleasant one?"

"Actually, my errand was about you." He looked at her. "I have some news for you."

"You do?"

"Yes. Actually, I guess you might say I've managed to solve your Lethean dilemma. I have found out who you really are."

Gillian released his hand, then wondered why she had done so. Had she thought by doing so, it would keep him from going on? She stared at him, frightened, and she didn't know why. "I see."

"Your real name is not Beatrice, of course. It is Gillian Forrester. Lady Gillian Forrester. Your father is Alexander Forrester, Marquess of Adamley."

"Gillian Forrester," Gillian said, as if saying her name might trigger a return of her memory. It didn't. "You mentioned my father. Is my mother still living?"

"Yes. Her name is Joanna, and she and your father live here in London, at Adamley House, with your three brothers and their families."

"I have three brothers?" Gillian remembered the voice she had heard that day in the cave back at Wyldewoode, the one that had called her "bratchet," goading her on. It must have been one of her brothers.

"Reginald is the oldest," Dante went on, "then Archebald and Marcellus respectively."

Gillian was silent, thoughtful, repeating the names of each family member in her head. *Reginald. Archebald. Marcellus . . .*

An image came to her then, a muted picture of a pair

of broken spectacles and a number of small children, boys and girls, of different ages.

"My family, they are here, you say, in London?"

"Yes. And they are very anxious to see you again."

"Then why are they not here with you now?"

"I haven't told them where you are. I wanted to tell you the truth about your identity myself first, to prepare you before . . . "

He hesitated.

"Before what?"

"Before I am to return you to them."

"Return me to them? It sounds as if I am a lost button or a book that you borrowed from this Marquess of Adamley person. Is that how you think of me? And why hadn't they come looking for me if I was kidnapped as they say I was? Didn't they care that I was gone? Didn't they care what happened to me?"

Gillian was growing upset now. Her whole body was trembling. Why did she feel this reluctance to return to her family and the life she had known? It was as if something were trying to tell her not to go, not to return. And suddenly she knew. Because returning to that unknown world would also mean leaving Dante, and Phoebe, and the only life she really knew.

"Gillian, I—"

"I don't remember them, Dante. They are like strangers to me. They are strangers. Will you simply set me on their doorstep and disappear? What if I never remember them? Am I to spend the rest of my days living with people I do not know. And what of Phoebe? Will I never see her again either?"

She was trembling, and Dante pulled her into his arms to calm her. He held her against him, whispering soft sounds into her hair. Gillian closed her eyes. She tried desperately not to cry, but the thought of leaving Dante and Phoebe filled her with a very real fear.

This will go a lot easier for you, Gillian, if you don't attempt to fight us.

Gillian pulled away from Dante. "What did you say?"

Dante looked at her. "I said nothing."

"But I just heard a voice telling me not to fight, that it would go easier for me if I didn't."

Dante's face stilled. "Did you recognize the voice?"

"No." Gillian added, "It wasn't a nice voice, though. It was threatening me."

"Listen to me, Gillian. Your father said he believes you were kidnapped from your bedchamber, and I guess that would explain why I found you as I did abandoned in the road. In truth, your father believes I am the one who kidnapped you."

"You? Why would he think that? You saved my life."

"That doesn't matter, Gillian. At least now it doesn't. I don't care what your father believes either. I want you to know I did not kidnap you, but I think you might know who did. I think it is locked away somewhere, the same place your memory has gone. My mentioning your family to you seems to have brought some of that memory forward in the voice you just heard. Perhaps, if you were to see them again, it would help to bring back your recollection entirely."

"And then I could tell my father who really kidnapped me," Gillian finished.

Dante smiled at her. "Precisely. Tomorrow morning, I would like to take you to Adamley House to meet your family. I will stay with you as long as you want me to. If you want to leave after meeting them, then we will. I will not abandon you there."

Gillian looked at him. She suddenly remembered something Dante had once told her. He had told her he didn't lie. And she believed him. She stood slowly. "You will not leave me there?"

"Not unless you ask me to. Trust me, Gillian. I give my word, everything will be all right."

Except, Dante thought as he walked with her toward the house, *when you regain your memory, you'll also find out the truth of who I really am.*

Chapter Seventeen

A peculiar chill hung in the air despite the late summer sunshine as the coach drove along the narrow London streets on its way to Adamley House.

Gillian couldn't deny the chill, nor, try as she might, could she reason it away. They were going to meet her family, but she didn't know them. They were as much strangers to her as any other. She pushed herself back farther against the cushions of the coach seat, trying to ward the unsettling cold off, but something kept nagging at her, as if trying to tell her something. It was not a voice, this disquiet. It was more a feeling, like dread. Why did she feel this foreboding? She should be overjoyed at the prospect of finally knowing who she was, where she came from. She should be eager to return to her roots. Why then did this feeling stay with her?

Actually, she had first sensed it when Dante had approached her in the garden the previous day, even before he'd disclosed her true name. She had been pleased to see him, yes, but there had been something in his eyes she'd never seen there before. She couldn't put a finger on it, this strange dark chill, but the sky had definitely clouded overhead and it hadn't cleared since.

Gillian realized then that the coach had halted in the front of a vast and imposing mansion. Trim rue bushes and shaped topiary flanked the wide front stairs that led up to an impressive double-doored entrance with

handles shining golden in the sunlight. A crest of sorts
was set in the stone above the door, bearing the design
of a lion, crowned with laurel and intertwined with an
elaborate letter *A*. A tall black iron gate separated the
street from the house, the top of which was set with
menacing-looking spikes.

This was her home? It looked more like an institu-
tion, with its strict and austere appearance. It looked
hardly lived in, and not at all familiar to her. The crest,
the house, even the two liveried servants standing at
the door, everything about this place looked foreign
and unwelcoming.

Gillian suddenly longed for Wyldewoode more than
she had since leaving. She yearned to smell the fresh
lime blossoms filling the air, to taste some of Mrs.
Leeds's sweet, hot gingerbread. She wanted to bury
herself beneath the rose-scented sheets in her bed and
never emerge.

Dante must have sensed Gillian's hesitation. He said
nothing to her, simply alighted from the coach and
handed her down. She held his fingers tightly, taking
with them his promise that she would not have to stay.
She would go with Dante inside the house and she
would meet these people who were her family, and if it
made her as uncomfortable as she felt standing before
this house, she would leave.

As they climbed the stairs that led to the door,
Gillian looked up at the three stories of gleaming windows. She spotted several tiny faces pressed against
the glass on the second floor, bright curious eyes
watching her closely from the other side.

An antiquated man, stooped in the shoulders, opened
the door even before the knocker had sounded.

"My lady Gillian," he said, giving her a yellow-
toothed smile. "It is wonderful to see you again."

Gillian looked at the man, then looked at Dante for
an explanation.

"This is Newport, your family's butler."

Gillian smiled kindly at the man. "Hello, Newport. I am pleased to make your acquaintance."

Newport flashed Dante an odd look before taking their cloaks. "The family has been alerted of your arrival and are awaiting you in the parlor," he said, directing them down a long hall. He pushed open a tall door and stepped back to allow Dante and Gillian to proceed.

Gillian hesitated a moment at the threshold, her apprehension mounting at the sea of unfamiliar faces that awaited her inside. She took a step closer to Dante's side, watching as an older gentleman dark-haired and with an air of command about him came briskly forward.

"Gillian, my girl, we have missed you." He embraced her tightly before she had any chance to react. When he released her, Gillian stayed silent.

Dante came beside her. "This is your father, Gillian, Alexander Forrester, the marquess."

Gillian smiled tentatively. "Hello, sir."

It felt odd, addressing this man who was her father in this distant and unfamiliar manner. She really didn't know how else to respond. She noticed, though, that he had gray eyes, very similar to her own.

A woman came forward behind her father, tears shining in her soft brown eyes. They were troubled eyes, and she was looking not at Gillian's face, but everywhere else on her person, it seemed. Gillian looked down, wondering if she'd spilled some of her breakfast chocolate on her gown, one of Helena's, a rich turquoise silk with pale blue underskirts edged in lace. It was spotless; what was wrong? Why was this woman, this lovely, elegant woman, looking as if she were ready to burst into tears?

"Oh, my dear child," she said as she threw her arms around Gillian and kissed her on the cheek, breathing a heavy sigh. "You look so very different. So grown up and lovely. I thought never to see you again."

Gillian looked at the woman as she finally released her and stepped back. "You are my mother?"

The woman didn't answer. Instead, she started to sob into her lace-edged handkerchief, and the man who was her father placed his arm comfortingly around her shoulders.

"It is all right, Joanna. She is the same Gillian, our daughter. It will just take some getting used to, her losing her memory."

"But she seems so . . . "

Gillian stepped forward and took the woman's hand. "I am sorry, madame. I didn't mean to upset you."

An image flitted through her mind, a picture of this same woman, younger-looking, gently smiling and holding out a small doll to her. As quick as it came, the image was gone.

A tall, handsome young man with spectacled eyes approached from the left, smiling. "You didn't upset Mother, Gillian. She cries at everything. When we were children, she cried the day you and I brought her home a toad we had found in the garden."

"I am sorry, but I don't remember," Gillian said, wondering what would have ever spurred her to touch one of those ugly little creatures.

He took her hand and squeezed it. "I'm Marcellus, the youngest of your brothers. I think you look stunningly well."

"And I'm Archie, another brother," said another man, older than herself and perhaps a few years older than Marcellus, with sandy blond locks that brushed his wide shoulders. He came forward to hug her, limping slightly and aided by a polished wooden cane. Gillian wondered what had happened to him.

"Don't bother about the cane. A result of a shot I took in the leg at Worcester. I'm the second of your brothers. That brooding ninny in the corner there," Archie went on, "is the third. Reginald. He's the oldest of us, and admittedly the most bullheaded. You were always rather fond of calling him Reggie."

Reggie looked at her, a small smile on his thin face. "It is good to see you, Gillian."

Gillian nodded, smiling politely. "I am pleased to make your acquaintance. All of you. I guess that is a rather odd thing for me to say, given that you are all my family. I am sorry."

All of them gave her the same look the butler, Newport, had earlier in the entrance hall. Why were they looking at her like that, as if they knew her, but they didn't? What was so very different about her?

The silence that followed was an awkward thing, and while still nervous, the chill Gillian had felt upon her arrival had begun to wane just a bit.

Marcellus took Gillian's hand, ending the silence, and led her more into the room. "It's all right, Gilly." He hesitated slightly. "Is it all right if I call you that? I don't think I've called you much else since we were in the schoolroom, except perhaps 'bratchet,' and well, that doesn't seem appropriate now."

Come on, bratchet, you're not afraid are you?

The voice she'd heard in the cave that day. It had been his voice.

Gillian smiled at him, relieved that she'd finally made a connection with someone in her family. "You may call me Gilly, though I may not remember to answer to it. And you, did I call you Marcellus?"

"Not often. Usually it was only in introductions. There were a few names you called me that our mother used to reprove you for, but mostly you just called me Mars, after the war god. You said it was more a fitting name for me than Marcellus since I used to fight with you constantly when we were children."

Gillian was beginning to feel a strange sense of familiarity with him. "How old are you, Mars?"

"I'm four-and-twenty."

"How old am I?"

"You are twenty. You will turn one-and-twenty in
March, on the twenty-third."

Gillian nodded, looking around at them. "Mars,
Archie, Reggie, Father, and Mother," she said, reciting
their names in order to better remember them. She
looked over then to where two women sat near the windows, apart from the rest of the family. "Dante did not
tell me I had any sisters."

"You don't. Allow me to introduce to you your sisters-in-law," Marcellus said, crossing the room. He
took the hand of a petite blonde who was in the very
late stages of pregnancy. She smiled warmly at Gillian.
"This is Dorothea, my wife."

Marcellus helped Dorothea to her feet, placing his
hand gently beneath her elbow.

"It is good to have you home again, Gillian,"
Dorothea said, standing close by Marcellus's side.
"And, please, I don't think anyone has called me Doro-
thea since I was a child. Dorrie will suit much better."

This woman who was the picture of loveliness,
looked happy, radiant actually, and it would appear she
adored her husband, for she peered up at him as if she
worshipped him. Indeed, one had only to look at Marcellus to see he felt the same.

"And this," Marcellus went on, "is Reginald's wife,
Clare."

The warmth Gillian had seen shining in Dorrie's
face did not seem to extend to the other woman. In fact,
Gillian felt a sense of wariness when introduced to her.
Despite the attention of the room now focused on
her, the woman remained removed. Her eyes were dark
and unclear, as if she would much rather be somewhere

else. Gillian also noticed Reggie did not come forward to stand beside his wife.

"Hello, Clare," Gillian said, trying to ease the tension she felt. Surely, this feeling was due to the awkward unfamiliarity between them. Hadn't the house appeared strict and austere as well, like this woman, at first glance?

Clare stepped forward and embraced Gillian stiffly. When she bent to kiss her on her cheek, she whispered softly in her ear, so quiet only Gillian could hear her. "Welcome back to Eden, Gillian. Do watch for the snakes, and be certain not to take a bite from any apples."

Her remarks, so insinuating and sharp, immediately took away any comfort Gillian had begun to feel in that house among her family. Why had Clare said that? Did she dislike her? Suddenly, the door burst open and several small children came charging in. A nursemaid followed after them, carrying an infant girl with lovely blond curls, sucking on two fingers.

"Aunt Gilly has come home!" the older children chorused as they came before her and started tugging everywhere on her skirts, surrounding her. Gillian simply stared at them.

"Johnny said you were taken by pirates to an island," said a delicate little blond-haired girl, older than the babe, who was the very image of Marcellus's wife, Dorrie.

"Did not," piped in a young boy who looked to be very close in age. He shot the little girl a frown that promised trouble.

"Anna, John," Marcellus broke in, his voice deep with fatherly authority, "let us not frighten your Aunt Gillian the very moment she returns home. Come over here, now, and mind your manners."

Anna and John left Gillian's skirts and marched

solemnly to Marcellus's side where they stood watching silently. Gillian smiled at them.

"The twins have been anxious to see you again," Dorrie said. "I'm sorry if they overwhelmed you."

"It is all right," Gillian said, then turned to look at the other children.

A second little boy, younger than the twins with a mop of white blond hair and a look of mischief about him, stared timidly at her with dark, soulful eyes. Gillian smiled at him and bent down to be closer to his height. "What is your name?"

"Am Sam-yule," he said softly.

"Samuel," Gillian repeated, "how do you do?"

She extended her hand to him. He hesitated a moment, then reached out slowly his own. Gillian shook his hand, then noticed one more child standing behind Samuel. He was older than the others and hadn't joined in on the initial raucous welcome.

Gillian rose up and started toward him. "Hello."

"Hello," he replied quietly, keeping his eyes downcast at his shoe buckles.

"What is your name?"

Still he looked down. "Alec. Alec Forrester." Finally he lifted his eyes to her. "You don't remember who I am?"

Something about the way in which he asked the question made Gillian feel the boy somehow believed she didn't know him because she didn't want to. His uncertainty was obvious on his face. "I'm sorry, Alec, I don't know you. I'm sure I will remember you very soon, all of you, but I don't remember anybody right now. You see, I hit my head very hard, and it has caused me to forget everything I knew before. Do you understand?"

He nodded, looking at the floor again. "Will you still play at fives with me as you did before, when you knew who I was?"

"I would be happy to, if I still remember how to play, that is. There are some things I know how to do and some things I have to learn again. You may have to teach me the game. Would that be all right, Alec?"

The boy's face began to lose some of its hesitant reserve. He even smiled a little, and nodded.

"Good." Gillian stood, looking around. "Is that everyone now?"

"Except the baby," Dorrie said, taking the infant, who looked about a year's age, from the nursemaid. "This is Lizzy, our youngest." She smiled. "At least until this next one is born a few weeks from now."

Gillian grinned at the tiny cherubic face set with large blue eyes so like her mother's. "May I hold her?"

"Of course you may," Dorrie said, handing the child to her. "You needn't ask. Lizzy is just beginning to walk, but she loves to be held."

"They are all yours?" Gillian asked, motioning to the children.

"Nearly, but not all," Dorrie said. "Everyone but Alec. He is Reginald and Clare's son. He is nine years old now, quite the young gentleman. John and Anna are our twins. They are five. Samuel just turned three. and Lizzy will turn two in eight months."

"But I'm older than John," added Anna proudly, "because Mama said I was born first."

"That doesn't make you older," countered John. "And I can still run faster than you can."

Anna glared at him. "No, you can't."

"I can."

"Well, perhaps, we'll have to have a race then, all of us, to see who really is the fastest," Gillian finished, effectively ending the argument.

Watching Gillian and the children with an admiring eye, Dante stood at the door, away from the others. She had a marvelous rapport with them that even the loss of her memory hadn't taken away. Communicating with them, understanding the way a child's mind worked was something Dante had never been able to master. Even now, when he would talk with Phoebe, he still felt as if they were from two very different worlds, separate worlds, despite that he was her father. Perhaps it was because she was a girl, and he had no experience with them. Yet. Even with Robert, his friend Hadrian's son, Dante had never felt completely at ease, constantly wary of saying something wrong or speaking of things irrelevant to a child.

But Gillian, Dante thought watching her, she was remarkably good at it. She had bridged the initial gap with Phoebe almost instantaneously, and now with these children she had done the same. She had the uncanny ability to sense a child's feelings, to realize that what they had to say mattered. Most adults didn't bother or care with such a thing. A child's opinion; it was disregarded by most of the world. Dante remembered his own father as a man who had adhered to the belief that a child was to do what was told and remain silent until permitted to speak.

"A word, Morgan."

Dante glanced up at the marquess's approach. He looked to where Adamley motioned toward a side door, nodded, and followed him toward it.

"Dante?"

Gillian's voice stopped him just as he reached the door. He turned.

"You are leaving?"

It was not simply a question. It was a reminder of his promise to her. A promise that he wouldn't leave her. Dante shook his head, indicating she needn't worry. "Your father and I have some"—he glanced at the marquess—"business to discuss. It shouldn't take long. Is that not right, my lord?"

Gillian's father did not look pleased, not at all.

"There are just a few things I need to discuss with Morgan in private, Gillian."

Gillian's desperate expression eased. She smiled. "I will see you when you are finished then."

Dante nodded, returning her smile before proceeding from the room.

"Brandy?" the marquess asked once he and Dante were alone in the study. He was decidedly more hospitable than the last time Dante had been here.

"No, thank you, my lord." Dante took the seat offered. He waited.

Lord Adamley did not immediately speak. He removed a key from his coat pocket, opened the top drawer to his desk, and removed something from inside. He tossed it in front of Dante. It was a letter. The Adamley crest was pressed in the red wax on the seal.

"What is this?" Dante asked. He didn't move to retrieve the letter as the marquess had so obviously intended.

"That, Morgan, is a letter instructing my solicitor to release to you the sum of twenty thousand pounds."

Dante looked at him. Still, he didn't move to take it. "A rather large sum, my lord. May I ask what it is for? As a gentleman, I certainly wouldn't expect any reward from you for returning your daughter safely to you."

"It isn't a reward, Morgan. Consider it recompense meant to secure your promise as a gentleman and a guarantee that after you leave Gillian here today, you will never again attempt to see her."

"You are paying me to leave your daughter as if I never before met her?"

The marquess nodded, completely serious. "Precisely."

"What makes you believe I would be willing to accept these terms? What makes you think I would just leave Gillian?"

The marquess laughed out loud. "Because you are

who you are. You are Dante Tremaine, the Rakehell Earl of Morgan. Your identity alone makes it likely, actually it makes it necessary for you to accept this offer, which is beyond generous, considering."

"Considering what, my lord?"

"Considering that if you do not accept this offer and with it my terms, I will have you brought up on charges of kidnapping. Scandal or not, I will make certain every person in London, including King Charles, knows Gillian was forcibly taken from her bedchamber that night, shortly after your return from France. I will make it known that this was your attempt at revenge against my family for the damage done your standing in that debacle involving Reginald and his wanton wife a number of years ago. With your reputation paired against mine, who do you think will be believed? You will be fortunate if His Majesty doesn't see fit to transport you to the other side of the globe, that is if he doesn't have you thrown into the Tower to rot instead."

Dante listened to Lord Adamley, and then out of it all something he had said stuck in his head, something the marquess most likely hadn't meant to reveal. "I have one question, my lord. Why was it, really, you didn't inform anyone of Gillian's disappearance?"

Lord Adamley took in a slow breath. "That, Morgan, is none of your concern."

"You say you believed your daughter was kidnapped, forcibly kidnapped from this house, and yet you never alerted the authorities. You never sent anyone looking for her, except one man you say, and obviously an inept one, because as far away as Warwickshire, no one had heard of Gillian missing."

"There were a dozen men looking for her, under the direction of my one man, only they were looking in the wrong places. And whether you believe me or not, I was on the brink of involving the Palace. Damn it, Morgan, I didn't know what I was dealing with. I didn't know what I should think. I considered she had eloped. I considered she'd been kidnapped. And if she had indeed been kidnapped, I needed to await a request for ransom. I have enemies—what political man doesn't?—and I didn't know if it was one of them who had done this in hopes of ruining me. When time passed and there was no request for ransom or word from Gillian, I began to grow very frightened. I knew I had been wrong to wait."

"How is it that you managed to explain away Gillian's sudden absence to your acquaintances?"

"Gillian's aunt, to whom she is very close, suffered an unexpected incapacitation. Gillian left immediately to be with her in Dorset. She has only just returned to London."

Dante shook his head. "You have everything thought out. And it was successful, wasn't it? After all, your political standing remains intact."

The marquess's face had turned red, very red. He looked as if he might explode. "It was also for Gillian's protection that I didn't raise a hue and cry, and now that I know with whom she's been all this time, I'm bloody glad of it. Damn you, Morgan, do you know what it would do to Gillian's good name if it were known she had spent a fortnight alone with the Rake-hell Earl? She would be ruined. My family cannot afford another scandal the likes of which you presented us with the last time. We've barely recovered from that ugly episode. I am simply a father who is doing what he must to protect his daughter's future. What man would want her for wife after she's known to have been with you?"

Despite his anger, which was fast reaching the boiling point with every gibe the marquess threw, and despite knowing Adamley was trying to turn him away from his own shortcomings, Dante did realize there was some truth to what the man was saying. Despite the fact that he had taken no advantage of Gillian, that she remained as chaste as the day she was born, everyone would believe he had defiled her.

Bloody hell, they already did.

He was, after all, the Rakehell Earl.

What person who knew anything about him wouldn't assume the same? It mattered naught that he had returned Gillian to them. It would become the scandal to surpass all previous scandals, only the repercussions of it wouldn't matter a whit to Dante's already tarnished name.

Instead, the brunt of it would fall straight on Gillian's shoulders.

The marquess was right. Gillian's future would be ruined. No decent man would accept her as a wife, and wherever she went, it would be whispered after her that she had been ruined by the Rakehell Earl. Unless . . .

Dante pushed the unopened letter back across the desktop in front of the marquess. "I do not accept your offer of recompense."

Adamley looked at him. "You want more?"

"Not at all, my lord. I would be willing to accept different terms than those you have indicated."

"Different terms? What is it you have in mind?"

"Quite simple, my lord." Dante watched him. "Instead of your twenty thousand pounds, my lord, I would ask for Gillian's hand in marriage."

Chapter Eighteen

The marquess stared at Dante. He didn't speak, not a word. Not at first. His leather chair creaked as he stood and walked to the window. His back was to Dante. The small brass lantern clock on the desk continued ticking. A horse and coach passed outside the open window. Dante simply waited.

He wasn't kept waiting long.

The marquess turned, flattened his hands against his desk, and roared. "Damn you, Morgan! Damn your eyes! Damn your teeth! And damn that blasted Tremaine arrogance that makes you think I'd ever entertain such an absurd notion. Just who do you think you are? I'll tell you who. You are the Rakehell Earl of Morgan, a man who has ruined more women than can be counted. Did you really think that three years away from court would change all that? My Gillian wed to you? I'd rather see her pass her remaining days climbing higher and higher on the shelves of the unwed. I'd see her enter into a life of spinsterhood before I'd sentence her to such an existence as she would have as your wife. Wed my daughter to you? Do you think me an absolute fool, Morgan?"

Dante ignored the stinging words and the insults against him, his body parts, his ancestors before him, but the man went on regardless, thundering now.

"You aren't a stupid man, Morgan. You no doubt realize that wedding Gillian would bring a sizable dowry.

'Tis no wonder you turned down the twenty thousand pounds I offered to be rid of you. You're simply holding out, seeking a greater sum."

Dante's anger was reaching its threshold. He was many things, yes, arrogant among them, but ambitious for an heiress he was not. Dante took a deep breath, calmly released it, and said in a low voice that immediately captured the marquess's attention, "I would expect no dower from you, my lord. I have no need of it. In fact, I would be willing to transfer to you the sum of twenty thousand pounds, a reverse dowry if you will, if you would but agree to the suit."

"So it isn't the money that you're after, eh, boy? Instead, you think to buy yourself respectability, do you, Morgan? Well, you can keep your twenty thousand pounds and go searching for some other fool. I'll not be bribed, and I'll not have you using my Gillian to affect yourself a proper place in society. You had that opportunity when your father died. You could have assumed the earldom, sowed your oats, and settled down as the rest of us did. You had every opportunity to prove yourself. Your earlier transgressions would have been forgotten, yet even then, you could not mend your ways. You ran about pell-mell, until you went too far. You involved yourself in the king's business, and with the king's mistress, and you finally were made to account for your actions. Now you suddenly are having an attack of the conscience? Well, my daughter will be no part of it. When my daughter weds, if my daughter ever weds, it will be to a man who loves her and who appreciates her for who she is. It will be to a man who knows honor, a man who will accord my daughter the respect she is entitled to as a wife. I'll not have my daughter pitied or ridiculed, her husband's conquests whispered about the moment she enters a room. As her father, I cannot, I will not accept any less."

Dante stared at the man. He couldn't fault the marquess for wanting to safeguard his daughter's future. Even with the short time he'd had Phoebe in his life, he knew he would feel the same. "What makes you think I do not realize and appreciate Gillian's true qualities? What makes you think I have no tenderness of feeling for her?"

"Because of who you are. To put it bluntly, Morgan, you are a man incapable of committing yourself to one woman. Bloody hell, you could not even commit yourself to a handful of them. I cannot leave Gillian to a life such as that."

"Why do you not simply ask Gillian herself?"

"Ask her?"

"Yes. Let us bring Gillian in here with us now and ask her if she would like to be my wife. Leave her to decide whether I would make a good husband for her. She is, after all, the one who would be, as you so eloquently put it, sentenced to an existence with me. Shouldn't she be the one to decide if it is a fate she would want?"

The marquess glared at him. "Perhaps, if Gillian were in her right mind, I would do that very thing, Morgan. The Gillian I knew was raised to have a mind of her own, to exercise good judgment, and to see things for what they are. But after witnessing what I have just seen in that other room, I would be a fool to do that. I have now seen her regard for you, her veritable awe of you. She would barely leave your side from the moment you came through the door. For all I know of it, you have most probably corrupted her to the point of worshiping you. What Gillian needs is to be with her family, without you around to influence her. Take my offer of the twenty thousand or not, but either way, you will be leaving this house today without Gillian."

"I am afraid that is impossible, my lord. You see, I made a promise to Gillian that I would not leave her here today if she did not wish it. It is a promise I have every intention of keeping."

The marquess grinned. It was a grin that knew supreme confidence. "Sorry to have to disappoint you, Morgan, but you have no choice in the matter. At this very moment Gillian is no longer even in the house. That carriage you just heard passing by the window, that was Gillian leaving. She is gone, so I see no further reason for you to remain in my house a moment longer."

A very real chill came over Dante at the marquess's words. He did not argue. He stood, walked to the door adjoining the study to the parlor, and threw it open. Just as Lord Adamley had said, Gillian wasn't there. Nobody was there. The room was empty.

"You are a bastard," Dante said, still staring out the door.

"Be that as it may, this is the way it will be."

Dante turned around. "Do you realize how much you are putting Gillian's health at risk? You may think you are protecting her from further harm, but in it you may cause her to lose her memory permanently. I hope you can live with that."

The marquess waved a hand at him. "Nonsense. I have checked with our physician, and I have been assured that all Gillian needs is peace and quiet and to be back among familiar surroundings and the people who love her. It is in the interest of Gillian's health that I am telling you now that after you leave here today, you will not attempt to communicate with her again. You will not see her. You will not speak to her. You will not even write a letter to her, for I have instructed Newport to destroy anything that comes bearing your mark. And if you do not adhere to my wishes, Morgan, scandal or not, I will have you brought up on charges of kidnapping. I will even add to that the charge of witchery, for you have most certainly worked some sort of spell on my daughter. Practicing witch-craft is nasty business in England these days, Morgan. The penalties for it aren't very pleasant either, so heed my word, or if it takes me to my dying day, I will see that His Majesty has you sent so far away from here you never come back."

Why had they come here?

It was that same question Gillian kept asking herself as she sat in the small antechamber at Madame Olga's shop, impatiently waiting to leave. Dorrie and Clare had convinced her to come along with them only be-cause they'd promised they wouldn't be long. They had assured her they would certainly be back at Adam-ley House before Dante had finished speaking with the marquess, her father.

But here they sat, fresh cups of jasmine tea now set before them. Dorrie had come after a gown she'd or-dered, at least that was what she'd said. It was taking quite a while.

While she waited, Gillian studied the faces of her sisters-in-law as they leafed through the pattern plates spread out on the dainty giltwood table before them. She searched every feature, trying to find the slightest hint of familiarity in the two. Dorrie was the picture of prettiness. Like Gillian, she was short and petite, with soft ash blond curls framing large eyes the color of bluebells, giving an image of kindness and warmth that her pregnancy only enhanced.

In contrast, Clare was tall, statuesque, with dark brown hair that was upswept and pulled back to best present her classical features. High patrician cheek-bones, a straight elegant nose, dark eyes that seemed able to look straight through a person and freeze them cold with their intensity. From the moment she'd met her, Gillian had gotten the impression that Clare wasn't all too fond of her as a sister-in-law. In fact, Gillian felt that Clare wasn't really fond of any of the family, and she seemed to hold her highest disdain for her husband, Reginald.

Clare looked up from the plates and her eyes locked on Gillian. Gillian looked quickly away.

"Gillian, dear, why don't you tell us what you did all that time while you were away, alone with Lord Morgan."

Gillian looked up, caught by the gleam in Clare's dark eyes. "There really isn't much to tell. After Dante found me in the road that night, he took me to his family seat, Wyldewoode, in Derbyshire. It's a most beautiful place with thick trees around it and mountains that reach into the clouds. And we weren't alone, not really. The staff at Wyldewoode is quite large, and Dante's friend, the Marchioness Seagrave, came to visit after a while. Lady Seagrave is a lovely and kind woman."

Clare smiled. It wasn't a genuine smile. Actually, it made Gillian feel even more uneasy. "Ah, yes, lovely, kind Cassia. Did you know she was accused of murdering her own father?"

"Clare!" Dorrie exclaimed, nearly choking on her tea. "You know Lady Seagrave was proven innocent of that charge years ago."

"Or so it was said, but then again, Cassia was friendly with King Charles. Most friendly. Who is to say he didn't conveniently arrange for that unfortunate duke to hang in her stead?"

Dorrie shook her head. "His Majesty would never knowingly execute a man unless he was certain of his guilt. And you seem to forget that Cassia is on close terms with Queen Catherine as well. She even helped to save Her Majesty's life when she became so ill that time a few years ago."

"Of course she did, Dorothea dear. It is rumored that Queen Catherine became ill from a poison in her tea. What better way to prevent oneself from becoming suspect than to help to heal the victim? And, too, what a doubly ingenious way to keep the queen from becoming suspicious of Cassia's relationship to the king?"

Gillian listened to all this with disbelieving ears. Murderess? Mistress to the king? Cassia had been so kind, so considerate. And she had appeared to love her husband, Rolfe, very much. She couldn't be all those terrible things Clare said. It all seemed impossible. It had to be.

"Was Lord Morgan kind to you as well?" Clare asked staring at Gillian.

"Oh, yes, very much so. He used to bring me tea with biscuits and jam from Mrs. Leeds's kitchen every morning. He wouldn't leave my bedside until I had eaten every thing on the plate."

Clare leaned forward. "He would sit at your beside, you say? So Lord Morgan came to see you while you were *en déshabillé*?"

Gillian looked at the two of them, knowing she'd just said something she shouldn't have. Both of them were poised at the edge of their seats, awaiting her reply.

"There never occurred anything improper, if that is what you're thinking. Dante just wanted to make certain I ate my breakfast so I could regain my strength. He was a perfect gentleman at all times."

"Certainly," said Clare.

"I think it would be wise if you didn't repeat that bit of information about your stay with Lord Morgan to your father, Gillian," Dorrie said. "What with the history between them, your father would be quite put out."

"History?"

Dorrie shook her head, trying to avoid the subject. "It is nothing you need to worry about. You were far too young to know what it was about."

"Oh, do go ahead and tell her, Dorothea," Clare

piped in. "Gillian should know everything there is to know about Dante Tremaine, her 'perfect gentleman.'"

"Really, Clare, it is all in the past, and I think we would be better served to—"

"Lord Morgan and I were once lovers," Clare announced, ignoring Dorrie's protests.

Gillian stared at her. From the look on Clare's face, she seemed almost proud of the statement.

"You were Dante's lover?"

"Yes, well, just so that you know the honest truth, he seduced me. It was five years ago. I was, like you, young and impressionable. Your brother and I were having a difficult time in our marriage. Reginald was spending more time at the gaming tables than he was with me. I was feeling unwanted, vulnerable, and Lord Morgan—Dante—knew this. He was most adept at seducing women. Ask anyone at Whitehall. He had made quite a name for himself doing just that. You know what they call him, do you not?"

Gillian frowned. "No, I do not."

"He is the Rakehell Earl, seducer of all women, committed to none. He knows exactly what to say. He told me he thought I was beautiful. He said he loved me, and I believed him. Only I didn't know until much later that he had told those same things to countless other women. And when I questioned him about it, he severed our relationship, but by then my reputation had been destroyed."

"Clare, that is enough," Dorrie said.

"I merely wanted to inform our dear Gillian about the truth of Dante Tremaine." She patted Gillian's hand. "Why else do you think he is known as the Rakehell Earl? He's made a career at court of seducing married women, ruining their names, their lives, and then discarding them like unwanted rubbish when he has no further use for them."

Gillian was confused. "But Dante told me he'd been

away from court, in France, and had only just returned to England after learning his mother had died."

"That much is true," Clare said, taking a sip of her tea. "I wouldn't suppose he told you the reason he was in France. Did he tell you that he was ordered there by His Majesty King Charles three years ago and was not allowed to return until now? And he only returned now because his mother died. The king couldn't very well prevent him from paying his respects.

"Do you know why Dante was sent to France in the first place? Because he finally went too far. He seduced one of the king's mistresses. A bold move, and a stupid one. The fact is, Gillian, Dante Tremaine is a blackguard and a rogue, and you should be glad your association with him ended as it did, for now that he has no further use for you, he will be gone from your life, as you will discover when we return to Adamley House and you see for yourself that he is gone."

"Dante will not leave me. He promised he wouldn't."

Clare laughed. "Promises mean nothing to him, Gillian. You will see."

Gillian didn't want to believe Clare, but she seemed so certain of what she was saying, and Dorrie certainly wasn't denying any of it either. Dante and Clare? Lovers? It couldn't be true. It had to be a mistake. But what about Phoebe's mother, Eliza? She had been married, and Dante himself had told her he'd done things, other things of which he was ashamed.

Still, there were two sides to every street, and one thing Gillian did know was that Dante was truthful. He said he'd always be honest with her. So she would simply ask him when they returned to Adamley House. He would be there. She knew he would. And even if what Clare said was true, even if she had had an assignation with Dante, it had been years ago, long before Gillian had ever met him. Dante wasn't the same man as he had been then. He had changed, and he would assure

Gillian of that once she returned to Adamley House. She didn't for one moment believe Dante wouldn't still be there waiting for her. He'd promised her he wouldn't leave her.

And Dante didn't lie.

It was true, all of it. Well, at least most of it. Gillian was faced with that reality when she returned to Adamley House with Dorrie and Clare a short time later.

The first indication of it was the absence of the Morgan coach on the street in front of the house. Clare hadn't wasted a moment in pointing that out to her when they rounded the street corner. She'd been watching for it and seemed most delighted to find the coach gone. Still, even then, Gillian had held fast to her belief in Dante's promise. Indeed, it was not until after her father had confirmed that he was gone, leaving, he'd said immediately after his meeting with him, that she had begun to consider that Dante wasn't coming back for her.

He had done what he'd said he wouldn't do. He had broken his promise to her.

Gillian spent an hour listening to her father as he accused Dante of every crime imaginable. He catalogued every despicable thing he knew about him, and Gillian couldn't help but think he was speaking of two different men. His Dante was ruthless and calculating, a debaucher, a rogue. Her Dante was honest and kind and giving. Her Dante had saved her life, and despite her father's words, despite the number of accusations, Gillian couldn't dispel the man she'd come to know. The man she now knew she loved.

Gillian left her father's study, feeling more confused and uncertain than ever. And she went straight to the one person she felt would tell her the truth.

"In all fairness, Gillian," Marcellus said to her from the other side of the cluttered desk in his study, a smaller, less resplendent version of her father's, "I have always held the private belief that Dante and Clare never did have any involvement."

Marcellus adjusted his spectacles on the bridge of his nose. Gillian wondered if he was uncomfortable discussing such matters with her. Yet he went on. "Still he is commonly known as the Rakehell Earl, a name that didn't just come about for nothing. The other things Clare told you, about Dante's other relationships with married women and the circumstances surrounding his being sent by King Charles to France, as far as I know, are all seemingly true."

Gillian was looking down at her hands, squeezing her fingers tightly together while trying desperately to make sense of it all. She just couldn't believe it. How could she have been so mistaken about him?

"Gillian, I must ask you something, and if hearing what I have to say will upset you, you do not have to answer me."

Gillian looked up at her brother.

"Did Lord Morgan ever do anything to you that he shouldn't have?"

She knew immediately what Marcellus meant. He wanted to know if Dante had seduced her as he believed he had the others. Gillian thought back to when Dante had kissed her, but his doing so hadn't ever seemed wrong or improper. Everything about their few kisses had felt so very right. Gillian decided not to mention it. "No. Dante was always a gentleman while I was with him, which is why I am having such a difficult time with what you have just told me."

Marcellus came around his desk and took Gillian's hands. He looked into her eyes. "You are most probably going to hear many unflattering things about Dante, from both within this house and without. That doesn't mean he is without virtue, Gillian. The truth is despite his short-comings, I have always found Dante Tremaine to be plain-spoken and foursquare, which is something I cannot say even about certain members of my own family. He has never tried to deny or disguise his faults, which is what led me in the first place to suspect Clare's accusations were false. Throughout the entire episode with Reginald and Clare, Dante would never admit to have taken Clare as his lover, and believe me, it would have been far easier for him had he done so. Reginald even challenged Dante to a duel. Dante is known for his skill with the rapier almost as much as his relationships with women. He could have easily run Reginald through and have been done with the whole mess, but even then he didn't."

"What did he do?"

"Dante walked away, even when Reginald publicly called him a coward. He also was the only one who could finally show Reginald the truth about Clare."

"The truth?"

Marcellus shook his head. "It is nothing you need to concern yourself over. Let me just say that the difficulties between Clare and Reginald go far deeper than any imagined liaison between Clare and Dante. Gillian, I want you to look at me. As a man who works with the law, I firmly believe in the presumption of innocence. As a Christian, I also believe in reform. I was in that room when Dante first came here to tell us he'd found you. While Father and Reginald and Archie were thundering at him, I listened to him. He was sincere in his concern for you. Dante seems a different man, and this is coming from someone who has known him many years. Perhaps he has changed since being away. Think of it this way. He had every opportunity to take advantage of you. He could have left you in the road, and you might have died. He could have had his way with you when he had you alone at his estate in Derbyshire. When he did learn who you were, he could have done any number of things to seek revenge on this family.

He didn't. He acted as I would, as any gentleman would, and because of that, I hope you will not judge him too harshly for his past."

Gillian smiled at Marcellus. "Thank you. I appreciate your honesty. It is very unnerving to lose one's memory and not know whom one can trust."

"You can always trust me, Gilly. One thing I will always give you is honesty." Marcellus stood. "Now, I have an appointment I must keep. I am sorry to have to leave you like this, but I must. If you have any other questions, I would be very glad to talk with you again later this evening. Would you like me to have Dorrie come sit with you a while?"

Gillian shook her head, knowing Dorrie had retired to her bedchamber as soon as they'd returned from Madame Olga's, her pregnancy making her exceedingly tired. "No, actually, I think I would prefer a little time to myself."

Marcellus smiled. "All right, I shall see you later then. And don't forget, tomorrow evening is the ball at the Palace."

"I'm sure it will be wonderful."

Gillian watched her brother go. How could she forget about the ball? It was all her father could talk about, once he'd dispensed with his attack on Dante's character, repeating the same things over and over, as if by doing so he could make her believe them.

The ball at the Palace was being held in honor of the death of the Protector, Oliver Cromwell, and with it, the end to his reign of terror. It was to be Gillian's informal return to society, after her fictitious sojourn to the country with her convalescing aunt. It would put to an end any question as to her whereabouts the past weeks. It would serve as protection against scandal. They must, after all, protect her reputation, or so her father had so earnestly said.

To Gillian it all seemed so ridiculous, putting on this

grand charade, when the truth was really quite simple. Nothing had happened that would damage this sterling reputation of hers. Gillian almost wished it had, just so there would be some credence to this nonsensical farce. But, her father, Marcellus, everyone had assured her these steps must be taken, that it was necessary, so Gillian had agreed to their plan. She found it odd, though, exceedingly odd, that they would put so much effort into this, her preservation, when they had scarcely bothered in looking for her while she'd been gone.

Gillian stood and walked over to the tall windows. She could see the street outside, the park across, the people milling busily about. Everything in her life was in such disorder. It seemed difficult to believe that only hours earlier she had first come to this place everybody assured her was her home, the one place where she should feel secure, where it was safe. She felt more frightened than she ever had.

Why had Dante left her here, especially after he'd promised to come back for her? Gillian didn't want to believe Clare when she'd said that Dante had just used her as he had so many others, and that he had now discarded her since she no longer held any purpose for him. Marcellus's depiction of Dante as the gentleman Gillian had believed him, albeit a bit tarnished, was certainly more appealing.

But there was one thing that Gillian couldn't deny. Dante had gone; he had left her there after promising he wouldn't, and, from all appearances, it looked as if he did not have any intention of coming back.

Chapter Nineteen

Dante watched his daughter as she entered the dining room with her usual swift gait and headed toward her place at the table. Until she noticed Gillian's vacant chair. Phoebe halted, looking straight from the chair to him.

"Where is Beatrice?"

Dante had been dreading this moment only second to the moment he'd left Adamley House without taking Gillian with him. He'd spent the past several hours telling himself what an idiot he'd been to have taken Gillian to Adamley House in the first place. He'd been even more of an idiot to have allowed them the chance to take her away. Why hadn't he listened to that niggling hesitation he'd felt when the marquess had asked him into the study? Why hadn't he refused to leave until they had returned her to him?

Dante already knew the answer. He had no right to Gillian. She wasn't his wife; nor would she ever be. He'd gone only because he knew the Forresters wouldn't bring Gillian back with him there. He'd had no idea where they'd taken her. Chaining himself to the marquess's study chair would have been senseless. She was gone, and now he must tell that same truth to his daughter.

Dante stood and walked over to Phoebe. "Beatrice is gone, Phoebe."

She didn't budge. "Where has she gone?"

How could he explain something he himself did not want to believe? How could he put it so she would understand? Dante needed Gillian there with him to explain to Phoebe in that way only she could, in words a child would understand, as she had when Phoebe had first come to them.

"Phoebe, do you remember how Beatrice explained to you why you had been sent to live with me?"

"She said that you were my real father, and that since my mother had died, I had come to live with you because that is where I belong."

Dante nodded. It had been the simplest and most obvious explanation. It actually made the most sense when one left out the truth of how Phoebe had been conceived. "Well, Beatrice has a mother and father and she even has brothers. She has been away from them because she forgot who she was."

"Because she can't find her mem'ry."

"That's right. But we know now who she is. I discovered what her true name is and where she came from."

Phoebe considered this. "Her name's not Beatrice?"

"No, it is not. Her name is Gillian. Gillian Forrester. Her father is the Marquess of Adamley."

Phoebe was silent a bit longer while she thought it out. "Like the other man? The one my mother was married to?"

Dante fell silent. Of everything she could have said, he hadn't expected that. "Gillian's father is a marquess like the man your mother was married to, yes."

"Is he mean to Gillian as the other man was to me? Maybe if he is, Gillian can still live with us."

Those words spoken in her tiny voice tore at Dante's heart. He took her hands, covering them with his own. "Phoebe, what did that man whom your mother was married to do to be mean to you? Did he ever strike you?"

Phoebe shook her head, biting her lower lip. "No. He used to call me names. He told me to stay away from him. He wouldn't let me talk about my mother." And then she added, "Miss Stoutwell hit me when I stuck out my tongue at her."

Dante pulled Phoebe to him, smoothing her dark curls down with his hand. "No one will ever strike you again, Phoebe. You have my promise of it."

Promise. The word stuck in his throat, reminding Dante of another such promise he'd made, a promise he hadn't been able to keep.

"Where is Gillian now?" Phoebe asked as she pulled away from him to look at him.

"She has gone back to her family, her real family. It is where she belongs. She will not be staying with us any longer."

Phoebe still stood in the same spot where she'd stopped upon noticing Gillian's absence at the table. The only difference now were the huge tears filling her dark eyes, streaming down her tiny cheeks. The pit that had formed in Dante's stomach at losing Gillian grew deeper at the sight of his daughter's tears.

"But I didn't tell her good-bye." She looked at him, her lower lip quivering. "I don't feel good, my lord."

Dante wiped the tears away with his thumb. "I know, Phoebe. I don't feel very good either."

Phoebe sniffed, rubbing her nose with her hand. Dante took his handkerchief from his pocket and held it to her nose. "Blow."

Phoebe did as he'd asked.

When Dante pulled the handkerchief away, Phoebe stared at him. "Are you sad, too, that Gillian is gone?"

"Yes, Phoebe, I am very sad."

"But you're not crying."

"That is because men do not cry."

"Never?"

Dante shook his head. "Hardly ever."

"Why not?"

Dante tried to pull her thoughts away from Gillian. "Men do not cry because it would wrinkle their neck cloths. Ladies don't wear neck cloths, so they must do all the crying for the men."

Phoebe looked at the floor, considering his explanation, and obviously found it a plausible one, for she shrugged and bit her lower lip again. Her tears had stopped. After a moment she looked at him again. "Who will have tea with me and Mrs. Fillywicket now?"

"Who is Mrs. Fillywicket?"

"She's my doll. Gillian helped me to name her."

Dante smiled, an image of Gillian sitting with Phoebe and her doll, sipping tea and exchanging female conversation, flitting through his mind. He stood and took Phoebe's hand, leading her toward her chair. "I'm going to hire a governess to come stay with us when we return to Wyldewoode. I will make one of the requirements of her position a daily tea party with you and Mrs. Fillywicket. You can help me decide who to hire if you would like, but that may take a little time, so, until then, perhaps I might join you and Mrs. Fillywicket for tea?"

"Where the devil have you been?"

Dante raised a shielding hand to his eyes against the glare of the sudden light coming through the door in the otherwise black room. The goblet of brandy he had poured upon coming there sat untouched atop the small side table. He didn't know the time. He didn't know how long he'd been there. Nor did he care.

The fire had died hours ago, not from lack of wood, for there was a small neat stack of it sitting in a scuttle alongside the hearth. The fire had died from lack of care. Dante had been sitting in that chair before the fire since just after sharing a somber meal with Phoebe, after which the Seagrave housekeeper, Mrs. Whitman, had taken Phoebe off to bed. It was a good thing she had, for if Dante had been forced to listen just once more to that same question Phoebe had repeated all through the meal, he'd have lost the meager hold he still had on his anger.

Why did Gillian have to go away?

Dante wasn't angry with Phoebe. He'd asked himself the same question countless times since that morning after he'd made the worst mistake of his life. He never should have left Gillian to go into the marquess's study, but his anger wasn't even directed at her family for their duplicitous success. He couldn't fault them for loving her; it was nigh impossible not to. No, his anger was directed at the one person who was responsible for the bad turn of events he now found himself faced with. His anger was directed at himself.

"Dante?" Rolfe said, coming into the room. Cassia stood at the door, holding high a burning branch of candles. "What is the matter? Have you taken ill?"

Dante finally moved, sitting upright from his comfortable unrefined slouch. His eyes were fixed on the floor. "No, Rolfe, I am not ill."

"We expected you at eight o'clock at Mara and Hadrian's. Did you forget we were supping there tonight? They were anxious to meet Gillian. Mara was very worried when you didn't come." Rolfe hesitated a moment, then said, "Has something happened to Gillian? Is she feeling out of sorts?"

If only it could be something so simple. "No, when last I saw her, Gillian was the very picture of health."

"What do you mean, when last you saw her? Dante, where is Gillian?"

Dante looked at his friend. "They took her, Rolfe. Gillian's family has her, and as for any further association with me, well, they have made their feelings on that end perfectly clear. The Rakehell Earl of Morgan is not considered acceptable company for Lady Gillian Forrester."

Cassia came into the room. "Tell us what happened."

Dante began relating the tale of his well-intentioned visit to Adamley House; yes, visit, for that was precisely what it should have been. It was to be the first of however many encounters it would take for Gillian to become acquainted with her family, until she felt comfortable with them. He described to Rolfe and Cassia how Gillian had been reintroduced to each family member, how she had shown no outward sign of having recognized any of them. He finished with his meeting in the marquess's study, where his offer of marriage was flatly refused and he was told to leave.

"What did you do?" Rolfe asked, having now taken a seat in the opposite chair.

"I left."

"You what?" Rolfe reached for the brandy glass and took a long draw.

"After I asked the bloody marquess for Gillian's hand, he told me he would rather fill an early grave than see his daughter wed to me, after which he accused me of seeking to buy respectability. That was never my intention, but I suppose, judging from my past association with the Forresters, I can understand his reasons for it. The marquess then ordered me out of his house. He said they would keep Gillian wherever they had taken her to until I left, that it would do me little good to fight."

"What did you do?" Cassia asked.

"As I said, I left. What more could I do? I had no choice. They had taken Gillian God knows where, anywhere just to get her away from me. I couldn't very well root myself to the chair and demand her back, especially with Lord Adamley threatening to have me thrown in the Tower for kidnapping and practicing witchcraft." He paused. "And, oh, yes, we're not to tell anyone the truth about where Gillian has been in the past weeks. He thought she might have been kidnapped by some political enemy of his, and he never said anything about it to the authorities, fearing it was what these supposed enemies would want. He was hoping for a ransom, which he would pay. His belief is that everyone has a price. Bloody hell, he even tried to buy me off."

"So what does he plan to do now?"

"Lord Adamley has explained away Gillian's sudden absence as a sojourn to visit a sick aunt in the country, so that her reputation will not suffer the consequences of being linked to me. He has promised, though, if I were to tell anyone the truth, especially that she was with me, he would have me arrested for her abduction, knowing that with my standing at the Palace still on the lower end of His Majesty's favor, the word of the Marquess of Adamley would most certainly be believed over that of the Rakehell Earl."

Rolfe was silent for several minutes. Finally, he looked at Dante. "In all this arguing over where Gillian really belongs, everyone seems to have overlooked one thing."

"Which is?"

"Someone obviously did kidnap Gillian, and that someone is still out there, free to do the same, or perhaps even something worse."

Dante frowned. "I've already thought of that and have begun looking into it. I believe Gillian is probably safer there at Adamley House than anywhere else. They will keep her under watch, only instead of the true culprit, they will be trying to keep her safe from me."

Rolfe nodded. "So what are you going to do now?"

"What the devil can I do? I'm caught. By now Gillian's family has most certainly filled her head with every detail, true and imagined, from my past. No doubt Clare headed off that particular task rather enthusiastically with Reggie more than willing to assist. Gillian probably thinks herself well rid of me by now. And, having thought about it for the past several hours, I've come to the conclusion they are most probably right in that particular opinion. I am the Rakehell Earl of Morgan, ruiner of women and overall defiler, aren't I? I made myself the name, and now I must live with its rewards. It wouldn't do well to burden Gillian with a legend of that proportion."

Cassia closed her eyes as tears started to spill down her cheeks. Her own past came vividly to mind. She knew well what society's perception of a person could do. She had faced the same rejection, the same ostracism at court, when her father had been killed and all the evidence had pointed to her as his murderess. It mattered naught if she had committed the crime. The people of polite society had judged her far more quickly than any court of law.

Her own reaction at that time had been much the same as Dante's now. She had secluded herself rather than face the accusing looks, and had even begun to question her own morality, wondering if, perhaps, everybody was right in their opinion of her. If one is told something often enough, one begins to believe it— until Rolfe came into her life, helping her to prove her innocence and giving her back her belief in herself.

Bless him his fortitude, Cassia thought, looking at her husband in the low candlelight. It hadn't been any easy task to undertake. Self-reproach was a characteristic that was deeply rooted. Cassia had recognized the beginnings of it in Dante when last they'd seen him in France the year before. Where he'd always held a glancing devil-may-care approach to life, he'd changed somehow into a solemn, unhappy shell of himself. Gone was the laughing light from his eyes. Instead, his expression had been shadowed by the toll that his past life had taken on him.

Cassia had expressed her concern for Dante to Rolfe during the journey back to England, but he had assured her his friend was simply homesick.

"He'll snap out of it," Rolfe had said, but when her correspondence to Dante, which had before been regular in its response, started going off unanswered, and reports coming back to her from friends in France described Dante as more remote than before, Cassia had grown more than concerned. She'd actually become frightened for him.

It was that same fear that had spurred her to traveling to Wyldewoode upon Dante's return to England. It was that same fear that evolved into delight when she saw the Dante that awaited her there.

The change had been noticeable the instant Cassia had seen him. The light had returned to his eyes. The grin had brought out those devilish dimples again, and it could only be ascribed to one person. Like an angel, Gillian had appeared, chasing off the demons that had filled Dante's world, presenting him with his chance at love, a love like the one that bound Rolfe to Cassia.

And now, Gillian was gone, and with her, Dante's last chance.

Unless . . .

Chapter Twenty

"Lady Gillian, there is someone at the door, asking to see you."

Gillian sat up in her chair, setting the book she'd been reading to the side. "Is it Lord Morgan, Newport?"

The expression on the butler's face darkened the moment she mentioned Dante's name. It was a reaction Gillian was growing accustomed to, for any time she mentioned Dante's name, whoever was with her at the time immediately did the same.

"No, Lady Gillian, it is not Lord Morgan. Your visitors are two ladies. The Marchionesses Seagrave and Kulhaven respectively."

It was Cassia, and she'd brought someone with her. "You may show them here to the parlor, Newport. And please arrange for tea and cakes for our guests."

Cassia's visit was an unexpected and a welcome one. Gillian was anxious to see a familiar face among so many unfamiliar ones. Despite what had happened, she still thought of Cassia as a friend. Gillian hoped she had brought Phoebe with her, for she missed the little girl terribly.

As she waited for Newport to return, Clare's words about Cassia unwittingly came to mind, how she had been accused of murdering her father, and her relationship with the king. Gillian had discounted them, along with Clare's remarks about Dante, that same day Marcellus had spoken with her.

"Gillian?"

Cassia's expression was hesitant until she saw Gillian's responding smile.

"Cassia, it is so good to see you."

Cassia entered the room and embraced Gillian, kissing her on the cheek. "I have been so worried about you my dear." She stepped back, but did not immediately leave go of Gillian's hands.

"I am fine, really. A little lonely, perhaps, but I read a lot and play my music. And no one here entirely leaves me alone. I think they are afraid I might just vanish again." Gillian noticed Cassia's companion, a striking woman with beautiful red hair. She smiled at her. "Hello."

Cassia turned. "Gillian, I wanted you to meet a very good friend of mine. This is Mara Ross, Marchioness of Kulhaven."

"You are married to Dante's friend, Hadrian Ross."

"Yes, I am."

"And you live in Ireland."

"Correct again." The woman extended her hand. "It is wonderful to meet you, Lady Gillian. Cassia has told me all about you."

"Please, just call me Gillian. I get confused enough having to remember that it is my name without having to remember proper address of it."

"And please call me Mara. I do not stand on formality either."

"Mara has just arrived from Ireland with her husband, Hadrian, and their four children," Cassia said. "Actually, you should consider yourself privileged. You are one of the few people on this earth who have seen Mara at a time when she wasn't currently increasing."

Mara slanted her friend a glance. "You are truly amusing, Cassia."

"When I met Mara, she was expecting her most recent child, which ended up being a matched set."

"Twins?"

Mara nodded. "I couldn't understand why I was so much larger with that pregnancy than the others. Hadrian told me it was my imagination. I realize now he was just trying to be kind. There is an old wise woman named Sabdh in the village near my home in Ireland who had predicted that I would be blessed with more happiness than I had ever known. She'd had a dream that I would have twins, but wanted it to be a surprise for me when they were born. And a surprise it definitely was."

Cassia broke in. "Hadrian is a big man, a veritable Goliath, and he was a soldier, so he lives a very regimented existence, at least he did before Mara entered his life. They were on a ship making the crossing to Dublin when Mara began to labor. It was in the midst of a terrible storm and the ship was tossing about so that they couldn't dock safely. They were forced to ride it out, during which Hadrian himself delivered Mara of the twins."

Mara smiled. "My maid, Cyma, who usually helps me to deliver, was bedridden with seasickness and couldn't so much as lift her head without losing whatever food she had managed to eat that day. So my husband and I were left to our own devices. It was amazing, really, for despite all his strength and stoic male reserve, Hadrian wept when those children were born."

"What are their names?" Gillian asked.

"Robert is my oldest son, then my oldest daughter, Dana, followed by the twins, two boys, the first named for his father and other named Morgan, which although it is Dante's peerage title, also means 'sea warrior' in

Gaelic. Fitting names, given the circumstances of their birth." Mara smiled and added, "We call young Hadrian 'Hayden' because when he was born, my daughter, Dana, who became instantly attached to him as if she was his mother and not I, couldn't say Hadrian. Hayden was the best she could do at the time, so Hayden it is."

Gillian smiled. "I should like to meet them all someday."

"You should be careful what you wish for," Mara said. "Cassia said that very thing once, and now, when we're together, my little demons won't allow her a moment's peace."

"I wouldn't mind, not at all. My brother Marcellus has four children with another one expected very soon."

Gillian walked with Cassia and Mara toward a pair of settees near the chair where she'd been reading. They were situated in front of the tall windows in the morning parlor which at that moment was filled with bright sunlight, the flowers from the gardens giving off a delightful sweet scent that drifted in with the summer breeze through the open windows. The room had reminded Gillian of the solar at Wyldewoode, and Gillian found herself spending a good deal of time here reading and thinking.

Newport appeared at the door, carrying a tea tray which he set on the boulle marquetry table. Gillian poured three cups of tea, arranging a tiny iced cake on the edge of each saucer before handing one each to Cassia and Mara.

It was quiet for several moments after Newport had quit the room. Finally, Gillian spoke.

"How is Phoebe?"

Cassia set her tea aside. "She is well enough, I guess." She paused. "She is confused. She acts so grown up, it is easy to forget she is still a child. Her little life has been filled with such disappointments. She misses you very much."

"And I miss her. I imagine she has a number of questions about why I disappeared without saying good-bye. Perhaps, next time you come for a visit, you might bring her along?"

"Of course. I would have brought her this time except I wasn't certain how things would be." Cassia looked at Gillian. "How are you really, Gillian?"

"Quite frankly, I feel like a stranger in a house I am supposed to have grown up in. I mean it is obvious I truly am Gillian Forrester. The gowns in my bedchamber fit me, and there is even a portrait of me hanging in the upstairs hallway. Everyone tells me things I have done through my life, but I just do not feel any connection to anything here. It is confusing and frightening, not knowing anything or anybody."

"But you know me, and Phoebe, and"—Cassia paused, testing the waters a bit—"you know Dante."

"I thought I knew Dante." Gillian looked away. "I'm not so confident of that any longer."

Cassia realized her worst fears. Gillian's family had obviously wasted little time in telling her about Dante's past, their version of it. Now to try to undo the damage. "You've been told things about him, haven't you?"

Gillian looked at her. "Are you going to tell me none of it is true?"

"I couldn't possibly do that, not at least until I know what you have been told. I promise you this, though, I will be honest with you to the best of my knowledge. You have a right to know the truth, favorable or not."

"Thank you." Gillian set her cup of tea to the side with a relieved smile. "I have been told that Dante has had many illicit assignations with women, married women, even one which involved my sister-in-law Clare."

Cassia took a deep breath before beginning. "I told you I would be honest. Yes, Gillian, Dante has had assignations with married women. You would be hard pressed to find a man among society who has not, especially when our own sovereign practices the same habits. Still, I would wager my favorite pair of dancing shoes that in Dante's case, it hasn't been quite as many as you have been told. As for Clare, I can state without hesitation that Dante never became involved with her."

"How do you know?"

"Because I asked him, and Dante has never lied to me. He has no reason to. You see, he and I have something in common. We have both been victims of our pasts, and have become social outcasts because of it."

Gillian looked at her. "You speak of your father's death."

Cassia had not expected Gillian to question her about the specifics of her past. It came as somewhat of a surprise that she was even aware of it. It had been a long time since anyone had asked her about her father's murder, a long time since she'd had to defend herself against the charges that she had killed him, a long time since she'd had to face the terrible memories.

After her innocence had been proven and the guilty person had been punished for the crime, Cassia and Rolfe had left London and the court, preferring a quieter life in the Sussex countryside. There, among the peaceful summer breezes and the secluded hinterland, Cassia had nearly forgotten that part of her life had ever existed. She should have realized that others would not be so willing to forget.

"My father was an abusive man, Gillian. The marriage of my parents had been arranged for financial reasons and was not by any means an amicable one. My mother tried to punish my father for his abuse of her by creating scandal. She carried on, openly, with other men, which resulted in her giving birth to an illegitimate child. My mother and the child died in childbirth. The enormity of the scandal drove my father to the bottle, which drove him to even more abusive ends. I was the only one left in his life, so naturally I became the recipient of his abuse. I never told anyone of it because I was too ashamed. I blamed myself instead. The night my father was murdered, he had beaten me unconscious. He was dead when I came to, and since I was the only one in the room with him, it was generally believed that I had killed him. You see, society assumed I had killed my father because they didn't truly know me. That was partly my fault, though, because I had never allowed anyone to really know me, the person I truly was."

Gillian frowned. "Why?"

"Because if they had known me, if they had truly known me, they would have known of my father's abuse, and that was simply too shameful to bear. It was far easier for me to hide behind a different persona. No doubt whoever told you about my father's murder also told you I was one of the king's mistresses?"

"Yes, but I was also told by someone else that it was naught but rumor."

"And indeed it was a rumor, a rumor that I initiated myself."

Gillian looked at her, confused.

"I found a certain protection in being thought of as the king's paramour," Cassia explained. "It was all part of a disguise I put on to hide the person I really was."

Gillian looked at her. "I am so sorry, Cassia. I didn't know. I wasn't told . . . "

"It is all right, Gillian. I have overcome that part of my life. In doing so, I also discovered who I really was. I learned I wasn't so terrible a person as I had made myself believe. I learned this because Rolfe showed it to me. I shudder to think what my life would be like now if Rolfe hadn't come into it when he did."

"It all has to do with perception," Mara said, breaking into the conversation. "Do you know that when I first met my husband, I hated him? I believed he had been responsible for the deaths of my family. You see, I am Irish. My mother had been killed when the Protectorate confiscated my family's lands. My brothers were killed in the fighting. My father was locked away in prison when he attempted to protest the loss of his property. He died before he was ever heard. Because of this, I hated everything English." She smiled. "My husband, Hadrian, is English. I had heard horrible stories depicting him as violent and cruel. When I learned he had been given my family's lands, I decided to avenge my family."

"But I thought you said you hated him. Why would you marry him?"

"That, my dear, is a long story, and one I'll tell you another time. Suffice it to say I did hate him. It was not until after I married him that I began to see for myself that he was not the horrible person I had been told."

Gillian considered this. "I was also told that Dante spent the past three years in France because King Charles ordered him to leave the country for an assignation he had with the king's mistress, Frances Stuart."

"That is true, although I don't know if the word 'assignation' would be entirely appropriate. Dante's connection to the woman was purely platonic. Frances was a young court beauty who had caught King Charles's eye and she wasn't the King's mistress. Again, everyone assumed she was. King Charles was attracted to her, but Frances did not return the king's affections, a tenuous position for any woman at court. She was having increasing difficulty in sidestepping the king's advances. She had come to Dante with a plea. You see, Frances was in love, and she applied to Dante for assistance in escaping Whitehall to elope with her true love, the Duke of Richmond. It was an odd match; the duke was nearly twice her age and had only just buried his first wife a few weeks earlier. Still, Dante agreed to help. He helped Frances to slip from the Palace late one night, escorting her to London Bridge, where her eager bridegroom awaited to whisk her away. Do you remember when I mentioned Lady Castlemaine the first day I met you?"

"You had said she was responsible for sending Dante to France."

"Yes, you see she informed King Charles of Dante's involvement in Frances's elopement. The king was furious. Frances and her bridegroom were banished from court, although it is rumored they will soon return. Dante was sent into unofficial exile in France."

Gillian's eyes were wide with disbelief. "It sounds vastly unfair. Dante had acted honorably, and for it he was punished severely."

"You can now see how rumors grow into full-fledged falsehoods."

"So you are saying I should not believe what my family says about Dante?"

Cassia shook her head. "Not at all. What I am saying is that you should trust in your own judgment before relying on that of others. Gillian, you saw a side to Dante different from that which other people know. You saw a side he hasn't shown anyone else. Rely on that when making your judgment of Dante. And if all else fails, you should consider just asking Dante yourself."

Newport came back into the room, carrying a silver salver. "Your day's correspondence, Lady Gillian."

Gillian took the small pile of letters. She waited until he'd gone, then shook her head. "I can't be left to my own for more than a half hour without someone coming in on some trivial errand. Newport could have left these in the hall. There really was no need for him to interrupt our visit with them other than to make certain you two hadn't carried me off."

Cassia smiled. "They are just concerned for you, Gillian."

"I would that they had been so concerned when I was gone." She shook her head. "I swear sometimes the walls have ears and eyes as well in this house. I cannot even read a book in peace." She showed them the letters Newport had brought in. "What's even worse is I receive letters from people I don't even remember. Friends, relatives, and even suitors like this one." She held up a folded and sealed parchment. "Another letter from Garrick Fitzwilliam, no doubt expressing his great fondness for me. I have no idea who he is. I don't know who any of these people are. There are people writing to me all the way from Scotland and I—"

Scotland.

Darkness, fear, and a strange peppery smell suddenly overcame Gillian. She was no longer sitting in the morning parlor, having tea with Cassia and Mara. She was in a carriage and her hands and feet were tied in front of her.

I told him to take the back alleys and byways to the east, in case we're seen leaving by anyone, then split off at the cross to the North Road and onward to Scotland.

"Gillian, are you all right?"

When Gillian opened her eyes, Cassia was kneeling before her, looking into her eyes, her own filled with frightened concern. "What happened? You looked as if you might faint."

"I heard something in my head. It was someone speaking about Scotland. I think it might have been the

person who kidnapped me, Cassia. He said he was going to take me to Scotland, by way of the North Road."

"Can you remember his name? What he looked like?
Do you know who he was?"

Gillian concentrated hard. She closed her eyes.
Nothing. She shook her head. "It was just here, in my
head, and now it is gone."

"It is all right," Cassia said. "At least you are starting to remember something. That is a good sign. I'm
certain very soon it will all come back to you. And
when it does, you can tell everyone the truth."

Standing outside in the garden, Clare turned from
her place near the window. She had been walking by,
on her way to search for Alec, when she had heard
Gillian inside talking. She had stopped, of course,
when she had heard the mention of Dante's name. It
hadn't taken her long to figure out to whom Gillian
was talking.

Cassia Brodrigan and Mara Ross. The noble marchionesses. Clare could still remember the day she had
first seen the two of them at Whitehall. Everyone had
whispered about them, fascinating things, but to Clare
they were really nothing more than a murderess and an
Irish upstart who'd wed themselves into respectability.
And now she had listened to them filling Gillian's head
with that drivel about what an honest and honorable
man Dante Tremaine was.

The misunderstood Earl of Morgan.

If it hadn't been for Dante, and what he had done to
her five years earlier, she would be happily widowed
by now.

Clare had chosen Dante on that long-ago day with
careful consideration. He was a man with a legendary
reputation that knew no bounds. No one would have
thought to dispute her allegations of an affair between
them, despite the fact that he'd refused one in truth.
Damnable fool. Dante's history with the sword was

legendary. Reginald would have had no choice but to call him out, and Dante would have had no choice but to face him off and ultimately run him through.

It had been a brilliant plan, except that Dante was so damnably honest, too honest to face Reginald in a duel based on a falsehood.

Dante was the root of Clare's failure then, and he could very well be the root of her failure now, for it was he who had brought Gillian back home. Why couldn't he have simply left her where he'd found her, where that idiot, Garrick, had lost her?

Clare had nearly fainted when Reginald told her Gillian had been found alive. She had managed to keep her senses about her long enough to learn that Gillian had no memory. And if she had no memory of who she was, she certainly had no memory of her kidnapping or of anything else for that matter. She knew nothing of her life before, thus she no longer posed a threat to Clare's plans. But for how long?

Garrick had assured her he would take the situation in hand, but he failed to realize that if Gillian was starting to remember as it now seemed she was, then she might remember who had kidnapped her. She might also remember other things, things she should never had stuck her nose into in the first place. She might remember what she had found that day before she'd disappeared. She might ask the same questions she had then. She might begin to fit the pieces together. And if she did, then all would be hopelessly lost.

Clare started for the door leading into the house. She walked slowly up the stairs to her chamber, thinking as she went, this wouldn't do at all.

Something would have to be done about Gillian.

Chapter Twenty-one

Garrick followed Clare from the overcrowded taproom of the Slaughtered Lamb Tavern into the small side chamber that served as storage. Wine casks were stacked against one wall, and smoked hams dangled from hooks set in the low, cobweb-strung ceiling. The sour smell of old ale hung heavily in the air.

Admittedly, it was a far cry from their last meeting place, stretched among the soft pillows of a bed, the air filled with the scent of their coupling. Clare seemed agitated, urgent almost when she'd arrived unexpectedly, tapping Garrick on his shoulder as he sat playing at piquet. He wondered how she'd known he would be there. Even more, he wondered what had brought her.

"You take a great chance in coming for me here."

"Yes, well desperate measures incite desperate acts." Clare latched the door, then turned to face him. Her lips, colored red with Spanish wool, were pressed in a thin frown.

"You must do something about Gillian."

Garrick leaned disinterestedly against a cask. "Me? What would I need to do about poor Gillian? She doesn't even know who I am, except some idiot swain who writes insipid tributes to her eyelashes. Bloody hell, she doesn't even know who *she* is for that matter."

Clare glared at him. He could see the angry glint in her eyes despite the small amount of light given off by the single candle lighting the space they occupied.

"You won't be so glib, Garrick, when I tell you that poor Gillian is beginning to regain her memory."

He stood aright. "Completely?"

"No, not completely. Not yet, at least. She hasn't confirmed that she is who everyone says she is, although I heard her say earlier today that she did think whoever had kidnapped her had planned on taking her to Scotland."

"Bloody hell!" Garrick turned and slammed his fist into the cask. The wood splintered. A small trail of wine, the color of blood, began trickling down its side, dribbling to form a pool on the dirt floor. "I thought you had assured me you had the situation well in hand, Clare. You were supposed to convince her that Morgan had been her abductor."

"Yes, well, obviously, despite her muddled memory, Gillian's wits are still as sharp as a sword point. She seems to have put aside everything I told her about Morgan. She still believes him to be some sort of hero straight out of one of those ridiculous French romances she reads. It would appear he outdid himself in charming her. No doubt he realized the fifty thousand she'd bring him. Morgan is no fool. He knows a ripe opportunity when he . . . "

Garrick barely heard her. He was already formulating a plan, a plan to rid himself of any involvement in Gillian's abduction whatsoever. He had been a fool to allow Gillian to have seen him in the coach that night. He'd never considered that she would escape. He had underestimated her, a mistake he wasn't about to repeat.

"What are you thinking?" Clare asked, eying him suspiciously.

"I was simply trying to come up with a solution to our problem."

"Well, I think I have a way to—"

"No, Clare. Your plans have thus far brought us

nothing but trouble. Because of you, I now find myself center stage in a production in which I was supposed to play a supporting role. Because of it, we are now both faced with the very real possibility that Gillian will regain her memory. She will recall that I am the one who kidnapped her. She will recall everything, Clare. Everything."

"Gillian is far too meddlesome for her own good. She always has been. Do you know that when she was eight years old she tried to sabotage my wedding to Reginald? She said she'd had a dream that his life would be very unhappy, so she set a greased and squealing pig loose in the church in the midst of the ceremony. It took six grown men a full hour to catch it, and not before it caused half the women there to swoon."

Garrick had to smile at the image that presented itself. "Sounds as if Gillian is far more perceptive than she is meddlesome."

"Don't you go off getting all moon-eyed over her now. That perceptiveness of Gillian's could lead you straight to a cell in Newgate when she remembers it was you who abducted her."

"Then we will simply have to make certain that Gillian doesn't remember my role in her abduction. Ever."

"And how do you propose we manage that? Seeing your face again may be the deciding factor in the return of her memory. If she does that, then we are both doomed. You certainly cannot wear a mask wherever you go."

A mask. A thought came to Garrick.

He looked at Clare. "Just leave Gillian to me."

"And what will you do?"

Garrick smiled at her in the candlelight. The return gleam in her eyes told him she already knew what he was going to say. It was the only solution they had left.

"We are left with little choice in the matter, Clare. I'm afraid we must kill Gillian."

Cassia's note arrived early the morning after her visit to Adamley House.

> Come to the swan's pond in the
> Spring Gardens at one o'clock.
> Phoebe would like to see you.

Gillian folded the note and tucked it inside the pocket attached to her gown. The Spring Gardens. She had no clue as to where, or even what they were. She only knew that she had to get there and by one o'clock so she could see Phoebe.

First she questioned Newport and discovered that the Spring Gardens were a leisure spot where one could walk among trees or watch the wildlife. It was where courtiers would often repair to escape the rigors of the Palace, where wandering minstrels performed dulcet ballads for everyone to enjoy.

Now, how to get there. Gillian sat down to devise a plan. How could she possibly slip away without anyone noticing? She couldn't so much as relieve herself without someone attempting to follow her to the chamber pot. While they tried not to be so obvious about it, Gillian would have to be blind not to notice that every person in the house was keeping close watch on her. She didn't know if their efforts were due to their fear that she might vanish again, or that she might somehow attempt to see Dante. She wasn't at all certain she wanted to know.

Gillian read the note again and thought of Phoebe. She felt so guilty at having left her without explaining the reasons. Phoebe had been through so much. Losing her mother had been terrible enough; but then to be uprooted and sent away from everything she had known?

No, she had to see Phoebe. She had to find some way to get to the Spring Gardens without anyone, especially the eagle-eyed Newport, knowing the better of it.

It was that moment which Dorrie chose to come into the room.

"Oh, Gillian, I didn't know you were here. I hope I didn't disturb you."

Gillian glanced at the case clock on the wall. An hour earlier, Newport had come asking if she'd like tea. The hour before that, one of the maids had come in on the pretense of dusting. She'd made short order of her task, leaving the writing table and most of the shelves untouched. And now there was Dorrie. At least they were a punctual lot.

Gillian smiled at her sister-in-law. "Was there something you needed?"

"Yes, I'm trying to find a book to read to the children." Dorrie came forward. "They are dreadfully bored."

Gillian watched as Dorrie peered at the shelves that lined the library walls. She was certainly making a good show of searching for a title, Gillian thought, waiting as Dorrie removed a book from the shelf and made to leave. A thought suddenly occurred to her.

"Dorrie, how would you like to take the children to the Spring Gardens for a picnic today? I overheard Reginald talking about the Gardens to Archie earlier this morning. They sound delightful, what with the trees and the swan's pond he spoke of. The sun is out, and it looks to be a lovely day. The children could run and play away their boredom, and we could read them the book there. It would be great fun, and I would so love an outing."

Dorrie looked at once agreeable to the suggestion, before the shadow of doubt began to fall. "It is a wonderful thought, Gillian, but I'm not so certain it is a good idea what with . . . "

Gillian had expected her misgivings. She had learned since her return that Dorrie seemed to prefer floating along whatever course was laid for her. She wasn't one to cause disturbances, nor did she ever seem eager to voice her opinion. Taking the children with Gillian to the Spring Gardens? To make such a decision on her own would be alien to Dorrie, but she really had little choice. Everyone else had gone out early that morning. Marcellus had left immediately after breakfast for his office. Reginald and Archie had gone with their father to Whitehall. Her mother had gone to the market stalls with the cook, and Clare, well no one ever seemed to know precisely where Clare went. Regardless, with the exception of the servants, that had left only Dorrie and the children at home with Gillian.

"Oh, come now, Dorrie," Gillian said, "you and the children have been holed up in this house too long. Think of it as an adventure for them. And for me as well. You just said the children were bored. Just think of how much they would enjoy an outing. I can have one of the kitchen maids pack us a basket of food, and we'll take along Marie-Therese to help with the children."

Dorrie thought a moment longer, then finally she nodded. "All right, as long as we return by four o'clock. That is when most everyone else is expected back to the house. Your father keeps a spare watch in his top desk drawer. I'll round up the children and help Marie-Therese to ready them while you arrange for the basket and fetch the watch."

Gillian wanted to shout, but managed to maintain a reserved expression as she went off to the kitchens to make her request for the food basket before hurrying off to the marquess's study.

They were off a half hour later in the Adamley coach, all eight of them, Dorrie, Gillian, Marie-Therese and the children, Dorrie's four and Reginald's son, Alec.

"Johnny," Dorrie called as they passed through the entrance gate and started walking along one of the main promenades, "I want you to stay close by us at all times. I don't want you to get lost on one of these pathways. They wind on and on to nowhere."

Johnny and Alec, followed closely after by Anna and Samuel, bounded along the graveled walkway, snapping twigs from the flowering bushes while paying their mother precious little heed. Dorrie shook her head, eyes fixed protectively to the four of them.

"This looks a pleasant enough spot," Gillian said as they came to a small stand of apple trees. She had chosen a position not far from the entrance and just off the main walkway. It would be easy to find again after she met Cassia and Phoebe.

Gillian wasn't sure where in the park the swan's pond was, but she decided she would ask someone once she slipped away from Dorrie and the children. Now, how to slip away?

Gillian removed her father's watch from her pocket. It was a quarter hour before one o'clock.

"Shall we eat first?" Dorrie asked.

"I would think it better to wait a little while." Gillian looked to where the older children were climbing on the low hanging branches of an elm. "They are much too excited to sit down for a meal just now, wouldn't you agree? And Lizzy is dozing there with Marie-Therese. Let's give them a bit to run and play, then we'll eat our lunch and go back home."

"That sounds like a good idea," Dorrie said. She smiled as she sat down on the blanket they'd spread out. "Thank you, Gillian, for suggesting the outing. I think it is just what the children needed, and it will give you a chance to get reacquainted with them."

Dorrie was quiet for a few minutes, watching the children play. She was leaning against a tree, and several pillows they'd brought were propped against her back. One hand rested negligently on her rounded belly. For a moment, Gillian thought she was dozing off, until she spoke again. "Gillian, is it terribly frightening, losing your memory?"

"It is more disconcerting than frightening really, only because I hold the belief that I will regain my memory in time. If I didn't have that belief, I'd surely expire from the fear. It is odd, though, losing your memory, especially when you know you've been a part of a family all your life, but you don't really remember anybody in it."

Dorrie nodded and looked back to where the children were playing. She pulled forward from the pillows. "Oh, my goodness, Gillian. Johnny is gone. I don't see him anywhere. Anna," she called out, "where is Johnny?"

The little girl stopped what she was doing and turned about at the desperate tone in her mother's voice. "I dunno."

Dorrie tried to get up, but her pregnancy impeded her. "I've got to find him before he gets lost."

"Stay here with the others," Gillian said. "I'll go and find him. We only just arrived. He can't have gone too far."

Gillian walked over to the other children. "Where did you last see Johnny?"

"He was watching a rabbit over by those bushes," Alec said, pointing.

Gillian headed off. She passed beyond the bushes and found herself on a secluded pathway. Johnny was nowhere in sight. She spotted an opening near the ground beneath where some trees had fallen. The earth around the opening was freshly dug out, making it to just the size of a small child.

"Johnny?" she called in a rough whisper. "Johnny, are you there?"

Silence, and then a moment later, she heard the rustling of leaves.

"Johnny, this isn't the time to play tricks. Come out from there at once before you frighten your poor mama."

A small face, brushed with dirt on the nose and cheeks, emerged from the cubbyhole. "You scared the rabbit away."

"And you scared your mother something terrible." Gillian frowned at him. "Come out of there."

Johnny crawled out slowly. His suit of clothes was sadly soiled, and he'd torn the fabric of his breeches at his left knee. In addition he was missing a shoe.

"Your mama is not going to be very pleased when she sees what you've done here," Gillian said. "Go on back to her now."

"But I lost my shoe somewhere in there."

"I will fetch it," she said. "Go now, before your mother becomes worried."

Gillian watched as Johnny ran back along the pathway. When she was certain he'd gone, she crouched down and looked inside his makeshift hiding place. Much as she'd expected, a small shoe was wedged between the ground and the fallen tree trunk. She worked it free, then stood to leave. She didn't head back toward the picnic sight. Instead, she continued along the pathway in the opposite direction.

As she rounded a curve, she spotted a man peering at a bird in a tree through a perspective glass. "Excuse me, sir. Do you know where the swan's pond is?"

"Aye," he said, never taking his eye from the glass, "you go down this pathway to its end. There's a turn, and then you'll find it. Have a care though, miss, 'tis easy to lose your way there."

Gillian thanked him and went on her way.

She was walking along the fringes of the pond when she first spotted Phoebe standing a few yards ahead.

"Phoebe!"

Gillian crouched down, hugging her tightly as the little girl came running into her arms. She set her back a space, looking at her. "I've missed you."

"Me, too." Phoebe peered at her. "Why did you go away?"

Gillian took Phoebe's hand and began walking with her. She found herself struggling to put simple words to a not so simple situation. "Remember how you came to live with your father when Miss Stoutwell brought you?"

"Uh-huh."

"And you remember I told you that you came to live with him because he is your real family and you belong with him. Well, I have a real family, too, and I had to return to them just as you returned to your father."

"That is very similar to how I put it."

Gillian looked up at the unexpected voice. It wasn't Cassia.

"Hello, Gillian."

Dante stood a few yards away from them beneath a huge oak tree. His arms were crossed over his chest, his booted feet set apart. His dark hair ruffled softly in the breeze. He looked so blessedly handsome. It was like a dream. If she closed her eyes, Gillian could almost believe they were at Wyldewoode again.

She stared at him. She had wondered many times in the past days what it would feel like to see him again. She wondered if the things she'd been told about him would change the way her heart would quicken its beat whenever he was near. They hadn't.

"Hello, Dante," she said.

"It is good to see you, Gillian." He came forward. "Phoebe isn't the only one who has missed you."

"You are regretting your decision then?"

"My decision?"

"Yes, your decision to leave Adamley House before I returned from Madame Olga's with Dorrie and Clare."

Dante smiled ruefully. "I was told to leave Adamley House, Gillian. Just after I was warned never to attempt to see you again."

Gillian knit her brow. "I don't understand. When I returned and saw you were gone, I naturally assumed you'd decided to leave me there and—"

"And, naturally, your family did nothing to inform you otherwise. You forget something, Gillian. I made you a promise. I said I wouldn't leave you unless you wanted it. I do not lie, so I would not have broken my promise to you unless I had been forced to."

"But you weren't there," she said, still trying to make sense of it.

"I wasn't there when you returned because your father had ordered me to leave. He'd had it all arranged before we ever arrived there that morning. It was stupid of me not to have expected that he would. Dorrie and Clare were instructed not to bring you back unless I had gone. I didn't know where they had taken you nor how they had convinced you to leave with them. I had no choice but to leave."

"Dorrie and Clare told me they had to go out on a quick errand. They invited me along and said you would probably be talking to the marquess for a while. They assured me we would return before you had finished. I thought it would give me a chance to get to know them, to see if I might remember them. I had no reason to disbelieve them. I guess I was the stupid one."

"You, Gillian, are the furthest thing from stupid I

have ever seen. You were trusting. And I hope you haven't lost that quality." Dante looked down at Phoebe, who still clung stubbornly to Gillian's hand. "Phoebe, would you please go down by the water for a few minutes? If you look closely, you might catch a glimpse of the great orange fish who lives in the pond. They call him Triton. It is said if you see him, you should make a wish and it will come true."

Phoebe looked at Gillian as if fearful she might disappear again.

"It's all right," Gillian told her. "I won't leave without saying good-bye this time. I promise."

"We'll join you there in a few minutes," Dante said.

"Yes, my lord."

Gillian watched as Phoebe walked slowly to the edge of the pond. Her black hair, tied back with a pale blue ribbon that matched her dress, shone in the sun. "She calls you 'my lord.' "

"Yes, although I have come to the conclusion that it is not because of anything she was told about me. I believe it is because she's never called any man 'Father,' even the one she knew before me." Dante was silent for a moment, then said, "You've been told things about me, too, haven't you, Gillian?"

Gillian continued to watch Phoebe as she walked along the water's edge looking for the orange fish. "Yes."

"Would you like to tell me what some of those things were?"

Gillian looked at him, silent.

"I will not lie to you, Gillian."

She looked at him a moment longer. She believed him. He would tell her the truth. "I was told you are called the Rakehell Earl because you have had many liaisons with wedded women."

Dante let go a slow breath. "Yes, Gillian, I have had relations with wedded women. It may not seem like it, and you probably will not understand this, but I actually do practice discretion in that aspect of my life."

"Discretion?"

"Yes, more so than a lot of other men at court, but I will not try to defend my past to you, Gillian. I have done what I have done. It cannot be changed. I will only say that I never ruined an innocent, and I never divided a happy union. The women I have known intimately in my life were all unhappily wed. I wasn't interested in a relationship that would bring entanglements. I had no plans to wed. I wasn't willing to mislead any lady into the impression that she might change my mind in that. I don't know what more I can tell you, Gillian. It happened, and it is my responsibility now to live with."

Gillian considered Dante's words. Somehow, it made perfect sense to her He was a man who had seen much of the world. No one could expect that he wouldn't have had experience with women. She decided to mention the rest of what she'd been told. "Clare told me you had a liaison with her."

"Look at me, Gillian."

Gillian looked into Dante's eyes. She saw something glimmering in the golden-brown depths, a fire that wrapped entirely around her. She took a breath and held it.

"I did not have any relationship with Clare. You were too young to know, but I called your brother friend before the events of five years ago. I have never been a man to boast of the women I have been with, but as is the way with such things, when Clare started the rumors of our having been involved, people began to talk. I was said to have had relations with women I'd never even met. But Clare, well, I had known her through Reggie. She made it very clear she wanted a more intimate relationship with me, but I refused her. I would never cuckold a friend. Clare became angry with me, and it wasn't long before ballrooms would hush when I entered them. It also wasn't long before Reggie came looking for me, pressing me to duel for Clare's honor."

"And you refused his challenge."

"Yes, I refused him, of course, but Reginald wouldn't let it rest at that. He finally pushed me too far one day. He pushed me into doing something I will regret for the rest of my life."

Gillian could see a sadness in his eyes now, a heart-felt regret. She touched his hand. "What happened?"

"I suggested that Reginald follow Clare one day when she took Alec to visit his true father."

Gillian gasped. "Do you mean to say Alec is not Reginald's son?"

"No, he is not. Despite that he bears the Forrester name, he is really the son of Viscount Limley."

Realization dawned on Gillian then. "That is what Marcellus meant when he said the troubles between Reginald and Clare went beyond what she'd said of you."

"Most everyone at court knew Alec wasn't Reginald's son. Somehow, unbelievably, Reginald didn't. I never should have told him the truth, though. It stripped Reginald of his pride and no man should have his pride taken away from him."

"Should Reginald have continued on believing Alec was his son?"

"It was not my right to make that decision for him, Gillian."

Gillian didn't answer. She didn't know what to say. Even without her memory, she had been able to see that Reginald and Clare's marriage was not a happy one. It obviously never had been if Clare had given birth to another man's child, allowing Reginald to believe the child his own.

Dante tipped her chin up so Gillian that was looking at him. "I would guess, then, you can now understand why your father arranged things as he did? It must have been difficult for him, learning that his only daughter had been alone all that time with the Rakehell Earl of Morgan. I mean, I destroyed his son's life. I suppose I can't fault him for believing I kidnapped you as well."

"No." Gillian stared at him. "You are wrong in that, Dante, because you did not kidnap me. If there is anything of which I'm certain, it is that. Someone else did, and I'll be damned if I'm going to allow my family to add another false blot on your name while the true culprit goes off scot-free."

Dante narrowed his eyes. "I'm afraid I don't know what you mean."

"As I view it, the two people who suffered most from the effects of your fictitious liaison with Clare are Alec and you."

"Alec's plight is obvious. That is precisely why I wish I'd never told Reginald the truth. Alec was innocent."

"As were you, Dante. You stood on the side of honor. You refused to cuckold Reginald, your friend, and you refused to face him in a duel after Clare spread her vicious lies. No doubt, some at court took your refusal as an admission of Clare's accusation. You tried to avoid a scandal, and for it you were rewarded with your notorious moniker. Even in this other instance, when you discovered me lying in that road, you acted with honor. You didn't know who I was. You took me in and helped me to mend, and again my family rewards you with unfounded accusations and slander."

"Somehow I get the feeling you are coming up with a plan."

Gillian grinned. "Precisely. I've been thinking about

this and in view of recent recollections I have had, as I see it, there is only one avenue left open to us. It is the only way we can clear your name and make my family see you for the truly honorable gentleman you are. Dante, we will have to sniff out the true culprit."

Chapter Twenty-two

Gillian felt much better during the ride back to Adamley House than she had upon leaving. Together, she and Dante had come to a plan. Well, not really together. Dante had listened to her idea of finding the person who had kidnapped her by smelling him out through his unusual choice of scent. Dante had even come up with several good ideas of his own. It was his slight unwillingness to allow her to help that had put a twist in her plans. If she remembered correctly, he'd actually refused her help, warning her that whoever it was, this person with the peppery scent she remembered, he had been daring enough to kidnap her. And he had stolen boldly into her bedchamber to do it. Dante didn't wish to risk how far the man would go a second time.

Unfortunately, Gillian hadn't had the chance to finish that particular disagreement with Dante, for they had been interrupted by the sound of Dorrie calling Gillian's name in the distance. Gillian had quickly said good-bye to Phoebe and Dante, knowing Dante would eventually see reason. Of course she would have to be involved in finding the true culprit. Only she knew the particular scent. Only she could identify the man through it. And Dante would certainly realize that, once he had the time to sit and really think about it.

The marquess was waiting on the steps outside Adamley House when Gillian and Dorrie returned with the children from the gardens. He eyed Dorrie with ill-concealed hostility as they alighted from the coach. "Where have you been?"

Poor timid Dorrie wilted under his stare. "We took the children on an outing, a picnic at the Spring Gardens."

"So I have heard."

Lord Adamley waited until Dorrie had ushered the children inside before speaking to Gillian who was behind the others. "A word, if I may?"

Gillian nodded. He was obviously angry, most probably because he had noticed his watch missing.

Inside, the marquess motioned down the hall. "In my study, Gillian."

Once there, he closed the door firmly behind them.

Gillian decided to be forthright. "I am sorry. You are displeased with me for having borrowed your watch." She took it from her pocket and held it out to him. "I should have asked, but Dorrie and I wanted to make certain we didn't stay over long at the Gardens."

Her father took the watch from her and placed it calmly in his desk drawer. "The watch is not the reason why I am angry, Gillian." He lowered himself into his chair.

"Why did you break Marcellus's spectacles, Gillian? You know he cannot see well without them."

Gillian closed her eyes. She saw her father before her, sitting in his chair, but he was a younger man, his hair not quite so gray. She heard herself answering him in a voice very similar to Phoebe's.

"He pulled my hair."

"It was not well done of you, Gillian. Not at all."

"Gillian, what is it? Are you ill?"

Her father's face had at once gone from angry to concerned.

"If he didn't have his spectacles, he couldn't see to pull my hair again."

"I beg your pardon?"

"I broke Marcellus's spectacles so he wouldn't pull my hair again. I'm sorry. I didn't mean to."

The marquess looked at her, confused. "Gillian, you broke those spectacles when you were eight years old. I should think I have forgiven you by now."

"But I heard you just now asking me why I had broken them."

"I didn't say anything about any spectacles."

Gillian thought hard. Vague images came to her as though through a fog. "After I broke the spectacles, did I hide them? In my pillow sheet perhaps?"

The marquess nodded. "Yes. That is how I learned you had broken them in the first place. We had thought Marcellus misplaced them; in fact, we punished him for being so careless. The maid found the broken spectacles in your pillow sheet and brought them to me. Poor girl was frightened near to death, thinking she had broken them."

"I remember it," Gillian said excitedly. "I remember she was dreadfully frightened you would dismiss her for having broken the spectacles. That was why you were so angry with me for it."

Gillian came around her father's desk and hugged him. "I remember it. I remember it all."

The marquess looked startled at her affectionate display. "Yes, well, the physician said you would most probably begin remembering such things from your childhood." He put on a serious face. "And that is why I must speak with you about where you went earlier today, Gillian. You saw him at the Gardens, didn't you?"

"Him?"

Deception was not Gillian's forte. It was not something she felt at all comfortable with. Obviously, she never had.

"You know well who I mean, Gillian." He paused as if saying the name upset his stomach. "Morgan."

The air in the room took a decidedly heavy turn.

"I saw Dante only briefly, my lord. I wasn't even aware he would be there. Actually, it was Phoebe I went there to see. He just happened to come along."

The marquess's face darkened. "Do you mean to say Morgan brought one of his mistresses there to see you? Whose wife is she?"

"Phoebe is far too young to be someone's wife. She's only five years old. And she is not anybody's mistress. Phoebe is Dante's daughter."

"Daughter? When did Morgan wed? I heard nothing of it. It must have been while he was in France. At least he is finally settling down. But then why did he ask me—"

"Dante Tremaine is not married."

Her father stared at her, mute. Somehow Gillian knew it was not often he fell speechless.

"Phoebe's mother died from the plague. Dante did not even know the child existed until she showed up at his doorstep, literally, bag and baggage in hand. The man who had been married to Phoebe's mother abandoned her. Dante did the proper thing in taking her in and assuming responsibility for her. Shouldn't that count for something?"

"Morgan fathers a bastard, and you term it responsible."

"Don't call Phoebe that word. She is an innocent child."

"I will not have you taking that tone of voice with me, Gillian. Regardless of whether you remember it or not, I am still your father."

Gillian lowered her eyes. "I am sorry, my lord."

The marquess sat down again. He was thoughtful for some time. Finally, he spoke.

"I had thought to delay in telling you this, Gillian. I hoped to give you time to adjust to living here again and perhaps fully regain your memory, but hearing of the existence of this child only causes me to realize I have taken the proper steps for you. You do not see it, Gillian, but I do. Morgan has a hold on you; he has influenced your thinking far too much. He even has you defending his indiscretions for him."

"Phoebe is not an indiscretion."

"Be that as it may, I have come to the conclusion that he had a purpose in his acquaintanceship with you. A reprehensible purpose." He looked at her. "I believe Morgan sought to wed you for the child. He needed a mother for her, someone who could help to dispel the air of illegitimacy surrounding her."

"Nonsense. He never made a proposal of marriage to me."

"Aye, but he did to me. The day he brought you here, when we left to come here to my study, he offered for your hand. He said it would keep you from facing any scandal at having been with him, but I refused him, just before I threw him out to the street where he belongs."

Gillian wasn't at all certain she'd heard her father right. "Dante asked your permission to wed me?"

"Yes, but I would be damned to perdition if I allowed such a thing to pass. He is a rogue of the first water, Gillian, a libertine. Why do you think they call him the Rakehell Earl? I'll tell you why. It is because he has made a career of ruining innocent young girls just like you."

"Name one."

"What?"

"Name a single innocent young girl Dante ever ruined."

The marquess struggled. "Well, I . . ."

"You cannot because you know very well he never ruined any innocent. How could he have when he has only had relations with married women."

"Good God, Gillian, do you hear what you are saying?"

She had to admit it had not been the most intelligent of things to say, but she'd said it nonetheless. "You do not know him as I do. He is not the same man you think him."

"You talk as if you have fallen in love with the cad."

Gillian fell silent.

The marquess looked at her. "Oh, dear God, you have, haven't you?"

The marquess turned and walked to the windows. He stood there for a long while. Gillian wondered what he would say next. She would never have expected to hear what she did.

"Your marriage has been arranged to Garrick Fitzwilliam."

"I beg your pardon?" she said, again thinking she must not have heard him right. "Who on earth is Garrick Fitzwilliam?" And then she thought about it and remembered the letters that had come, ridiculous letters attributing her toes to rose petals. "Surely not him?"

"He is the son of an associate of mine, the Earl of Handley."

"I will not consent to this, my lord. I know nothing of the man, except of course that he writes bad poetry."

"You do know him, Gillian. You just don't remember it. You had expressed a fondness for Garrick at one time. Surely, you can find that fondness again." He returned to the desk. "Garrick will be at the ball at the Palace. You will meet him and, God willing, you will remember him. And you will wed him, Gillian, unless you want Morgan to be thrown into the Tower to rot for the rest of his life."

"What do you mean?"

"I am of the belief that Morgan orchestrated this whole abduction and memory loss debacle. I believe he did it in his efforts to seek revenge against this family. Of course, I cannot be entirely certain until you regain your memory and can tell us who it was who truly abducted you. I had hoped to delay your marriage to Garrick until that time, so you would see what I say is true, that Morgan is a vile rogue, but it appears that I will not be able to do so. I will therefore make the arrangements. You and Garrick Fitzwilliam will wed as soon as possible. And if you fight me on this, Gillian, I will have no choice but to have Morgan brought up on charges of kidnapping, rape, even witchery if necessary."

"Dante never touched me!"

"How could you know? You can't even remember your own name?"

"I'm telling you, Dante was nothing except honorable in his association with me."

"Honorable, ha! That scoundrel doesn't have an honorable bone in his body. I stand by my warning, Gillian. If you refuse to wed Garrick, I will see Morgan brought up on charges. And with his reputation, who do you think the king will believe?"

Gillian tasted fear. It was sour and unpleasant, and she tried to swallow it back. There was nothing she could do to stop him. "Why are you doing this? I am your daughter. I thought you loved me."

"I do love you, Gillian. That is precisely why I am doing this, to protect you from further endangerment by him. Marriage is the only way I see to solve this once and for all. Do you know what a connection to the Rakehell Earl will do to your name?"

"Stop calling him that."

"I have made my decision. You understand my terms. Don't think I will not see them through either, Gillian. I will not allow you to be used as a means to an end for that reprobate. He may think he can avoid the fires of perdition by stealing his way to heaven through you, but he is wrong. He must face what his actions have brought on him. One cannot escape the past. We all must account for our sins, all of us. Someday, when your memory has returned, you will thank me for it, and you will realize what I have done is for your own good."

Dante stood the moment the footman opened the door. He watched the tall, dark-haired man who entered afterward, admitting reluctantly that he was more nervous than he'd like to be. He tightened his hand into a fist.

King Charles II motioned his manservant away, then regarded Dante. "Morgan, you are either very brave or very stupid for coming here."

Dante knelt reverently and bowed his head, taking the king's hand and kissing his ring in a display of respect. "I had the opportunity to ponder that same question greatly during the past three years, Your Majesty, and I have come to conclude I am both, though probably a little more of the latter than the former."

Charles's mustachioed mouth curled into a subtle smile. "At least your arrogance has remained intact." He stepped away. "Get up on your feet before I begin to believe you truly humble."

Dante stood. He waited for the king to speak.

"Brandy?" Charles asked.

"If His Majesty will join me in a glass, I would be honored."

"Please, Morgan, enough of the mouth honor. It is, after all, your brandy."

"A gift for His Majesty in gratitude for bringing me home."

Charles shook his head and glanced in the general direction of one of the many manservants who flanked the door. In moments two glasses of French brandy were set before them. "How does my French cousin, Louis, fare?"

"His Majesty is well. Your Majesty's sister sends her fond regards across the Channel, as well."

Charles turned anticipatory eyes on Dante. "Minette sent her felicitations with you?"

"Yes, she did, Your Majesty, in the form of a letter."

Dante removed a folded and sealed parchment from his coat, knowing he held in his hand the final key to his reacceptance at Whitehall's court. King Charles's relationship with his sister was intimate and far-reaching, far closer than any other in his life. Minette occupied the highest position in her older brother's esteem, above his most trusted friends and lovers, even above his queen.

While at Versailles, Dante had befriended the English princess who had wed Louis XIV's brother, the ugly and notoriously cruel Duc D'Orleans. While Minette had been welcomed and accepted by the French people, she knew it was a conditional welcome. She was still an outsider from a country whose relationship with France seemed ever tenuous, and for that reason, she had scarce few she could truly trust at the glittering French court.

Minette had come to trust Dante during his time there. He had entertained the princess with stories of Whitehall's most notorious contemporaries, reacquainting her through his words with her brother whom she hadn't seen for many years. When Dante had learned of his grant to return to England, his first action had been to visit Minette and offer his services to her as trusted courier.

He handed the letter to Charles, who opened it immediately. Dante waited in silence, sipping his brandy, while the king read. Charles was grinning like a fool by the time he reached the last line.

"I do so miss my Minette," he said, refolding the letter and tucking it in his pocket. "Louis keeps her to himself since she left to wed that swine, D'Orleans. I think he fears I wouldn't allow her to return were he to grant her leave to visit us here at home. Her letters to me have always been vague because she knows they are all read before they leave France. I had suspected what she has just confirmed in this letter. D'Orleans is abusive to her. Knowing now how my sister's husband treats her, I must admit King Louis's fears of my keeping her would be justified."

Dante nodded. "If it is any ease to you, Your Majesty, the princess lives a peaceful life at Versailles. She has her own court made up mostly of English transplants, and her husband rarely sees her. You would be relieved to know she has come to a sort of arrangement with him so that they only interact when politically necessary."

Charles smiled. "Yes, that does allow me a bit of relief, but I will do whatever it takes to see her again." The king wandered off into his thoughts and reminiscences for a moment, then returned his attention to Dante. "I offer my condolences on your loss, Morgan."

Dante nodded. "And I my gratitude for granting me leave to return and pay my respects to my mother."

"As well as your acrimony at keeping you waiting so long, no doubt."

Dante looked at the king.

Charles grinned. "It is all right, Dante. I was unjust in leaving you there so long. I prevented you from your mother's last days, a thing even I have no right to do. As you know, I was not able to see my father before they killed him. I hope you will accept my apologies and forgive my neglect through these many months. It has been a trying time."

Dante inclined his head. "It is in the past, Your Majesty, and I am of the recent opinion that the past is best forgotten."

Charles swallowed down the rest of his brandy. He set the glass aside. "Cassia has told me of your interesting visitor these past weeks."

Dante hadn't known that bit of news, or expected it for that matter. He sat up, ready to defend himself. "I sought only to aid Lady Gillian."

"It is all right, Morgan. I value Cassia's judgment very much. She seems to think you have turned a new page in your life's book." He paused. "You must have come to care a great deal for the girl if you managed to remain honorable throughout all that time you were alone with her. I daresay I wouldn't have had your willpower."

"Yes, well, whether I did or not matters naught, Your Majesty. Her family, as you know, are not to be so easily swayed to my favor. I even offered marriage, but her father refused. He believes me responsible for her abduction and subsequent loss of memory."

"And are you?"

Dante looked at the king. "I swear to you, Your Majesty, I had no part in it."

Charles raised a hand. "At one time I may have been easily convinced to the belief that you would have resorted to kidnapping, but now, I think not. Even in your past entanglements, you never acted out of dishonor. Including that last little bit of abduction."

Dante had hoped the elopement of Frances Stuart and the Duke of Richmond would be a subject he could avoid when speaking to King Charles. "My intentions were nothing if not honorable in that instance as well, Your Majesty."

"I am aware of that, Morgan. Now. I had no right to keep Frances here against her wishes. The girl had a right to wedded bliss, and from all appearances she seems to have found it with Richmond, difficult as that may be to believe. You needn't worry that I would give

Adamley an ear to listen to his baseless accusations. So if you wish to pursue the girl . . ."

"You can take great store in that I have every intention of doing just that, Your Majesty, as soon as I can discover who really kidnapped Gillian that night."

"You are something of an investigative proficient, Morgan. I seem to recall you were very helpful to Cassia in that little mess involving her father a few years ago. Your skills may be a bit rusty, after resting untested for the past three years, but I place my odds on you emerging the victor in this particular contest."

Chapter Twenty-three

Gillian stood atop the three steps that descended into the glittering and hopelessly crowded ballroom— "The Pit" as Dorrie had called it upon their arrival at White-hall Palace. Flanked by Dorrie on one side, her mother on the other, Gillian could but stare below at the hundreds of richly decorated gowns swirling about so many elegant ladies, decorously dressed men posing beside them. It was an overwhelming and truly splendid array.

The Forrester ladies had arrived separately from the men, who had come early to the Palace for card playing and would join them soon after the beginning of the dancing. It was all part of the plan to make Gillian's return to society as seemingly insignificant as possible. Were the entire clan to arrive together, a thing they rarely if ever did, it might draw questions, and questions, Gillian had been told, were to be avoided at all costs.

Clare had mysteriously excused herself the moment the ladies had arrived at the Palace, vanishing around a darkened garden corner on what she had termed a quick errand to find a friend. She hadn't reappeared since.

Standing among the resplendent guests in the ballroom, Gillian was suddenly very glad Dorrie had pressed her into wearing the brilliant royal blue silk gown with the pale yellow underskirts. Though not nearly as lavish as what most of the ladies were wearing, or the men for that matter, the blue bowknots that lined its bodice were a lovely complement to the necklace Dante had given her. Gillian reached up and touched the Blue John pendant, which rested just below the hollow of her throat, thinking to herself that she would definitely have her work cut out for her. With so many people in attendance at the ball, ferreting out the peculiar scent of her abductor might prove difficult.

Perhaps even impossible.

"Is it always like this?" Gillian asked as they waited for the milling crowd to disperse so they could move onward into the ballroom.

Dorrie laughed. "You mean so like the busiest day at a cattle auction in Lincolnshire? That is what you used to call it, and, yes, dear Gillian, it is." She motioned across the expansive room. "Here, on the southern wall, we have the young misses who sadly aren't attractive or well-dowered enough to command the attention of their more privileged sisters, the young ladies who are all but surrounded by eager swains in the immediate center of the room. But those ladies you see there, are, like me, fortunate enough to have already wed, and are thus allowed the freedom of strolling about the entirety of the room. You will be too, once you have wed Garrick."

Gillian frowned. Marry him? The very idea of spending her days listening to his ridiculous poems were enough to send her head spinning. This, and she had yet to see him. Her father still insisted that she would wed Garrick, after which he renewed his threat to have Dante arrested and charged with kidnapping her.

Gillian, however, had other plans.

"And the older set," Joanna said, breaking into Gillian's thoughts, "like your mother, are relegated to the balcony and the northern wall to sit on exceedingly uncomfortable chairs while watching our youth pass away like smoke up a chimney before our very eyes."

"Goodness," Gillian said, eying a grandly dressed gentleman with a wig of bushy red curls that nearly eclipsed his head, "it seems more like a circus than a cattle auction."

"That is a very good description of it," Dorrie said. "And what that man is wearing is considered fashionable. Shall we proceed to the dancing bears, then?"

A few heads turned as the trio started down the steps to enter the painted and powdered crush. Their progress was slow, giving Gillian a chance to search every face she saw, looking, studying each feature. Perhaps, if she came face-to-face with her abductor, her memory would return. Surely, she would know him the instant she saw him. And wouldn't it be grand if she could expose him here before all these people? Dante would be publicly resurrected. But, as Gillian moved slowly through the room, one face seemed to blend into another. No one looked at all familiar to her.

"Remember, Gillian," Joanna said, "you have been away in the country visiting with your ailing aunt. Should anyone approach you, either Dorrie or I will whisper their name in your ear, or somehow convey their identity to you through conversation. Your father insists that no one know of your memory loss."

Gillian wanted to tell her mother she thought it would be far easier to just tell the truth, but she never had the chance. Joanna smiled brightly as just then an older woman came forward from the throng. "Ah, Lady Dowlinger, how are you this evening?"

"I am suffering from a headache the likes of which the world has never seen, Joanna, which is making me as ill-tempered as ever." She glanced at Dorrie. "And you are looking pregnant as ever, Dorothea. Should you even be seen in public? Joanna, can you not convince your son to leave the poor girl alone long enough to recover from birthing the previous child?"

Before Joanna could respond, Lady Dowlinger looked at Gillian. "Haven't seen you about lately, Gillian. How do you expect to snag yourself a husband if you insist on hiding your pretty face behind a book cover all the time? Where have you been concealing yourself?"

Gillian frowned. "I was away in the country, visiting my aunt. She was ill."

"Your aunt . . ." Lady Dowlinger narrowed her eyes. "Which aunt would that be—Perdita, your mother's sister, or Edna, your father's?"

Gillian glanced at her mother. They had never specifically named the aunt she was supposed to have visited. She certainly didn't want to attempt a guess and come up wrong.

"Perdy took ill and sent for Gillian," Joanna broke in. "You know she has always favored our daughter. Gillian was great companionship for her while she was repairing."

Lady Dowlinger seemed satisfied by the response, for she moved on in conversation. "My boy, Humphrey, is here tonight, Gillian. Like your Aunt Perdy, he favors you, as well. I hope you'll at least favor him with one dance."

"Well, I . . ."

"Don't fret, my dear. I'm not asking you to betroth yourself to him for heaven's sake. You would be far too much for the boy to handle. You've a brain, you see. But, just perhaps, if he is seen with you, some myopic creature will think he has merit and take pity on him."

Gillian looked at her. Was this woman speaking about her own son?

"He certainly isn't having any luck in trying to catch

himself a wife on his own," she went on. "I swear I'll be feeding that boy till I die if I don't get him wed soon."

"Of course, Lady Dowlinger," Gillian said. "I would be more than happy to dance with your son."

"I shall inform Humphrey directly."

Joanna eyed Gillian. "Perhaps we should move on, away from the door to allow the others easier access to the ballroom. It was good speaking with you, Lady Dowlinger."

Joanna broke away, and the three of them continued on through the ballroom. It was difficult to move, for the crowd was growing thicker by the second, countered by the multitude of servants weaving in and out of the throng with trays of refreshments.

"Oh, dear," Joanna said, "had I known it would be this much of a crush tonight, I would have suggested we wait to bring Gillian out for a less crowded affair. Everyone seems to have returned to the city, and they are all in attendance here tonight. I hope we will not run into any trouble, what with Gillian's memory loss and—"

"Gillian!"

A pair of shrill, excited female voices broke through the din of the crowd. Gillian turned just as two young ladies came rushing forward, squealing in delight. Actually, she thought they sounded rather silly.

"The one in the yellow is Felicity St. John, and the other is Prudence Fairchild," Dorrie murmured quickly. "They are two of your closest friends."

"They are?" Gillian turned and smiled cheerfully. "Felicity, Prudence, it is wonderful to see you."

Gillian heard Dorrie take in a breath. What had she done wrong already?

"Such formality, Gillian dear," Prudence said, peering at Gillian as if immediately noticing a difference in her. "You haven't called me 'Prudence' since we met ten years ago at Miss Skidmore's School for the Young and Impressionable. And no one calls Lettie 'Felicity.' That's her mother's name."

"Girls," Joanna broke in, coming straight to her daughter's rescue, "I understand Her Majesty is planning to attend the festivities this evening. Have you seen her yet, Pru? I hear tell she will be wearing Madame Olga's latest creation."

"No, Lady Adamley, Her Majesty has yet to arrive, but the general buzz is she will come out sometime after the king's arrival, to assume her rightful place now that 'La Castlemaine' is on a definite decline in His Majesty's affections. 'Tis said it is only a matter of time before poor Barbara Palmer's reign will be over."

"Aye," continued Lettie, winking at Gillian, "but wagers are already being placed on the books as to who will take Barbara's place as chief mistress to His Majesty. Some even say Frances Stuart may return to court."

"Unthinkable," Gillian's mother said. "After she wed His Grace, the Duke of Richmond, it was said she could never show her face again at Whitehall."

"Especially after their scandalous elopement, which involved none other than the Rakehell Earl of Morgan."

Gillian's attention was immediately snared. "Did you say the Earl of Morgan?"

Dorrie eyed her cautiously.

Joanna simply frowned.

"You've heard of him, haven't you, Gillian?" Prudence asked. "But, then, perhaps not, since Lettie and I were brought out at court a year before you, and, well, then came the plague. By the time you arrived on the social scene, that scandal had died down. His name is Dante Tremaine, and they say he was the most notorious rake at Whitehall not a handful of years ago.

Handsome and charming, his number of lovers can surely attest to that. He was banished to France several years ago for his part in helping Frances Stuart to escape from the Palace and elope with the Duke of Richmond. He hasn't been seen or heard of since."

"It would seem his punishment was far more severe than the duchess's," Gillian said. "That certainly doesn't seem fair."

"Gillian . . . ," Joanna said.

Lettie was already responding. "Yes, Gillian, but His Majesty was doubly annoyed with Lord Morgan because he knows that a woman like Frances Stuart could not have helped but to have become one of the Rakehell Earl's many ladies." She giggled into her hand. "Given His Majesty's failure to bed her himself, his anger is most understandable."

"Girls," Joanna broke in, her tone scolding now, "such talk is not to be heard from proper young ladies. It is unseemly."

The chatter ceased. Gillian frowned. She had wanted to hear more, so she could defend Dante without anyone realizing she knew him, of course. But perhaps it would be better if she just kept quiet. It wouldn't do, after all, for her mother to fall in a swoon here in the middle of the ballroom.

"Would anyone care for some refreshment?" Joanna asked.

"A lemonade would be nice," Gillian said, hoping if her mother left, she could question her friends further about Dante.

"Oh, yes," added Dorrie.

"I shall be back in a moment. Prudence, Lettie, perhaps you would like to come along?"

Gillian frowned. Joanna really gave them little choice but to go with her. Soon Dorrie and Gillian were standing alone.

"That certainly was awkward," Dorrie said. "I had

forgotten to tell you that you were fond of calling them 'Pru,' and 'Lettie.' "

"We seem to have successfully averted any suspicion," Gillian said with sarcasm that was lost on Dorrie.

She watched, stifling a grin as a man, tall, thin, and with a copious periwig made of sandy brown curls that covered his shoulders, came forward carrying three glasses of lemonade. His face was heavily powdered beneath the two black patches shaped like a moon and star on his left cheek. He wore a short coat of bright yellow sateen bedecked with wide green ribbon knots at the elbows and shoulders over a frilly lawn shirt. Lace-flounced cannons fell in layers at his knees beneath his yellow-and-green striped petticoat breeches. Black hose stretched over his legs to his shoes, shoes that had red heels and wide windmill bow ties. He was quite a sight.

"Lemonade, ladies?" he asked in a mincing sort of voice that reminded Gillian of a peacock's cry.

"Oh, thank you," Gillian said, taking two glasses from him and handing one to Dorrie. "My mother just set off in search of one of you."

"My lady?"

"You are serving, aren't you?"

"Gillian," Dorrie broke in, "this is Garrick Fitzwilliam."

"Oh, dear." Gillian tried to recover. "I guess I didn't recognize you at first."

Actually, she prayed Dorrie was joking. This . . . this fop was the man her father expected her to wed? But then, when she thought of his poetry, it made perfect sense, for only a coxcomb like this would think of likening someone's earlobes to butterfly wings. In fact, he looked rather like a butterfly, fluttering his hands as he was, looking like he might swoon. Gillian didn't know whether she should laugh or cry.

She looked at him again.

He smiled, his brightly painted lips curling upward.

Dear God. Gillian quickly glanced at Dorrie, who wisely kept silent.

Finally, Garrick spoke. "I met with your father earlier today, Gillian, and he has told me you—"

"There you are!"

Reginald and Archie came forward through the crowd, stumbling. Reggie held a goblet of brandy in his hand, Archie a half-filled bottle. Marcellus followed, seemingly reluctantly, moving immediately to Dorrie's side. He kissed her affectionately on the cheek.

"Mother said you were over here. Do you believe the crush tonight?" Reginald's voice was slurred, and he flung his arm outward, gesturing in an animated fashion and spilling most of his brandy on a passerby's wide skirts. "Won this bottle at the tables. The second of three. Archie had the other." He frowned, then added, "Obviously, my wife isn't with you."

"Clare excused herself shortly after we arrived," Dorrie said. "I believe she said she needed to speak with someone. She probably just hasn't been able to find us in the crowd to rejoin us."

"More likely she hasn't even tried," Reginald said sourly. He looked at his glass with glazed eyes. "Archie, my glass is empty."

Archie laughed and leaned forward on his cane, tipping the bottle to Reggie's glass and filling it nearly to its rim. He then swallowed a mouthful, finishing off the bottle.

Reginald turned to Garrick. "Is that you, Garrick? Good God, I guess it is. Have you changed tailors?" He took a swallow of his brandy. "Say, Garrick, doesn't our Gillian look exceptionally fetching this evening?" He sniggered, dribbling some of his drink on his chin.

Gillian glared at her brother. At that moment she wished she could punch him.

"Yes, she does, Reginald," Garrick said, "but then, Gillian is always lovely." He took in a deep breath, puffing up his lace-covered chest, and began reciting, " 'She is like a blossom in spring, so lovely, so new. I am a fortunate man, honored to be her—' "

The musicians struck a collective chord, effectively cutting off the rest of Garrick's poem. Gillian couldn't have been more relieved. The crowd "oohed" expectantly and began leaving the dancing area. A footman appeared atop the same steps where Gillian had come in. He stood straight and tall, preparing to make an announcement.

"My lords and ladies," he called out, "I present to you His Royal Highness, King Charles II."

Trumpets blared from the musician's balcony. The crowd parted, and the double doors near the entrance swung wide. Gillian strained to see, standing on her tiptoes to get a view above everyone else's heads. She could see nothing. Since she was a head shorter than everyone standing around her, she'd be lucky if she could so much as see the plume in his hat.

Several minutes passed and then everyone around her tensed. The air grew thick with expectation. Silk skirts rustled. The room fell silent, so silent Gillian heard the sound of someone's hairpin falling to the Italianate tile floor. Before Gillian realized what was happening, the people standing around her lowered themselves and she suddenly found herself standing taller than the rest.

"Good evening, my lady."

Gillian turned about at a deep voice speaking to her from behind. A man of great height and a most impressive presence stood before her. His hair was arranged in a profusion of black curls that reached down beyond his wide shoulders. His suit of white and gold winked in the candlelight. He smiled at her, and his dark eyes danced with ill-concealed amusement at her look of confusion.

It was then she realized he was the king.

A tug on her skirts was followed by Archie's whisper beside her. "Curtsy, Gillian, curtsy before you do us all in."

Gillian lowered into a nervous and uncertain curtsy. She looked up when the king came a step closer to her.

He held out his hand, taking hers and kissing it gently. His curled mustache tickled her fingers.

"You are Lady Gillian Forrester, are you not?"

Gillian looked around her for help, but everyone was still poised low. She felt ridiculous, the only one standing amid a sea of elegantly coiffed and lowered heads.

"Yes, Your Majesty, I am Gillian Forrester."

"I had thought as much. I was made aware of your situation by a close friend earlier today. I understand you have just returned to court." He winked. "A sick aunt in the country, I believe?"

He was made aware of her situation? What did that mean? Gillian didn't know what she should do. Something told her she should simply agree with anything the man said. "Yes, Your Majesty."

"We are pleased you could return to court to once again grace us with our loveliness, my dear." He glanced at her necklace. "A pretty stone, Lady Gillian. Might I inquire how you came by it?"

Gillian reached up and touched the Blue John pendant. "It was a gift, Your Majesty, from a friend."

"I would guess a very special friend?"

Gillian looked into the king's eyes, searching. "Yes, Your Majesty."

The king smiled. "We hope you will always cherish

such a rare and valuable gift. Good evening, Lady Gillian." Charles stepped back, waving to the musicians. "Please, play. Let us commence with the dancing before everyone's back becomes fixed in a crick."

Laughter followed his pronouncement. The king moved on. Conversation resumed. Everyone around Gillian finally rose to their feet.

"Good heavens, Gillian," Dorrie said, "do you realize that you were just speaking with the King of England?"

Gillian couldn't answer. She was still trying to decipher what exactly the king had been saying to her.

We hope you will always cherish such a rare and valuable gift.

Somehow she didn't think he was speaking exclusively of the necklace.

"You know, Gillian," Marcellus said, "His Majesty may have just labeled you as his next conquest."

Garrick turned to stare at her, his rouged mouth pursed in a pickled frown.

"Nonsense, Marcellus," Gillian answered, herself frowning. "He merely wanted to remark on my necklace. That is all." She pointed across the ballroom to where the king was now kissing the hand of a lovely young brunette before taking her onto the dance floor. "See, he has already moved on."

Joanna returned with Lettie and Pru.

"Was I seeing things," her mother asked, "or was Gillian just speaking with the king?"

"Our Gillian enchanted His Majesty to his toes," Marcellus said, winking playfully at his sister.

"I hope you didn't say anything untoward to His Majesty, Gillian."

"How could Gillian do that, Lady Adamley?" Pru asked.

"You needn't worry," Gillian broke in. "Any of you.

His Majesty and I just exchanged a few pleasantries. Nothing more."

They chatted a bit longer until the first round of dances came to an end. Gillian turned and noticed a young man with carrot-red hair fast approaching. Beside him, like a warship charging through a sea of smaller crafts, came the hulking Lady Dowlinger.

"G-good evening, Lady Gillian."

No doubt this was Sir Humphrey. Gillian smiled, studying him. She must have known him before she lost her memory; their families seemed to be well acquainted. Perhaps he'd even been a suitor. She wondered. Could he be her culprit? He certainly didn't look like someone given to abduction. Actually, he hardly looked old enough to be allowed out of bed at this hour of night. Still, there was only one way to be certain. "Sir Humphrey, how good it is to see you."

Gillian put her hand out to him. He took it and quickly kissed her fingers with tightly pursed lips. His hand shook nervously, his palm damp and hot. "You look lovely this evening, Lady Gillian."

"Sir Humphrey, what is that on your shoulder?"

Before he could look for himself, Gillian leaned forward on the pretense of brushing something away. She took in a deep breath, and with it, effectively crossed the first name off her list of possible culprits.

"There you are, Sir Humphrey," she said, stepping back. "It was just a bit of lint."

"Gillian, I told Humphrey you had expressed a wish to dance with him."

Garrick, who had heretofore remained to the side, suddenly stepped forward. Actually, Gillian had completely forgotten about him until his bright clothing announced itself to them all once again.

"I believe I was to have this dance with Lady Gillian."

"Actually, gentlemen," came a deep and commanding voice from behind, "I believe the next dance has already been promised to me."

Chapter Twenty-four

Dante suddenly stood there, holding out his hand to Gillian. "Will you do me the honor of this dance, Lady Gillian?"

Pru and Lettie let out a collective gasp. Joanna cleared her throat loudly. Gillian glanced about the crowded ballroom. It seemed as if the attention of everyone was fixed upon Dante. She could almost hear their thoughts aloud.

The Rakehell Earl of Morgan had returned from exile.

Gillian had to school herself against her initial reaction, which was, of course, to go with Dante and dance with him. It would be wonderful to be with him now before all these people, to show them he was not what they believed him. But it would also do nothing to help her in her quest. She already knew Dante hadn't kidnapped her, and with so many people in the ballroom, any one of whom could be the culprit, she would need every dance and every minute left to the evening to seek him out. She had to find the man who had kidnapped her.

From the warning gleam Gillian now saw in Dante's golden brown eyes, she read that he knew what she was up to. In approaching her for the dance, admittedly taking a risk with her family there, he was attempting to prevent her from it.

"Nay, my lord," Gillian responded, smiling politely.

"Thank you, but Lady Dowlinger is correct. I have already promised this dance to Sir Humphrey."

Pru and Lettie stared at her, mouths gaping. Gillian looked over at Humphrey, who seemed to inch closer to his mother's skirts. In fact, his face was beginning to turn as red as his hair while Dante glared down at him.

"I, uh, if you prefer, Lady Gillian, you may, of course . . ."

"By Cob's body," Dante said, clearly annoyed now, "dance with me, Gillian, before the poor puppy ends up wetting his breeches."

Gillian didn't have a chance to respond, for Dante grabbed her hand and proceeded toward the dance floor, pulling her behind him. She thought back to that day in the village square when Dante had pulled her into his arms and had kissed her before all. A shiver of excitement went through Gillian. Everyone else crowding that ballroom seemed to melt into the background. She no longer cared whom she was supposed to be dancing with. Discovering who had kidnapped her could wait a little longer, too.

She was going to dance with Dante.

A hush came over the crowd as they walked out onto the floor. All eyes were fixed on them.

She smiled up at him. "Your effect on the tongues of society is remarkable, my lord. I don't think I've ever seen such a vast number of people struck dumb all at the same time."

"Well, madam, it isn't every day the Rakehell Earl of Morgan rises from the dead."

They positioned themselves at the end of the line of dancers just taking the floor for the bransle and awaited the first chord.

Gillian watched Dante as she stood across from him in the line. He looked particularly handsome this evening. His coat, dark blue, nearly black, fit his broad shoulders well, complemented by a starched white neckcloth turned over in his usual way, once very simply at his throat. Buff-colored breeches stretched over his long legs, complete with polished black jackboots that reached just below his knees. Not a single ribbon or row of lace was to be found upon him.

But it wasn't simply his attire that drew Gillian's attention, and the attention of everyone there. There was a light in his eyes she'd never seen before, a reckless, challenging gleam that made Gillian's heart pound with excitement. It was no wonder the ladies' eyes followed him appraisingly as he had walked her across the room. Dante was a legend, indeed, dashingly notorious, scandalously mysterious, and he was dancing with her.

The musicians began, and Dante bowed, sweeping his hand while Gillian curtsied. Into the first turn Gillian spotted her family and friends standing on the fringes of the dance floor. They were watching them. Pru and Lettie were chattering like excited hens. Reginald and Archebald looked fit to kill. Her father, who had suddenly appeared, looked apoplectic. Marcellus was obviously attempting to diffuse the situation, though he didn't appear to be having any success, for they were, all of them, staring straight at Dante with the promise of physical punishment in their eyes. Garrick in all his finery had thankfully disappeared.

"You may soon regret you insisted on this dance, my lord," Gillian said as she took Dante's hand and together they stepped in time to the dance. "You should not put your life at risk like this."

"I should say the same for you, madam. You, too, put your life at great risk." Dante frowned. "Why are you refusing to listen to me, Gillian?"

"I can hear you quite clearly, my lord, despite the music."

"Apparently not, for otherwise you wouldn't have come here this evening with the intent to dance with every man present in hopes of sniffing out your abductor's peculiar scent. I told you I would take care of everything. I do not want you to get hurt."

"I'm sure I don't know what you mean, my lord."

"Gillian . . ."

They had come to the end of the line of dancers, at the opposite side of the ballroom from her family now. There was a break in the dance where those who wished to leave could make their bow and curtsy and do so. Dante seized the opportunity, taking Gillian's hand and backing from the line. He ushered her quickly from the ballroom, passing all the inquiring eyes and assuming smiles, to the outside balcony. He released her only when they reached the shadows that fell on the weathered stone railing.

Gillian turned and smiled brilliantly at him. "My lord, you will be pleased to know I have already narrowed down the list of possible culprits. Sir Humphrey couldn't have kidnapped me. He favors cloves, not the peppery spice of our culprit."

"Really? And I was certain he was our man." Dante frowned at her in the moonlight.

"You are teasing me again, my lord, but that is all right. I'm beginning to grow accustomed to it."

"I'm so glad to have pleased you. Now I want you to listen to me, Gillian. I am already in process of finding out who it was who kidnapped you. Rolfe and Hadrian are helping me, and the three of us have the situation well in hand. I am telling you now to stay clear of it. I do not want to see you smelling any other men."

Gillian giggled at him, confirming that, yes, that had sounded as ridiculous as he'd thought it had.

"My lord, it really is all right. Sir Humphrey never knew what I was up to."

"Sir Humphrey wouldn't know if his shoes were on the wrong feet unless his mother told him."

"Yes, well, just think of how much swifter our work

will be once I have eliminated a good number of the gentlemen present here tonight."

"Gillian—"

"And I will not need to dance with them all. There should be a number of them present at the supper to announce my betrothal to Garrick Fitzwilliam tomorrow evening at Adamley House."

Dante stared at Gillian. "I beg your pardon Gillian? Would you mind repeating what you just said? I wish to make certain I heard you aright."

"Oh, do not worry, my lord. There will be no wedding. It is merely to keep my father from pursuing charges against you. You see, the marquess learned of our meeting at the Spring Gardens the other day, and when I returned, he told me if I didn't agree to wed Garrick, he would have you thrown into the Tower on charges of kidnapping."

"And you agreed to this?"

Gillian shrugged. "Actually I never told my father I have no intentions of wedding Garrick. I refused, of course, at first, but he was rather adamant. It is much better if my father believes he has brought it all off. I had no other choice. Had I continued to refuse, my father would have seen his threat through. He would have had you brought up on charges. I could never allow that to happen. It would create a horrible scandal, not so much for me, for I care little about what people would say about me, but for you, my lord. You have been mistreated and maligned enough, and I could never live knowing I had brought more down upon you. It doesn't matter anyway, because once I"—she paused, smiling—"once *we* unmask the real culprit, my father's threats will be groundless. He will see you are truly a gentleman, that you didn't kidnap me, and I won't have to wed Garrick Fitzwilliam at all."

"And then what will you do, my lady?"

Gillian stared at him, caught by his intense gaze. "That will depend, my lord."

"On what?"

"On you."

Dante reached for Gillian and brought her against him. He looked into her eyes a moment before lowering his mouth on hers. Gillian was startled at first by his sudden embrace, but soon relaxed and parted her mouth, kissing him with all the emotion and passion she felt for him. The rest of the world—her family, the foppish Garrick Fitzwilliam, the five hundred or more people standing on just the other side of that door—all of it vanished as Dante eased her back until she was half sitting on the stone railing, clutching at his shoulders to keep from falling.

She loved the feel of his arms supporting her, of his body pressed close to hers. She loved the taste of him as he deepened the kiss, and uninhibited, she touched her tongue to his. A tingling sensation raced through her when Dante groaned into her mouth and pressed his hips against hers. As his lips moved down from her mouth, along her throat, pressing urgent kisses against the swell of her breasts, she felt herself losing all strength in her legs.

Memories of another night, and another kiss, came to her. Rain, cold, then warm arms holding her close. Dante's face, so concerned, so worried. About her.

Dante slowly lifted his head. Gillian looked at him through half-open eyes, her lips parting to allow a soft sigh. "You kissed me that night."

"Which night is that?"

"When you found me in the road, when I was injured, you kissed me. I just remembered it when you were kissing me now. Why did you kiss me?"

"It is the only way I could think of to shut you up about the ridiculous notion of your wedding Garrick Fitzwilliam."

"No, I didn't mean just now. I meant that night. Why did you kiss me when you first found me?"

Dante stared at her. "I don't rightly know."

Gillian smiled. "Do you often kiss ladies the moment you first meet them?"

"I don't usually meet ladies lying in the middle of a dark roadway, soaked to the skin. And don't go off trying to change the subject from Garrick Fitzwilliam. Listen to me, Gillian. I do not want you placing yourself in any further danger. I expect within the next few days to have found out who abducted you." He shook his head. "You will not wed Garrick Fitzwilliam. And you will no longer attempt to find out who kidnapped you. Do you understand?"

At that moment Dante could have told her the sky was striped as yellow and green as Garrick's petticoat breeches, and Gillian wouldn't have contradicted him. He was wonderful. He was magnificent. And she loved him.

"I see you are wearing the necklace I gave you," Dante said, still holding her close, touching his fingers lightly to the pendant at her throat.

"Of course I am," Gillian replied, smiling. "What else would I wear, my lord?"

"That's sure a pretty piece around your neck, Lady Gillian," said the maid, appropriately enough named Abigail, who saw to Gillian's personal needs. She picked up the gown Gillian had just stepped from and draped it over a chair. "Did your Garrick give it to you as a betrothal gift?"

"No, Abbie, he did not."

Gillian leaned her chin in her hand and frowned at her reflection in the glass at her dressing table as Abbie began removing the pins from her hair. The evening had been a dismal failure. After her dance with Dante, and their kiss on the ballroom balcony, he had left. Actually, he had slipped over the railing when her brothers and her father came storming through the doors, ready to kill him. From there the evening had taken a decidedly dreary turn.

Gillian had had no luck at all in finding her kidnapper. All evening she'd searched, suffering through dance after dance with men who, if they weren't treading on her toes, were ogling her breasts as if they were ripe plums, or crushing her skirts as they tried to press her into darkened corners in efforts to grope at her with their meaty hands. The vulgar Lord Chumley had even pressed her hand against the crotch of his breeches to demonstrate to her proof of his "tender feelings" for her. Tender? Well, that part of his anatomy most probably was feeling a bit tender now, after having been intimately introduced to the heel of her elbow moments later. There was something to be said for her lack of altitude after all.

When all was said and done, none of the men, not one she'd encountered had favored the peculiar peppery scent of her abductor. Adding to her suffering was the unpleasant discovery that a number of them, like that awful Lord Wallingford, smelled as if they rarely bathed at all, and half of them no doubt now thought she was seeking a dalliance with them.

What was she going to do? Gillian glanced at the small clock on the table as if to confirm that her time was fast running out. She had to find the real kidnapper. She had to prove Dante's innocence, or else . . .

"I was a bit surprised when I heard you were going to wed the likes of Garrick Fitzwilliam, miss," Abbie said, pulling a brush through Gillian's hair and pulling her from her thoughts of the evening as well.

Gillian looked at the maid in the mirror. "Why is that, Abbie?"

"I had always thought you didn't favor him before, that's all."

Gillian turned to stare at Abbie straight on. "What do you mean, Abbie? My father told me I was most fond of Garrick."

"If you call referring to him as 'Lord Ratface' fond, I guess you were then, but I swear I thought you'd put him on the list with all the others."

"What list?"

"You used to keep a running tally tucked in your diary of all the young bucks you'd come across who you said you'd never marry for one reason or another. Most of them were listed because they just weren't smart enough for you, miss. Others had been added after they'd done something to offend you. You know, such as trying to steal a kiss or other things . . ."

And a good portion of those men she'd encountered that night could now be added to it, Gillian thought as Abbie went on.

"I don't recall exactly what it was Garrick Fitzwilliam did to make himself an addition to your list, miss, but I felt certain he was there along with all the others."

Gillian considered this bit of news. A list. A list she'd obviously made of rejected suitors. That sort of a list could be very helpful in seeking out her abductor, very helpful indeed, for whoever had kidnapped her certainly had known her. Perhaps that was his reason for stealing her away. Perhaps she'd angered him by rebuffing his advances. It was a possibility. At least it was a start. "Do you know where this diary is, Abbie?"

"Yes, miss. You keep all the diaries you've written in that chest there where you store all your personal items."

Gillian moved over to kneel before the small teak-on-walnut chest near the foot of her bed. A small brass lock on its front shone in the light from the hearth. "It is locked."

"Yes, miss. You always kept it that way to prevent the little ones from getting into your personal things."

Gillian frowned. "And I don't remember where I keep the key."

Abbie opened a small silver box set on Gillian's dressing table. "It's right here, miss." She handed the key to Gillian. "I hope you won't be angry with me, but when you were away and no one knew what had become of you, Lady Clare asked me where you kept your diary. When I told her, she asked for the key to open the chest. She said it would help to find you, so I gave her the key. I'm terribly sorry, miss."

Gillian was concentrating on fitting the key into the lock. She barely heard her. "It's all right, Abbie. I know you were only trying to help." She released the latch and lifted the chest's lid. Inside were various objects: hair ribands, letters bound with string, a small pewter cup filled with colorful seashells . . .

"Wait for me, Mars."

"Stay back, Gilly. Mother won't be pleased if you get the hems of your skirts wet and sandy."

"But I've never seen the ocean before. It's so endless and blue . . ."

"Miss? Are you feeling faint?"

Gillian opened her eyes. Abbie's concerned face was staring down at her. She was sitting on the floor before the open chest, holding the cup filled with seashells close against her chest. "No, I'm fine, Abbie, thank you. I was just thinking about the ocean."

"Oh, yes, you have always loved the ocean so, miss. Said you'd marry a sailing man so he could take you far away. Your father wasn't happy to hear that. He wanted you to wed a titled gentleman, and it looks like he's going to get his wish with Garrick Fitzwilliam. Well, mayhaps he will. Mr. Garrick has got those brothers in line in front of him when his father kicks off this mortal coil, but odder things have happened, and then you'll be a countess."

"Abbie!"

Abbie smirked. "Mayhaps Mr. Garrick will take you on a wedding trip somewhere away from England, so you can see the ocean again. That is why you wanted this chamber when you came here to Adamley House you know, because it faced the river. Even though you can't see it, you said you knew it was there, and it led to the ocean, so you wanted to be as near to it as you could."

"Yes, mayhaps he will." Gillian's spirits fell at the reminder of her impending marriage to Garrick Fitz-william. Her supposed impending marriage. Picturing him in all his finery made a shudder pass through her. She just had to find the kidnapper. She reached inside the chest and searched through its contents. On the bottom, lined in a neat row, were a number of small books. Her diaries. While she may not remember very much about her life, she could at least read it. She lifted the book farthest to the left from inside and turned to the first page, reading.

March 23, 1666
Mother received a letter from Father telling us it is safe to come to London. The plague has finally gone and the king and court have returned to Whitehall. We will leave at week's end to stay for the season. I am to be presented at court. I will finally see Pru and Lettie. They have promised to introduce me to all their friends at court. It sounds most exciting. Mother says if any young man tries to make improper advances I should reprove him. I wonder if planting him a bob on the chin would be considered bad form. Father says Dorrie is with child again. Mars is well and Archie is spending too much time at the gaming tables. Reggie continues ill, the physicians know not why. Mother grows

increasingly worried. Perhaps, when we get there, he will improve. I entered my twentieth year today.

August 1, 1666
Went to the assembly at Lord and Lady Markson's. Sir Ozwell Gilhooly was there and pretended to sneeze so he could look down the front of my dress. What a ninny. I'm putting him on the list. I'm not certain yet about Garrick Fitzwilliam. Will have to wait and see. Reggie grows worse each day. Mother is worried. Clare says it is nothing. I went to the book stalls and purchased the latest translated copy of Mme. de Scudery's new novel. Mars brought me a new viola bow since Samuel broke the other one. Tomorrow we go to a masque at Whitehall. I have never attended such a thing. Does one wear a mask to a masque? I will ask Dorrie in the morning, and I will tell Clare what Lettie's mother suggested about the tea for Reggie. Perhaps it will help. I pray it does.

Gillian reached the bottom of the last page in the last of the diaries from her chest. It was late, and Abbie had long since retired. The candles were guttering down to their last, and Gillian sat on the floor at the foot of her bed, leaning against the tall carved post.

While reading her diaries hadn't brought her any closer to discovering the identity of her kidnapper, she had gained insight of the person she was, the person she had been before she'd lost her memory.

What she had found was that she really wasn't any different from the Gillian she had been before. She still loved reading and playing her music. She adored the children, but there was one distinct difference between the Gillian she'd read about in the diaries and the Gillian who sat on the bedchamber floor now.

The Gillian she was now loved Dante Tremaine, the Rakehell Earl of Morgan.

Gillian started to close the book to place it with

the others back in the chest. It was then she noticed the
date on the last page. It was a full two weeks before
her abduction. She'd written every day for nearly six
months. There should have been another diary started
the following day. Gillian looked inside the chest.
There were no others. And the list of her rejected suitors, it wasn't there either. Abbie had said she had kept
the list in whatever diary she was writing in at the time.
There must have been another diary with entries for the
two weeks before she'd been kidnapped. Why wasn't it
there? Someone must have taken it. But who?

It was then Gillian remembered Abbie's confession,
of how she had given the key to Clare in hopes of helping to find her.

Chapter Twenty-five

"Tomorrow is the day," Dorrie suddenly announced with a tentative smile at the breakfast table. "It will be wonderful, won't it, Clare?"

Gillian glanced up from her book, but that was all the notice she gave the conversation. She would have preferred to have been left to her own, to read in peace and nibble on buttered rolls while she sipped her cup of chocolate. It was for that reason she'd come to the solar, instead of the main dining room, for breakfast. Still, despite getting up early enough to see the sunrise for much the same reason, not three pages after sitting down, Dorrie had come into the room. A half page after that came Clare.

"What wonderful thing that is to occur tomorrow are you talking about, Dorothea?" Clare asked, taking a quiet, disinterested sip of her coffee.

"Have you not heard?" Dorrie provided. "Gillian is to wed Garrick Fitzwilliam tomorrow morning."

Clare choked on her coffee, sputtering, her eyes watering. "And when did this all come about?"

Gillian shook her head. "I knew Garrick had spoken with the marquess recently, but it would seem Dorrie is mistaken about when the wedding is to take place. The wedding is not to be tomorrow. The banns have yet to be published. It will be at least two months before—"

"No, Gillian, Marcellus said the wedding is to be tomorrow, and he should know, for he arranged for the special license himself. It was at your father's request, of course, but he said you knew of it. He said you'd agreed to the match. He said it is to be a quiet ceremony, performed in the marquess's study with only the marquess and Joanna, and Garrick's father, of course, present as witnesses. An announcement of it will be made after the fact, as will the assembly honoring the marriage."

Tomorrow morning? In contrast to what Dorrie said, her father had mentioned nothing of it to Gillian. The only thing he had said was that he wanted the marriage performed as quickly as possible. But this quickly? They would never be able to find who had kidnapped her before then. Perhaps that was precisely what her father wanted. Perhaps he already knew Dante was innocent and was planning to wed her off to Garrick before the proof could be found.

Gillian's first instinct was to find her father and tell him exactly what she thought of his scheme, but then she realized he would only put forth more of a defense to keep her away from Dante. No, instead, she would have to act as if she was agreeable to the match, while she figured out on her own what to do to stop it.

"Well, I guess, the sooner the better," she said. "Why wait when there really is no need?"

Clare turned to Gillian. "But I had always held the belief that you weren't overly fond of Garrick."

Gillian wondered if Clare had gleaned that impression after reading her missing diary, but kept that thought to herself. With any luck she would soon find out. For now, she played at ignorance. "I really don't remember Garrick favorably or unfavorably, although Father assures me I did like him very well before I lost my memory."

Clare narrowed her eyes. "What about Lord Morgan? You were so defensive of him. One would have thought . . ."

"I have decided you were right about Dante, Clare. He is a rogue. He even admitted to his indiscretions when I asked him about them."

Gillian said nothing more. She didn't want to be overly critical of Dante. Expounding further would look a bit suspicious, and transparent. Brevity was certainly the better course.

Clare looked at her a long moment, then said, "Well, I would guess then congratulations are in order to you, Gillian."

Clare stood.

The congratulations, Gillian noticed, were never given.

"You are leaving?" she asked.

"Yes," Clare said, already headed for the door. "I've an appointment that I simply must keep."

"At this hour?"

"Yes. Actually, I had forgotten about it until just now. Tell Alec I will not be able to take him with me today after all."

"Oh," Dorrie said, "he will be so disappointed."

"Yes, well, some things cannot be helped. Life is filled with disappointments, and Alec may as well learn that particular lesson now. You will tell him for me, won't you, Dorothea dear? He can spend the day in the nursery with the children and Marie-Therese. I will be back later today, in time to go with you all to the assembly at Halsey House this evening."

Gillian and Dorrie watched her go.

"Well," said Dorrie, taking up her cup of chocolate the moment they were alone, "Clare certainly does seem in a bit of a hurry, doesn't she?" She grinned. "Do you think it was something I said?"

Gillian barely heard Dorrie's words. She was thinking instead that Clare's absence would give her the opportunity she needed to look for the missing diary.

Gillian waited until she had finished the last of the

chocolate in the pot before rising from the table. "Please excuse me, Dorrie. I've a few things to see to before tomorrow."

"Gillian?"

She turned. Dorrie was looking at her with a strange light in her soft eyes. "I'm sure you and Garrick will come to care for one another very much. When I wed your brother, I barely knew him, and now I cannot imagine my life without him. I hope you will find the same happiness in your life."

Gillian smiled. "I have every intention of it, Dorrie."

That same thought stuck in Gillian's head when she slowly opened the door to Clare's bedchamber a short time later. After checking that no one was inside, she slipped past the door, closing it softly behind her.

The room was everything Gillian would have imagined when thinking of Clare: austere, imposing, untouchable. Dark green velvet and gold brocade draped the tester bed and tall windows, the furniture made of rich laburnum inset with elaborate marquetry. The plasterwork ceiling was carved with trefoil and laurel leaves in a design more befitting a palace, and an Anatolian rug with an intricately woven pattern covered the polished wood floor. There was nothing out of place, no hint that any real person had ever dwelt there.

Gillian started poking about in search of the diary. The drawers to Clare's writing table contained nothing more than blank sheets of foolscap and a few spare quills, the crystal inkwell appearing more as a decoration than an everyday implement. She searched everywhere, in the chest of drawers, the wardrobe, even in Clare's dressing table. The diary just wasn't there. Finally, just before leaving, an afterthought really, she decided to check the small drawers in the night table beside the bed.

Gillian pulled the drawer out. It was empty. She

frowned at having failed to find the diary. When she pushed the drawer to close it, though, she heard a sound, something moving, rolling in the drawer. An empty drawer. Gillian moved the drawer again, pulling and pushing. Again the sound.

Gillian tried to pull the drawer out. It stopped halfway, refusing to go any farther. She pushed against the back of it. The wood shifted, as if it wasn't totally fixed in place. Gillian lifted the drawer just a little, and it pulled free from the table.

A small compartment was revealed underneath, hidden behind the front part of the drawer. A false side separated the two sections. Inside the smaller portion lay a glass bottle. Gillian picked the bottle up and inspected it. Her vision began to grow cloudy.

"Was there something you needed from me, Gillian?"

Gillian turned around. Clare stood framed in the doorway. "I, uh, was looking for some extra quills. I've run out. I didn't think you'd mind . . ."

Clare came into the room. "Of course not, Gillian. Did you find what you needed?"

"I hadn't looked yet. I . . ."

Clare came forward, stopping before Gillian. "What is that in your hand, Gillian?"

Gillian looked down at the bottle she held. "I just found this in your drawer."

"Oh, yes," Clare said, swiping it from her hand, "that is a bottle of scent. A special blend I had made."

"I've never seen a scent bottle like this before. It looks more like an apothecary's bottle."

Clare stared at her. "Yes, well, as I said, it is scent and it is very expensive, so I'll just put it away so it doesn't get spilled. Now if you wouldn't mind, Gillian, I find I'm a bit tired. I should like to rest now."

Gillian turned to leave, completely forgetting the quills she'd come for. She stopped when she reached

the door. "Clare, I saw the physicians here again ear-
lier today. Does that mean Reginald's condition is im-
proving?"

"What do you think you are doing, you bastard?"

Clare's shrill voice drew the attention of the other courtiers standing near to Garrick on the crowded bowling green. Garrick, noticing their sudden interest, lifted his monocle to his eyes, smiled at Clare politely, and spoke with his mincing fop's voice.

"Lady Trisbane, isn't it? Was that your slipper I just stepped on? Oh, Gemini, but I am so clumsy sometimes. I hope you will accept my apologies, dear lady. Perhaps we should walk a spell, to assure you are not injured in any way?"

Garrick swung his arm outward with a flourish, motioning toward the crushed shell walkway that followed the river along Whitehall's south side. "I would suggest you limp," he murmured under his breath, "unless you wish to set tongues to wagging and destroy everything we've worked for thus far."

Clare made a good show of it, favoring her left foot as they moved away from the crowd of courtiers watching the king at play on the green.

When they were out of earshot, Garrick spoke. "Now, madam, perhaps you can explain what it is that possessed you to do what you just did before half the court?"

Clare stopped walking and stared at him. "You look like a fool in that ridiculous costume."

Garrick looked down at himself. "You do not like my new fashion? I am wounded." He posed, setting his hosed leg forward to best show off his wide-bowed shoes. The many gold buttons that lined the front of his lively purple jacket blinked in the sunlight. He toyed with a beribboned ringlet that fell over his lace collar. "I am told Lady Gillian is rather fond of my wardrobe."

He grinned, his painted lips curling into a sneer. "She cannot recall ever having seen the like."

"Very amusing." Clare frowned. "You had better hope this disguise of yours lasts until the wedding. Of course that shouldn't prove too difficult for you, given that I understand are to wed Gillian on the morrow."

Garrick didn't look at her, but stared out beyond Clare at the river. He dropped the shrill affected tone to his voice. "Yes, I am."

"And was I present when this little part of your plan was decided upon?"

He looked at her. "No, Clare, you were not."

Actually, there had been a woman present when Garrick had made up his mind to offer for Gillian, but it hadn't been Clare. Althea. Yes, that is what her name had been, at least that's what he thought it had been. He really didn't bother with such trivial details. Whatever her name, he did know she had been a pretty blond with lush breasts, soft, smooth thighs, and she fit tighter than a glove two sizes small around his rod.

Ah, Althea—if that is what her name was—had been good. Very good. She'd been open to things no other woman had. She had even allowed him to climax in her mouth, a thing Clare had always refused. Garrick found himself wondering if Althea might still be unengaged for the evening . . .

"Garrick!"

He looked over at Clare, who at that moment looked as if she'd just swallowed a whole lemon. He released an impatient breath, assuming his roll of fop once again. "Yes, my dear?"

"You are still planning on staying with our original objective, are you not?"

Garrick took up the small mirror he had suspended from a chain at his waist and checked the condition of his face paint. "You speak in riddles, madam. I know not what you speak of."

"Then allow me to put it in plainer terms for you. You are still going to get rid of Gillian before she can tell anyone the truth of the events leading up to and following her abduction, aren't you, a truth that would see us both thrown into prison?"

Garrick smiled. He ran a finger along the line of her tense jaw. "Of course, dear Clare. That is what I said I would do, is it not?"

He started walking with her again, his mind drifting to his plans for Gillian, to the things he was going to do to her. "I believe I shall play the role of the grieving bridegroom most convincingly. An accident, I think. Yes, while we are off, Gillian and I, on our wedding trip. It will be night. We will have almost reached the inn. The carriage will slip down a rocky ravine most unexpectedly. I, of course, will be thrown clear, but Gillian . . ." He shook his head. "I'm afraid there will be little hope, little hope indeed for her surviving." He smiled again. "Alas, poor Gillian won't stand a chance when I'm finished with her. And no one, not even the heroic Lord Morgan will be able to save her this time."

"I believe that is checkmate, Your Majesty."

King Charles looked at Cassia with an expression as unreadable as a book with blank pages. She waited. Very slowly, a wry smile curved upward at one side of his mouth. "Well played, my dear. Very well played, indeed. Shall we have a go at another round?"

"I'm afraid I must be getting back to my husband before he begins to think I do more with Your Majesty than play at chess."

She made to rise from her chair. The King reached for her hand.

"Just one more game, Cassia."

Cassia lowered herself to her chair. She knew well that tone in the king's voice. He had something to say to her, something he'd been waiting until just this moment to tell her. "Well, perhaps just one more game . . ."

Charles set up his pieces on the board. "I hear tell there is to be a private marriage performed at Adamley House on the morrow."

"Is that so?" Cassia said, eying the king curiously as she set her own pieces.

"Yes, the marquess requested a special license. He was in quite a hurry to have it off and done with as soon as could be arranged. He was so hurried, in fact, I wondered if the bride even knew of it herself."

Cassia moved her pawn. "And the bride would be . . . ?"

"Lady Gillian Forrester. The marquess's daughter, of course."

Cassia waited for Charles to make his play, then moved her own piece. "And who is Lady Gillian to wed in so much of a hurry, Your Majesty?"

"Garrick Fitzwilliam. You know who he is, don't you, Cassia?"

Cassia hardly noticed when Charles captured her queen's knight. "Isn't he the Earl of Handley's son?"

"Aye, that he is. Fifth in a line of ten, I believe. It came as a bit of a surprise to me, especially since I had thought the girl's affections given to another."

Cassia lifted the king's bishop off the board. "I, as well, had that impression, Your Majesty."

"One can never tell when others may enter the fray," Charles said as he took her king's pawn with a knight.

"An interesting observation, Your Majesty."

"Ah, but I am of the belief that true love will eventually persevere, for without love, we are nothing but flesh and bone and emptiness, and no one should be made to live an existence such as that."

Cassia moved her queen to king two. "I would have to agree with you on that point, Your Majesty."

"Things do have a way of working themselves out,"

Charles said, moving his own queen to face hers. "Of course, a little aid to keep true love on its course can do no harm . . ."

Cassia stopped, her hand resting on her queen as she deciphered the king's innuendo. Gillian had assured Dante she had the situation with her father in hand. While she hadn't refused the proposed match with Garrick Fitzwilliam, she had no intention of actually wedding him. Obviously, she hadn't foreseen her father's determination. They would have to act fast. And they would need all the help they could get.

Cassia moved her queen again. "Thank you, Your Majesty. This has proven to be a most enlightening game."

Charles grinned. "You shouldn't thank a man, Lady Cassia, when he's on the very brink of taking you."

He glanced at the chessboard.

Cassia did the same.

She read the positions of the pieces remaining on the board. She looked up at the king.

Charles smiled. "I daresay I will checkmate you in some six moves, my dear."

"I daresay you are right, Your Majesty. Perhaps even in five."

Chapter Twenty-six

"Explain to me again why we are doing this?" Hadrian asked as the three of them—Dante, Rolfe, and himself—crouched behind a hedge of rue bushes. Hadrian sneezed; he always did whenever he came near rue.

"We are going to prevent Gillian from having to wed Garrick Fitzwilliam on the morrow," Rolfe said, adjusting the coil of rope that hung from his left shoulder. "Isn't that right, Dante?"

Dante wasn't listening to them. He was peering through the trees at the stone balcony that led to Gillian's bedchamber at Adamley House. At least he hoped it was Gillian's bedchamber. He removed his small spyglass from his coat and began to mentally design their strategy.

Thankfully, the moon was full, low and fat in the night sky, providing more than enough light. It was late, and activity within the house had ceased a good two hours before. The streets were otherwise deserted. The time, it seemed, was ripe for abduction.

"All right," Dante said, looking at the other two, "we will move around that line of trees toward the alleyway. There's a service gate at the rear of the Adamley garden. From there, we'll move to Gillian's balcony. There is a trellis that covers the wall just to the side of it. One of us will scale the wall and secure the rope to the balusters so another can follow. The last of us will remain on the ground to keep watch on the area and give warning should the need arise. Have you any questions?"

"Yes, I do," said Rolfe. "Who will be the one climbing the trellis?"

"I hope you're not to thinking of me," Hadrian said, objecting before anyone else could. "I'm too old to be scaling walls, Dante. I've not done anything of that sort in a decade or more. I'm not even certain I still can. I also have children to consider. I'm better suited to keeping watch." He added, "On the ground."

"Well, I can't climb the trellis," Rolfe piped in. "I have a wife who is with child. And that old injury to my leg has been kicking up lately." He flexed his leg outward as if to emphasize his statement.

Dante frowned. "What injury to your leg?"

"You remember the one I got when . . . "—Rolfe paused—"but then again you weren't there that time when I nearly crippled myself after jumping from one rooftop to another in order to avoid a particularly tenacious Roundhead in pursuit."

"No, Dante wasn't there," Hadrian broke in, "but I was, my friend, and that's quite a canard you're spinning. You were far from crippled. It was a mild sprain, which certainly didn't keep you from entertaining a pert little tavern wench in your room later that same evening. And as for your having leaped from rooftop to rooftop . . . "

"By God's dines!" Dante drew a slow breath. "I will climb the trellis, despite the fact that I, too, have a child, for whom I am solely responsible. The two of you would probably whine poor Gillian into a stupor anyway." He shook his head. "It's a wonder to me you were once celebrated soldiers in service to the Crown. Even more remarkable is that King Charles ever regained the throne at all, having to rely on soldiers like you."

"As Hadrian said," Rolfe broke in, "our military

days were nearly ten years ago. And you are younger than either one of us."

Dante nodded. "Yes, that six months that separates you and me in age makes a world of difference, Rolfe. That argument might prove reasonable for Hadrian, his being our senior by several years and all."

"I could still whip both of you, despite my advanced age."

Dante grinned, knowing, despite their protests, his friends would walk through fire for him if they had to. They would even climb a trellis. "Let's get on with it."

Dante slid around the hedgerow and moved silently, keeping his back along the stone wall at the rear of the Adamley property. Rolfe and Hadrian followed. Dante didn't hear anything, not even the crunch of gravel beneath their boots as they skirted the perimeter. It was all in the way one positioned the feet, toes first instead of heel as was the usual practice. It had been one of the first maneuvers Hadrian had taught them when they'd been at Oxford. Back then it had helped them to avoid detection when sneaking away from their rooms at night to the local tavern. During the wars it had saved their lives when scouting in enemy territory. They could, any one of them, probably still bound between rooftops as well.

They came to the service gate, and Dante went for the latch. It held fast. He reached over top of it to the one adjoining on the other side.

"Damnation."

"What is it?" Rolfe asked, close behind him.

"The gate is padlocked . . . "

"So pick it."

" . . . from the other side."

Dante turned to them. "One of us is going to have to scale the wall to pick the lock."

"Which one of us?" Rolfe asked, subtlety indicating it wouldn't be him.

Dante looked at Hadrian.

"You're off your chump," Hadrian said. "You expect me to climb that wall? It's at least ten feet tall, and there are iron spikes along the top of it!"

"You're the best lockpick among us," Dante said. "You know you've scaled walls twice as treacherous. Remember when we had to extricate Rolfe from the gaol after he was taken in that tavern at Worcester?"

"Yes," Hadrian continued, "and after we dragged ourselves through miles of swamps, slipped over the curtain wall, then the inner wall, and scaled three stories to his cell window, we found him playing All Fours with that Roundhead captain, gambling for his release, which he'd just won moments before our arrival."

Dante looked at him. "You are still the best lockpick among us, Hadrian."

"Perhaps, in my younger days, but I haven't picked a lock since we stole into Colonel Whitby's quarters, looking for Cromwell's dispatches. That was quite a while ago."

Rolfe and Dante stared at him, silent.

Hadrian frowned even as he took the rope from Rolfe's shoulder and began forming a slip at its end. It took him only three tosses before he looped it on one of the stone finials that topped the rugged wall. He pulled the rope taut, bracing himself. "I'll toss the rope back once I reach the ground on the other side. You two can follow me over and start up the trellis to Gillian's balcony while I work the lock on the gate free."

Hadrian set his foot in an outcropping and with the aid of the rope, hoisted himself up the garden wall. A few minutes after he'd lowered himself down and out of sight, the rope came flying back toward them.

"All right, Rolfe, I'll hold the end while you go over first." Dante pulled the rope. "Then when I reach the top, I'll release the slip and toss the rope down to you."

Five minutes later, Dante and Rolfe were skirting the edge of the garden toward the south side of the house and Gillian's bedchamber. Hadrian was involved with the padlock.

"Uh, didn't you say there was a trellis on the wall beside her balcony?" Rolfe asked as Dante came up beside him.

Dante looked to where Rolfe indicated. The trellis had been removed, no doubt after the last midnight escapade at Gillian's balcony.

"Bloody hell," he muttered.

"Any idea what we should do now?"

Dante looked around the garden. An ancient elm with sturdy fat boughs stood about ten yards away. One of the boughs stretched very close to the balcony, within leaping distance. It would be chancy, but what choice did they have?

"Wait here in the shadows so no one sees you. When I give a whistle, come beneath the balcony and toss the rope up to me."

"What are you going to do?"

Dante was already turning away. "I'm going to climb a tree." Then he bent his knees and jumped, grabbing hold of the nearest limb. He didn't look down as he climbed, not even when he reached the bough that stretched near to Gillian's balcony. He only focused on where he was going. He wasn't interested in where he'd come from.

Straddling the thick bough, Dante slowly made his way toward the end of it. When he reached the point where he thought his weight might break it, he grabbed onto the upper branches and stood. The bough made a cracking noise as he pushed off from it and jumped for the edge of the balcony.

Dante grabbed onto the balcony railing with both hands, legs dangling beneath him. He swung himself up and over the edge, dropping onto the balcony floor.

He stood and turned, then froze when he saw someone standing in the doorway.

"I was wondering when you'd find your way up here."

Chapter Twenty-seven

Gillian walked slowly from the shadows. "I'd nearly given up on you, my lord."

Dante stared at her. He was amazed. "How did you know I would be coming for you?"

"Really, my lord. Have as much faith in me as I do you. I knew you would never have allowed me to wed Garrick Fitzwilliam. You've seen him, haven't you? So you realize I could never be wife to someone who looks like that. Besides, Cassia sent me a little note, wishing me well on my marriage. I figured something had to be done tonight."

Dante grinned at her. She was dressed appropriately in a simple dark gown. Her hair was tied back from her face, and she held a small traveling valise in one hand. "Then you should know never to give up on me, my lady. Never."

Dante looked over the balcony railing and whistled softly. Rolfe stepped out from the cover of the trees. He tossed the rope up to him, and Dante secured it to a balustrade before turning back to Gillian.

"I was thinking, madam," he said, taking her valise and dropping it down to Rolfe, "that I have seen enough of London. I will be returning to Wyldewoode now and wondered if you'd care to join me? That is, if you haven't any pressing engagements."

Gillian came before him, smiling. She leaned against him, placed her hands against his chest, and looked straight into his eyes. "There is nothing that would keep me from going with you, my lord."

Gillian closed her eyes as Dante lowered his lips to hers. She could feel his heart beating beneath her hands. She could feel her own heart racing just as quickly. Dante had come back for her. He had kept his promise. She wanted to laugh and cry with the realization of it.

"Now," Dante said as he reluctantly pulled away from their kiss, "much as I would enjoy continuing what we just started, we will need to get you down from here first. The last time I did this, I was sent away for three years. I have no intention of that this time." He climbed on the railing, looping the rope behind his back. He set Gillian before him, supporting her with his legs, and slowly lowered the two of them to the ground.

"Before we go," Dante said to her once they had reached the ground, "I need you to do one more thing for me."

"My lord?"

"I want you to scream."

"I don't understand . . ."

"You know how to do it, Gillian. It's inherent to your gender. Just open your mouth and let out a yell that would wake the dead, or at least those who are sleeping heavily."

Gillian looked at him as if he'd lost his mind. "You wish me to scream?"

"There's nothing to worry about. I have the situation well in hand."

Gillian looked at Dante one last time, then turned back to face her balcony. She opened her mouth and let out a scream that indeed would have woken the dead.

"Now let us just hope Hadrian was successful with the lock," Dante said, taking her hand as he raced with her to the service door.

Hadrian had sprung the lock and was waiting for them. "I was beginning to wonder if you'd been caught."

"Not yet, my friend. But we are still hopeful." Dante turned around. Candlelight was already burning in almost every room inside the house. The sounds of confusion and panic soon followed. Several moments later, the marquess appeared on the balcony, his nightcap askew, glaring at them in the moonlight.

"He's got her. Bloody hell, Morgan has taken Gillian again!"

Reginald, who had come out behind his father, was already turning back toward the house. "After them!"

"That is our cue," Dante said, and they hurried through the service door to the street.

As they came around the corner, Gillian noticed three coaches that were parked in a line in front of Adamley House. Mara stood beside one, Cassia another. Rolfe and Hadrian joined their wives and got into their respective coaches. Dante took Gillian to the last coach in the line.

"Your chariot, my lady," he said and helped Gillian inside. He climbed in behind her and pulled the door closed. "Stubbs, be off, man! Quick as you can!"

As they rolled away from the footpath, Gillian looked out the coach window and watched as the other two coaches carrying Rolfe and Cassia, and Hadrian and Mara, started off in opposite directions. One headed north, the other south. Their coach rolled off for the west.

Dante sat back in the seat. "That should certainly help to confuse our pursuers."

"That is why you asked me to scream, so they would see the coaches leaving. That way my family would not know which coach to follow first." Gillian smiled at him. "Very clever, my lord. Where are you really taking me?"

"To Wyldewoode, just as I said."

"But wouldn't that be the first place they would look for us?"

"Not at first, only because I am wagering they will think that is the last place I would take you for much the same reason. By the time they come to Derbyshire, after having exhausted every other alternative, I expect to have everything in readiness. Phoebe will remain in the city with Mara and Hadrian until any threat of danger has passed."

"Then you have discovered who kidnapped me?"

"I am awaiting confirmation, but I have my suspicions."

"Is it Clare?"

Dante looked at Gillian. "Your sister-in-law? What makes you believe that?"

"I learned that she stole my diary after the night I was taken. My maid, Abigail, told me of it just yesterday evening. I went to look for the diary in Clare's chamber earlier today, but I found something else instead. There was a small glass bottle hidden in a secret compartment in her night table. At first I did not know what it was, but then I remembered something. I suspect I had found the bottle before and had questioned Clare about it. I read in my diary that Reginald had been very ill. I think I might have thought the bottle had something to do with his puzzling sickness."

"What sickness was this?"

"I still am not certain. I questioned a few people, Dorrie and Abigail, among them. Reginald had started to become ill just shortly after my father and brothers returned to London after the plague. At first they feared his illness was the plague, but a physician discounted that. From his headaches and the stomach distress, they considered a gastric fever, and then, as he deteriorated, they even considered jaundice. However, the physician could never really pinpoint what was ailing Reginald. He seemed to improve shortly before my disappearance."

Dante listened carefully to her. "Jaundice you say? Gastric fever? Do you still have this glass bottle?"

Gillian shook her head. "I left it in Clare's night table because I didn't wish to arouse any suspicions before I knew exactly what Clare was about."

"That was good thinking, Gillian. It is better Clare believes you don't remember anything of it. From what you have told me of Reginald's symptoms, it would appear to me that she was slowly poisoning him."

"The thought had occurred to me as well, although I was hoping I would turn out to be wrong."

"I'm afraid not. I would guess her particular choice arsenic, though not in its purest form, for Reginald would have surely died from its effects long before now. There are ways to adulterate it, so it would be less detectable; the death is a lingering one so as to avoid suspicion. I have heard of arsenic being fed to toads, and a liquid form of it is then distilled from the body of the dead creature. Most often this sort of thing is made by a perfumer, one who is skilled in the art of distillation."

"When I questioned Clare about the bottle initially, before my disappearance, she told me it contained a uniquely blended scent she'd had made."

"Scent, you say?" Dante thought a moment. "I would have to wonder if the perfumer who created Clare's unique arsenical scent might also have been the one who made the peculiar scent favored by your abductor."

"You are thinking Clare arranged to have me kidnapped so I couldn't tell anyone I suspected her of poisoning Reginald? I had considered that, but then I wondered why the man who kidnapped me would have planned to take me to Scotland to wed me?"

"It would all depend on who it was who kidnapped

you, and what the true motive behind the abduction was, which we will concentrate on more once we are safely arrived at Wyldewoode. Rolfe and Hadrian will continue the investigation in London. They have been instructed to send word to us at Wyldewoode once it is safe for us to return. We will, and with us we will bring the name of the real culprit. I had hoped to stay in London to see to it myself, but then I received the information that your father had arranged to have you wed to Fitzwilliam on the morrow."

"So you received my message telling you about my father's plan?"

"No, I never received any message from you. It was Cassia who relayed that bit of news to me, after His Majesty, King Charles, mentioned to her in passing over a chess game your father's request for a special license. If it hadn't been for the King, I never would have known it. I never would have come for you tonight. And you probably would have been forced to marry Garrick Fitzwilliam in the morning."

"I did entertain the thought of dressing my maid, Abigail, in my mother's wedding gown and placing her at Garrick's side in my stead."

Dante smiled. "I should have liked to see that. It is of no matter now. You are no longer in any danger of having to wed Garrick Fitzwilliam, nor do your father's threats against me have any bearing either. I have spoken with the king and have explained everything to him. He, in turn, has assured me that he would not entertain any accusations made against me."

"How long will it take us to reach Wyldewoode?"

"We will be riding along back roads through the night and tomorrow. We will stop at an inn tomorrow night to sleep and change horses. We should be at Wyldewoode sometime late the following day. And, then, all we will need to do is wait for the summons from Rolfe and Hadrian."

* * *

Gillian watched Dante come through the trees and into the clearing, carrying a basket in one hand, a bunch of wildflowers in the other. She had chosen a spot for their afternoon picnic beside a secluded brook where the sunlight filtered down through the thick trees.

She smiled as she watched Dante trying to maneuver his way across the brook on stepping stones while keeping hold of the basket and flowers. She sat up when he succeeded and came over to where she waited on a lap rug that had been stowed in the coach seat.

"I hope you're hungry, for Cassia's cook packed enough food to last us a week," he said, sitting beside her.

Gillian came forward. "I'm famished."

They chatted a bit while they ate cold chicken and cheese and shared a bottle of claret, drinking from crude pewter cups, which afterward they rinsed in the brook. The claret, and the food soon made Gillian feel sleepy. She had rested very little since they'd left London late the previous night, only dozing a bit on Dante's shoulder in the coach.

"We've a little time before we need to start off again," Dante said to her. "I told Stubbs to water the horses where the brook runs alongside the roadway, then let them graze a bit on the sweet grass beside it. Come, you look tired. Why don't you rest a bit before we must leave?"

Dante leaned against the tree trunk and pulled Gillian to him, setting his arm around her as he fiddled with a lock of her hair, hair that shone red-gold in the late afternoon sunlight. They were quiet for some time.

Dante finally spoke. "Gillian, I need to say something to you."

"Hmmm?" Gillian closed her eyes, the warm sunshine beaming down on her face.

"We haven't yet discussed what the future might hold for either of us, but it is something I have lately considered quite often. At first, when your father first took you from me, I thought I could forget you. I thought that perhaps your father was right in saying you deserved a man who could give you a respectable life, a life in which you would never have to bear the brand of having married a man with a past quite as extensive as mine. But I found I was wrong. I couldn't forget you. I came to realize that I cared for you more than I have cared for any other woman in my life. Even when you weren't with me, I saw you everywhere, in the small ways you'd come to touch my life. I saw how much Phoebe had come to care for you. I saw how you were with her. I wanted you to be there for her at those times when an girl needs a woman, a mother." He smiled. "Even to have tea with when she plays with her dolls. I came to the conclusion that no other woman could satisfy those needs. Only you. I know I haven't lived the most exemplary life. Looking back, it seems as if I was looking for something, but was searching in the wrong places. I found that something the moment I found you."

Dante hesitated, searching for the proper words. He'd never spoken so seriously with a woman before. He wanted to do it right. "What I mean is I don't want to lose you again, Gillian, and if you'll have me, I would consider myself the most fortunate of men if you would agree to become my wife."

There, he'd said it. It had been occupying his thoughts since he'd danced with Gillian at the Palace, when she'd told him of her father's wish that she wed Garrick Fitzwilliam. Losing her was not a risk he ever wanted to take. Wedding her would ensure he wouldn't. Dante awaited Gillian's response.

"Gillian?"

Dante looked down at her. Gillian's eyes were

closed, and her breathing was even and slow. He smiled. She had made a valiant effort. Several times during the ride from London, she had started to nod off, only to lift her head moments later, assuring him all the while she wasn't the least bit tired.

It was one of the things he admired most about her, her determination to prove her mettle against any odds. He had seen it that first day when she'd woken in his mother's bedchamber at Wyldewoode to discover that she had lost her memory. It was that same spirit that drove her to master an instrument as difficult for her as the viola da gamba.

Carrying that thought with him, Dante smiled, leaned his head back against the tree, and drifted off to sleep.

The coach pulled into the courtyard of the Golden Goose Inn just after moonrise.

"We'll stay here tonight," Dante said. "Tomorrow we will sleep at Wyldewoode."

The innkeeper either assumed they were married, or simply, from experience, refrained from asking. In any case, it mattered naught, for there was only one room to let. The other had already been taken by another nobleman traveler.

"It is our best room, my lord," said the innkeeper, a man named Crutch, who wore a patch over one eye, as he opened the door to them. He quickly lit a branch of candles sitting on the chest near the door. "We can send supper up for you if you prefer to take your victuals here in your room instead of in the taproom. It can get a bit rough down there once the boys get a few jacks of ale down their gullets."

Dante nodded. "A good idea, Mr. Crutch."

Gillian looked about the room. It was surprisingly clean. The bedding appeared fresh and free from vermin, and a vase full of flowers graced the crude wooden table near the window that faced the courtyard. The water in the washbowl was also clear and clean.

"Will there be anything else, my lord?" asked the innkeeper.

Dante looked at Gillian. "My lady?"

"Can a bath be arranged?"

"Of course, my lady," the innkeeper said, already starting for the door. "I'll tell Margaret, my wife, to get the water heating right away. She just finished making some of her lavender soap. I'll have her bring you a cake of it, too, my lady."

"Thank you, Mr. Crutch. That would be lovely."

Gillian remained standing, facing the door even after it closed. An awkward silence came over the room as she searched for something to say, other than the thoughts that were running through her mind. Would they share the bed? The thought of waking in the morning, wrapped in Dante's arms, even if she shouldn't even consider it, gave her a bit of a thrill.

Finally, Dante spoke. "I apologize for the scarcity of rooms, Gillian. I have never stayed at this particular inn before. Of course you will take the bed, and I will go to sleep in the stables with Stubbs."

"No."

Dante looked at her.

"It is not as if we are strangers, Dante. The bed is really quite large; there is more than enough room for the two of us. I have just spent the past two days confined alone with you in a much smaller space inside the coach. I trust you as I trust no other, and I would feel far more at ease with you lying beside me than sleeping with the horses."

For a moment Dante looked stunned. She trusted him with herself, with her life. He would never break that trust. Neither of them spoke. A knock on the door not a moment later broke the silence. Dante opened the door.

"We've the tub for your bath, my lady," said a young boy of about fifteen, who, with the help of another, carried in a wooden tub likely used more for laundering than bathing. The second boy produced a cake of soap.

"Mrs. Crutch said to give you this. We'll bring up the water real quick."

With that, the boys left.

"I will retire to the taproom while you have your bath," Dante said and followed them out.

Dante sat in the crowded taproom, watching the flames flickering in the crude stone hearth while nursing an ale that was far too sour to do anything more than sip. As he sat there, he tried failingly to dispel the image of Gillian immersed waist high in the tub while the fire crackled in the hearth beside her. He tried not to think of how the fire would glow against her skin as the water trickled down between her breasts, over her taut nipples, running down her flat belly to . . .

"Would you like anything else, milord?"

The inn's serving girl was suddenly standing before him, saucily pressing her bosom under his nose as she reached for his empty blackjack.

Dante shifted, trying to ease the terrible discomfort in his breeches that had come about while he'd been thinking of Gillian. He waited silently while the girl wiped the still clean table with a cloth.

"Another jack of ale?" she asked again.

"No," Dante said, standing and tossing her a shilling, "Thank you, but I think I've been here long enough. Tell Mr. Crutch to include a bottle of claret with supper when he sends it up to my room."

Dante halted when he reached the door to their room. He listened for sounds of water splashing on the other side of the door. He heard nothing.

"Gillian?"

There was a silent moment before the latch jiggled, freeing the door.

"I was beginning to wonder if you'd decided to spend the night with the horses after all," Gillian said.

Dante stood in the doorway, staring at her. She walked over to a chair by the fire and started to dry her hair, wet from the bath, with a cloth. She ran her fingers through the damp strands, pushing them back from her face. She wore a chemise, nothing more, and when she had walked past him at the door, he caught the scent of her lavender soap.

Dante took in a slow, deep breath. "I can return later, if you are not yet finished . . ."

"No. I am done with my bath, and Mrs. Crutch will be sending up our supper very soon." She looked at him and smiled. "You may, of course, remove your coat, unless you have plans to sleep in it."

Dante removed his coat and draped it over the back of his chair. He turned toward Gillian and froze. She was standing now in front of the hearth, still drying her hair. Her body was clearly outlined beneath her chemise in the light from the fire, her legs, her hips, her breasts. The room seemed to grow warmer by the second.

A knock on the door revealed the innkeeper's wife with their supper.

"I hope your ladyship liked the soap," she said, setting out a meat and vegetable stew served in bread trenchers, cheese wedges, and apple tartstuff.

"Yes, thank you," Gillian said.

Dante tried to concentrate on the meal as they sat across from one another at the small table near the fire. What the devil was wrong with him? Why was his head filled with only one thought, to sweep Gillian up and carry her over to the bed and have his way with her. Why couldn't he even share a meal with her without his pulse racing and his palms sweating? Even more so, how was he supposed to sleep in the same bed with her and not touch her?

"Is anything the matter, Dante?"

Besides the fact that I can't sit comfortably and that your skin is beckoning me to taste it?

He looked up from his stew of which he eaten precious little. "No, not at all."

"You seem preoccupied."

That was an understatement. "I am just anxious to get back to Wyldewoode." *And anxious to get out of this room before I expire from the need to have you.*

Gillian stood. "I guess I wasn't as hungry as I thought I was." She looked at Dante's trencher. "Neither were you, from the looks of it."

If only you knew, madam . . .

Gillian went over to the bed. She pulled back the covers and climbed onto the mattress. "I think I'll retire now. Stubbs said we've a long day's journey ahead. Will you join me?"

That was it. He could stand no more. The sight of her sitting on the bed, inviting him over to her was nearly Dante's undoing. "No, Gillian. I've decided that I should sleep in the stables after all."

"Why, my lord? Have I done something to displease you?"

"To put it to you plainly, Gillian, I simply cannot trust myself to sleep in the same bed with you and not touch you."

Gillian smiled. "It isn't that large of a bed that I would expect you not to touch me at all."

"When I said 'touch,' I really meant something more than the literal sense of the word. I do not trust myself to be that close to you when having you completely is all I can think about. You are far too lovely tonight, Gillian. I am attempting to live a decent and moral life now, but there are limits to the strength of my conviction. If I were to sleep with you, things would happen, and everything you've heard about me will then be true. You are an innocent, and I will not take advantage of that. One thing I can say with surety about myself is that I have never taken an unmarried woman to bed, and it is not something I wish to start now."

Gillian looked at him and said matter-of-factly, as if it was the most logical solution to their problem, "So, then, marry me."

Chapter Twenty-eight

Dante stared at Gillian. "I beg your pardon?"

Gillian looked calmly at him. She stood and started walking toward him, talking as she did. "Yes, my lord. You heard me aright. I asked you to marry me. You see, I cannot help but feel partly responsible for the awkward situation we are now in. I would never wish for you to compromise your principles. I agree that sleeping in the stables will probably be the better choice tonight, but it is beyond that which concerns me. We could very well end up together for some period, and I certainly don't wish to have you sleeping in the stables the entire time. If the fact that I am not wed is what troubles you so much, then the easiest way to dispense with that is for me to wed, and the only man I would ever wish to wed is you."

Gillian was standing so near to Dante now that his head was filled with the sweet lavender scent of her. Her hair had dried and was hanging in a twisting, curling mass about her shoulders. It took every ounce of strength within him not to gather her up in his arms, married or not, take her to the bed, and make love to her until the sun rose.

Somehow, with the grace of whichever saint was watching over him, he didn't.

"You did not answer me, my lord."

Dante stared at Gillian. "I can think of no other woman I would rather wed than you."

Gillian smiled. "We have solved our dilemma, my lord. What will you do now?"

Dante turned away from her, for if he stayed with her another moment, looking as inviting as she did, he would not be able to stop himself from having her. "I shall see you on the morrow, my lady. We leave at dawn, for I do not wish to wait a moment longer than I have to in order to make you my wife."

Gillian watched him go. Even after she'd doused the candles and had gone to bed, she wondered why she'd done such a ridiculous thing. It was not that she regretted proposing marriage to him. Wedding Dante would be like living a dream that she had hoped for but hadn't dared believe might happen. She wanted to wake in his arms every morning. She wanted to share her life with him. She wanted to have his children. No, it was her having agreed with his wish to wait until they were wed before they should be together that she was beginning to regret. Lying in the bed, unable to sleep, unable to do anything but think of him lying in that stable, wanting him there with her, she wondered if she might have convinced him to forgo his convictions just this one time.

But even as she speculated, she knew that in this one instance, with her, Dante needed to be able to say, to anyone and everyone, that he had remained a gentleman after all.

The coach pulled off the road and rolled to a stop in the clearing of a copse of tall elm trees. It was nearing dusk. Gillian looked out the window and saw a small stone building set back from the road. Dante, who had ridden outside on Fury since they'd left the inn that morning, was just walking inside.

Gillian opened the door, but didn't step out. "Stubbs, why have we stopped here? Lord Morgan said we'd be arriving at Wyldewoode near nightfall. Have we lost our way?"

The coach listed a bit as Stubbs clamored down from the driver's seat. "N-no, my lady. W-we aren't l-lost. W-we are v-very close to W-Wyldewoode now. Sh-should only t-take another hour or m-more to g-get us there. H-His lordship just s-said he needed to s-stop here to s-see to s-some b-business of his."

Business? Gillian wondered what it could be, and then, almost at the same time, she remembered how Dante had been helping the residents of that poor plague village before they'd left for London. No doubt, he had stopped here now, before they reached Wyldewoode, to see how things were faring there.

"Thank you, Stubbs. I'm sure his lordship will only be a moment."

And, indeed, he was.

"Would you come with me, please?" he said to her as he pulled the coach door open most unexpectedly.

"What is it, my lord? Has something happened? Are the villagers in need of more assistance?"

Even as she answered, Dante took her hand and helped her down from the coach. "Villagers?"

"Yes, didn't you stop here to see how that plague village was faring?"

"The name of the village is Eyam, and no, I did not. But since you are so concerned, the last report I received on it indicated that the number of plague cases were beginning to drop substantially. I was able to send in some herbal remedies suggested by Mara while we were in London. This village we are in now is not Eyam, though. It is called Peak Forest and lies between Tideswell and Chapel-en-le-Frith. It is known for many things, its canal among them, though its most recent notable point is its church, which we now stand before, dedicated to King Charles the Martyr, our late sovereign. It was built less than a decade ago by the wife of the Earl of Devonshire, and the window over the altar is made of Venetian glass. The church does not welcome any one faith and therefore is independent of episcopal jurisdiction. This means many things to many people, but among them it gives Derbyshire its own little touch of Gretna Green, where banns are not required, and if you so desire, you can be wed within the space of an hour. That is, if you still want to be my bride?"

Gillian smiled at him.

The ceremony took less than an hour, fifty minutes actually if the tall clock in the antechapel was precise, and they were back on their way to Wyldewoode just as night began to fall. Fury was relegated to the rear of the coach, tethered there when Dante joined Gillian inside.

"Come here, wife," Dante said and pulled Gillian into his arms so that she was sitting across his legs. He kissed her urgently, like a man who'd been denied food a long time but who suddenly had a veritable feast set before him.

Gillian clung to his shirt front as he moved his mouth down along her neck and throat, nibbling at her ear, kissing her chin, sending wondrous tremors racing through every inch of her. She felt his hand moving up along her leg, over her knee, fingers racing lightly over her thighs. She felt a sensation of warm expectation deep inside. She wanted to feel him against her. His mouth had kissed a trail to the tops of her breasts, his hand cupping her, enticing her. She felt him releasing the hooks at her bodice, felt the fabric give, and she took a deep breath as she waited for him to continue.

Gillian cried out as she felt Dante's mouth then, wet and hot, tugging at her breasts, teasing her with his tongue, driving her to distraction. His hand had moved higher on her thigh now, stroking her sensitive skin, sending tingles of raw awareness to the very center of her, where a need so real and so desperate for release began to build and build. His hand moved higher still between her legs, and when she felt his finger nudge against her, parting her, delving, she wanted to scream with the pleasure of it.

Dante moved his finger over her, and Gillian was taken up by a tempest of feelings and reactions, her body rocking with the movement of his hand. He flicked his tongue across her taut nipples, then drew on them, filling her with an urgency that left her trembling. The movements of his fingers increased, and with it, his mouth on her breast, and Gillian knew a strange and wonderful soaring sensation that grew and grew in intensity until it burst into a shower of tremors and spasms that rocked her to her soul.

Gillian screamed and squeezed her fingers tightly in Dante's hair, throwing her head back as the tremors slowly subsided into exquisite shivers. Dante held her tightly, burying his face in her breasts as she fluttered back to reality. And when she lifted her head, staring at him in mute wonder at the gift he'd just given her, he touched his lips to hers in a soft and tender kiss.

Dante held Gillian against him, her head resting contentedly against his shoulder, until the coach reached Wyldewoode.

Gillian could hear the sounds of the servants emerging from the house to welcome home their lord.

"Welcome home, Lady Morgan," Dante said as he refastened the hooks at the front of her dress and pulled her skirts down from where they were still bunched at her hips. "I mean to finish that which I began the moment I get you to my bed."

Finish? There was more? How on earth could anything surpass what she'd just experienced?

Dante set her away so he could climb out first. As Gillian emerged, Dante came to her and swept her into his arms. He smiled and whispered into her ear. "Tradition dictates the groom carry the bride over the threshold."

Holding her against him, he started up the stairs to the door. Renny, Mrs. Leeds, every servant it seemed, had come out to meet them. Dante nodded to them, saying nothing, and proceeded into the house, taking Gillian up the stairs to his chamber door. A fire was crackling in the hearth inside and the bedcovers had already been pulled back. Still holding Gillian, Dante turned and kicked the door closed.

"Do you have any idea, madam," Dante said as he lowered her to his bed, "how desperately I want you?"

Gillian couldn't answer. She just stared at him as he lifted her leg, one then the other, and slowly removed her shoes, her ribbon garters, her stockings, tossing them to the floor.

"I ache with my need to have you," he went on, unfastening the hooks on the front of her bodice, the same hooks he'd just closed moments before in the coach. As he did, he kissed her along the hollow between her breasts, her belly. The heat of his mouth aroused her senses even through fabric of her chemise.

"I have wanted you from the first moment I found you," he murmured against her neck as he released the ties on her skirts at her waist. "That, my lady, is the reason I kissed you that night in the rain." He whisked the layers of fabric away. "I have dreamed of having you here, Gillian, in my bed, dreamed of what I would do to you, of how I would touch you and taste you."

Dante stood back, pulling his shirt over his head and tossing it aside. The muscles in his chest and arms rippled seductively in the firelight. He was beautiful, every inch of him defined. Gillian watched as he removed his boots and hose, then loosened his breeches. She stared as he stood before her, magnificently naked.

"Oh, Dante, I have wanted you too."

Dante held out his hand to Gillian. He guided her up to sit before him on the bed, legs dangling over the side. He lowered his head and kissed her softly. He gently pulled her chemise up and over her head. He lifted her against him, reclaiming her mouth while pressing her body close against his.

They were close, so close, breath to breath, flesh to flesh. The mingling heat of their bodies was beyond intoxicating. Gillian locked her hands behind Dante's neck and let herself be lost to him. She could feel his hardness against her and clung to his shoulders as he lay her back onto the bed, coming over her.

Dante lifted his head and looked down at Gillian in the firelight. "Do you know what happens when a man and woman come together, Gillian?"

She nodded, blinking.

"Do you know there will be pain for you this first time when I come into you?"

She nodded again.

"I promise you I will try to make it as easy for you as I can. There are certain things a man can do to lessen the pain. I cannot take it completely away. I would that I could take it upon myself in your stead. Do you trust me, Gillian?"

"Yes," she whispered.

"I need your trust, Gillian. The pain will be sudden, but it will not last, and I will try to bring you to pleasure again so it will fade quickly."

He kissed her mouth. "You are beautiful, Gillian." He kissed her again, deeper this time, moving his tongue in soft thrusts. Gillian parted her legs, and Dante moved between them. He pressed himself intimately against her. Gillian moved her hips, lifting her knees, and felt him at the center of her. She felt an overwhelming need to have him inside of her. Now. She yearned to feel as one with him. She moved her hips again, seeking him.

Dante smiled against her mouth. "Slowly, my love. We've the entire night ahead of us."

Before she could respond, Dante dipped his head to her breast and captured a nipple with his lips, biting softly at it with his teeth. Gillian raked her fingers over his back as a strong shuddering spasm came over her. Dante stroked his hands down the sides of her, cupping her buttocks and lifting her upward as he slid down the length of her, trailing wet kisses downward over her belly, nipping at her side.

Gillian nearly screamed when she felt Dante's mouth, hot and moist, tasting her there.

Waves of pleasure rioted through her as his tongue entered her and he cupped her with his hands, squeezing her hips. He moved his tongue, flicking over her, and Gillian tightened her hands into fists on the sheet, losing all reason. The sensations she had felt in the coach built again, only stronger this time, more intense. She cried out his name and lifted her knees higher, gasping as his tongue continued to flutter over her, quickly, relentlessly, teasing her. He took her, bringing her higher and higher with him until she came nearer to that last exquisite place, and she arched her back, lifting her hips from the bed, and begged Dante to release her from the sweet torment. When she thought she could stand it no more, he did release her and she gasped as the tremors took her, pulsing through her.

Gillian vaguely realized it when Dante rose up on his arms over her and was lifting her knees again, moving between them. She felt the pressure of him as he slowly entered her. He hesitated and parted her legs wider. He covered her mouth with his and took her cry as he pushed through her maidenhead and buried himself within her.

Dante's arms were trembling as he held Gillian tightly to him. Oh, God, he felt he could die from the pleasure of feeling her around him. He held himself still, allowing her to adjust to him inside her. The muscles in his back and neck were tense. Dante pulled himself back. Gillian reached for him. Slowly, languidly, he pushed his hips forward again. Gillian opened her eyes, and watched Dante as he moved against her.

His eyes were closed, and his face reflected his struggle. Slowly he moved, then faster, until he lost the struggle of control over himself and his movements increased and he was thrusting into her. Over and over he came into her, and his breathing was labored until he was gasping out her name and he gathered her to him, burying his face in her hair, her neck, his hips driving now, fast and hard, and finally he shouted out and thrust forward one last time. His body shuddered as he spilled his seed deep inside her. Gillian wrapped her arms around his neck and held him tightly to her as he fought to catch his breath.

The room was suddenly so silent Gillian could hear the sounds of the fire in the hearth. Dante's breathing slowed and he lifted his head, placing his hands on either side of her face. He smiled softly.

"You are an angel, and I thank God for sending you to me. If it takes the rest of my days, I will find a way to show you how much I love you."

Gillian smiled as tears began to form in her eyes. "You just did that very thing, my lord."

When Gillian awoke, the sun was beating brightly through the windows and the sounds of the awakening day filled the room. Dante lay beside her on his back, the sheets tangled furiously in his legs, one hand curled around her back and resting on her bottom. His face was shadowed with a night's beard, his hair tousled around his neck.

God, but he was beautiful.

And he loved her.

Gillian sat up and traced a fingertip softly over his mouth, caressing his bottom lip. She stroked her hand down the side of his face and over his chest, moving her fingers downward to his belly. She moved even lower until her fingers met the sheet at his waist. She took the sheet with her fingers and lifted it slightly to look at him.

"I don't think I've ever been awakened in quite so delightful a manner."

Gillian looked at him. He was staring at her, a wide grin on his mouth. "I was just . . ."

"You are curious by nature, Gillian. It is one of the things I love most about you."

Gillian bit her lower lip, looking at him again. She placed her hand on his belly. Dante closed his eyes, his mouth relaxing its smile. She moved her hand lower, watching the way the muscles in his stomach contracted under her touch. She traced a finger slowly over the velvet hardness of him. Dante sucked in a sharp breath. Gillian pulled her hand away.

"Did I hurt you?"

"No," Dante said, taking her hand and placing it back. "I have never known such pleasure as your touch gives to me, Gillian."

Gillian grew more confident. She closed her fingers around him. It was a potent feeling, this effect she had on him. She stroked her fingers over him, amazed at the strength of him, the maleness of him. She watched the way his body reacted in response to her touch. The excitement it gave her was heady. She remembered the pleasure he'd given her with his hands and his mouth on her. She wanted to give him the same. She moved her hands over him as she rained light kisses on his chest and his belly. She looked at him when he caught her hand and held it away from him. He rolled her beneath him.

"If you persist in what you are doing, my lady. I will

surely embarrass myself in front of you. While I would love for us to continue this little lesson in learning, I do not wish to hurt you. You will more than likely feel a bit sore after last night. We've a lifetime of mornings ahead of us to wake and make love to each other."

He kissed her, slow and long, before moving from the bed. Gillian watched him as he walked over to the washstand and poured some water in the bowl there. He brought it with a cloth to the bed.

"What will you do?" she asked.

"There will be blood from your maidenhead."

Dante laid Gillian back and parted her legs, pressing the damp cloth against her thighs. The cool water soothed her.

Dante stood again and pulled on a dressing robe that lay on the bench at the foot of his bed. He moved to the wardrobe and brought out another for her.

"Are you hungry?"

"Famished."

Dante's robe fell well over her feet, the sleeves completely covering her hands. Gillian didn't care. The silk caressed her skin and the scent of him emanated from the fabric as she walked with him down the stairs to the dining parlor. She never wanted to remove it.

"Good morning, Renny," Dante said as they entered the room together.

"My lord." Renny smiled at Gillian. "Good morning, my lady. I would like to offer my congratulations on your marriage."

"Thank you, Renny. I already feel as if Wyldewoode is my home."

"And it is," Dante said, taking up his cup of coffee.

"A letter arrived by courier early this morning, my lord," Renny said, placing it before Dante. "He said he'd come from London."

"Most likely it is from Rolfe and Hadrian." He opened it, nodding as he read it. "Rolfe indicates your brother Reginald was not pleased when he finally caught their coach only to find him and Cassia inside."

"What did Reginald do?"

"Well, it seems . . ." Dante read a bit more. He chuckled. ". . . it seems they had pulled the coach beneath some trees away from the road. They didn't even hear Reginald approaching. They were in a rather intimate embrace when Reggie threw open the door, expecting to find us inside."

"Oh, dear," Gillian said. "I imagine Reginald was a bit disconcerted."

"To say the least." Dante read on. "Rolfe says he thinks he has located the perfumer who made the odd scent for your abductor. A man named Briggs who works out of a shop on the east end of the city. I should think that by now he would have paid him a visit. We may even have some news by tomorrow. Apparently, Garrick Fitzwilliam was so distressed at your disappearing on the eve of your marriage to him, he has gone into seclusion. Your father wasn't so discreet. Seems he has had a warrant issued for my arrest."

"Oh, dear."

Dante took her hand. "There is nothing to worry about, Gillian. It certainly isn't the first time I've had the authorities looking for me. Derbyshire is a long way from London. I'd wager with Cassia's influence, King Charles will convince the good sheriff that he has matters far more urgent that require his attention."

Chapter Twenty-nine

Gillian was sitting at her dressing table, brushing out her hair when Dante came to her, appearing in the open doorway that joined their chambers.

She caught her breath at the sight of him. He wore naught but his dressing robe, his long legs bare beneath it. She smiled at his reflection in the looking glass. "How do you find your new bedchamber, my lord?"

During the course of the day Dante's belongings had been moved to the master's suite, which adjoined what had been his mother's chamber, now Gillian's. It had been no small task, for the room had remained unused since his father's death, virtually shut up and forgotten. The bed, an ancient piece of box work made of crude dark oak that had been crafted during the previous century, perhaps even earlier, had been dismantled and placed in the garret storage. The other furnishings—chests, tables, assorted chairs—had been relocated to various other parts of the house.

Dante's huge tester bed with its thick carved walnut posts and rich blue hangings, was taken down, only to be reassembled in its new place, the spacious chamber that had always been occupied by the Earls of Morgan since Wyldewoode's beginnings. The hangings and the linen were cleaned and freshly aired, the rope supports were tightened, and the mattress stuffed with fresh down.

"I had thought it would be strange, moving into the

chamber my father had once called his, but owing to my wife's diligence, it looks nearly the same as my other bedchamber, only larger."

Dante came to stand behind Gillian and kissed the top of her head. "The only difference is I need no longer walk down a flight of stairs to find you. There is one thing I wish to make clear, though. I hope your efforts won't prove wasteful, for despite that we now have adjoining chambers, I want you to know I have no intention of sleeping alone. I will give you the choice, though of which bed we will share."

"Why not both?" Gillian said, smiling. "That way when we grow bored with one, we can simply move to the other."

Dante looked at her, his eyes intensely golden-brown. "If there is one thing that is certain, my lady, it is that I will never allow you to grow bored when sharing my bed."

Gillian immediately understood. She stood and turned, pressing her body close to his. "And how will you manage that, my lord?"

Dante grinned. "Ah, my curious wife, a wise man never reveals his secrets too soon. Allow me to say there are countless ways for me to keep you from tedium." He kissed her hand. "Shall I show you one of them now?"

Gillian slipped her hand beneath his dressing robe, splaying it against his bare chest. She caressed his warm skin. "I should be most disappointed if you did not, my lord."

"You have merely to name which bed you prefer."

Gillian smiled mischievously. "I have a mind to sample them both."

"I have married myself a wanton."

"Indeed, my lord, you have."

It was later that night, much later, when Gillian finally asked Dante the question that had been playing on her mind all day.

They had made love first in Gillian's chamber, a fervent love that left them both breathless and excited. The second time, after they had moved to Dante's bed, they had lingered, taking every touch to its utmost peak, where Gillian had finished satisfying her curiosity of her husband's body, before culminating in a mutual climax that held them spellbound as they drifted off to sleep, the last flames flickering slowly in the hearth.

"Dante?"

Gillian felt him move behind her. Her back was pressed up against him, and his legs were hooked over hers. One hand cupped her breast. The other covered her hand.

"Hmm?" Dante's voice was muffled against her hair.

"There is something I must ask you."

Dante chuckled softly. "No, Gillian, I could not possibly return to your bed now. You've worn me out. It is a physical impossibility."

Gillian smiled. "That is not what I was going to ask."

Dante must have sensed her seriousness, for when he spoke again, his voice was no longer sleep-soft. "What is it, Gillian?"

"I was just wondering what we will do if we never find out who really kidnapped me. My family will never believe it was anyone but you now. My father will have you arrested, and we will have nothing to prove he is wrong." She hesitated. "I am beginning to think I will never recover my memory in full. What small bits of it I had begun to regain seem to have all but vanished. I think if I were going to recover it, it would have come back to me by now."

Dante tightened his arms around her. "Gillian, I have every confidence we will find out who it was who

kidnapped you and very soon. No one is that clever not
to leave behind a clue. Faith, he already has with his
peculiar choice of scent. There is nothing more for us
to worry about. I promise you whoever it is will never
again be able to hurt you. As for your memory, there is
nothing I can do to get it back for you. If it were possible, I would. But I hope you can find promise in that
there will be other memories to fill that emptiness,
memories like those we have just made together."

Gillian squeezed her fingers around his. She rolled
onto her back and peered into his eyes. She touched her
hand to the side of his face. She loved this man with
everything she had. "You always seem to know what to
say to take away my fears. It is no wonder I love you as
I do."

Dante's answer was lost in a kiss that was both tender and passionate, a kiss that gave Gillian his promise
to protect her for the rest of his life.

They were sitting at the breakfast table early the following morning, sharing a feast only Mrs. Leeds could
have created, when the first coach came rolling up the
drive.

Gillian set her cup of chocolate back in its saucer
and looked to the open windows where Dante was already standing. "Who is it, Dante?" And then she
added reluctantly, "Is it my father?"

"No, Gillian, it is not. Nor is it the sheriff or even
Reginald. But I still think you'll be very pleased at who
it is."

Gillian walked to the window to join him. The coach
door opened, and Phoebe quickly scampered down.
Following her came Mara with her two oldest children,
Robert and Dana. A second coach had pulled up behind
them, and Hadrian, with the twins, emerged from it.

Before Gillian could reach the front door, Phoebe

came tearing inside, dark curls flying about her laughing blue eyes. "Gillian, you're here!"

She flung her arms around Gillian's skirts. Gillian looked down at her, smiling. "Yes, I am, and now so are you. Isn't that grand?"

Hadrian came through the door next, a wiggly twin on each arm, following by Mara, Robert, and Dana.

"Phoebe begged us to bring her, so we decided to leave the city a little early. Rolfe and Cassia should be arriving on the morrow."

"That is good news." Dante led them into the dining parlor. "Then I guess I am to assume Rolfe has already met with Briggs, the perfumer who made the kidnapper's scent?"

"Yes, actually we both did," said Hadrian as he set the twins down with a playful pat on their heads.

"And did he reveal to you who had purchased the scent?"

Hadrian smiled. "With a bit of Rolfe's particularly persuasive coercion, yes, he did. Funny thing about that, too. Seems we were in the right church all along, but we simply had the wrong pew. It wasn't Garrick Fitzwilliam who kidnapped Gillian that night after all."

Gillian turned to Dante. "You believed Garrick was the culprit?"

She had managed to get the children into chairs and had Renny fetching them fresh chocolate and rolls from the kitchen.

Dante nodded. "I grew suspicious after his sudden marriage proposal, especially when I learned you could barely stand to be in the same room with him before your memory loss."

"My father told me I was fond of Garrick." And then she added, "But then Abigail said I called him 'Lord Ratface.' "

"Two friends of yours were particularly helpful

along that vein. Ladies Prudence Fairchild and Felicity St. John to be precise."

"Pru and Lettie? But how did you convince them to tell you anything?"

"That," Hadrian broke in, "was Cassia and Mara's doing. They happened to attend a small ladies' gathering where the two young ladies were also present. Mara is somewhat of a master at getting people to divulge information. You should see her sometime. She could put a military interrogator to shame. Your friends told her that Garrick had had designs on you before, but that you had rebuffed him. They were very surprised to hear you had agreed to wed him. I believe they said, 'He was the last man they would have thought you'd ever wed.' "

Gillian took this in. They were sitting at the dining table, the children happily munching on Mrs. Leeds's gingerbread. "So if it wasn't Garrick, then who?"

"Sir Ozwell Gilhooly."

"Who?" Dante and Gillian had both responded at the same time.

"Gilhooly," Hadrian repeated. "A rather remote figure at court, a baronet, I believe, from somewhere in Scotland. It has been all but confirmed by the fact that he has been little seen since the night of Gillian's abduction. In fact, he was found nosing about in lower Derbyshire, asking some very interesting questions not long after you found Gillian, Dante."

"Then it would stand to reason that it was Sir Ozwell," Gillian said, "especially since I remembered that the kidnapper was planning to take me to Scotland. What else do you know of him?"

"We really haven't found much else," Mara said. "Cassia was going to check into it further, through Cordelia, of course, but we left the city before she had returned from the Palace. We had wanted to get an early start, and Phoebe was quite anxious to see you both."

"Why did you leave without me?" Phoebe piped in.

"Because," Dante said, "Gillian and I had to make certain we weren't followed first." He looked at Gillian, smiling. "And we had some other business to attend to."

"Business?" Hadrian said. "What business?"

"The business of getting wed."

Mara laughed. "I thought I detected a certain change in you both. How truly wonderful."

Hadrian clapped Dante on the back. "Leave you alone for even the smallest amount of time, and you still manage to find trouble." He winked at Gillian. "Congratulations to you both."

"So Gillian won't be going away?" Phoebe asked, already down from her chair and standing beside Gillian.

"No," said Dante assuredly, "Gillian will not be leaving us ever again."

Gillian awoke the moment Dante slid into bed beside her. She started to turn from her side to face him, but he placed his hand on the small of her back, stopping her.

"Shh. Lie still, madam."

He kissed her lightly on her earlobe.

"You and Hadrian were downstairs quite a while," she said drowsily. "I tried to wait for you, but then I fell asleep. I was having the most wonderful dream. You and I were lying in a field filled with flowers and . . ."

Her words dropped off as she felt Dante's hand reach around to the front of her and begin to untie the ribbons of her nightrail. She tried to sit up to assist him, but Dante locked his arm over her.

"I said lie still, Gillian."

There was something in his voice, an impatient and passionate urgency, that made her realize he was planning to do something delightful to her. She felt his fingers fumbling with the ribbons, struggling, then finally yanking on them as he buried his face in the nape of her neck and nibbled exquisite kisses there.

Gillian took in a deep breath when she felt his fingers on her breast, his thumb rubbing against her. She knew a shiver of anticipation when he reached his other hand downward and pushed the hem of her nightrail up, past her thighs, bunching it at her waist.

"Lift your leg just a little and move it forward," he whispered into her ear, guiding her slowly. "That's it."

Gillian gasped when she felt his finger slide slowly inside of her. He caressed her, sending waves of delightful pleasure rushing through her as he teased her, making her wild with the need to feel him deep inside her.

And suddenly he was inside her, deeper than she could have ever imagined, as he pulled her back against him and entered her. The feeling was unlike anything she could have imagined. It was stronger, more vivid, blindingly erotic, and Gillian arched her back to feel him even deeper.

Dante's fingers returned to her breasts, setting her body on fire as he kissed along her neck and shoulder, while he remained buried within her. He withdrew from her slowly, then drove back, and his hand slid down from her breasts, over her belly. The heat, the fervency she felt as he resumed that same torment he'd began earlier was almost too much to bear. She wanted to scream from the riot of sensations that were taking her, rocking her with each movement of him within her as his fingers worked their delirious magic on her.

She stuffed a fist into her mouth as Dante continued his desperate impulse, driving deeper and deeper until she was writhing with need, begging him for release, and gasping out his name. And when he did give her that final release, she cried out his name one last time as the force of her climax took her over the edge, showering her with tingles of blinding pleasure.

They lay there together, silent, joined as one, for some time while Dante rained featherlight kisses along Gillian's back and shoulders and neck. He pulled himself from her and moved her gently to face him. Gillian could only stare at him, beyond words, beyond knowing, at what she'd just experienced. A wondrous calm descended upon them, like the aftermath of a great and unbelievable happening, and indeed, it had been both great and unbelievable.

"It would be my greatest joy, Gillian, if a child were conceived this night," Dante said and kissed her once before drawing her against his chest, stroking his fingers over her forehead as together they drifted off to sleep.

Gillian opened her eyes. The room was dark with only a sliver of moonlight filtering through the trees outside the window. Dante's breathing was slow and even in sleep. His arm was carelessly flung about Gillian's waist.

She didn't know what time it was, but figured it quite late, or very early. She realized then what had woken her. She was hungry. She hadn't eaten much supper, not that the roast duckling with orange slices Mrs. Leeds had prepared wasn't appetizing to her. She just had been too busy seeing that Mara and Hadrian and the children had freshly aired chambers, and that another chamber was waiting for Rolfe and Cassia's arrival sometime the following day. She had personally selected the flowers from the gardens to scent the rooms, conferred with Mrs. Leeds on the menu, and even took Mara and the children on a tour of the house while Dante and Hadrian rode about the estate.

By the time they had sat down for supper, Gillian had simply been too tired to eat. Now, hours later and having rested after her husband's glorious lovemaking, she was famished.

Gillian slid off the bed and out from under Dante's arm, pausing to make certain she'd not woken him. She would just go down to the kitchen and fetch herself a late-night snack to keep her until morning.

As she walked across the courtyard toward the outside kitchen building, she glanced up at the sky, a sky lit by thousands of glittering stars. She loved feeling so at home here, so untroubled. She never wanted to leave Wyldewoode again. Lighting a candle on the huge block table that stood in the center of the room, she searched the kitchen cupboards.

Beneath a basket covered with a cloth she found some soft bread rolls left over from supper. A tub of butter was in the larder, and some apples were stored in a wooden bin by the door. She sliced into the apple, chewing the first piece of it, then cut the rest of it into wedges. Sitting on the tabletop, she ate her late-night feast in silent contemplation.

She didn't hear him approaching until he was standing right behind her.

"Dante, I—"

Gillian's words were cut off when a gloved hand clamped down hard over her mouth. She took in a sharp startled breath and the smell, the peppery smell that she'd been searching for so long, nearly overcame her.

"Don't move or make a sound, or I will have to kill you right here on the kitchen table. It will not be a pretty thing, Gillian. The servants will wake to find your blood on the table and the floor. It will be quite a mess."

Gillian's heart was pounding. Sir Ozwell had come for her.

"Is that clear, Gillian?"

She nodded. She remembered the knife she had used to slice the apple. She slowly inched her fingers across the table, searching for it. Until Sir Ozwell grabbed her hand, squeezing her fingers together so forcefully she thought certain they'd snap.

"That was not a very wise thing to do."

He twisted his other hand in her hair, tugging sharply. "Next time you try to take a knife to me, I will use it to remove those same fingers. Now I am going to take you out of here, Gillian. I have you tightly by your hair so you cannot run off as you did the last time we were together. That wasn't well done of you, Gillian. You delivered me a setback by tossing that brandy in my eyes so you could jump from the coach. You very nearly escaped me, until you made the mistake of returning to London. Things were moving in the right direction again, until that bloody Morgan interfered."

Sir Ozwell tightened his hold on her hair and pulled her head back. Gillian nearly buckled beneath the pain that was shooting through her scalp. When she saw the face of her abductor, she did buckle.

It took her a moment or two to recognize him, without all the bright colors and powder and cosmetic addition. This man wasn't Sir Ozwell Gilhooly. Her abductor was Garrick Fitzwilliam, the man her father had wanted her to wed.

"Are you surprised to see me, Gillian? But, then, you believed the culprit who kidnapped you that night was Sir Ozwell, didn't you? He may have purchased the scent, but it is only because I had him do it. You see, Ozzie will do anything I tell him. If you knew anything about Ozzie, you would realize he is too stupid to mount a horse without proper assistance. Ah, but I can mount a horse. I can mount a good deal more than just that."

He pulled his hand away only long enough to cover

her mouth with his, shoving his tongue deep as he plunged his hand into her nightrail and squeezed her breast, the leather of his glove pinching her skin painfully. He yanked on her hair as he pulled away. "Ah, the things I have planned for you, dear Gillian. Did you think the manner in which Morgan entered you from behind was unusual? Did you like the way it felt to have him impaling you like a beast of the field? I think you did. I saw your eyes glazing with the pleasure it brought you. I was there, in the shadows of your bedchamber, watching the whole thing. I heard you gasping as he drove himself into you. As you see"—he squeezed his fingers against her breast hard—"pain can ultimately bring great pleasure. I will teach you the ways of pain, Gillian, the methods you can use to control it so that you can taste the real pleasure of it. In time, you will come to beg me for it."

Gillian gasped as he increased the pressure on her. "Please . . ."

Garrick smiled, delighted with her response. "See, you are already begging me to give you more." He released her and Gillian had to grip the edge of the table to wait for the blinding pain to pass.

Garrick came up behind her, covering her mouth with his hand as he bent her forward at the waist so that her face was crushed against the table. She felt his hands on her legs, lifting her nightrail, exposing her to him. "I'm of a mind to take you right here and now, just as Morgan did, so he will smell the evidence of it when he comes looking for you on the morrow. Scent is a truly telling thing, isn't it, Gillian? Despite not recognizing my face through all the face paint, you knew my particular scent. I, of course, had to refrain from its use while I was composing that drivel and dressing up like an effeminate fop, standing aside while Morgan danced you out in front of everyone right under my nose. I wanted to kill him right there, but I had to keep silent and play my Ganymedean role just a little longer, so you wouldn't know. You had no idea it was me all along, did you, Gillian?"

Gillian tried to shake her head. She could not move, not even her hands, for her arms were pinned beneath her against the edge of the table. She shuddered with revulsion when she felt Garrick's hand sliding up the back of her leg. He grabbed her thigh hard, wrenching her legs open wider.

Gillian fought to stay conscious, despite the fear that was threatening to overtake her. She swallowed back the bile that rose in her throat from the sickening peppery scent of his glove that was suffocating her. She could hear the sound of him fumbling at his breeches with his free hand. She closed her eyes, praying silently.

Oh, dear God, please do not let him do this. Please help me.

Chapter Thirty

A distant voice broke through Garrick's sexual frenzy just as he managed to free himself from his breeches. "Garrick, there's a light coming from inside the house."

Garrick froze over Gillian. "Bloody hell." He quickly rearranged his clothing. "It seems we will have to wait a bit before your initiation into the mingling worlds of pain and pleasure, Gillian."

"Garrick, do you hear? I think someone might be coming."

"Yes, you idiot," Garrick shouted, and he pulled Gillian up from the table by her hair. He pushed her before him. "It is time for us to take our leave now, my dear."

Outside, a figure lingered in the shadows. "What were you doing in there? I thought you were just going to get the lass and we were going to leave."

"I was showing our dear Gillian what she can expect of her life in the days to come. Gillian, allow me to introduce your abductor, Sir Ozwell Gilhooly."

Gillian stared at him. She hated that tears were springing to her eyes from the painful grip Garrick had on her hair. She didn't wish either of them to see the fear that was running through her.

"I'm sorry things have to be this way, miss," Sir Ozwell said. "I never wanted—"

"Shut up, you fool!" Garrick cracked Ozwell across the mouth with the back of his free hand. "Gillian is going to get what she deserves. She treated us poorly. She made as if we weren't even there. Well, she can ignore us no more. We shall all get to know one another. Intimately. And that can begin as soon as we get away from here. Where are the horses?"

Dante woke just after dawn. He wasn't surprised really to see that Gillian had already risen. She was most probably making last-minute preparations for Rolfe and Cassia's arrival. They'd sent a message by courier indicating they had stopped the previous night at an inn in Wirksworth. They should arrive sometime this morning. The Earl of Devonshire would be coming from Chatsworth as well, to join them for an early dinner. Afterward, he and Dante could discuss the current state of affairs in Eyam. He would most probably remain the night. It was going to be a busy day.

Dante doused his face with cold water from the washbowl in his chamber and quickly shaved. Penhurst, his valet, would also be coming from London, but would most probably not arrive before week's end since he was seeing to the purchase of certain toiletries and provisions before leaving the city for Derbyshire. Until then, Dante would need to fend for himself, unless he simply abandoned shaving until his valet arrived. Dante drew on a fresh shirt and breeches, wondering if Gillian would find him appealing with a beard. He yanked on his boots before heading down for breakfast.

A crowd of hungry guests awaited him.

"Renny," Dante said as he made for his place at the table, "you can inform Lady Morgan we are now all assembled and ready for the morning meal."

Renny nodded, pouring Dante a cup of steaming

dark coffee at the sideboard. "And where would I find her ladyship to tell her this, my lord?"

"What do you mean?" Dante asked. He wondered what game the steward was up to. "Surely, you've seen her. She must have risen with the sun, and you've been up for hours, haven't you, man?"

"Yes, my lord, I did arise at my usual hour, half past four o'clock, but I have not seen Lady Morgan about at all this morning."

Dante looked to the clock on the wall. It was nearly half past nine. Five hours and Renny hadn't seen her? Where was Gillian?

"Perhaps she is in the kitchens," Mara interrupted.

"Yes, most probably," Dante said. "Will you check on it, Renny?"

The steward bowed his head and turned to leave.

"Actually," Dante added, "I will go and find her myself as I'm sure I will have to force her to stop seeing to everything and sit long enough to eat a full meal."

Dante started for the kitchens, walking straight across the courtyard outside. As he drew near, he wondered why he did not detect any of the familiar smells of food cooking. Usually at this time of morning, the air was filled with the mingling aromas of bacon and bread, while kitchen maids scurried about. He found Mrs. Leeds standing outside on the far fringes of the courtyard, speaking with one of the footmen.

"Mrs. Leeds, can you tell me where to find my wife?"

The rotund cook looked at him oddly. "My lord? I have not seen her. She was supposed to come to the kitchens early this morning to give me instruction on what to prepare for today's meals, but she never came about. I was just asking after her now. I thought she had come to the kitchens, because there is a plate and knife . . ."

Even as he listened to her response, Dante was turning toward the kitchen building. Inside the main chamber everyone was still as he ducked his head through the low door. Two maids stood beside the center table, staring at him. A small plate with an apple, sliced, lay upon the table. The apple looked to have been there a while, for its flesh had grown dark from exposure. A buttered roll with one small bite taken from it lay beside it.

Mrs. Leeds came up behind him. "We found the plate just as it is when we came here this morning, my lord. The knife was lying on the floor, and the door was standing open. I told Renny of it, but he said he felt sure her ladyship was still abed, because she hadn't asked him for her morning chocolate like she always did. And you weren't about either, my lord, so we knew she must be with you."

Dante shook his head. "She was gone from bed when I awoke."

"We also found this." The cook held out a twisted and frayed bit of pale blue ribbon such as one would find decorating a gown.

Or a nightrail.

A wash of cold fear came over Dante's entire body.

"When we saw the apple, we thought perhaps her ladyship had come down last night for a small bite to keep her until breakfast."

Dante shook his head. Gillian would never have left the food sitting out. She may have come down for a snack, but she would have tidied up after herself. That was just her way of doing things. And she would never have gone to her own bed alone. She would have come back to him.

Dante turned about, closing his fingers around the scrap of ribbon.

"Stubbs," he called to the coachman, "saddle Fury and another horse, a good and able steed, for Lord

Kulhaven. Bring them to the front of the house immediately."

Dante walked straight to Hadrian when he entered
the dining parlor. The children's chatter ceased at the
sight of him. "Gillian has disappeared."

Hadrian stood. "What do you mean?"

"She's gone. No one has seen her this morning, not
at all. A snack plate was left, virtually untouched, in
the kitchens."

Mara raised a hand to her mouth. "Oh, good Lord."

Rolfe suddenly appeared beside him. "Let's go after
her, Dante."

Dante didn't even stop to ask Rolfe when he'd arrived. He spotted Cassia standing behind her husband,
her eyes wide with dread.

As the three men started for the door, Phoebe came
up in front of them. "Where has Gillian gone, my
lord?"

Dante kneeled down to her. "I cannot say, Phoebe,
but I will find her, and I will get her back. I promise
you. Now I am counting on you to stay here with the
other children and to help Lady Kulhaven and Lady
Seagrave."

Phoebe stared at him, tears already forming in her
eyes. She nodded, bravely biting back her fear.

"That's my girl. I expect to see you waiting at the
top of the steps out front when I bring Gillian home."

Grabbing their swords from Renny, who stood at the
door ready with them, the men left the house. They
mounted their horses on the front drive, wheeling about
and galloping off in a cloud of dust and gravel.

They pulled up at the crest of the first hill.

"Rolfe, tell me this isn't Gilhooly's last-ditch effort
to get his hands on Gillian somehow."

"I wish I could, Dante, but I can't. When I went to
Sir Ozwell's lodgings to have a talk with him about his
peculiar choice of scent, he was already gone. The

landlady said he'd vanished almost a week before, leaving without paying his rents. She allowed me into his rooms. They were left empty after what appeared to be a hasty departure."

"Bloody hell!" Dante stared out at the expanse of rolling green that stretched before them. They could be anywhere. The hills went on forever, and the thick woodland forests even farther. Derbyshire, with its wild terrain and remote locale was the perfect place to conceal oneself.

"Where would he have taken her?" Dante asked, more to himself than his friends. "He doesn't know Gillian and I have wed, so he might yet try for Scotland. It had to be very early in the morning hours when he took Gillian, for she was still with me at three. I don't think he would have taken to the roads, knowing we would be fast on his trail. If he's a man of any thought, he's probably hiding out somewhere, waiting for a time when he can get safely away."

Dante pointed to the north. "Hadrian, there are ruins of the former house beyond that rise. Some of the rooms are still habitable. With the proper provisions they could hide out there for days. You check there. Rolfe, the nearest village is Castleton. There is a man named Huggins who owns the livery stable there. Tell him I sent you, and ask if any strangers have recently come about. I will search the caves and woodland along the eastern fringes. That should take us the day. If we haven't found them by nightfall, then tomorrow we will start along the northern border."

The three of them split from there, each heading off in their appointed direction.

Dante made slow progress, stopping often to listen so that if Gillian were calling out to him, he would hear her. His frustration grew with each stretch of land he covered. Nothing, not even a track to indicate anyone had recently been that way. He hated that he might be wasting time. He hated even more that he hadn't protected Gillian. He'd thought the situation well in hand. And now, he might well lose her. Perhaps he'd been wrong in thinking they would be hiding somewhere close by. Perhaps they had indeed taken to the road and were now so many miles away he'd never find them. What would he do if he lost Gillian now? He couldn't. He wouldn't even consider it.

The day passed quickly, and the sun rose swiftly in the late summer sky before starting its nocturnal descent. Dante hadn't seen sign of Rolfe or Hadrian since leaving them that morning. Dante wondered if they'd found Gillian. Even as he hoped they had and were back at Wyldewood awaiting his return, Dante still refused to give up his own search.

He just had to find her. Somehow, some way he would get Gillian back.

Dante found the first hint of Gillian's trail within the hour.

A small bit of lace lay fluttering in the breeze on a tall reed of dry field grass. Dante dismounted to retrieve it. He looked at it a long time, as if trying to see to Gillian through its delicate pattern. He folded it in his gloved hand as he started back for Fury.

The second bit of lace was dangling from a low oak branch several roods away. This time Dante noticed two sets of hoofprints in the moist earth. He dropped from the saddle and examined them closely. One set was much deeper than the other, indicating that the horse carried some additional weight. Two riders? If it was so, and Gillian was riding with Ozwell, who was on the other horse? There had to be someone else with Sir Ozwell, someone who was part of the scheme. Gillian might have been able to escape had there only been Sir Ozwell. With two, though, her chances of success were twice as lean.

Dante followed the tracks as they headed deeper into

the wood. Tree twigs were snapped and seedlings had been trampled along the path that was now quite easy to see. Gillian must have realized this, for she left no other bits of lace. Dante would have smiled at her foresight, if not for the fear that was gripping him.

He came to where the foothills began to grow steeper and more rocky. They were very near the caves where Dante had played with his brother as a child. He remembered the day he'd brought Gillian here, how curious she'd been about the caves, how he'd promised to bring her back someday. When he'd said that to her, he had never thought it would be under these circumstances.

Dante dismounted. Given the position of their tracks, they must have stopped for a spell at the small brook nearby to water the horses. More than likely they also had to decide on a course to take from there. Their progress would be hindered by the rocky landscape. In fact, at the point where they were, they would descend a rugged gully and would be coming straight to where a smaller ridge met the lower Pennines forming a cragged cirque. Sir Ozwell wouldn't know this until it was too late. They would be surrounded on three sides by jagged cliff walls. The only way out would be to backtrack to where Dante was now.

And where Dante would be waiting.

Dante knelt by the brook and cupped water in his hands to drink. The water was cold and clear. If felt good running down his throat. Fury sipped negligently beside him. Dante washed some water over his face, then pulled on his gloves. He walked to where the tracks had faltered and surveyed the surrounding area.

It was then he heard the voice, an angry voice, cursing, threatening. It reverberated off the rocky cliff walls. And when Dante heard Gillian's responding scream, the chill that had stayed with him since discovering her gone vanished, became hot, boiling rage.

Dante left Fury drinking at the brook and started toward them.

Chapter Thirty-one

"Watch now, Gillian, for it is because of you this worthless piece of crow bait will die."

Garrick removed his sword from its hip scabbard and raised it up.

The horse reared fearfully, the whites of its eyes showing stark against its lathered chestnut coat.

"No, Garrick, you cannot do this!"

Garrick turned on Gillian, the point of his blade dangerously near to her. Sir Ozwell, standing to the side, took several steps away.

"Is that so?" Garrick said. His voice cracked with rage. "And why is it I cannot kill the horse, Gillian, this horse that isn't even mine? I stole him from Morgan's own stables, you know? I should kill him for that one reason alone. I had heard Morgan was a good judge of horseflesh. I was misinformed. The beast is lame. He is lame because you led us on this merry little chase, and he twisted a leg on these bloody rocks. He cannot bear our weight any longer. He is suffering because of you, Gillian. I am merely going to put the animal out of its misery."

Garrick raised the sword again, preparing to thrust forward into the horse's chest.

"Wait!"

Garrick didn't lower the sword. He kept it poised, ready to deliver the killing gesture, but he did turn to Gillian.

"He may be able to walk off the inflammation," Gillian said quickly, desperate to convince him. "Perhaps if I soak his leg in the brook, it will help to ease the soreness. We will need the horse once we have gotten through this area. We've a long way to go if you still intend to travel to Scotland."

Garrick laughed at her. "Scotland? Pray tell me why I would wish to take you there?"

"To marry me, of course. That is what you wanted, isn't it?"

"I had wanted it, yes, at one time."

"What has caused you to change your mind?"

"Let me just say that the idea of dragging a woman bound and gagged to the marriage altar is less than appealing to me."

Gillian looked at him. A thought struck her. "What if I do not resist? What if I go along with you and marry you willingly? Surely, you must have had a purpose for wanting to wed me, a purpose strong enough to have driven you to abduction. Was it a dowry, perhaps? Was the marquess planning to dower me handsomely?"

Garrick didn't need to answer. The affirmation of Gillian's suspicion was written all over his face. "That may be all well and good, Gillian, but in order to wed you in Scotland, we will need to get there, and we certainly will not be doing it on the back of this worthless nag."

Gillian tasted the beginnings of success, albeit a tenuous one. "I will walk, Garrick. Spare the creature's life, allow him a chance to walk off the lameness, and I will walk along without any resistance."

Garrick laughed at her again. "You will walk? Look down at your feet, Gillian. You are without shoes."

"I do not care. I will manage, just, please, do not kill the horse."

Garrick stared at her a long moment before he finally lowered the sword. His voice dropped to a tone that almost sounded regretful. "Would that you had been as cooperative before, the first time I took you. None of this would be happening now." He shook his head. "The first time I took you, you were dressed in your nightrail and barefoot, just as you are now. I find there is a certain irony in that."

Garrick dropped down on a large flat rock that jutted from the ground. He looked very tired. His eyes were shadowed and owlish. Gillian watched him as he ran a hand through his hair in frustration, short-cropped sandy hair so different from the bushy wig she'd previously seen.

It still amazed her, this Garrick she now saw without all the gimp and galloon and powder. The copiously bushy wigs, the blinding costume, the effected tone to his voice, he had fooled her completely. Without the additions, Garrick really wasn't unappealing. She wondered what had brought him to become a man who would consider abduction—and murder.

Garrick was becoming agitated, talking softly to himself, as he tried to come to a decision about the horse. But it was more than the horse that agitated him. What he was going to do with Gillian? How had things progressed this far? It was supposed to have been a game. Now he was faced with having to kill Gillian, but even if he did, what of Morgan, and what of Clare? Sooner or later the truth would come out. He leaned his arm on the cup of his sword, balancing the point on the rocky floor. He stared at the ground as he wrestled with his thoughts.

Gillian looked over at Sir Ozwell, who now sat cross-legged on a bed of heather. He looked as if he might nod off at any moment. Even now his head was beginning to droop. Perhaps . . .

Gillian slowly approached Garrick, sitting tentatively beside him on his rocky perch. She didn't say anything at first, just sat there, trying to show Garrick, that she meant him no danger.

"Why did you do this, Garrick?" she asked softly, trying not to start when he picked up his head so suddenly.

Garrick smiled, a rueful, sarcastic gesture that made his features appear even sharper. "You mean you haven't figured it out yet, Gillian? And I believed you a quick-witted creature."

He peered at Gillian.

She said nothing.

"You really haven't regained your memory, have you?" Garrick laughed. "And Clare was so very certain you had."

"What does Clare have to do with any of this?"

Garrick looked as if he might refuse, but then he shrugged and turned a little toward her, resting the sword against the rock behind him. He bent one knee and even leaned his chin upon it. This gesture, so childlike, made him appear a great deal less frightening.

"It was Clare who came up with the idea of kidnapping you in the first place, Gillian."

"Why would she do something like that when I was family to her?"

Garrick chuckled mirthlessly. "Family, Gillian, means very little to Clare. I guess that is something she and I have in common. Another is our driving ambition. Clare wed your brother Reginald for nothing more than the money and social stature she believed he would give her. She was less than pleased when she learned he was stubbornly tight-fisted with them both. He didn't parade her out before the court as she'd believed he should. He didn't allow her to entertain the *ton* with lavish parties that would have quickly lifted her to the very heights of society. He refused to live separately from your family when she wanted to set up her own address. Reginald even put dear spendthrift Clare on a allowance that wouldn't have fed a squirrel."

"Reginald was a cruel husband?"

Garrick shrugged. "No, you know, I cannot really blame him, for he is simply a husband who refuses to be ruled by his wife. Unfortunately he didn't know what he was getting in Clare. It all has to do with control, and Clare is at her worst when she feels she is tethered by the rein of any man. She decided the only way to remedy her sad state of living would be to remove Reginald from her world. Her first attempt at that was five years ago when she tried to have him killed in a duel. Clare figured that Reginald would be run through and she would enter widowhood fat in the purse with her jointure."

Gillian already knew the answer to her next question, but in the interest of keeping Garrick as unaware of the true state of things as possible, she asked anyway. "Reginald won the duel?"

Garrick shook his head. "There was no duel, and so Clare was left with her husband and the mess she'd made of things. She behaved herself for the next few years, most probably so when she tried a second time to get rid of Reginald, no one would suspect she had had a hand in it. And, indeed, they didn't. She procured a form of poison from my perfumer, which she began to feed to Reginald in small doses, so it would appear he had contracted an unknown illness. She'd nearly done him in, too, until you happened to discover her little secret sitting in the drawer of her writing table."

"The small bottle," Gillian said. "She told me it was a scent she'd had made."

Garrick looked surprised at what she'd said. "You do remember then."

"Only that I had seen the bottle in her drawer."

"When you so innocently questioned Clare about the

bottle that first time, she began to fear that she would fail in her efforts to rid herself of Reginald again, only this time she would not be able to walk away so easily. You may have suspected something was up, but you hadn't yet figured it out. Clare had to do something about you, Gillian. She knew she could not poison you as well. That would look very suspicious. She needed you gone, not for good, but long enough for her to finish Reginald off and clean up any evidence of it. She hatched a scheme. She convinced me to kidnap you so she could finish what she had begun with Reginald in the delivery of one final, fatal dose of the poison. I was to keep you away long enough so that Reginald would be dead and buried long before you came back."

Gillian shook her head. "Why would you have agreed to this?"

"Clare and I were lovers. And you had rebuffed me once. I didn't much like it."

"My family would have known I was kidnapped. Didn't you think they would come looking for me?"

"Not when they couldn't rule out the possibility of your having eloped. That would have been confirmed, in fact, after they read in your diary that you had fallen in love with me and that we had stolen away to wed because you knew your father would never consent to a match between us."

"And your reward in all this would have been my dowry." Gillian was fast fitting the pieces together. "That is why Clare took my diary. It was not because she wanted to keep me from reading something. She wanted my family to believe I had run away with you to wed so they wouldn't come looking for me."

"After she learned you had escaped from me, she never did give your father the diary indicating an elopement, but she planted enough of a seed of it to cause him to wait in reporting you missing. When you returned with Morgan, she then made your father believe Morgan had kidnapped you, especially since you could not remember anything. It fit in rather nicely with her plans."

Garrick looked at her. "Unfortunately, things got out of hand, and now I have no choice. Even if we were to wed, Gillian, Clare would find a way to somehow make me her scapegoat, when she is really the linchpin who holds this all together. I have no choice really but to—"

"What if we returned to London together?"

Gillian knew that if Garrick had finished what he had started to say, there would have been nothing more she could do. He would kill her. Unless she convinced him to try another plan, a plan that would at least secure her more time.

Garrick looked at her. "What do you mean—we should return together?"

"We could go to the marquess and tell him the truth, all of it. We could tell him how Clare had been poisoning Reginald, and I will assure him you now regret what part you unwittingly played in this."

Gillian watched Garrick carefully. He was listening to her as if he might consider her suggestion. She went on.

"We will tell him everything, of how she stole my diary and how she was trying to make it seem as if Dante had kidnapped me when—"

"Morgan!" Garrick stood, the expression on his face turning at once from one of willing consideration to furious disgust. "That is all you are concerned with, isn't it? You don't care what happens to me. You only want to make certain your lover is cleared of any implication in it."

Garrick snatched the sword up, swinging it recklessly. "I was an idiot. How could I have ever thought you might have cared about me when it's been Morgan all along?"

"No, Garrick, listen to me!"

Garrick lunged at her with the sword. "I am through listening to you, Gillian." He lifted the sword up. "It is you who should have listened to me, but instead you chose Morgan, the Rakehell Earl. Where is your precious Dante now?"

"Turn around, Fitzwilliam," came a voice from behind, "and you will see for yourself."

Dante stood on a rocky ledge, his sword drawn, its blade flashing in the sun that was setting on the mountains behind him. He looked magnificent. Gillian wanted to run to him, but held herself from it. Garrick still held his sword dangerously close to her.

"You don't really want to kill Gillian," Dante said, stepping down. "You want to kill me. Here is your chance. Let us see if you can manage to pull this one off more successfully than you did Gillian's abduction."

Garrick swung around and came at Dante with an animal growl, lunging forward with his sword.

Dante deflected the blade. Garrick came back at him, and the two continued to parry and riposte, sword blades clashing with lightning speed. Gillian could do nothing but stand and watch as they fought. They separated and circled each other. Dante never took his eyes from Garrick's. He stared at him, deadly calm, and deflected Garrick's next lunge, slicing his blade back to cut Garrick high on his arm.

Garrick looked down at the wound. His eyes grew wide and enraged. He lunged at Dante again, coming back at him relentlessly after each parry. They parted again, and Dante simply stood and waited for Garrick to charge him again. He seemed to know each play Garrick would make before he ever executed the move, and each failed thrust of his blade only provoked Garrick more.

Garrick retreated and Dante took his first lunge, catching Garrick sharply on his side. Garrick cried out more from anger than the injury itself and ran at Dante full-tilt, blade aimed straight for Dante's chest.

Dante ducked, then spun about, slicing Garrick on the cheek. They parted, and Dante waited for Garrick's next offensive. It was then Gillian saw Ozwell coming up behind Dante, arms raised high, a small boulder held in both hands.

"Behind you, Dante!"

Dante spun about just in time to avoid the falling boulder. It would have hit him on the head and levelled him. Garrick took full advantage of the distraction, coming up quickly behind Dante.

"No!"

Gillian saw Garrick ready to send his sword blade into Dante's back and ran at him, grabbing his sword arm. She didn't know what she would do; she just wanted to keep him from running Dante through.

Garrick growled and grabbed Gillian by her arm. "I should slice your throat for that," he said, before he swung her around, shoving her away from him.

Gillian fell, striking her head on a large rocky formation that jutted from the ground. Through dazed and blurred eyes, she watched as Dante thrust his blade forward, sinking it to its hilt into Garrick's chest. She then saw Garrick crumple to the ground before darkness overtook her.

"She's coming around now, Dante."

Gillian opened her eyes, blinking quickly. She was lying on her bed in her chamber at Wyldewoode. It was night, and the room was shadowed by candlelight and moonlight mingling. She could see Mara standing over her, a gentle smile on her worried face. She reached over to press a cool rag that smelled of an herbal mixture to Gillian's forehead.

"You gave us quite a scare, Gillian."

"What happened?" Gillian said softly. "Where is Dante?"

"He is fine. He is right here, waiting to see you. I told him I would stay to see if my herbal had done its work, but he refused to leave until you awoke."

Dante came forward, his golden-brown eyes filled with fearful concern. "Hello, wife."

Gillian smiled. "I am so glad you are all right."

"I could say the same for you. That was a rather nasty-looking rock you fell against. Luckily, the blow to your head wasn't serious. You'll have a lump there, but it didn't break the skin. How are you feeling?"

"I am fine now that you are here." She closed her eyes as he laid a hand softly against her cheek. She looked at him again. "Garrick?"

"He can no longer threaten you, Gillian. And his friend, Sir Ozwell, is in the custody of the authorities. They will deal with him. I really don't think he presents any threat to you, for he hasn't the wits to do anything more than what he is told by somebody else. There is nothing more to fear now."

Gillian closed her eyes. The danger was finally gone. The mystery was at last solved. Now nothing could come between them.

The door across the room suddenly burst open. Gillian's father and Reginald stood framed in the doorway.

"Get away from my daughter," the marquess said, marching forward. "You have kidnapped Gillian not once, but twice. I will see you hanged for this, Morgan."

"No!"

Everyone turned as Gillian sat up on the bed. "No,

Father, you are wrong. Dante did not kidnap me that first time. And as for the second time, I went with him willingly. He was only trying to save me from the real culprit."

The marquess looked at her. "Who?"

"Garrick Fitzwilliam. Only Garrick followed us here and tried to kill me so I wouldn't tell Reginald the truth about Clare. You should be thanking Dante, not cursing him. He saved my life."

Reginald came forward. "What do you mean, Gillian? What truth about Clare?"

"Clare was poisoning you, Reggie. That is why you were so sick all those months. But I discovered her bottle of poison. She keeps the poison in her night table, in a secret compartment at the back of the drawer. That is why she arranged to have Garrick kidnap me, so she could finish what she'd started before I was able to figure out what she was up to."

Reginald's face began to turn a very odd shade of white. Stunned, he dropped into the chair behind him. "How do you know this?"

"I began to suspect something wasn't right after I first found the bottle of poison in her room, even though she said it was scent. This was before I was kidnapped. I remember I had found it odd that Clare had been so calm when she'd come upon me in her chamber that day. She wasn't even angry with me, Reginald. That wasn't like Clare. She used to look for reasons to quarrel with me. Don't you remember that time she said I had stepped on her foot purposely? She had stumbled and had blamed me for her clumsiness because I was the one standing closest by. I had apologized to her, even though I knew I hadn't tripped on her, but she didn't speak to me for weeks after that. That is why I knew she was lying about the scent bottle."

Reginald looked at her. "How can you remember her

getting angry with you like that for thinking you had tripped her, Gillian? I barely recall—"

He stopped talking and simply stared at her. "Your memory. Gillian, you've gotten it back."

Gillian thought for a moment. The memory of the incident with Clare was so clear in her mind. She smiled. "You're right, Reggie. I have. I can even remember that your birthday is the second of June and that you used to hide your peas from dinner in your coat pocket so you wouldn't have to eat them."

Reggie laughed. It was good to see him smile again. It made him look younger, healthier. But that smile vanished as quickly as it came. "I should have realized what Clare was about. I knew she hated me, but I guess I never thought she'd want to kill me."

"That is why Clare lied to you about Dante all those years ago, too," Gillian went on. "She wanted you to challenge him because she thought Dante would run you through in a duel. What she didn't count on was Dante's refusing to meet you at all, thereby ruining her plans."

Reginald stared at the floor, struggling to come to grips with the realization that his wife had tried to murder him, not once, but twice.

"No wonder she tried so hard to convince me you'd eloped," the marquess said, coming forward. "I was a fool to have listened to her at all. We will deal with Clare when we return to the city, Reginald. She will soon be out of our lives for good." He turned to Dante then. "It would appear we owe you a debt of gratitude, Morgan, for saving Gillian's life not once but twice now. I also would like to offer my apology for our treatment of you." He turned to Reginald. "Tell the coachman we will be returning to London as soon as we bring Gillian down."

Dante didn't move from his place beside the bed.

"I'm afraid I cannot allow that, Lord Adamley. Gillian will be staying here, at Wyldewoode."

The marquess colored. "That is improper. Regardless of what has happened, Morgan, you still have no right to decide where my daughter will go."

Dante stared at him. "As her husband, and knowing that she wants to remain here at Wyldewoode with me, I have every right, my lord."

Epilogue

"Here they are!"

Dante yanked on the strap handle of the small trunk that was wedged in the space beneath the garret roof. He set it down and opened the lid, removing the small wooden soldiers from inside.

"Cavaliers, just as I told you, Phoebe. Scores of them. See, they even carry their swords."

"Like you when you fought that bad man?" Phoebe asked, her eyes alight as she examined every one of them. "Gillian told me you were very brave."

Dante and Gillian sat down together on the garret floor, watching Phoebe as she arranged the Cavalier soldiers before her. Gillian smiled and rested her head contentedly on Dante's shoulder.

Her father and Reginald had left early the previous morning, bound for London—and Clare. They had stayed the night, and the marquess had listened while Gillian had explained to him how Garrick had gotten involved in Clare's scheme and how he'd told her everything about what she had planned for Reginald. And when she had finished, her father had looked at Dante with sincere regret in his eyes.

"I never thought I would say those words, but my daughter has found herself a man worthy of her," he had said shortly before taking his leave. "She is a very special woman. I only hope that someday, when your daughter is grown, you will come to understand my reasons for what I have done."

Dante had simply nodded, shaking the marquess's outstretched hand.

Gillian looked at Dante now, this man she loved more than life itself, knowing they were destined to spend eternity together. She looked at Phoebe, whose small face was set with two dimples so like her father's. Despite that she wasn't her daughter in blood, she felt a special bond with her, a bond that only grew with each day they were together. As Dante's wife and Phoebe's stepmother, Gillian knew a feeling of complete happiness.

"She is such a special child," she said as Phoebe concentrated on the soldiers.

"That she is," Dante said. "I only wish my mother could have known her."

Phoebe looked over at them, grinning. She was surrounded on all sides by the soldiers. "See, they are all ready for the battle now. But I just wish Mrs. Fillywicket could see them, too." She frowned. "I forgot her in London."

"Then we will simply have to go back for her," Gillian said.

"I miss her now, though."

Dante narrowed his eyes. "You know . . ."

He stood and moved toward a small chest that stood against the wall. "My mother used to have someone who might just do while Mrs. Fillywicket is away visiting our friends in London."

He opened the two doors at the front of the chest. "Yes, here it is. Just as I thought."

Phoebe stood and hurried to his side. Dante turned and handed her a small doll that wore a splendid ball gown of shimmering pink. "This was my mother's doll when she was a young girl. She had saved her to give her to my sister, but I think she would be very happy to see you have her now."

Phoebe took the doll. "She is so pretty. Look, she even has shoes to match her gown. What shall I call her?"

Dante smiled. "You could call her Helena. That was my mother's name."

"Helena." Phoebe nodded, holding the doll close to her. "Did your mother look like her doll? Momma used to say that my doll looked like me."

"I guess my mother resembled the doll a little. She had dark hair like the doll, and she had blue eyes like yours." Dante turned, looking about the garret. "I think there is a portrait of her here somewhere."

He searched for several minutes until he found it, stored with a number of others beneath a light cloth. He lifted the portrait up, dusting it off with his hand. "This is my mother, Phoebe. Your grandmother."

"That is the 'Nice Lady!'" Phoebe squealed. "Remember I told you about her, Gillian? She used to give me presents when Momma took me to see her in London."

Dante stared at Phoebe, wondering if he'd heard her correctly. "Your mother took you to see this lady in London? You are certain it is she?"

"Yes, Momma used to write to her all the time, and the lady would write to Momma asking about me. She was very nice."

Gillian suddenly remembered something, the bundles of letters she'd seen in the trunk when they'd first come to the garret, searching for the soldiers that long-ago night. Could they possibly be . . . ?

She found them and read the first one. "Look, Dante. These are Eliza's letters to your mother. They begin at Phoebe's birth and tell all about her, when she started to walk, her first words, everything. Your mother saved them all. It would appear she saved them for you."

Dante took the letters and read them. "My mother did know about Phoebe. She knew about her, and yet she never said anything to me. Why wouldn't she have told me, even if Eliza hadn't, that I had a daughter?"

Gillian placed her hand on his arm as he read through several more of the letters.

"She knew about Phoebe, Gillian, even before I left for France."

"She most probably didn't tell you because she loved you, and she didn't want you to change who you were. It is the same reason Eliza never told you the truth, Dante. If you had known about Phoebe any sooner, you might have tried to take Phoebe and her mother away from Lord Overton, even though Eliza was married. That would have caused only more problems for you, and you wouldn't have been happy living that life. Eliza and your mother knew you; they knew the man you are, and they loved you for it. As do I. Telling you about Phoebe would have meant that you would have changed from who you are before you were ready for the change. Even worse, you might well have come to regret it."

Dante looked down at Gillian, a smile of love in his eyes. "And it would also have meant something else as well."

"My lord?"

He gathered her into his arms, saying before he kissed her, "It would have meant, my dear wife, that I would never have found you."

Author's Note

Once again, as with the previous two books of this trilogy, I have chosen to blend a bit of factual history in with my fiction.

The plague was a very real event in England's history, and the figures mentioned in *Stealing Heaven* of those who died are as accurate as my research could find. It is written that a blazing comet appeared in the night sky on the eve of the New Year, 1665. Some said it foretold the coming of the end of the world, and, indeed, those who lived through the plague, which came within months of that comet's sighting, probably felt it was. Imagine their fears when, at a time they believed they had just survived the worst, a fire began in a bakery at Pudding Lane in London shortly before midnight on the first of September, 1666. That fire would destroy a greater part of the city, and with it five hundred years of history.

One hundred and sixty miles away lies the small Derbyshire hamlet of Eyam, whose one quiet street winds along a tree-shaded hillside. Plague was but an afterthought to the good people of this village, who had likely never seen the busy streets of London in their lifetime. Ignorance is bliss, or so the saying goes, but Eyam's carefree days of ignorance were to be short-lived when the plague came upon them in early September, 1665.

Due to the efforts of William Mompesson, the village rector, they managed to keep the disease within their bounds, and thereby prevented it from spreading to any of the neighboring villages. Their heroism did not, however, come without its price. When the plague first arrived, Eyam had a population of barely three hundred and fifty. Fifty of those evacuated the village before the quarantine began. When the plague departed Eyam in October, 1666, two hundred and fifty-nine of those three hundred villagers who remained had died.

The Earl of Devonshire played a vital part in Eyam's eventual survival. Through his efforts, the villagers were assured of food and other essentials. The gritstone slab covering the spring at Mompesson's Well in Eyam today remains as a reminder of where food and money were exchanged during the plague quarantine.

Marshall Howe, mentioned the night Dante had encountered Mackie and the torchman outside Eyam, was the giant of a man who as parish burier declared all possessions of the dead without heirs his own. He was also an actual figure in history. Though his wife and young son succumbed to the disease, he survived to enjoy his ill-gotten fortune another thirty years. His legend lived on even longer when for generations afterward, the villagers would caution naughty children to behave lest they would send for Marshall Howe, Eyam's own "Bogeyman."

The small chapel where Dante and Gillian were wed in the village of Peak Forest was indeed built due to the efforts of Christian Bruce, the wife of the second Earl of Devonshire. It continued to offer its "Gretna Green"–style marriages until early in the nineteenth century, and brought in a tidy income from it. The church was eventually rebuilt in 1878 as an imposing Victorian structure, and the original seventeenth-century Venetian window and porch were put to use again in the village reading room.

As well, the pendant that Dante gave to Gillian is

crafted of a real stone, called "Blue John," and is naturally striped with violet, blue, and yellow. Purported to have magical powers, it has been found nowhere else in the world except the misty hills of Derbyshire.

The rest of the story comes from my imagination. I do hope you enjoyed *Stealing Heaven*, reacquainting yourselves with old friends Mara and Hadrian, and Cassia and Rolfe, and making new ones with Gillian, Dante, and the others. I would love to hear your thoughts, so until we meet again, feel free to write to me at P.O. Box 1771, Chandler, Arizona 85244-1771.

WE NEED YOUR HELP
To continue to bring you quality romance
that meets your personal expectations,
we at TOPAZ books want to hear from you.
Help us by filling out this questionnaire, and in exchange
we will give you a **free gift** as a token of our gratitude.

- Is this the first TOPAZ book you've purchased? (circle one)
  YES   NO
  The title and author of this book is: _____

- If this was not the first TOPAZ book you've purchased, how many have you bought in the past year?
  a: 0 - 5   b 6 - 10   c: more than 10   d: more than 20

- How many romances in total did you buy in the past year?
  a: 0 - 5   b: 6 - 10   c: more than 10   d: more than 20 ___

- How would you rate your overall satisfaction with this book?
  a: Excellent   b: Good   c: Fair   d: Poor

- What was the main reason you bought this book?
  a: It is a TOPAZ novel, and I know that TOPAZ stands
     for quality romance fiction
  b: I liked the cover
  c: The story-line intrigued me
  d: I love this author
  e: I really liked the setting
  f: I love the cover models
  g: Other: _____

- Where did you buy this TOPAZ novel?
  a: Bookstore   b: Airport   c: Warehouse Club
  d: Department Store   e: Supermarket   f: Drugstore
  g: Other: _____

- Did you pay the full cover price for this TOPAZ novel? (circle one)
  YES   NO
  If you did not, what price did you pay? _____

- Who are your favorite TOPAZ authors? (Please list)

- How did you first hear about TOPAZ books?
  a: I saw the books in a bookstore
  b: I saw the TOPAZ Man on TV or at a signing
  c: A friend told me about TOPAZ
  d: I saw an advertisement in_____magazine
  e: Other: _____

- What type of romance do you generally prefer?
  a: Historical   b: Contemporary
  c: Romantic Suspense   d: Paranormal (time travel,
     futuristic, vampires, ghosts, warlocks, etc.)
  d: Regency   e: Other: _____

- What historical settings do you prefer?
  a: England   b: Regency England   c: Scotland
  e: Ireland   f: America   g: Western Americana
  h: American Indian   i: Other: _____

- What type of story do you prefer?
  - a: Very sexy
  - b: Sweet, less explicit
  - c: Light and humorous
  - d: More emotionally intense
  - e: Dealing with darker issues
  - f: Other

- What kind of covers do you prefer?
  - a: Illustrating both hero and heroine
  - b: Hero alone
  - c: No people (art only)
  - d: Other_____

- What other genres do you like to read (circle all that apply)

  Mystery   Medical Thrillers   Science Fiction
  Suspense   Fantasy   Self-help
  Classics   General Fiction   Legal Thrillers
  Historical Fiction

- Who is your favorite author, and why?_____
  _____

- What magazines do you like to read? (circle all that apply)
  - a: *People*
  - b: *Time/Newsweek*
  - c: *Entertainment Weekly*
  - d: *Romantic Times*
  - e: *Star*
  - f: *National Enquirer*
  - g: *Cosmopolitan*
  - h: *Woman's Day*
  - i: *Ladies' Home Journal*
  - j: *Redbook*
  - k: Other:_____

- In which region of the United States do you reside?
  - a: Northeast
  - b: Midatlantic
  - c: South
  - d: Midwest
  - e: Mountain
  - f: Southwest
  - g: Pacific Coast

- What is your age group/sex?   a: Female   b: Male
  - a: under 18
  - b: 19-25
  - c: 26-30
  - d: 31-35
  - e: 36-40
  - f: 41-45
  - g: 46-50
  - h: 51-55
  - i: 56-60
  - j: Over 60

- What is your marital status?
  - a: Married
  - b: Single
  - c: No longer married

- What is your current level of education?
  - a: High school
  - b: College Degree
  - c: Graduate Degree
  - d: Other: _____

- Do you receive the TOPAZ *Romantic Liaisons* newsletter, a quarterly newsletter with the latest information on Topaz books and authors?

      YES   NO

  If not, would you like to?   YES   NO

  Fill in the address where you would like your free gift to be sent:

  Name: _____
  Address: _____
  City:_____ Zip Code: _____

  You should receive your free gift in 6 to 8 weeks.
  Please send the completed survey to:

Penguin USA•Mass Market
Dept. TS
375 Hudson St.
New York, NY 10014